STORIES FROM
THE BLUE MOON CAFÉ IV

Edited by Sonny Brewer

MacAdam/Cage
155 Sansome Street, Suite 550
San Francisco, CA 94104
www.macadamcage.com
Copyright © 2005
ALL RIGHTS RESERVED.

Library of Congress Cataloging-in-Publication Data

Stories from the Blue Moon Café IV / edited by Sonny Brewer.
    p. cm.
  ISBN 1-59692-142-0 (alk. paper)
  1. Short stories, American--Southern States. 2. Southern States--Social
life and customs--Fiction. I. Brewer, Sonny.
  PS551.S744 2005
                              2005013940

Manufactured in the United States of America.
   10 9 8 7 6 5 4 3 2 1

Book and jacket design by Dorothy Carico Smith.

Several of these stories have appeared elsewhere, in some cases in a different form:

"Those Summer Sundays" and "An Explanation" by Andrea Hollander Budy in
The Other Life (Story Line Press, 2001); "Taking off from Welty" by Ellen Douglas
in *Witnessing* (University of Mississippi Press); "Spleen, Ole Miss, Late August" and
"Where, Beneath a Magnolia" by Ann Fisher-Wirth in *Blue Window: Poems*
(Archer Books, 2003); "Ghost Dance" by Chip Livingston in *Boulder Planet*; "Talk"
by Diane McWhorter in *The American Scholar* (Vol. 73 No. 1, Winter 2004);
"Rehab" by Janet Nodar in *Georgia State University Review* (Fall 2001); "Chicken
Bone Man" by Anna Olswanger in *The Memphis Music of Berl Olswanger*; "Down
There on a Visit" by Charles Simic in *New York Review of Books*.

STORIES FROM

THE BLUE M<u>OO</u>N CAFÉ IV

Edited by Sonny Brewer

MacAdam/Cage

TABLE OF CONTENTS

INTRODUCTION

Sonny Brewer

"There's your introduction to the next *Blue Moon Café* book," Joe said to me.

He, Joe Formichella, and Suzanne Hudson and I sat in the kitchen at one of those old Formica-top tables with the aluminum strip around the edge. The appropriate mismatched chairs were pulled up close, and we were eating a little of Suze's homemade spaghetti, salad on the side. The house belonged to Everett Capps. He was in the living room watching something on the television with a friend. Just down the hill on the banks of Fish River, bullfrogs were singing up a rain.

Joe writes. Suzanne writes. Everett writes. I write. Four out of five people in the house called themselves writers. We were talking about writers. About books, and raw manuscripts and copyedits, about submissions and deadlines and how quickly a book can disappear from the Books-in-Print database. We counted ourselves lucky to have books published, still available at your local bookstore, and not yet mulched back to paper pulp.

Suze lit a cigarette. I'd already pushed back my plate. This was not a nonsmoking house, but Joe and Suze waited until I twirled my last forkful of noodles before firing up. Joe poured me a glass of red wine. Something nice, not expensive, from one those really good vineyards in Argentina.

Some chatter went around the table about the *New York Times* article that reported there were more manuscripts submitted for publication in 2003 than there are people who claim to read books on a regular basis. They always say that writers should never give up their day jobs, that about 5 percent of published authors actually make a living from writing.

"It's not about the money," Suzanne said.

"No kidding," I said. "Every day it seems I get a query about a manuscript or story from an unpublished lawyer, doctor, engineer, architect,"

I said. "People who've got the good jobs, drive the Hummers. Good stable folk. And they want to do this crazy thing that we do." They smoked, I sipped. We got quiet and could hear the TV like it was on the counter by the bread box.

We fell into a round of talk about why so many people want to write a novel, about those who say they are going to write a book as if it's easy as ordering at the drive-up. The single most common misconception about writing good fiction is that it is easy to do. "But it's really hard work," Suzanne said. Joe and I both knew how many hours she had spent in solitude turning out the six hundred pages of her next novel, *In the Dark of the Moon*.

But, like playing the piano, you don't just walk up to a Steinway in the corner of the room and bang out a concerto in a full bloom of excellence. It takes skill and study and practice. A lot of it. And there is a big difference between arranging a subject and verb between a capital letter and a period and conjuring with words well chosen a life that stands up on a page and slaps the hell out of you. The latter is worth sacrificing the trees to make the page.

Besides, why would somebody in the Rotary Club want to wreck his life with all that writerly angst, ever pressing the back of a damp wrist tight to a wracked and wrinkled forehead looking for another clever turn of phrase, the kind of metaphors that will elicit "furiously original work" from the *Dallas Morning News*?

It's not easy to write.

It's easy to talk.

The coin of the realm for both writers and talkers is a word. But, some easy talkers are bankrupt storytellers.

I broke the silence, easy talker that I am. "I got a call today from a dentist. He said he'd written a book. He asked me if I'd read it and tell him what I think." I told Joe and Suze I was in a mood when he called. As I talked to the dentist, I found myself thinking about John D. MacDonald's introduction to Stephen King's *Night Shift*, a collection of great short stories.

"MacDonald said in his intro that it really pissed him off when somebody came up to him and said they'd been thinking about writing themselves a novel. He said he wanted to say, 'Yeah, and I've been thinking about doing some brain surgery.'"

MacDonald's incredulity was how anyone could have the audacity to think they could write a book instead of, say, watching television for a night or two.

Everett came in to get a beer from the refrigerator. He lost his grip and dropped the slippery wet bottle back into the vegetable crisper drawer on top of its longneck mates. Nothing shattered. "I gotta invent a soft beer bottle," he said. Totally to himself. And walked out of the room. We watched him go, all grinning.

And then got serious again: Who the hell do these people with their unlicensed laptops think they are?

"So I asked the dentist calmly, 'What makes you think you know how to write a novel?' I wanted to know," I said to Joe and Suzanne, "if he'd studied writing, if he'd stacked up ten thousand manuscript pages getting to the three hundred he wanted to call a book, maybe even why he wanted to write a book in the first place."

"What'd he say," Joe asked. "You want some more wine?" He nodded toward my empty glass.

"Sure," I said, handing him my glass. "He said that when he and his brother were little boys they used to write stories to each other, used to read to each other all the time, used to promise each other that someday they'd write a book together. Then he told me that his brother died before they got around to it. Then he told me he wrote the book for his brother. 'To keep my promise to him that we'd write a book. I'm here and I can and he cannot. So I wrote the book.' And you know, guys," I said, looking from Joe to Suze, "that's as good a reason to write a book as there is."

And the book may not be any good at all. But it may so damn full of heart and honesty and longing that it is just, by God, fine.

"I hope to hell he brings the book to me," I said.

"There's your introduction..." Joe said.

He's right. What clicked for Joe, clicked for me at the same time.

Yes, it is very hard to write a good book. Damn few people can do it.

And yet.

And yet there is sometimes an alchemical transformation of lead into gold that occurs in the crucible of one's love for reading. You don't love to write if you don't love to read. You cannot write worth a whit if you don't get as hungry to read as you do for good homemade spaghetti, if you don't enjoy it as much as a glass of good pinot noir. But if you do really love to read, and you think you want to write, something magic might happen. It just might be that your urge to write fiction is accompanied by some talent.

And John D. MacDonald would be sorry if he ever yelled at you.

'Cause you are the real deal. You've got the audacity to face a blank page and come away with the upper hand. One in a million.

And if my belly ain't down in the dirt fielding the queries, how am I going to catch that little sparkle in your prose, grab you up, and see you backlit by the sun?

God, lay me low. Keep me down there looking for the other half of Emerson's man, who is half himself and half his expression. I want to get my hands on the expression of the man. (And if it's good, it too will have been a sifting in the frothy dark waters of the soul of a writer.)

That's the joy of putting together this anthology we like to call *Stories from the Blue Moon Café*. To go panning for gold knee-deep in the inky sluice and come up with something that shines. Bright.

For now, for this time, for these stories or essays or poems, we've found the men and women who read good stories and good books and decided they needed to do that too. Promised themselves they could do it. Would try really hard to write something fine. The contributors to this collection have done it. Or we think so. If you're in agreement, then we've got ourselves a book worth the trees that were felled, hauled, chipped, cooked, and pressed into the pages in your hand.

ACKNOWLEDGMENTS

Right down to the wire, on top of the deadline for this fourth volume of *Stories from the Blue Moon Café*, Joe asked me, "Do you know who Charles Simic is?"

Joe was helping me get the lid closed on the book, and we still had some tails hanging outside the box. Particularly, there were a couple of bio sketches missing from authors, Charles Simic among them. Joe had been trying to get in touch with Charles.

"No," I said, "except for his piece in the *New York Review of Books*."

"Listen to this," Joe said, and read to me:

> Charles Simic was born in Belgrade, Yugoslavia, on May 9, 1938. As a boy, Simic received what he quotes Jan Kott as calling "a typical East European education"—an education, that is to say, in which Hitler and Stalin taught us the basics.
>
> Toward the end of the war, Simic's father fled the country, and it was to be ten years before his family would see him again. He had made his way to America, where his prewar work for an American company (he was an engineer) had given him numerous contacts. However, his wife and children were unable to follow until 1954.
>
> After a year in New York, the family moved to Chicago. Simic attended Oak Park High School, an earlier alumnus of which had been Ernest Hemingway. He graduated in 1956, but instead of going to college, like most of his peers—his parents had very little in the way of savings, but in any case seem not to have given any thought to the possibility—he found work, first as an office boy, and later as a proofreader, at the *Chicago Sun Times*.
>
> It was during this period that Simic started to write poetry. Simic has since published more than sixty books, won the Pulitzer Prize for Poetry, been a National Book Award finalist, and received numerous other grants and awards. Simic

and his wife, who have a son and daughter, live in Strafford, New Hampshire.

Hmm. After confessing that we really should know our American poets better, we admitted 'tis also nobler to pick something for these *Blue Moon Café* stories based on writing, and not the notoriety of the author. Still.

And then I was thinking about skipping the acknowledgments for this fourth volume because, if you look at the acknowledgements page in the blue book, our first, and the red one and the green one, the second and third *Blue Moon Café* books, I'd be thanking all the same people again.

And then this bio came in from Charles Simic, not all of which is included here. At one point, before the first of his poetry collections was published in 1968, Charles, after a stint in the army in the early sixties, threw away everything he had written up to that point, calling it, "no more than literary vomit."

That set me to thinking about the writers who work for beans, or grapes (oh, look, see what a constant effort to get the words right), toiling in the quiet vineyards of their fertile imaginations. And, as we read in Charles's story, so often it's frustrating work.

And the pay's inconsistent. Here our writers even give back their fee to the Fairhope Center for Writing Arts. For that, then, in the mood of our introduction to this volume, I thank all the writers.

Here in this book, and abroad in books of their own, and in other anthologies and collections, for the sake of the ideas bound together and preserved with your words, for the stories, I thank you, the writers. And, especially, writer Joe Formichella who helped me with the reaching and gathering and sorting (and the squeezin') it took to get this book to press.

Sonny Brewer
Fairhope, Alabama

Our Uncle Willem Stanfield

June 1949

Howard Bahr

Aunt Maeve, lithe and red-haired, came down to the house at the fall of evening, just as the first cicadas were tuning up in the oaks. She was barefoot, in a housedress printed with flowers. She smelled of oil paints and lipstick. In the kitchen, she poured a cup of coffee and lit a Chesterfield, and settled herself at the enameled kitchen table where I was doing algebra.

I was fifteen, a year younger than Mother when she married Jack Stanfield. I had failed algebra in the regular term, and this was summer school, and I fully expected to fail again, for the subject made no sense to me. I was not able to see then, and cannot see now, how X plus Y equaled anything at all that could be worth the trouble of getting to it. I had never progressed beyond whole numbers and multiplication up to, but not including, "times twelve," and felt it unlikely that I ever would. As it turned out, I was correct in this. Mother said it was the atomic age now, and I would never amount to anything if I didn't "buckle down" in math and science. I never did, and proved her correct as well. One is never free of the disciplines, however. When, in September of 1954, I became a brakeman of the Southern Railway, I learned:

Useful mathematics: The tonnage of a freight train may be calculated by multiplying loads times one hundred tons; empties, including the caboose, times twenty-five tons. If Train A leaves Point A with 125 cars, and Train B leaves Point B with 35 cars, and the dispatcher issues orders for Train B to wait for Train A at Point C, then Train B better have his ass tucked away on time or a world of shit will happen.

Useful science: If a train leaves Point A and moves at sixty miles an hour toward Point B, and a gasoline truck, or gravel truck, or a school bus fully laden is stalled on the crossing ahead, and the engineer is telling for the hundredth time about a strumpet he met in East

St. Louis on the CB&Q—and if you and the fireman holler loud enough and wave your arms, and the engineer looks up at the last possible moment and slams the brakes into emergency ("dynamite" was the term we used)—at that juncture of events, the laws of physics—friction, motion, momentum, etc.—will immediately apply themselves and cause a world of shit to happen.

But Maeve, our aunt. She crossed her freckled legs, dangling a shapely foot damp with dew and adorned with blades of new-clipped pasture grass. She held the cigarette between the tips of two fingers, as she had learned in the sorority. Whenever I was up at her house, she always let me smoke. Mother knew, of course, but never said anything about it. Aunt Maeve winked at me. "Jackie, can I trouble you for an ashtray?" She had a beautiful husky voice of the kind associated with coffee and cigarettes in after-hours cafés. I found a red plastic one that said "Old Milwaukee" and slid it across the table. Aunt Maeve drew deep and let the smoke jet from her mouth. "What are you doing, anyway?" she said, pushing the ashtray back toward me. It is odd how people will move an ashtray around.

I was about to answer when Mother said, "He is going to pass algebra, is what he's doing." She was at the coal oil range, making spinach and brussels sprouts and beef liver for supper—a vile concoction, especially the liver, which tasted like river-bottom mud to me. She turned and leaned against the stove and crossed her arms and glared at me, though I knew she meant nothing by it. She had silky black hair and a fine, sultry face. Mother and Aunt Maeve both took after their father, Mister Lane Ryder, though each had chosen a different part of him, if you can choose such things. Mother took the practical, stoic, shadowy part, and Maeve the romantic and free-thinker. Mother never cried, and Maeve hardly ever laughed. It was a mystery where Maeve's red hair came from—maybe an Irish girl somewhere in the old times, back when our generations were still wearing horned helmets and raiding the coasts, before they became Englishmen and, later, Cavaliers, or so it was told, anyhow. I have no doubt they could ride horses and were good Church of England and

King's men, but Cavaliers always smacked too much of genealogy to me. Whatever they were, at least they were not Puritans—and if any of them were, I don't want to know about it.

I learned early to be suspicious of genealogy, for I found that it is magnetized toward romance. Our great-grandmother was said to be a Cherokee Indian, and I used to enjoy believing it, for the very word dripped of romance. I would examine my face in the mirror to see if I had "high cheekbones"—I didn't—and try to make myself walk with one foot in front of the other like the Children of the Forest. Then, after I became more or less sociable, I learned that *everybody's* great-grandmother was a Cherokee Indian, and they all walked the Trail of Tears, and so on. Romance. A great-grandmother is a useful personage if she is dead, for in that condition, she is just distant enough to be obscure and can be fashioned into anything. Still, I have yet to find a person who claimed a Digger or a Flathead in his blood.

Maeve moved the ashtray around with her little finger while the ash on her cigarette grew longer and longer. It finally dropped off on the table. She took a deep breath and said, "Well, Sister, I have come to tell you that Willem is putting his car down the goddamn septic tank."

"Is that right?" said Mother. She was a great stoic, the only thing I ever faulted her for. Some people mistake stoicism for dignity, but I have found little virtue in the former. It is only another way of showing off, in my view.

Aunt Maeve said, "He took the lid off about daylight—my god, you ought to of seen the *roaches* down there!—and said he had to get the car in there before tomorrow."

"Did he say why?" asked Mother.

"No."

Mother looked up the hill toward Maeve and Willem's house. "I don't see him now," she said.

"Well," said Aunt Maeve, "that is because he unscrewed everything he could unscrew, and hacked off everything he could hack, and now he's taken the truck and gone to Sneed's for a cutting torch."

Mother consulted the kitchen clock. "He won't make it before they close," she said. "You want some supper?"

Aunt Maeve snuffed out her cigarette. She snuffed and snuffed, rubbing little circles, moving the ashtray around and around. "Sears will still be open," she said, and then she began to cry, the tears running in long, silent streams down her face, falling on the linoleum tablecloth. My sister Nancy was there then, standing outside the screen door, watching. She was thirteen and looked just like the picture of Mother at her age standing on the running board of an Essex. I looked like Father. There is a picture of him in the Book of the Dead, as we call it, taken not long after Normandy. In the picture, he is leaning against a burned-out German tank, his helmet pushed back, sleeves rolled up, holding an M1 rifle. He is looking off, grinning at something. That could be me standing there, grinning. Later it *would* be, only the tank would be a North Korean T-34, its gun tube drooping forlorn, the red star on the turret plainly visible.

Mother came and sat at the table, her eyes dry and clear. She leaned across and touched Maeve's arm. "You ought to eat something," she said.

"I don't *want* to eat anything," said Maeve. Her voice was strong, with no crying in it, though the tears went on rolling down her cheeks. "I just want to understand what happened." She raised her face to the window and let the twilight fall across it. "Why is he doing that?"

We were all quiet then. Outside, the cicadas were in full voice, and fireflies were beginning to rise from the grass. Uncle Willem's three white-faced cows had gathered in the lot and were bawling for their own supper. There wasn't much to say, for everyone—Maeve too—knew what the matter was. It was just that we had spent a long time thinking it would get better, trying to forget that some things can't get better.

It was a story so plain and straightforward that we knew it was true. Willem Stanfield himself never told it but once, in its broad outlines, to an army psychiatrist at Walter Reed; the details came from another boy who had gone off to Europe with Father and Uncle Willem—Ward Bond was his name, like the actor. They had all been pals since primary school, and joined the National Guard together, and now here they were in the Hurtgen forest, lost on a scout, on an afternoon with a light snow falling. Father was behind the wheel of their jeep, a carbine in his lap, watching for movement. Willem was puzzling over a map that didn't seem to have that particular road on it, or any other road since Napoleon's time. Ward had gone up ahead to see what he could see. They hadn't slept in three days, which is how the Kraut, a *Panzergrenadier* about sixteen years old, was able to walk right up behind the jeep. He dropped a stick grenade between Father's legs and shot Uncle Willem in the head with a Luger. The slug spun inside his helmet and lodged in his temporal lobe. Meanwhile, the boy went on staggering up the road, lost and sick and exhausted himself. Right then, he didn't know he only had about forty-five seconds left to him. They ticked away, and Ward cut him to pieces with a tommy gun. Thus, Father was in the Book of the Dead, and Uncle Willem was putting his beautiful chromed cream-and-maroon 1948 Chevrolet coupe in the goddamned septic tank.

"Sister, why didn't you come down here sooner?" said Mother.

Maeve tipped her head back. "I believed I could handle the situation," she said. That was logical, for she had handled many such situations in her four years of marriage to Willem Stanfield. "I called the police. They talked to him a while, tried to get him to quit. Then they said it was his car and his septic tank, and there you are."

"Yes," said Mother, "there you are." She looked up the hill again and ground her teeth together. That was her way of swearing, whereas Aunt Maeve was more forthright.

Maeve had learned to swear in the navy. During the war, she was a WAVE in Washington—a cryptographer. She talked glibly of WAVE Quarters "D" and the navy yard. She traveled to great cities: Philadelphia, New York, Boston. Once, in Pennsylvania Station, she was nearly trampled to death when a sudden gate change was announced. I thought that to be an example of urban romance. She was beautiful in her uniform, her white cap cocked over one eye, her red hair pinned up.

"Well," Mother said, "I see the truck. We better get up there."

The two houses belonged to the same hundred acres of pasture and woods along the Southern Railway. It was out in the country once, but now the edge of town—represented by a greasy Esso station, a feed mill, an ice-cream factory, a lumberyard—lay just beyond the trees along the creek bottom. That suited me, for we could walk to town on hot summer nights, or go to the picture show, or Woolworth's. The houses were built by our great-grandfather and great-uncle, one on the hill and one down below. They were both in the vernacular of the 1880s: two-story, white-painted, broad galleries on three sides, two chimneys, tin roofs shaded by oaks and hickories. In the yards were bunches of chinaberry trees and crape myrtle. In the spring, yellow daffodils appeared dutifully along the walks, and old-time blue iris grew thick in the flower beds. Summer had lantana and nodding Old Maids of every color. Midway, where you could see it from either gallery, was a cemetery inside an iron fence. Everybody who had lived in these houses was there, except us and Father. In fact, something of Father was there: the flag that had covered his coffin in Germany, and a Purple Heart, and a banner with a gold star; the fatal telegram and the letter beginning, "Dear Mrs. Stanfield, It is with deepest sorrow that I must inform you—." These things Mother buried in a corner of the cemetery fence, digging the hole herself.

The one who was supposed to be a Cherokee was buried there too. The name on her stone was Sarah Osborne Stanfield. You may decide for yourself.

The gravel road to town crossed a bridge just below, then crossed the railroad so that the trains had to whistle for it. With thirty or so trains a day, that meant a lot of whistling, though in time you didn't hear it unless you listened—like a clock ticking in the back hall that no one has really heard in fifty years, unless it stops. Then you hear the silence back there, and you go wind it so you can't hear the ticking again. If you listened, though, as we did sometimes, in shallow sleep or in a sudden moment of aloneness, the sound of the trains could move you deeply, could make you believe that everything in the world was passing away, no matter how beautiful it was, or how strong, and you couldn't catch it, no more than you could the red marker lamps that blinked out around the distant curve.

Years later, after we lost the place, I would go by in the cab of a diesel locomotive, or in the cupola of a caboose. By day, I would see laundry on the lines, strange children waving from the yard, strange cars and trucks parked under the sheds. The land was subdivided, and new brick houses had sprung up here and there, treeless, anonymous, baking in the sun, with no galleries to sit on. The graveyard was still ours, but the current owners—"developers," they styled themselves— wanted us to move it since it put a pall over the property value. Apparently, young families did not care to live with dead people they didn't know.

By night, the lights in the houses lit the lives of strangers, and at first I would wonder if they ever heard us blow for the crossing, now paved, or if we were only a clock they never listened to. After a while, I quit thinking about it and didn't look anymore, but kept my eyes fixed on the block signal ahead, which was always yellow for the yard limit.

Nancy and I went ahead up the hill. "Jack and Jill went up the hill," sang Nancy. We hadn't gone far when Mother hollered, "You all put some feed out, make those cows shut up." Mother did not care for cows, nor did Maeve. Uncle Willem only kept them out of a sentimental attachment to the vanishing agrarian life of his youth, when the farm really was a farm, when the steak or beef liver you cooked for supper had been walking around in sight of the house a few days before. Willem gave all his cows names—Doris, Sunflower, Daisy, and so on—and when they dropped calves, he gave them names too and kept them all so long that it broke his heart when he finally had to take them to the sale barn. He got the calves by a bull named Bluto he rented every spring. I had no liking for Bluto and stayed out of the pasture when he was around, though Nancy had no fear of him. Once Maeve, a little in her cups, handed me a .45 pistol and said, "Jackie, I will give you ten dollars a head to shoot those goddamn cows." I couldn't do it, of course, for I didn't mind the creatures, and Nancy liked to look at them and walk among them where they grazed. She saw things, she said, deep in the soft brown depths of their eyes—moving shapes, reflections out of a time we didn't know about. She always cried when Uncle Willem carried one away in his truck, crying himself for all we knew, for he always went to the sale barn alone.

I might have shot Bluto for free, only he wasn't ours—and then only with a rifle, and from a long ways off.

Uncle Willem did not make his living from cattle, then. He was a supervisor at the big Flintkote lumber mill on the other end of town, along the Louisville and Nashville Railroad. On the side, he was a representative for Mason shoes, and each year pestered everyone with his "new line" of products. Of course, we all wore Mason shoes, and they *were* pretty good. In their house, he had two things that, even now, I consider the most fascinating artifacts in my history. One was a fluoroscope, where you could slide your feet in and see the actual bones of your toes and how they fit in the shoes. The other was a gigantic cutaway of a Mason shoe, showing all its innards. He would carry both these marvels on his selling trips, and did pretty well, for people would buy shoes just to see their bones in the fluoroscope. In time, however, his dedication to the product—and his eternal refrain, "Say there, how you like them shoes?"—grew to be an irritant. He asked it of all his customers every time he saw them, even at funerals. He became a zealot, and it was embarrassing to us all. Once, after he had taken two of her favorites to the stockyard, Nancy asked him how he'd feel if the cows he sold ended up with their hides at the Mason shoe factory.

"What if that's Madeline?" she said, accusing his polished loafers.

Uncle Willem gave her a hard look. "Little Sister, don't ever think that again," he said, in such a way that she never did.

Of all the things in Uncle Willem's life, he was most proud of his Chevrolet coupe. Much of his shoe money went into accessories: a windshield visor, fog lights, an adjustable rearview mirror and a search light on the door, a custom-made genuine staghorn steering wheel.

He washed and waxed it every Saturday, and never drove it on gravel roads—except the one to town, and then only about five miles an hour—and you could not drink a Coca-Cola in it, or eat in it, and you had to wipe off your Mason shoes before you got in. Sometimes he would go off in it at night, all by himself, and drive the highways until morning. No one ever asked where he went, for we all knew well enough. He went nowhere, anywhere, so long as it was dark and solitary. I used to wonder why he did it, what he thought about during all that time, if he saw beyond the headlight beams the same mysteries Nancy saw in the gentle eyes of the cows. Much later, I understood that he did it so he wouldn't have to think at all, just fall alone into the vacant darkness, the fat white-walled tires humming beneath him, headlights reaching out, and through the open window the night sounds and the cool air over bridges.

Later, later, later. In time. In the course of events. Understanding never comes when you need it the most.

Now Uncle Willem was ruining his beautiful car, and I did not want to think about what that meant. I told myself, as we climbed the hill, that Maeve must be mistaken, but, of course, she wasn't. I told myself that no septic tank could hold an entire automobile, but this one did.

When we got to the yard, Uncle Willem was manhandling an acetylene bottle out of the back of his truck. He paid us no mind, but worked feverishly, muttering to himself. His white shirt was filthy with sweat and grease, and his tie was loose at the collar. He always wore a tie, no matter what, and a white shirt with khaki trousers, and polished shoes, and he was wearing them now, though they were no longer clean or polished, and even the crystal on his wristwatch was broken. His hands were bloody from cuts and skinned knuckles. We looked at him without saying anything. Then we saw the car, and even Mother let out a gasp.

It was a skeleton car. The windows and headlights were smashed out, tires gone, brakes gone, seats gone, bumpers and dash and doors and trunk lid, even Uncle Willem's custom-made steering wheel with the red suicide knob—all gone down into the septic tank. Only the round shape of it remained, and the waxed maroon paint that gave back of the twilight like a pool of dark water.

Uncle Willem was struggling with the tank. I said, "Sir, let me—"

Mother said, "You all go feed those cows like I told you."

Willem turned and looked at us then, as though he were seeing us for the first time in years, maybe the first time ever. "What?" he said.

"What!" cried Aunt Maeve. She raised her fists and pressed them to her forehead. "Willem, what the *fuck* are you doing!" It was the first time I had heard an adult use that word.

Mother's face turned the color of Reddi Kilowatt. She stabbed a finger at Nancy and me, then at the lot. "I'm not going to tell you all again," she said.

So we went to the lot. Nancy poured a bucket of sweet feed into the trough, and I pitched a little hay. The cows ceased their bawling and crowded close, docile as old dogs. Nancy rubbed the pink nose of her current favorite, Eleanor. "Hey, Jackie," she said, "what does 'fuck' mean?"

It was a shock to hear Nancy say it. I didn't like the sound of it in her mouth. "I'm not sure," I said. "It has to do with the Seven Deadly Sins. Don't be saying it around Mother, or she will boil you in oil."

"Well, she is not boiling Aunt Maeve in oil," Nancy pointed out.

"Well, she might yet," I said. "Anyhow, don't you be saying it at all."

Nancy tossed her head, which made her ponytail swing. She wore a checkered shirt and blue jeans rolled at the cuffs, white socks and oxfords—the plumage of all the girls that summer and for some time to come. "Don't be telling *me* what to say or not say. Anyhow, I won't because, whatever it means, it is an ugly word, like 'sibling.' And 'foyer.'"

I thought a moment, trying to pick out a word I hated. "'Gubernatorial,'" I said. "That sounds worse than anything."

"'Snot' is worse," said Nancy.

"'Piss' is worse than that," I said.

Nancy crossed her arms on the rail and rested her chin on them. "Look at Eleanor," she said. "She don't think she's ever gonna die."

I didn't say anything then—because I didn't know to—but in time I might have answered that nobody does. We are born with a firm belief in our own immortality, and no amount of wisdom or evidence can ever convince us otherwise. By then, of course, I would not have had to answer at all, for Nancy would know it too. She would know it long before me. She might have known it then.

Nancy said, "You know why Willem is doing that to his car?"

"Because he is crazy," I said. "Like when he shot the phonograph and plowed under his record collection. Like when he burnt up all his pictures and—"

"It's what his head is telling him to do," said Nancy. "It makes perfect sense in the place where he is."

That was the sort of novel idea Nancy was always coming up with. "What do you mean, 'the place where he is'?" I said. "He's right over there in the yard."

"He is not in the yard," said Nancy. "He is someplace else, and we can't follow him."

"*That's* crazy."

"Go ahead and try," Nancy said. "Try and follow him." She scooped up some feed and let Eleanor nuzzle it out of her hand.

"'Slobber,'" I said.

"That's pretty bad," agreed Nancy, and wiped her hand on my shirt.

We went back to the yard. Willem had his cutting rig all set up: tanks on a hand truck, red and black hoses, a shiny brass torch, a welder's mask. Now he was running an extension cord out of the house for a floodlight. Maeve and Mother were sitting on the back steps.

"God knows what all this cost," said Maeve.

Nancy was looking at the car. She was crying now, a little. I wanted to cry myself. You couldn't look at it and not want to. Meanwhile, Uncle Willem plugged in the new floodlight. It came on, brightening the twilight. You could hear the metal hood tick-ticking, and it smelled like burning paint.

In the sudden illumination, Uncle Willem stood transfixed. "Aw," he said. He looked at the shell of the car, then down at his hands. "Aw, mankind," he whispered, and in that moment, you could see in his face the full understanding of what he was doing and where it would lead— too late, of course. The same awareness settled over us all for the first time, and spread away from us into the fields, the creek bottom, the town, upward to the evening star and the stars waiting to appear, and the moon, and the coming night, to all the broad universe—to the end of time, and back to the vanished lives in the Book of the Dead. The women rose from the steps. Aunt Maeve stumbled forward, but Mother caught her and held her back. Uncle Willem put out his hand and touched the roof of the car. We watched him take out his hand-kerchief and brush softly at the dust that had settled there.

Nancy came and stood beside him. "It's all right, Uncle," she whis-pered. "You can get another one just as fine."

"No," he said. "No, I can't." He looked down at her then, the first time he had looked at any of us. "It don't matter, Little Sister," he said. "Don't ever think it does."

Then he was gone again. You could see his face change, his gaze turn inward away from us. Among the things I learned that day was that a man can only take so much memory. It is like hunting for some-thing in a trash can: you keep going until you get to the spit, then you stop. Uncle Willem had been hunting for a long time, and he was fin-ished. He put the helmet on his head, visor up. He turned valves and took up the striker: *click click click*—and the torch came to life— *Pop!*—with a long blue tongue of flame. When Uncle Willem put the visor down, he turned toward Nancy again, the torch spitting in his hand. He was only turning toward the car, but the sight of him terri-fied Nancy, and she screamed, and I snatched her away and, for the first time in my life, pressed her against me. She smelled of sweat and hay, and something sweet. I passed my hand over her hair and found a pink strand of bubble gum stuck in it.

We lay in bed that night and listened to the popping and hissing of hot metal and the voice of the torch. The strange light must have bothered the whip-poor-wills, for they were silent, and even the crickets were subdued, as if they were whispering in awe or puzzlement. No frogs sang in the creek bottom, no owls queried from the woods. Once I rose and went to the window. Up the hill I saw the black, masked silhouette of Uncle Willem. He was surrounded by thousands of bugs, all swirling in a mad dance, frantic for the light, while nighthawks darted in their midst. The harsh white glare of the floodlight threw long shadows and lit up Uncle Willem's house, and the torch made it flicker like a shorted-out neon sign. On the back steps, Aunt Maeve sat with her head in her hands, watching.

The next morning, after breakfast, Mother and I went up the hill again—Nancy wouldn't go, and Mother didn't try to make her. No Nancy to sing this time, going up the hill. We found Aunt Maeve sleeping in the porch swing, Willem's filthy handkerchief clutched in her hand. Where the car had been was an empty place of scorched and trodden grass. Everything, even the torch and the floodlight, was gone, and the cover was back on the septic tank.

Inside the house, Uncle Willem was in bed, still in his clothes and shoes. We came in, all of us, and stood around the bed in silence. Uncle Willem stared at the ceiling. After a moment, Mother put her hand on his leg and said, "Willem?"

He stirred then, sat up, fumbled for the counterpane with hands burned and pitted by the torch. When he had it, he lay down again and pulled the cover over his face.

"Goddamn you, then," said Mother, and began to cry.

From that day, Uncle Willem never spoke again but once, just before he died. I was not present to hear his utterance, nor walk behind the hearse bearing his flag-draped casket. The day after I graduated from high school, I forged Mother's name on a document that allowed me to enlist in the United States Marines at seventeen. I was not sure why I was doing it at the time, and am not sure yet. Perhaps I thought that I, too, might be caught in a wartime crush at Pennsylvania Station. But I never saw New York, only California, and six months later, I was a private in a rifle company in Korea where I learned:

Useful mathematics: The M1 rifle weighs nine-point-five pounds, holds eight rounds, and is accurate to a thousand yards. The M1 carbine will accommodate a box magazine of fifteen to thirty rounds, the Thompson submachine gun a box magazine of twenty to thirty rounds. The magazine of the Browning Automatic Rifle holds twenty rounds, and if the sear is broken, and you charge the bolt, the magazine will empty itself, and there is not a goddamned thing you can do about it. Beginning at twenty-two pounds, the weight of the BAR increases exponentially the farther you have to carry it. The M1911 .45 pistol holds seven rounds and is mainly useful for shooting cows and threatening prisoners of war.

Physics: The BAR recoils backward, and when the sear breaks, and you charge the bolt, the twenty rounds will knock you on your ass. The Thompson pulls left and upward. The bolts of the M1, the carbine, and the BAR are piston-operated by gas produced by the round as it departs the muzzle on its way toward a Chinese or Korean, who is carrying an ugly PPD submachine gun that fires a million rounds, all of them at you personally.

Medicine: Penicillin will cure the clap, but not the memory of how you caught it.

Biology: The human body, headlights smashed out by any of the above, or by artillery, or a mortar, or run over by a track, will appear cream and maroon against the snow. Frozen blood is the crystalline red of Uncle Willem's suicide knob (illegal now in all states), and there you are.

Mother was so mad, she would not write to me for over a year, and she forbade Nancy to, but she did anyhow, and so did Aunt Maeve. However, Nancy and Maeve agreed not to write about Willem's passage into the Book of the Dead as long as I was a candidate for it myself, so I did not learn of it until I returned.

I was not yet twenty on the cold afternoon when Maeve and Nancy met the train at the depot. When I saw them, I was shocked at what a mere two years had wrought—how time had carried them both forward, when all the while I had thought it was standing still, waiting for me to take it up again. Maeve was still beautiful, but her hair was streaked with gray; she was lean and fragile, and her overcoat seemed to drape on her bones. Nancy—I would not have known her had I passed her in Pennsylvania Station. She wore a tam and her hair was long, and a red coat and her legs were shapely, and red gloves, and lipstick, and eyes long of lash that held, deep in their blackness, a knowledge of time as it was, with no belief in the promise of tomorrow. She was already long past where I was. When I embraced her, she felt like what I imagined a woman would.

At home, the pastures were locked in winter. By their shagginess, I perceived they had not been clipped in a while, and no cows remained to graze. When we got out of the car, Nancy said, "You go ahead, Brother. I am right behind you."

The kitchen was warm and smelled of grease and coffee. Mother was leaning against the stove, arms crossed, staring across at the pie safe—but she had put on a pin-striped dress with padded shoulders, and she wore the pearl necklace and earrings Father had looted from a house in France. She was unchanged as far as I could tell; in fact, she looked fresh and new—like when you find something at the bottom of a trunk that you thought you'd lost. She looked damn good. I took off my overcoat and garrison cap and pulled down the skirts of my tunic. I thought I looked damn good too. "Well, Ma," I said, "are you still mad?"

"Yeah," she said. Then she pushed away from the stove and looked at me. "Where have you been?" she said, grinding her teeth together.

"To barber college?" I said.

She bit her lip. She shook her head, then crossed the linoleum and gave me one of those sideways hugs—her arm around my waist, my arm around her shoulders—that you were lucky to get, if you got one at all. "You are looking good, Ma," I said.

"Don't call me 'Ma,'" she said.

Nancy and Maeve came in then, figuring the coast was clear. It was easy, really. I knew Mother would always be mad at me, like she was at Father—but not so mad that she wouldn't wear his gift earrings when he came home. That's why she was wearing them now—not for me, but for him.

We sat at the table and drank coffee, and Maeve and Nancy and I all smoked, and even Mother took a cigarette and held it in her fingers. After a while, I ventured, "How is Uncle—" and stopped. I looked from face to face, the three women I loved, each one so different, each one strong enough to have chosen for herself who she would be. I knew then that Uncle Willem was dead. It was left for Mother to tell the simple details, while Aunt Maeve traced her fingers through the ashes on the tabletop.

Later, I went alone up the hill to the place where the septic tank used to be. The cover was hidden under a mound of dark soil that Aunt Maeve had hauled up from the creek bottom, and surrounded by a low rampart of brick. The dead stalks of marigolds and Old Maids testified to its planting, and a single white pansy that had borne all the winter and would persist, somehow, to see the spring.

A northbound train came by, a long string of flats loaded with Pershing tanks and quarter-tons and a battery of 105s shrouded in canvas, behind a quartet of growling black diesel locomotives of a kind I'd never seen. They looked like big alligators, and there was something vaguely sinister about them. I listened, and when the lead engine neared the crossing, a melodious horn raised its voice in the darkening afternoon—not the melancholy of a steam whistle, but beautiful in its own way, and still lonesome. I watched the whole train pass, and waved to the trainman on the back of the caboose. Then I knelt, and in the brown grass spied, as if it had been waiting all that time, a single lug nut with the chrome flaking off. I held it in the palm of my glove and tried to connect it to the car that lay under the perished flowers, that Uncle Willem had loved and so had to destroy. I couldn't do it. I could not make it be more than what it was.

After a while, I rose, my knees aching. I thought about saluting, but decided that was silly. Uncle Willem was not here, but in the cemetery down the hill, and this, I told myself, was not his monument. Instead, I dropped the nut among the dead stalks of summer flowers and turned and walked down the hill again. I told myself I wouldn't stop at the cemetery, for the day was gray and cold, and I had been too long cold, and too long among the dead. I wanted to be in the warm kitchen again, and look at the pictures Nancy had taken on her trip to England, and pet the cat Mother had taken in. Still, as I passed the little forlorn enclosure, I could not keep from looking, and once I looked, I had to stop. It was only a moment after all, and the kitchen, I knew—I believed with all my heart—would always be there. We believe in immortality. We insist on it.

Within the fence, a flock of blackbirds and starlings were rooting around, ignoring me. I clapped my hands, and they flew away. I took hold of an iron spike and looked at the cold gray stones so familiar, with Uncle Willem's now among them. He had a VA marker, a flat marble rectangle, which told that he had lived for a certain time, and that he was a corporal in the 365th Infantry Regiment, First Division, World War II. I heard Mother's voice again, telling the story so plain and straightforward that it must be true.

They went to visit Uncle Willem at the VA hospital for the last time. He lay in a ward in an iron bed, staring at the ceiling. He was shriveled up to almost nothing, for he had quit eating and had to take nourishment through a tube in his arm. He'd had a stroke, and his face was twisted up so that he looked like an aged Popeye, his skin the color of ashes. They stood around the bed for a little while, and all at once Uncle Willem stirred. He looked at Nancy and smiled and beckoned with a little scarred claw of a hand. They had to bend close so they could hear him. "Say there, Little Sister," he said. "How you like them shoes?" Then he pulled the covers over his head and left us forever.

GOOD NEIGHBORS

John Boyer

It was the year after they moved in that the Rudkus children went missing. I remember that day like it was yesterday. It was the last Sunday in August of 1991, one of those Alabama days where you know you have to get out in the morning, or be ready to spend the whole day inside until it cools off in the evening. Later in the afternoon when you hear the cicadas calling each other like someone's shaking maracas in your ears, you know it's time to get inside before the daily thunderstorm comes and dumps its load of water like the next Great Flood.

Ken's work brought them down here from Chicago. Ben and Macy, the children, were two of the most precious little flowers you'll find in the Lord's paradise, but they were as Northern as they come when they first moved here. Every speck of Southern politeness those children learned was taught to them by my Roy and me.

Last year, Judy joined my Bible study group, and I know it's been good for her to speak her mind about things. Why, my own faith in the Good Lord has been strengthened, seeing how even something unthinkable and awful like what happened to the Rudkuses can bring people together, making us all stronger. With the Lord's help, we'll get her through this trial.

I just wish we'd had more time with those two little babies. I hate the thought of them in hell, but they did not find the Lord before they passed on, and we all know where the road of good intentions leads.

Judy told it that she figured they had a few hours before the humidity made it impossible to be outside. Summer break was almost over, and she needed to get the kids out of the house. Just up the road is a real beautiful place we used to call Oak Tree Park. There's a nice set of playground equipment at the top of the hill, protected by a great big live oak that must be three hundred years old if it's a day. That old granddaddy tree looks like he's stretching his great, thick, moss-covered arms wide over the jungle gym and picnic tables that rest in his shade. Judy liked to read at the tables while the kids played on the jungle gym. Most days she'd pack a lunch, which they'd eat before getting themselves back home and out of the heat.

Just past the reaches of the great oak tree, the hill makes its way down to the bay, gradually easing on for about a hundred yards or so. On both sides of the hill from top to bottom are some of the thickest woods you'll ever see. The slope of the hill conspires with the tall trees to make it impossible to see the bottom until you're just about there. Once you get down there, dirt and grass give way to a wide, sandy beach that slips away to the water.

The Oak Tree Park community pier was built there going on twenty years ago. People love to fish off that pier, and all kinds come to enjoy that beautiful park, even on Sundays in the summertime. Used to be that the water was so full of redfish and trout that all you had to do was drop your line in the water, and you'd catch something. My Roy said that once or twice a year when he was a boy, he'd sneak away with his friend Donnie Fife and horse around at that very spot. If you must know, I think a lot of what he caught in those waters as a boy ended up in that special fertilizer formula of his.

My Roy, God rest his soul, had a beautiful head of hair the color of sand. It got a little thin as his years got on, just as most men's hair will, but it suited him fine. Gave him the look of the grandfather I know he always wished he could be. When he was in a mood to fool around, he'd take a basketball in each hand and mill them around fast as he could go. Those basketballs looked like honeydews would in my hands. Ben and Macy loved when he did that. Those two little angels would just fall to stitches laughing.

That gentle bear of a man had no idea how strong those hands of his were, so it's not really fair to say that Roy broke my arm bones. Truth of the matter is my arm got broken, and I was as much at fault as he was. He had just returned from one of his five-day trips into the woods, which is about how long he'd stay every time he just wandered off like that, and his usual routine was to take a great big nap. Before he came in the house, Roy would always stop off in the shed to clean things up. That shed was his private place. He always kept it locked up tight, and I never saw the inside of it, which suited me just fine. It was where he applied his genius.

Roy supported the two of us quite comfortably with a fertilizer formula that he himself developed. "Just the right mixture of shit and love" was all he would let on about his fertilizer, then he'd give a queer smile and turn his head away. That was another thing to admire about the man. Never went out of his way to insult another person. Whenever he said something he thought was clever, he'd just get that little smile on his face and turn his head away. Didn't like to make other people feel bad. A month or so before he died, the shed burned to the ground, and all of its secrets went with it.

On the day my arm got broke, when he was done with whatever business he had in the shed, he came right into the house and marched into the shower. Didn't say a word of hello to me.

As the shower water got started, I walked back to the porch and looked out to the shed. It was hard to believe my eyes, but the door to the shed was wide open. Standing where I was on the porch, I thought I could even see some into it, but the lights were turned off. I knew he took a lot of pride in whatever he did out there, and never before had I even seen the closed door without a lock, let alone the door standing wide open for all to see. I just knew he wouldn't want it to be that way.

Thinking back, what I should have done was wait for him to get out of the shower, then tell him about the door. Silly me, though, I have the tendency to try to do too much for people, even when they don't want things done for them, and I just took it upon myself to walk out to the shed and close the door. It was a little way from the house, maybe a hundred yards or so, and the grass was wet, so I was in no great hurry to get there, and before I got two thirds of the way to the shed, Roy had caught up with me. He was still dripping from the shower, wearing only his big old white drawers.

He could have just called out my name, asked me to stop, and I'd have turned right around. It all happened in a flash of the mind, but I did register the slapping of feet on muddy grass, then he had my arm in his great big bear paws, and I heard the bones snap. Like two cheese straws. He had me in his hands, and my arm had a new joint.

His eyes were open wider than you would think possible, like the eyeballs would fall out, and the pupils were opened up big as saucers. His whole face was flat. I knew my arm was broken, and so did he. "I'm sorry, Roy, the door was open, I knew you didn't want it like that, I was just fixin' to close it" was what I said to him.

His eyes slowly got back to normal, sort of faded back into his head as the lids closed down, and he told me, "I know you was, baby. I just came out to thank you. But look at your arm now, baby doll. Why don't you go back to the house, let me close this old shed up, and we'll get that arm taken care of." The sweetness and love and caring were so true in his voice that I just wanted to cry, and I turned right around and walked back to the house so I could wait for him to come back and help me.

Ken Rudkus was a different kind of man, and I do not believe Judy knew the kind of love I shared with my Roy. My Roy never was much of a golfer, praise the Lord, but I know there are some who treat it like a religion. So, on that awful Sunday, like every other Sunday since I had known them, Judy was left with the kids, and they had to fend for themselves while the man of the house and his cronies looked for their salvation in that little white ball.

Now, I know what I would have been doing if they were my kids. After all, this was a Sunday. This part always makes me shake my head. It just seems so obvious. What kind of person do you expect to run into at a place of entertainment when all the good Christians are in church? And what good do you think can come of playing when you ought to be praying? So it was that after about an hour on the jungle gym, Ben and his sister wandered down to the pier. Judy, bless her heart, stayed up on the hill, reading her novel on the picnic bench in the shade of the oldest known live oak in the county.

Ken has never said anything accusing to her, I just know it. You have to know he has thought about it, though. Who wouldn't? Judy has spoken often about the guilt that eats away at her. You can't help but think that those two lovely children would still be alive today if only Judy had put her book aside and walked down the hill with them. I have never told her that she should've been in church in the first place. Fate is fate, and no amount of wishing can change what has happened, no matter how much we might want to. It was just God's will that moved those two to descend unprotected to meet their destiny.

When the kids first went missing, everyone just assumed that they must have wandered a little too far into the woods and couldn't find their way out. So when Judy first called 911 all in a panic, the first thing anyone did was start searching through those woods. I'm here to tell you, we had quite a community response. It was like folks dropped everything else they were doing to come out and help. Volunteers even came in from other states, I think from as far away as California, believe it or not. Little Macy's and Ben's pictures were all over the newspapers and television. Ken and Judy had several interviews on the national news, and I think Judy even got to meet Katie Couric. It seemed like months before you could turn on the TV or look at the newspaper without being reminded of the anguish of the Rudkuses.

The search parties kept on looking, day after day, around the clock, good weather or bad. I was very proud of my Roy during this time. He was one of the search leaders, and proved to know a lot about those woods, on account of all the time he spent playing in them as a boy. Those dadgum woods are so tricky that one or two of the search parties even got lost themselves, and Roy and his crew had to break away from the Rudkus search to find them. Everybody got found eventually; except, of course, the children. This went on for two weeks or so, when we all got a surprise we'd rather not have gotten.

It seems Ben and Macy weren't the first ones to go missing around here. Some black lady in Lagniappe, a town about twenty minutes south from here, told one of the reporters that her daughter never showed up for supper one day, and hasn't been seen since. That was two years before all this happened. Nobody thought much of it back then, because this girl was older, about sixteen, and everybody figured she had just run away. Once her story got on the news, though, all kinds of missing people were getting mentioned, though all the rest were either homeless, or ladies of ill repute. We all had to wonder if something terrible wasn't going on in our peaceful little community.

Donnie Fife, Roy's old childhood buddy, was our sheriff. He always impressed me with how well he handled the responsibility of the job, but now as I think back about it, he never had much policing to do in a quiet place like where we lived. Once all this mess came about, though, Donnie changed for the worse.

When the kids first went missing, he was in the habit of coming over to the house in the evenings after a full day of searching. Donnie, Roy, and I would sit out on the porch, have some cold drinks, and talk over the day's events. Two weeks after the kids went missing, right around when that black lady from Lagniappe was spouting off about her missing daughter being ignored until two white kids disappeared, our old family friend developed an attitude my momma used to call contrary. He just seemed more agitated than usual. This particular night we weren't sitting more than ten minutes when Donnie says to Roy something like, "You and me, we've got a long history in those woods."

Then Roy says, "Yeah, Donnie, I guess we do."

"It's a good thing, ain't it, Roy, that you know so much about those woods? You've sure been a real help finding all those lost searchers," Donnie said to him, only his voice didn't sound right. "Shame we ain't found any sign of those lost children, though, ain't it?"

"Donnie," Roy said, and he patted him on the arm, real friendly, trying to soothe whatever was bugging his old friend. "I ain't no better than you. You've made things real easy for me all the years I've known you."

Donnie jerked his arm away from Roy, knocked over his iced tea, but didn't move to pick it up. "Look Roy—" but he never finished whatever it was he had been fixing to say. I was starting to get a little uncomfortable, and it was a relief when Roy turned to me and said, "Baby doll? It looks as though Donnie has gone and knocked over his tea glass. Would you mind fixing him another one?" But by the time I got back with the tea, Donnie was driving off in a big hurry, and Roy did not look like he wanted any company, so I turned around and took myself back inside.

Roy didn't come into the house right away. I didn't know what to do, so I just made busy in the kitchen, but I did catch a glimpse of his face as he stood out there, flexing those big old hands of his, eyes open wide and fixed on the spot where his old friend had been standing.

A week later, Roy had his first stroke. We were both home when it happened, and I was sure he had died. Eight o'clock in the morning, both of us were out on the porch enjoying the cool. "Baby? Can I get you some more coffee?" Roy asked me as he stood up, mug in hand.

"No thank you, Roy, I believe I've had enough. There's still some left for you, though." That was when I noticed he had stopped moving. Just stared into nothing. "Roy? Is everything all right?"

Then he fell over. Lost all control of body functions, coffee mug clattering along the brick floor, but somehow it didn't get broke. The doctors later told me he suffered a minor stroke, but the fall split some great big vein in the brain, and caused him a blood clot inside his skull. Two days after the fall, it had grown to the size of an orange, and he had to have brain surgery to clear it out. They couldn't tell me if he would live or die.

We finally got him home a month or so after it all happened, and with his motivation, it wasn't long before Roy was out tooling around in his shed again. The doctor was very clear about one thing: Roy was not to go out into the woods alone any more, or else there would be a time when he would simply not return. A lesser man might have felt himself a victim, or questioned his faith, but not my Roy. We had the time together those last few months that most married people long to have, but few ever get.

Months passed, and winter came and went. The two lost children were not found. Roy had another stroke that winter. It was a small one, but it did slow him down some, and he took to staying around the house more, what with his left leg being pretty weak. He spent most of that winter and spring in the shed, tending to the flower garden. He was a good Christian man to the very end.

I ran into Donnie Fife one more time. He at least had the decency to appear at Roy's funeral. I know now that he couldn't have brought on Roy's stroke, but it just happened so close to their falling-out that I couldn't help blaming him some, and I know that is not right. Still, neither Donnie nor his wife came to visit during Roy's year of sickness and that is not how friends treat friends. When we talked at the funeral, though, all was forgiven.

But nothing changed. He and Elizabeth walked away arm in arm, and I never heard from them again.

One final blessing came out of Roy's shed before it burned to the ground. It was early spring after the kids went missing, and they had been formally declared dead only the day before. Roy came out of that shed of his with two of the loveliest little flowers you have ever seen in pots. He had them decorated special with bows, one blue and one pink, and we took them over to the Rudkuses. It was just about the sweetest thing I've ever seen a man do. He didn't go on much longer after that; you could see how the strokes were eating him up. He fairly limped over to their house. I tried to help him carry the pots, but he wouldn't have it. "Myorchids" was all he said, and he repeated it a few times. The way he ran the two words together made it sound funny. Roy passed on a short while later, but Judy keeps those beautiful flowers on proud display in her living room. It gives me no end of joy to see the comfort she feels when she holds those flowerpots in her hands and calls them "my orchids." I know Roy would be so proud.

DEAR FRIEND

Rick Bragg

Dear Friend,

I never know what to say in a time of loss. Everything turns to ashes in my mouth, and words seem so trite and useless. But in such times you are moved to say something the same way you are moved to knot a choking scrap of silk around your neck and squeeze into grown-up shoes and a black coat. It is how we mourn, in Alabama. Sometimes, of course, we also pitch a good drunk, but that is mostly the Catholics.

But we will have no funeral for Cormac, because he is not gone, only lost, and there is a big difference there. Most likely he is not even lost.

He is, I believe, stole.

Somebody saw him, saw his fine red hair and his well-formed body and broad, intelligent head, and stole him. Sons of bitches.

Because Cormac is not a mean soul, he allowed himself to be stole. Somebody said, "Hey, boy," and he bounced on over, and was took.

And we are left here to be sorry.

But there some things that need to be said to you from a friend, and I have never been quiet in my life.

In his days with you and your wife and your boys, he was warm and well-fed and loved as much as any beast can be, and a whole lot better than a lot of children.

He suffered no cruelties. He was not beaten into compliance.

He lived fat and easy in a house on the hill.

The last time I saw him, with you, he literally jumped for joy.

Over and over, he hurled his body into the air, higher and higher.

It almost made me cry.

I had no luck with dogs. The wheels of cars took them, mostly. Feists, beagles, mixed-breed hounds, all perished on the Roy Webb Road. The only dog I had for any length of time died from heartworms because I lapsed in my care of him, because I was too busy. I should tell people that, when they say nice things about me.

But I had no luck, as to dogs.

So, when you told me how Cormac lay at your feet every single day as you wrote your novel, I was touched but also a little jealous. I am sorry now, for that envy.

Cormac seemed to sense that in me. He followed me around your house, insisting to be loved, and when I sat quietly in an otherwise empty room, he came in and laid his head on my knee, and just left it there.

Only when he heard your voice did he even twitch, and then he was gone, chasing the sound of your voice up the stairs.

I hope, someday, he just comes walking back up in the yard.

I hope he makes one of those miracle treks home.

I would like to think that whoever took him will have an attack of conscience, but that is unlikely. A man who would steal a dog is a low man, and it may be that all we will ever get from him is a darker satisfaction.

We will learn who took Cormac. We will not kill that man—because even though he is a thief, he may have cared for the dog, gently.

But I think we should take him to the swamp. I think we should tie him to a tree, and ask him some questions. We should scare him a little bit.

And if he laughs, or sneers, we will chop off one of his toes.

One of the big ones.

We will take him to the doctor, and leave him in the parking lot, and if he threatens us with legal harm, we will remind him that he has nine more toes.

That day, and that satisfaction, may never come. All that is left, in the end, is this.

He was not a lawn ornament, not an animal you bought to be fashionable. He had two acres of trees and fence line to mark as his own, and he did so with great determination. When you left the swimming pool gate open, he dove right in, no matter how many times you hollered, "Cormac, damn ye," and chased him out.

He terrorized squirrels and tolerated cats. He woke your two boys up by jumping into their beds. He listened as you read to him from words you wrote. He always, always thought it was fine. He thought you were Melville. He thought you were Faulkner.

He did not, for a big dog, greatly stink.

He loved you back, all of you. You could just tell.

I envy you, still.

Your friend,
Rick

THOSE SUMMER SUNDAYS

Andrea Hollander Budy

Sundays my father would join us
at the club pool, his skin
white and delicate as cigarette paper

on the one day he took
from the women who lined
his waiting room

month after month.
I waited at the shallow end.
He rose from the board

and dropped
straight as a table knife
without a splash. Always

the women stared, women
from whose bodies he had pulled
daughters, released sons.

And never
would he surface
until he had maneuvered through the depths

to the place where I stood. Giddy, I would close
my eyes as he hoisted me
from the flawless water

on his shoulders, the two of us
one thing, perfect and tall.
I did not know then

of the sometimes dangerous
entrances of men, how some will lift
what others slowly drown.

AN EXPLANATION

Andrea Hollander Budy

*Frank was missing something, and women would do anything to
find out what it was.*

—James Salter

It's nothing, really, just a kind of trick I use
to keep them. I look up from their bodies

with a tenderness I've maintained after we've made love
wishing to extend even further

that welcome moment of grace that settles in
just after the inevitable diminishment

over which neither of us has any control.
I look up from their bodies and glance

toward a window, if there is a window,
or a closet door or a calendar on the wall, perhaps

a candle on the bedside table with its rarefied flame.
If there's a painting above the bed, I make sure it's safe

before we even begin to undress or lie down
to undress one another. Once

it was one of those portraits of Jesus
naked and bleeding, which ruined everything.

I'm all there when I'm there. Yet sometimes, I've learned,
it's better to lift them out of themselves by giving

a little bit less. I don't mean to be cruel,
cutting them off from my pure attention. I only want

the deepest they'll give me, the thing you can't ask for—
they don't know where it is themselves. I think

of Valentino who was forced to use only his eyes to speak
and his body, the sound of his voice kept irretrievably

from us, that incomplete circle that wanted finishing,
and we, of course, supplied the best.

That's it, really. Leaving something necessary
out that they'll fill in. Something small, of course,

but important, something at first you don't withhold
so they'll notice right away when you do.

Remember the page in the children's magazine
that displayed a kitchen or a yard and asked you to find

the ten things wrong? An upside-down
clock, say, or a dog in a tree?

It's taken me years to learn this, and it works.
A woman will nest herself for as long as I want her.

She gives me more and more of everything, tries
to fill my gaps, plug holes in my conversation.

When she finally tires of her own failures, and leaves,
it never hurts. I always have at least her sympathies

and her longing. There are so many beautiful women
lighting this world. It's the only way I've found

to possess them.

In the Thirteenth Year of the Jonquil

David Campbell

Julie Ann stared across the road at the clumps of jonquils adorning the woods. Jonquils are a stupid flower, she thought; one day of sunshine and they will shoot up a bright yellow flag, just as if it were spring, never mind that it is just a warm February day in south Mississippi. She sat in the porch swing in her wedding dress, an hour past the time for her wedding.

This was the thirteenth year she remembered watching the jonquils bloom. Things were supposed to be different in 1949. It was after three o'clock and a light drizzling rain filtered across the landscape following a short downpour. If she wanted, Julie Ann could have walked across and picked a bouquet, and the light rain would have hardly wet her.

"Julie Ann, get in here with the rest of us; I don't know what you expected. How many times? Ah, all right, I ain't gonna say nothing else," Julie Ann's sister, Vola Mae, called out in a harsh, gruff voice through the screen door. Julie Ann could hear the others talking inside, about her, she suspected.

The voices came from what was known as the front room. It was located through the door at the other end of the porch from where she sat swinging. The door by the swing led from the porch to a bedroom where her siblings, Monroe and Brother, slept. She shared the bedroom behind that space with Monroe's two children. Her papa slept in a bed in the front room by the fireplace. He had bought the house before the Depression with money he earned as a carpenter employed by a large sawmill to build housing for an influx of workers. Most of his adult life had been spent as a tenant farmer. He had not worked much after a glancing nail struck him in the eye while he was working for the sawmill.

Julie Ann knew her papa was not in there talking about her, and he would stop the others if he heard, but at seventy-nine, he did not

41

hear much. He was probably in the kitchen at the dinner table reading his Bible. Her mother had died fifteen years earlier of pneumonia.

"Jesse'll be here, y'all just hold your horses," Julie Ann hollered back at Vola Mae.

Her sisters sitting in the front room lowered their voices. "She ain't got no business marrying anyway. Who gonna take care of Papa?" Mary Louise said, sitting up on the edge of her chair and leaning toward the others.

"If she marries and leaves, Monroe's gonna want to send them young'uns to stay with one of us," Vola Mae shot back. Monroe's wife had died a year earlier, and he had moved in with Brother and Papa so Julie Ann could help take care of his children.

"I ain't taking them. I got young'uns myself," Mary Louise said. "Besides, what if I have another baby and need her to stay with it while I work in the field?"

"Y'all hush, that preacher'll be back in here any minute," Emily, the oldest sister, said. Brother Reed had stepped out back to the outhouse. "Did y'all know she bought lime with egg money and poured it in the toilet?" she said. "That ain't been done since we was chaps. Guess she wants everything smelling perfect too," Emily said and chuckled.

"I don't care, she's almost forty. Like Mary Louise said, she ain't got no business marrying," Vola Mae said. "Anyhow, how come she got a wedding dress and we didn't? We just as poor now as then."

"'Cause she sewed it herself," Emily answered.

"I know," Mary Louise mocked. "She saved her egg money, bought the material little by little, and sewed it over the last fifteen years. Started it when she thought she was gonna marry that Hudson boy."

"Thirteen years," Emily corrected.

"Where the men at?" Mary Louise asked.

"I bet they're out at the barn in that dern plum wine Brother made," Emily answered.

"I hope they get the squirts," Vola Mae said.

At the barn, five men sat around a crock container almost as big as a barrel and served wine with a gourd dipper. Children played on the back porch where they had taken refuge from the misting rain. Most of Julie Ann's family had come to see her get married. Jesse's family was not planning to come although he had said that his mother might ride with him in his old truck to the wedding.

On the front porch Julie Ann made slow, calculated swings. She sat with her left foot dangled to the floor and the other folded up under her. She would study the porch floor, look over her shoulder down the road, bring her eyes back to the porch floor and then gently push off with the foot for a slight swing. The old swing creaked once each time she repeated this motion. Julie Ann did this even though she knew she would hear Jesse's truck if it came up the road, that popping sound it sometimes made.

Julie Ann was a tiny, frail thing, short and not big enough around to make a shadow except at the hips. She had a pretty face, dark brunette hair with even darker eyebrows over saucer-size brown eyes. Her papa said that once you knew her, you never noticed her right eye. When she looked straight ahead her right eye faced slightly off-center to the right. Her papa said it could have been fixed with enough money. The dress had a round neck and fitted sleeves. The center front of the bodice was accented with ten little ball buttons and one oval button. Thick lace wrapped over the shoulders on each side of the buttons. The ends of the sleeves and the bottom of the dress were edged with the same lace. Her hair was pulled behind her ears, tied with a ribbon and hanging between her shoulder blades.

Julie Ann shut her eyes and remembered when she had started the dress. It was the Depression, and she was working in the sewing room in Pickering, the only public job she had ever held. She had only finished the fourth grade, they moved around so much, but her mother always said, "Tell that you finished the sixth grade."

Charles Hudson was in the CCC Camp at the lake. It was one of the Civilian Conservation Corps camps that President Roosevelt had set up to help those without work, and it was the nearest one to Charles's home. He was from Grant County, about fifteen miles below

Pickering. Charles was a long, lanky man, six years older than Julie Ann, and wore a small moustache. She smiled as she thought of how they would hold hands and take long walks on the railroad track on Sunday afternoon. He had saved her one afternoon from what her mother called a coach-whip snake. Her mother taught her that the black snake with a tail that looked as if it were plaited would catch you and whip you to death with its tail, she remembered. Charles walked more than five miles every Sunday to see her. She knew he would eventually suggest marriage.

She gave all of the money she earned in the sewing room to her papa, but sometimes she saved a small amount from the sale of eggs that she toted to town and sold to Mr. Smith at his grocery in Pickering. She set aside that money and used it for little extras she thought the family needed. "Brother and Monroe will take my money and spend it on liquor if they know I got it. If something happens to me, the money is in one of your little tobacco sacks, pinned to my step-ins," she told her papa. Once, she saved for a coffeepot, which she hid and only used when visitors came. "People'll think we're really poor if we use that syrup can for a coffeepot when they come," she explained to her papa.

She had always wanted a real wedding dress for her anticipated special day. The Freeman family, whom Julie Ann sometimes did ironing for, gave her an old pattern for a dress during the time she was being courted by Charles. She kept it hidden in her pillowcase.

During the eighteen months Charles courted her, Julie Ann saved enough money to buy the unbleached cotton material that would become the base of her wedding dress. In the days leading up to when she marched into Smith's Grocery and bought the cloth, she walked with her right hand clutching the little tobacco sack pinned to her side. She hid the joy she felt from her brothers and sisters, who might think the money should be spent on the family. Her papa knew and approved. "You do enough for us. Do something for yourself," he assured her.

It was in the spring when Charles left the camp to go visit his family. He told her he would be back, but weeks went by, and she did not hear from him. Julie Ann waited patiently, even wrote a letter and waited by the mailbox to make sure it left safely, but no answer came. Someone at the sewing room said, "I heard he run upon a woman he was supposed to marry before he went to the CCC. They in New Orleans now."

Julie Ann pretended she did not hear the remark, but later she stood outside with her back to the building and quietly sobbed.

The cotton cloth remained wrapped in plain brown paper, just as Mr. Smith had handed it to her across the counter in his store. It was hidden under the mattress on her side of the bed, safe, she knew, since everyone else in the house left it to her to make the beds.

After Julie Ann had given up on Charles coming back, it crossed her mind to use the dress cloth in a quilt, or shirts for her papa. All of her dresses and the shirts for her family were made from flour and feed sacks. But Julie Ann never seriously considered using the material for anything but a wedding dress.

Even before she met Rufus "Catfish" Morris, Julie Ann sat one sunny afternoon in a patch of jonquils and picked through the button jar for something suitable for the wedding dress, just in case. The jar was a quart container in which buttons from any discarded garments were deposited. Many of them were from dresses worn by her mother. She found only ten of the little ball buttons she needed. So she substituted an oval button for the eleventh.

Catfish had brought Brother home one Sunday morning from a Saturday-night drunk at the pool hall, Julie Ann remembered. He was handsome and witty, but more important, he seemed attracted to Julie Ann. A daredevil, Catfish once attempted to walk atop the picket fence surrounding the yard. Julie Ann gasped when he fell, then burst into laughter when she saw he was not hurt. He was always doing things meant to be funny and watching to see if Julie Ann was looking.

Finally, one Saturday afternoon he walked over and sat by her in the double rocker on the porch. "Brother ain't the reason I come over here so much," he said without looking at her. Julie Ann thought he did not seem brave when he was serious. She sat still and stiff, holding her breath. He seemed to study something a long time before speaking again. "I really would like...want to court you," he said, then turned and looked straight into her eyes. It must be like Papa said, she thought, he doesn't seem to notice my bad eye.

"You would, huh?" Julie Ann said. "I think I would like that too."

Catfish was Julie Ann's age and had finished the eighth grade. He had a full-time job at the sawmill but also still lived with his family. He hung around the pool hall, but not for the drinking that went on in the parking lot. Catfish just liked to play dominos.

They talked a lot and took long walks. Catfish would not let her frown, she remembered. If he could not get her to smile with some story, he would dance around in front of her, making faces. It was a happy time when she was with Catfish.

Julie Ann did not think of it as premature to start the dress even though they had not talked of marriage. While everyone was out of the house, she carefully spread the cloth and opened the pattern out on the dinner table. She took small pins from a matchbox and pinned the pattern to the cloth. It was just as beautiful as she remembered. She cut some of the pieces that day, but waited several months to finish cutting it out. She still needed lace to complete the dress.

It was a cold Monday in December when the awful news came. Julie Ann chopped stove wood that day and Catfish worked at the sawmill. Her papa did not hear President Roosevelt's actual speech, but he heard later that the Japanese had attacked Pearl Harbor on Sunday. Catfish joined the army. Monroe was drafted into the army, and Brother joined the Coast Guard. Before Catfish left for overseas, they made plans to marry when he returned.

Julie Ann shoved back hard in the porch swing and bit her lower lip as she remembered that Catfish hadn't come home. She remembered how she felt, how she wanted to burn the unfinished wedding dress in the weeks after she learned that Catfish had been killed. She caught the oval button, sewn on only a month earlier, between her thumb and finger and began to gently rub it.

In the front room, the sisters were still talking about the unful-filled wedding.

"Like I said, what did she expect?" Vola Mae said. "Here's a man who arrived at her doorstep tied on the flatbed of a pickup truck." Brother had brought Jesse home with what he thought was a broken leg after pulling him from a drunken brawl over an ex-wife at the pool hall. He had tied him to the truck bed to keep him from rolling off and to keep the leg straight.

"Yeah, she fed him biscuits with syrup and cream," Mary Louise said. "Least little thing, she brightens up and falls in love."

"How many wives done left him? Two, and he's twelve years older than her," Vola Mae said. "Ain't nothing but a drunken house painter."

"He's a carpenter and he's done quit drinking. Besides, there ain't nothing to them other wives," Emily said.

They don't know Jesse, Julie Ann thought. She shifted in the swing and twisted her shoulders. "They woudden here the night he made Brother leave me alone when he wanted to drag me out of bed at midnight to make a pan of biscuits," she said softly through puck-ered lips. He wants things, like owning our own place, and he cares what happens to me, she thought.

In the kitchen Brother Reed pulled out a ladder-back chair and sat down at the dinner table. He laced his fingers together and gently laid his hands on the red-checkered oilcloth table covering. The old man looked up from his Bible. "Mr. McDonald, I don't want to cause any heartache, but that man ain't coming," Brother Reed said. "I know she's been hurt so much over the years, God knows it was awful for that boy to get killed in the war."

"It ain't been but a little over an hour," her papa said, looking at his pocket watch.

"I know, but he'd be here if he was a-coming," Brother Reed an-swered. "Besides, I got to get back to town," he explained. Mary Louise, Vola Mae, and Emily listened from the front room.

"This is gonna hurt," Vola Mae said. The others sat silently as Brother Reed passed quietly through the room and pushed the screen door open.

Julie Ann heard the screen door creak and looked. Brother Reed stood framed behind the door, part of his face obscured by a cotton ball stuck in a hole in the screen to keep flies out. He held the door and spoke through the screen.

"Julie Ann, I'm sorry, but I'm fixin' to have to go back now. I'm sure something has happened and he'll come later." Julie Ann sat silently, still rubbing the button between her thumb and finger. "Y'all just come get me on another day," he suggested.

Julie Ann nodded.

Brother Reed then stepped onto the porch and eased the door shut, trying unsuccessfully to close it without the telltale squeak. He walked softly across the porch to the steps like a man leaving the sick-room of a patient who had fallen asleep during a visit.

Julie Ann watched as he walked along the brick walk to the gate, watched his hand reach for the latch, watched him carefully push the gate open, but turned and looked away as he hurried to his car. She listened as the quick thump, thump, thump sound reported that Brother Reed's car was passing across the cattle gap guard over the road at the end of the driveway. No sounds came from inside the house. She no longer heard children playing behind the house. Just silence hung in the air; so silent she could almost hear the steps the Dominique rooster made crossing the yard.

Soon she heard her sisters mumbling in the front room. She used her finger to catch a tear in the corner of her eye and then crossed her arms tightly. The evening temperature drop had not arrived, but she suddenly felt cold.

In the distance, she heard a car horn blowing. She looked but did not see anything. Then she heard it again. Brother Reed was coming back tooting his horn. He turned into the driveway; the tires gave the thump, thump, thump sound across the cattle gap guard, and the sedan sped up the driveway. He was waving his arm from the window and shouting something. Julie Ann rose from the swing and walked across the porch to the steps. The screen door creaked and three heads popped out. She could hear her papa's cane tapping the floor as he moved across the room inside.

"Look what I found," Brother Reed shouted from the window of the car as he stopped at the gate. A man with a despondent look on his face sat inside the car beside Brother Reed. Julie Ann gazed with no emotion. Her family watched silently from inside. Brother Reed swung the door open and hurriedly got out of the car. Then he harnessed his enthusiasm and waited as a short, slim man without a sign of a waistline crawled from the passenger-side door. The first thing Julie Ann saw was a wiry arm that led to fingernails stained yellow by cigarettes. Then a head of dark wet hair emerged, showing graying around the ears. Jesse, soaking wet, slowly got out of the car and carefully placed his steps toward Julie Ann. He wore a khaki shirt with a wide flowery tie and gray pants. No one moved until Jesse reached the bottom of the steps in front of Julie Ann.

"I'm sorry. My truck wouldn't crank. I took a shortcut up the railroad track and it started raining…"

"Hush," Julie Ann said reaching down to touch her finger to his lips. "It don't matter. You here now."

"Yes, it does," Jesse said. "I got out of the rain in that old tenant house down on the Truman place. It's vacant. We can live there."

Jesse and Julie Ann lined up for a wedding, she in the beautiful wedding dress, Jesse shivering a little and with a ring of water slowly forming at his feet. The men had finally left the plum wine and were gathered in the yard watching the porch wedding. "I knowed he'd come," Vola Mae leaned over and whispered to Julie Ann.

Julie Ann glanced across at the jonquils, still waving their yellow flags.

JOE AND SHEILA

Marshall Chapman

"Life's either too short or too long, I can't decide which."

Joe was lying there smoking a cigarette. He always did that after they made love. Sheila sometimes wished they could just snuggle. Her skin always felt so vibrant after a good lovemaking session—smooth and warm, like hot silk. But Joe never seemed to notice. It was like his big brain would take over his little brain the minute his little brain finished its business. He'd come, then immediately reach for a cigarette, roll over on his back, and start waxing philosophical. Oh, he was generous enough while making love. Sheila couldn't complain there. Joe was a considerate lover, always making sure she came before he did. But the minute he came, he would disappear into his own thoughts.

Sheila and Joe had married young. Right out of high school. There wasn't much to do in Plainsville, Arkansas, but get married right out of high school. Nobody in Joe's family had ever been to college. Joe's father owned the local hardware store, and his mother had spent her whole life providing a good Christian home for her three children. Joe's older brother, Rufus, had settled comfortably into life in Plainsville, working alongside his father at the hardware store. He and his wife, Betty Lou, had three children and attended Mount Zion Baptist Church every Sunday with their families. Rufus was now in his late-twenties. Joe was twenty-five, and Caroline, their younger sister, was twelve. Joe and Rufus laughingly referred to her as "Love Child." Caroline loved both her brothers, but Joe was her favorite.

Joe had always been "the sensitive child" growing up. When he was but two years old, his grandmother, Mayleene, had referred to him as an old soul. "That child's got an old soul. Just look at him!" said Mayleene.

Rufus and Joe were both good athletes. Rufus had played halfback on the Plainsville High varsity football team, breaking three school records that still stand today. Joe surprised everyone when he turned his back on football and bought an old Gibson guitar at Billy Mac's Pawnshop with money saved from mowing yards the summer he turned fifteen. After that, he would sit in his room for hours with the door shut, listening to the radio while strumming on that old guitar. One day, out of the blue, he wrote a song called "It Hurts Me to Lie to You," but he didn't tell anyone. Especially his mother because she had sort of been the inspiration.

It hurts me to lie to you
I don't know what to do
If I can't tell you how I feel
Who can I tell it to?
I talk to God and wait to hear
What He has to say
But all I hear is silence
And it's driving me insane

Joe and Sheila started dating toward the end of their senior year. Sheila had high cheekbones and long, straight hair like Mary Travers in Peter, Paul & Mary. Most of the other girls teased their hair and wore it in a cute little bubble that flipped on the ends. Sheila was quiet and didn't run with the crowd. That's what caught Joe's attention. He liked that she was quiet and not a chatterbox like all the other girls. He felt like he could trust her. He figured she was deep in thought just like him. He'd always heard that "Still waters run deep." But five months into their marriage, he began to wonder if, in Sheila's case, still waters didn't just run still. Sheila was no rocket scientist. But she was steadfast and loyal. Whenever Joe talked about his dream of going to Nashville, Sheila didn't bat an eye. She'd just pour Joe another cup of coffee and sit there quietly while he went on and on about it. And she'd sit there quietly while he played her his songs too. After each one, he'd ask, "What do you think?" Sheila would smile and say, "That's really good. I like that one." She'd say that after every song. Joe knew that some of his songs were better than others, but Sheila's response was always the same. Sheila had been the very first person he had *ever* played one of his songs for. And when she said, "That's really good. I like that one," that first time, Joe thought his heart might burst from happiness.

Joe loved to drink coffee and smoke cigarettes while he was writing songs. He had to hand it to Sheila. She could sure perk up a good pot of coffee.

After a brief honeymoon in Memphis, Joe and Sheila had returned to Plainsville where they lived with Joe's parents for a while. Sheila worked as a nurse's aid at the local clinic, while Joe worked construction in nearby Jonesboro. By the time they had saved enough money to buy a used Dodge Dart and a tank full of gas, they took off for Nashville. As they pulled out of the drive, Caroline ran after them crying just like that little boy at the end of the movie *Shane*. "Don't go, Joe!!" she wailed. "Come back!!! Don't go-o-o-o!!!" For the next three days, Caroline was inconsolable.

Sixty miles outside of Nashville, at the Hurricane Mills exit, Joe had pulled off Interstate 40 to get some gas. "Hurricane Mills... Honey, I believe that's where Loretta Lynn lives," he said matter-of-factly as he hopped out of the car at the self-serve pumps.

"That's nice," Sheila said.

"I bet she's not home. She's probably out there on the road somewhere with her band."

"Probably," Sheila said.

Once in Nashville, Sheila and Joe checked into the Loveless Motel. The woman behind the counter had smiled when she saw Joe's guitar.

"First time in Nashville?" she asked.

"No, ma'am," Joe replied. Joe had been to Nashville twice in the past six months, walking up and down Music Row, hanging out at the Tally Ho Tavern and the Red Dog Saloon, playing his songs for whoever would listen.

One night at the Red Dog, a woman named Judy Baretta had given him a calling card that said JUDY BARETTA MUSIC PUBLISHING.

"Call me some time," she said. "I'd like to hear some more of your songs."

Joe thanked her and slid the card in his back pocket.

"You a songwriter?" the woman at the Loveless continued.

"Yes, ma'am."

"Well, I'm puttin' y'all in number six," she said, as she handed Joe the key. "Chris Gantry wrote 'Dreams of an Everyday Housewife' in that room. It was a big hit for Glen Campbell." Then she winked. "Maybe it'll bring you luck."

Later, as Joe and Sheila lay naked on top of the sheets after taking a shower together, a soft summer breeze blew over them, billowing the white curtains in the window. Normally, they would have made love, but the smell of frying chicken from the nearby restaurant was too alluring to ignore.

"Damn! That smells good!" Joe exclaimed. "Let's go get us some before they run out!"

"All right," Sheila said.

The restaurant was full, even though it was getting on toward the end of dinnertime. Joe and Sheila sat on a cushioned bench in the enclosed front porch, as they waited for their table to be called. Like everybody else, they gazed up at the walls, which were covered with framed publicity shots of every kind of celebrity you could imagine. There was Tammy Wynette, some politician named John Jay Hooker—Joe got a chuckle out of that one. "What a perfect name for a politician," he laughed, then pointed, "Look, honey…there's Gomer!" The black-and-white photograph revealed a surprisingly handsome and sophisticated Jim Nabors, a far cry from the character he played on *The Andy Griffith Show*. Oh, there were luminaries, has-beens, and wannabes. But they were all united in their praise of the delicious down-home cooking at the Loveless Café Restaurant. Especially the biscuits.

Their first night in Nashville had been a special one. Sheila had never seen Joe so happy as he was that night. They had splurged staying at the Loveless. Joe knew he would have to get a job soon doing *something*, even if it meant washing dishes. But on this night, they weren't thinking about that. They were eating fried chicken at the Loveless Café, and to hell with Plainsville, Arkansas, or Plainsville anything! This was Nashville, Goddamn, Tennessee, where anything could happen at any time. You just *never* knew! Why Johnny Cash might cut one of Joe's songs and they'd be livin' in high-cotton in no time! So *fuck* a bunch of poverty. Poverty could just go fuck itself to death in the Cumberland River for all anyone cared. But Joe wasn't consciously thinking these thoughts. He was too busy making Sheila laugh with his funny comments about things, like the seven fluffy biscuits he had eaten *after* his fried chicken dinner. Sheila had made some comment about something, and Joe said, "Huh?" Whereupon she repeated what she had said, and Joe again said "Huh?" Sheila didn't know what to think. Then Joe said, "Damn, honey, I've done ate so much, I can't hear!" Their sides nearly split from the laughter that followed.

Later that night, as they again lay on the sheets, the soft summer breeze was still fluttering softly through the window while outside the sky was full of stars beyond the neon of the Loveless Motel sign. Sheila eyes were shining with happiness as she lay propped up on a pillow while Joe sang part of a song he'd been working on. It was called "Don't Wake Me Up When I'm Dreaming."

Don't wake me up when I'm dreaming.
I'm happy out here with the stars.
The world with it's plotting and scheming
Seems so very distant and far.
Don't wake me up when I'm dreaming,
And I'll sing you a lullaby.
Then maybe you'll join me in dreamland,
But first you must close both your eyes

As he was singing, like magic Sheila drifted off to sleep. Joe pulled the covers up over her bare body, then quietly slipped out into the night air for a smoke. For a while, the moments seemed to string together like shimmering pearls, all the world humming in perfect harmony as Joe sat there on the concrete stoop just outside their door, listening to the crickets while gazing at the stars beyond the red-orange glow of his cigarette.

It's hard to know why things happen like they do. Or *don't* happen, as the case may be. Within the next five months, Joe got a job singing in the lounge at the Holiday Inn on Trinity Lane. He and Sheila moved into a one-bedroom apartment just north of Nashville in Gallatin, Tennessee. Joe signed a publishing contract with Judy Baretta. The contract gave Judy 100 percent ownership of Joe's songs, with the stipulation that she would "promote" them to the record companies. So far, none had expressed an interest. Joe was beginning to think maybe he'd made a mistake. Sheila had not trusted Judy from the start, but, as was her nature, she never said a word. Besides, she was busy working days in the claims department at the State Farm Insurance Agency. At first, she had enjoyed going to Joe's gigs at the Trinity Lane Holiday Inn. But after a few weeks, the long hours began to wear her down. She had to stop going weeknights so she could get some decent rest for work. Joe played from happy hour until well after midnight, six nights a week. The manager at the Holiday Inn had made him cut his hair and told him he couldn't wear jeans. The crowds were mostly traveling salesmen in red double-knit pants, leering at the waitresses in their black miniskirts and high heels. Every now and then, Judy Baretta would show up and buy Joe drinks between sets while encouraging him to keep writing songs. Joe had never been a heavy drinker. He'd have an occasional beer, and that was about it. When he first started playing at the Holiday Inn, the customers would buy him shots of Jack Daniels, and as the months wore on, he began to drink more and more. Many nights, he'd go to the bar after his last set and drink until the lights were turned on and the chairs up on the tables. Sheila was beginning to feel helpless, but what could she do? Maybe a visit home would do them both some good. Joe was becoming more and more withdrawn. Where was the fun-loving guy she'd married? Sheila realized she was lonely—more lonely when she was *with* Joe than when she was alone. She was also homesick. But for where? She wasn't sure anymore.

Joe quit his job at the Holiday Inn one night after the lounge manager had ordered him back up onstage only seconds after he'd stepped down off the bandstand to take a break.

"My bar just filled with customers and you're taking a break?"

Joe mumbled something about their agreement—"forty-five minutes on, fifteen minutes off"—and how he'd get back up and play another forty-five minutes as soon as he took a short break. What Joe failed to mention was his bladder, which felt like it might burst at any second.

The manager was livid. "If you don't get back up there right this minute"—his words were coming out like spit—"I guarantee you, that'll be the last forty-five minutes you ever play in my lounge!"

"Wrong," Joe said with surprising steadiness. "I just *played* the last forty-five minutes I'll ever play in your lounge." And with that he packed up his guitar and walked out into the parking lot to his car.

The next morning, Sheila called in sick, and they took off for Arkansas. For a while, Joe seemed like his old self, laughing as he reenacted for Sheila the drama of night before. But the closer they got to the Mississippi River, the quieter and more withdrawn Joe became.

Back in Plainsville, it was a hero's welcome. Joe's mother screamed out the minute they pulled in the drive, "Lord, look at you, son. You ain't nothing but skin and bones. Come on in this house and let's get you something to eat. Don't that wife of yours ever feed you none?" Sheila cringed, but kept smiling. Quite frankly, she was relieved to have Joe's mother taking care of him. Maybe now she could relax.

That evening, Rufus and Betty Lou and their kids came over for dinner. Caroline was beside herself as she followed Joe around like a puppy dog. At one point she ran headlong into the bathroom door, unaware that Joe was closing it behind him. "Hey, Love Child, watch your step now!" Joe said as he lifted her up and gave her a big hug. Thank God the only thing hurt was her pride, as everyone in the family had burst out laughing.

Joe's mother really put the food on the table that night: chicken and dumplings, mashed potatoes, green beans with artichoke relish, sweet rolls...the works. After dinner, Joe surprised everyone when he excused himself to go out with one of his old high school buddies, Billy Ray Rogers. "We're just going out riding for a bit. I won't be long."

And that was the last time Sheila, or Caroline, or anyone else in the family ever saw Joe alive. He and Billy Ray had roared off into the night in Billy Ray's brand-new 1974 Trans Am, stopping off at a couple of pool halls on the outskirts of town, where they downed a few beers. At one point, Billy Ray said, "Here, take this," as he handed Joe a couple of Dexedrines. Joe had always been a careful young man. Careful about himself and the people he cared about. But that night, he took the pills without even asking Billy Ray what they were. That was not a normal thing for Joe to do. Now, everybody knows that "normal is a cycle on a washing machine" and that's *all* normal is. But this was obviously no night for normal. They drove around some more, then pulled up in front of Billy Mac's Pawnshop, where a brand-new Sunburst Gibson J-200 stood gleaming in the window. Then someone threw a broken cinder block through the plate glass.

When the police arrived, Billy Ray was in the back of the store somewhere, and Joe was standing there in the broken display window holding the guitar. Nobody's entirely sure what happened next. The police yelled, "Put your hands up! Get 'em up!! Let's see some hands!!!" But Joe just stood there, frozen like a mannequin, holding the guitar. The police were nervous. There'd been an armed robbery earlier that evening. Within seconds, shots were fired. One ripped through the middle of Joe's heart, making a gaping, massive hole as it exited underneath his left shoulder blade. The officer who fired the shot would later testify he'd seen a gun in Joe's right hand. Ironically, one was found near the body. An old Colt single-action army pistol that Joe's grandfather—Mayleene's husband—had carried during World War I. The gun was not loaded. Later, there was testimony it hadn't been fired in over fifty years. It'd been stored away in a closet at Joe's parent's house all that time.

LIKE KUDZU

Ryan Clark

Del and I laugh long and hard. That's Del for you.

At first I'd just been trying to fill the silence with noise, the way people do when they need to break up the monotony of space. But then I told the story about my first time, and the way the girl had a pet guinea pig in her room, scurrying everywhere, and how I was allergic, and how the whole time I was trying to perform but I had to keep wiping my nose, wheezing like an old man on account of the guinea.

Del loves that story.

He coughs again, covering his mouth with a balled-up fist, and I worry about him like I always do. I try to keep my eyes on the road, try to make sure both hands stay on the wheel, try not to think about what we're doing or if we'll make it in time.

And Del? He sits shotgun, coughing, hacking up something that's probably going to kill him. He looks so pale now, his skin is like milk—the kind that's hanging on before it sours. Del's always hanging on.

He finally stops coughing and squints as the morning sun invades his eyes.

"You know you can't joke like that," he says to me. "I can't take it. I get to coughing and I can't stop, and then you get all worried. If you don't want me to cough, don't make me laugh."

Out of the corner of my eye, I see a smile stretch wide across his face, and I smile too. He's such a good person. He's got that blond hair, just like mine, sprouting every which way underneath the ballcap. And he's got those too-skinny arms poking out of his T-shirt. Wow. We don't even look like we're the same age anymore.

I remember years ago, when Del was trying to play T-ball, trying to be just like all the other kids. His jersey billowed around him, and he'd totter up to the tee and take his swings. He'd never hit the ball.

Never. And the other mothers and fathers in the stands would look away, uncomfortable at the sight. Some wiped away tears when he'd strike out. I watched it all from the dugout.

Del learned early that life wasn't fair, that people weren't nice, and that moments, real moments, are special. Even those moments when people look at you funny because they can see you're sick, and they can see there's no goddamn chance in heaven you'll ever hit the ball.

Even then, he'd already been sick for two years. God, that seems like so long ago.

Why do bad things happen to good people?

I snap back to the present. The story. Del laughing, Del coughing.

"Well, if you wouldn't laugh so hard, maybe I could tell a simple story," I say, looking ahead at the road. "But that's the way it always was, right? You remember third grade? Every day I'd try to say something funny at lunch to make milk come out your nose. I damned near did it everyday too. I'd always wait to tell the punch line of the story, wait until you started to drink, and you'd laugh and spray every time."

"I know, I know. Every time." Del smiles again. "All's I'm saying is, show a little common courtesy. I'm dying here."

That's Del for you. Taking a serious topic like his death and trying to joke about it. I hate it when he does that. He knows I hate it, but he does it anyway.

I look over to him and I shake my head. We've always been different.

He can write a poem, or tell you about symbolism in Salinger. He can discuss philosophical differences in science and religion. He can do math equations as long as the highway.

In high school, I had soccer practice in the fall, and Dell would have to wait for me because I was his ride. He'd sit on the bleachers, the sun in his face and a chemistry book on his lap. He'd do his homework there, and sometimes, after practice, he'd help the other players with theirs too.

He became our mascot. We should've been called the West Clayton High School Dels.

He's the artistic one, the serious one, the studious one, and the overachiever. He's the one that could've gotten the full scholarships, cured the cancers, and saved the world. He's my brother, and for all of these reasons, I love and protect him.

Like when that bastard Troy Lee McCarver and his gang jumped him after school. I found Del in a Dumpster, naked. They stole his wallet, blacked his eye, and separated his shoulder.

The next day, eighteen soccer players waited for Troy Lee and his friends outside detention.

I remember Troy Lee's eyes, wide with wonder and fear, when I crushed his face with my hand. His nose bled all over my yellow jersey. I let him have it again, then three more times. His forehead split open, his left eye swelled shut, and he fell to the ground. Del never worried about him again.

I grip the wheel tighter, my knuckles white. I still fill up with fury when I think about Troy Lee. But I feel pride too, because it may have been the most honorable thing I've ever done.

Because I am everything Del is not. I'm the fuck-up.

And I know this.

I'm the soccer star, the partier, the skirt-chaser. I'm the one that got the looks, the one that could schmooze anyone into anything, the one that got by on pure charm. I'm the one that has it all and can't do anything with it.

And now I'm lost.

Literally.

"Del, do you know where we are?"

His brown eyes open wide and he stares out the window of the car, scanning empty tobacco fields and miles of lonely interstate.

"I thought you knew where we were going!" he says. "I thought you knew! I can't keep up with this now, I—"

He coughs again, and I feel like I'm failing him.

"Del, calm down, calm down. We'll find our way. I think we may have gotten on the wrong road is all. We can just pull over and take a look at the map and maybe have a sandwich or something."

It's 11 A.M. now, and the sun isn't quite directly overhead. Still, it's hard to see the road very well because of the glare off the back windows.

Not that it really matters, so long as we're heading west.

The engine gurgles.

Boy, the car has been a real trouper. It really has.

Buy American, Dad used to say, so we did.

Ten years ago, we bought the car for Mom. It was snowing outside, and as we were coming home, Del blew hot breath on the inside of the window. Then he wrote his name with his finger. Dad told him to stop because he said he was putting fingerprints on the glass. I leaned over and smeared Del's name away. Del was mad.

I guess that was a pretty shitty thing to do.

Now, the car is ours. The other was demolished in the crash. So we have the puke-green '87 Escort with 135,000 miles on the odometer and a burned-out taillight. But it can still haul us around.

Again, back to reality. We're lost. We need to look at the map.

I pull over to the side and flip on the emergency lights, just in case anyone else might be on the road, though I doubt it.

I grab a peanut butter sandwich and a Bud from the cooler and give it to Del.

"Thanks," he says, and takes a swig. "Hey, I know you're going to get us there—I trust you. That's all I'm saying. I trust you."

I smile. "I know."

I open the map and scan it for any familiarity. I remember seeing several road signs for no-name towns: Martinsville, Cedarsburg, Cottonton, Dawson.

Those places are nowhere in sight.

A small wave of panic runs through me like electrical current. What if I don't get him there? What if his dying dream goes unfulfilled because of me?

My only hope is to keep driving west, to head to that town where it all can come true. Then he can pass in peace.

I study the map, and I see my eyebrows in the rearview mirror.

They're the kind that go all the way across the forehead and connect in the middle. Mom used to make fun of them and how they arch in one motion, saying they look like that monument in St. Louis.

Maybe I just need the distraction for a moment, because I look at the map again and see a familiar town name.

I think I know where we are.

Thank God.

"We're right here!" I say, proudly pointing to an almost nonexistent dot. "I think that if we just keep on going a bit, then get off on 27, we'll be okay. Then again, we could—"

"You know what?"

I stop talking. Del is looking out the side window. That's Del for you, always thinking and interrupting.

"What?"

"Look at it all. Just look at it. It's beautiful, isn't it?"

I look and see a wave of green blanketing the side of the highway. It looks like leaves, but it's covering everything in sight.

"What is it, Del? The leaves? Is that what you think is so special?"

"It's not leaves," he says, never taking his eyes off the sight. "It's kudzu."

I sit, waiting for the inevitable explanation.

"Kudzu grows around here, wild and unruly," Del says. "It'll overtake anything in its path—cars, houses, other plants. Nothing stands in its way."

He looks back at me.

"Can't you see? Can't you?" He has tears in his eyes. "That's us out there," he says. "That's us, wild and unruly. And nothing can stop us." He smiles.

"That's right," I say. "Nothing."

"You know, in the summer the kudzu blooms flowers, bright and purple. At first they're hidden, but after a while they grow bigger and become more noticeable."

I nod. I didn't know this at all. I look back at the road.

"That's us," he says again. "We're like kudzu."

He pauses.

"That's all I'm saying."

He coughs again, a wet, heaving sound from somewhere deep inside his sick body. Spent, he leans back in the seat, which is a mess of duct tape and cracked upholstery.

That's Del, being smart, knowing things no one else would know.

And I guess that's why I want to do this for him. Because he's everything I'm not and everything I want to be. Because he's dying, and he's not getting a fair shake. Because I love him.

I pull out a sandwich and start to eat, feeling more comfortable about life now that I know where we are. We sit in silence in the car, chewing, letting the quiet wash around us like a cool rain.

"Do you miss them?" Del asks, breaking the spell. "Are you thinking about them right now?"

"Yeah," I say. "I guess I am."

"Me too. I think about them a lot. I wonder if I'm going to see them sometime soon, and if we'll all be happy again."

I can't stand the conversation and hope Del gets quiet again. He doesn't.

"I want to see them again, really," he says. "And you know what's funny? I hope they're not mad at us."

"They wouldn't be mad at us," I say. I am not sure if this is true.

"I hope I can see them soon."

It had been two years since the accident took the lives of our parents. Two long years that I'd been taking care of my terminally ill brother.

And I never thought I'd be here with him, on this lonely interstate, sun shining high and his body close to giving up. He didn't have much time left.

"So..." he says.

"Yeah?"

"Do you think she'll be pretty?"

I'm taken aback by the sudden change in subject—relieved, really—and I smile.

"Yeah, we'll find you a pretty one. Promise. I bet there's tons of pretty ones there."

"Do you think there are as many lights as we've imagined?"

"I hope so, Del. I hope so."

"Do you think we're crazy?"

I laugh again. "Maybe. Maybe."

It's a strange thing, the dying wish of a kid in his early twenties, a kid who's had to fight his whole life, a kid who's stricken with an incurable disease and whose parents are then killed in a horrible car accident.

Del doesn't want to die a virgin.

He wants to taste a woman before he leaves this world.

And by God, if that's what he wants, that's what I'm going to give him.

"Yeah, we'll find you a pretty one," I say. "She'll knock your socks off—if you want her to."

And Del laughs, and I laugh, and I turn off the emergency lights and pull back onto the road, heading west.

Only a few hundred miles to Vegas, I think. We can make it in two days if we hustle.

As the engine keeps time, I look over and notice Del dozing. He looks peaceful, happy.

I press the pedal down, look out again and notice the sprawling kudzu. Small flower buds glimmer in the midday sun.

I think to myself that Del may be wrong, that I'm the kudzu, crawling over everything with no direction, and that he's actually the flower, my sole purpose in life to let him bloom. I know that sometimes you have to let something wild produce something beautiful.

I look again and see he's not asleep. He's staring outside too, thinking.

He looks to me.

"Tell me the one about Brenda Sue," he says, coughing again. He wheezes. "And about how her dad caught you two naked in his hammock."

And even though he's heard it three dozen times, I tell it again, because he wants me to.

And we talk on, driving, with the windows rolled down and the sun all around us. We're growing wild, Del and me, all over this countryside. Together. A team. Unstoppable.

PULP FISHIN'

Jim Dees

*

*Though boys throw stones at frogs in sport, the frogs do not die
in sport, but in earnest.*
                    —Bion, from Plutarch, *Water and Land Animals*

"HAULING ASS, HAULING ASS!—*click*!"

That was the message on the machine. Twice a year, every spring and fall, my friend Truck and I come to the Pearl River in central Mississippi at the urging of our old fishing mentor, Key Zanzibar, whom we call "Skip." Twice a year we both get that same message on our answering machines. Those cryptic words mean the fish are moving and Skip is planning "Operation Full Freezer": crappie (white perch to you), bass, and of course, catfish. This simple mode of bait and hook is dismissed as cretinous by "anglers" who can't fathom the beauty unless designer vests are involved. Hauling in a gnarly ten-pound catfish out of the Pearl River may not exude lyrical spirituality, and, it's true, Brad Pitt doesn't make pretty movies about it, but a close encounter with the bull of the bottoms affords a song all its own…it's just smellier.

Our modus leisuri entailed putting a minnow on a hook, throwing the line out, and then slotting the rod down into a rod holder. We would rig up five lines in this fashion, the frisky minnows swimming the river bottom from a lead line attached to a weight. The rod and minnow did all the work, which freed us up to ponder existentialism and maybe work in a few cold beers and the Saints game. In this way we achieved our own poetry—call it "My Liver Runs Through It."

Our buddy Skip Zanzibar is a fisherman, sculptor, welder, boater, philosopher, and perhaps the poet laureate of the Pearl River. Still, despite such attributes, one is filled with mixed emotions upon receiving his biannual "Call to Rods." You know you'll catch fish, that's not the problem. The cause for trepidation is the dreaded "X factor," an unpredictable, if not sinister, aura that surrounds Skip and his milieu. As an adolescent, young Key, already possessing a childhood propensity for trouble and physical harm, began a lifelong love-hate affair with danger. Regarding his penchant for the raw deal, his being prone to accident, his kinship with catastrophe, he has said, "I always picked the black marble."

He has suffered numerous broken bones and close calls with limb and organ. He's burned half his body and abused pharmaceuticals of every schedule. I once saw him go fishing while wearing a body cast after one particularly heinous car wreck. Some years ago, the toil and tumult took their toll and Key decided to get off the land and get on the water. That simple impulse changed his life forever and, whether he realized it or not, he became an artist. He had bounced around making big money on oil-rigs and workboats, learning the ropes (literally) and the ways of water. His twenties had been spent in and around the Intra-Coastal Waterway in southern Louisiana. That's roustabout country, where America ends and the rest of the world begins...on the edge of the continent. It is on the edge that Key "Skip" Zanzibar remains.

"Hey boys, glad you made it," Skip said as we walked in. "Y'all ready to go? I have a couple stops before we get on the water."

Truck looked at me as if we'd just paid admission to the Haunted House. "Here were go."

We gathered up our tackle, about twenty rods of various lengths and line strengths, plus five huge ice chests for Skip's light beer, and crammed ourselves back into Truck's truck. The first stop turned out to be Vicksburg, an hour away. Skip intended to pick up his 1963 sky-blue Cadillac, which his friend Laidlaw had worked on. Laidlaw is a culvert tycoon. His company, Pipe Down, rakes in big bucks building roads, pouring concrete, and installing drainage culverts while collecting the requisite kickbacks. On the side he restores old cars and collects snakes.

We drove over and found Laidlaw sitting in his garage, listening to a country music radio station, his feet propped up on the bumper of the Caddy, smoking a joint. Several aquariums surrounded him, each containing an exotic-looking viper. We walked up and he exhaled a plume of blue, pungent smoke and handed the joint to Skip. Skip took a Herculean toke that made the doobie burn up in a long streak like a mobile home on fire. The joint disappeared and Laidlaw rolled another one.

"How's the Caddy, Laidlaw, you got it by the ass?" Skip said. "I promised these boys a trip to the casino in style."

Laidlaw nonchalantly reached into the Cadillac with one hand and turned the key while hitting the joint with the other hand. The car came to life and hummed contentedly.

"Is that a champ or what?" he asked proudly, handing the joint to Truck. Truck and I took our puffs while nervously keeping one eye on the snakes. Kinda creepy when nothing moves but their tongues.

Skip grinned like a possum. "Yeah, you right. Sounds good. Well, what you boys think? I mean while we're over here in Vicksburg and everything, if y'all were wanting to hit a couple of those casinos, hell, I guess I'd ride with you. We can take the Caddy."

Truck eyed me ruefully. "Here we go. I guess we're fishing now."

"Well, come on and go with us, Laidlaw," Skip said as we loaded the car. "Wear some pants with deep pockets."

"Naw, I can't make it tonight," Laidlaw said, "but y'all go ahead and take a couple of pulls for me."

Merle Haggard was singing "Big City" as we left Laidlaw in a haze of dope smoke and coiled serpents. He was in his element. So was Skip. Cruising to the slots, behind the wheel of his Caddy with the windows down and the night air rushing in, is perhaps his favorite situation. Of course, a circuitous trip to the Vicksburg casinos wasn't exactly what Truck and I had had in mind, but we both hoped a hot night of high-speed gaming might soothe the savage Skip and tomorrow we could get on with "Operation Full Freezer."

Vicksburg has three casinos, all sitting on the Mississippi River. We arrived at the Beau Mirage and Skip walked into the sprawling room like he was back home. A couple of bartenders waved at him.

"Give me room, boys give me room…time to pick some cherries."

He perfunctorily played video poker to warm up and to get the first of the free drinks, then he was ready.

With drink in hand, he headed for the quarter slots and prowled the aisles, rubbing the tops of various machines. Skip's theory is that if a machine is warm, it's been played numerous times and the wheels have clicked around and it's possibly ready to pay off. It sounds reasonable and indeed he has won several jackpots this way. As he walked from machine to machine he resembled a New Age prospector. He not only caressed the machines but cocked his head and squinted as if trying to divine their secrets.

He found a couple he liked and began playing one, all the while having his eye on an old favorite that was occupied. Truck and I got distracted with throwing our own money away and lost track of Skip. The waitresses came by all too frequently, wearing tropical mufti and bearing free drinks, and we got more and more distracted, and we weren't the only ones: A drunken line began forming at the ATM machines. Finally, Truck took a break and sat down next to me. A passing waitress handed him another whiskey. I gestured toward the lines at the ATMs.

"I guess being broke is the best discipline." Truck nodded.

There are no clocks in a casino and few windows—only noise and color, simulating happiness. The whole scene is a well-thought-out conspiracy of constant computerized cacophony. It's a contained environment where time seems to stand still even if you can't.

So I wasn't sure how long we had been there when Skip walked up and said it was time to go. He was up $300 and in accordance with his "system," well, it was time to go. Truck and I were game and as we sauntered toward the door, sipping the last of our free drinks, the spell was broken by the most unlikely of occurrences: Skip was paged.

"Call for Skip Zanzibar, telephone call for Skip Zanzibar."

He really was at home. He looked at us with bewilderment. "What fresh hell is this?" he sighed. He went to take his call and Truck sat down at a video poker game and just watched the colors and graphics dancing on the screen. A waitress brought us another round.

"You ain't gonna believe what that was," Skip said when he returned.

"I'm sure you're right."

"Laidlaw said we got a python in the car. He said his python, Samson, got out of his aquarium. Laidlaw says he couldn't have gotten out of the garage and he's sure he slithered up in the Cadillac somehow. Wants us to go out there and check under the hood."

Right. As I've said, any trip with Skip is more than you bargain for, but this was turning into *Fear Factor*. Of course we had to go out and look. But if Samson was in the engine, what would be left of him now? We had done ninety miles an hour the whole way over. And if he wasn't in the engine, where was he? And, worst of all, if the snake *was* still alive, what kind of mood would he be in? We pondered all this as we walked out into the parking lot. Approaching the car gave new meaning to *apprehension*. Skip seemed more annoyed than afraid. He walked right up to the car and raised the hood. We couldn't see anything.

"Truck, reach in that glove box and get that flashlight will ya?"

The free whiskey had obviously numbed Truck fearless because he went right into the car and opened the glove compartment. He hardly changed expression when the long, slimy tail flopped out.

"Damn," he said shaking his head, "we fishin' ain't we?"

*

Extreme terror gives us back the gestures of our childhood.

—Chazal

"All right, Ray, time to go fishin'."

Ray and Floyd had been killing time at Tiffany's, a Gentleman's Club, and now they killed their beers. The dancing was fine but now it was time to head to the casino for "work." It was a simple gig. They hung out in the parking lot and preyed on drunken gamblers as they left the casinos. By choosing their spots prudently, Ray and Floyd had managed to stay ahead of security and no one had been hurt. So far.

Usually just brandishing the pistol yielded results. It was kid stuff, sticking up people like this. They didn't tell the other members of their gang about this moonlighting. But it kept them in beer money and supplemented their income from their day job, which was selling crystal meth up and down the Gulf Coast.

But there was more to it. The crystal meth gig was professional criminality and involved stress and split-second timing as well as depending on the other gang members. It had turned into a job. For Ray and Floyd these casino holdups were a relief, a little "play crime" to cool out after a long night of edgy dope deals with crankheads. They had even managed to work a little fun into it. While they sat vigil in the parking lot, sizing up potential victims, they indulged their real passion—playing Monopoly. The two pulled into a remote area of the Beau Mirage parking lot and cut the engine.

"Well," Ray said as he set up the game, "I guess we've come to that part of the evening where you can be a nice guy or your usual self."

"You mean, am I just going to let you have the race car as your token?"

"Correctimundo."

"You won the other night with the top hat, I don't understand why you don't want to keep your streak going. Baseball players do it all the time."

"Use the top hat?"

"No, superstition. Haven't you ever seen how they step over the foul line? Sometimes they wear the same socks or won't shave if they're in the middle of a streak."

"I've just always had the race car, it's more than superstition, it's...a way of life."

Floyd knew the discussion was moot, they would do what they always did.

"You ready?" he asked, holding a quarter on his thumb.

"Heads," said Ray.

Floyd cut on the dash light and flipped. "Tails, big boy, grab your hat." They played for a while until Ray landed on the Community Chest. He picked the top card.

"'You have won second prize in a beauty contest. Collect $10.'"

"Ten dollars sure seems cheap for second place."

"Well," Floyd said, "the game was invented during the Depression; ten bucks was big money."

Ray nodded solemnly. "You start the game with fifteen hundred, that must have seemed like a fortune to those poor people."

"You bet."

"Just imagine how they must have felt when they landed on Boardwalk or Park Place."

"Aces up."

They fell silent again as the game intensified. Houses and hotels sprung up; Ray spent a couple of rounds in jail and then flirted with bankruptcy. Several rounds later, Ray had a hotel on Boardwalk, the legendary, most expensive property on the board. But he wanted more.

"I'm going to put a second hotel on it," he said placing the second hotel on the space.

"No can do," Floyd said, removing it. "Check the rules, only one hotel per property."

Ray looked through the box but the rules were missing.

"The rules are the first to go," he said exasperated. "Look, Floyd, you can put four houses on a property, let's just say you can put two hotels. It makes sense. We'll make our own rules."

"Forget it, Ray," Floyd said, shaking his head like a schoolteacher. "If we don't have rules, where are we as a society? Rules are what separates us from jungle beasts." He took out his pistol and checked the chamber. "Without rules, we're just dumb animals."

Ray shook his head and peered out over the parking lot. Maybe there'd be no action tonight, he thought. He scanned over the great asphalt expanse, incensed at Floyd's relentless sermonizing and convenient rule making.

Then he saw a sky blue antique Cadillac with the hood up. He grabbed the binoculars, put them to his eyes, and focused. He saw three drunks lurching around the huge car, talking, gesturing, and generally looking like fish in a barrel.

"Hey, Floyd," Ray said smiling and nodding, "bag up the game; I think we got us some suckers."

When Truck opened the glove compartment looking for a flashlight, he found it, but he had to reach around three feet of python snake tail to get it. "Here you go, Skip," Truck said, calmly handing him the flashlight. "You might want to check this out."

Skip shined the light into the glove compartment and saw the snake tail.

"Sweet Mother of Moses in the Morning."

We stood there in the awe of the moment, unable to speak. There's nothing quite like being in the presence of a stowaway python. Laidlaw had called and said there might be a snake in the car, but we had figured he was stoned and crazy. He was also right. Skip poked the tail with the flashlight and it sucked into the paneling out of view.

"Damn," Skip said, "I reckon that's your Full Monty Python."

At that moment a black Chrysler New Yorker pulled up and two burly men sporting too much hair gel and bad jewelry got out.

"Saw the hood up, boys," Floyd said. "Need some assistance?"

"As a matter of fact," Skip started, "we got—"

Ray flashed the pistol. We all froze and Skip's face hardened.

"Now that we got the social amenities out of the way, boys," Floyd said, "let's see how you hayseeds did tonight."

We didn't move.

Ray turned the pistol toward Skip.

"Come on, beer gut, toss me a salad." Nobody moved, stupid with fear and confusion.

"Okay," Floyd said sighing, "It could have been easy, but let's do it this way...get in."

They herded us into the sofalike back seat of the Caddy as Ray trained the gun on us. Floyd got behind the wheel and the five of us, well, six of us, sped off.

How could a simple fishing trip have gone so desperately awry? How was it we were on our way to some desolate Louisiana backwater to be executed and probably tossed in the swamp like gator chum and the closest we had come to a fish was the buffet at the Beau Mirage?

The one called Ray had the gun on us and watched us with something approaching a smirk. I looked down the barrel of the gun and suddenly hated that I had watched my cholesterol. I became totally pissed I had given up omelettes. I was sorry for every night I went home before last call, every James Brown album I didn't buy, and to all the girls I never loved before...I would never see Paris, hike the Swiss Alps, sail the Great Barrier Reef, or take a safari in the wilds of Africa. Hell, at this moment I'd settle for a beer in Batesville.

We left the main road, and the one called Floyd drove us deep into the woods. After too many long, terrifying miles, he stopped the car, got out, and reached into his coat pocket. This was it. Skip gasped, Truck's eyes grew out of their slits, and I messed my pants. Grace under pressure would have to wait for another day.

"Time to dump freight, Ray. Let's shoot this one here first," he said pointing at Skip. "He got so much skin on him he may take all six rounds. How much you weigh, anyway, round man?"

"Eighth of a ton, maggot breath," Skip said defiantly.

"Get 'em out, Ray."

Ray opened his door and let out a scream that echoed across the bayous, marshes and sloughs, then reverberated in the car so loudly we thought we'd all been shot. In an instant, he was on the ground writhing and wrestling and screaming.

Samson, the puissant ten-foot python, had quietly wrapped himself around Ray's leg. The opening of the door had frightened the mighty viper and he had now tightened his death grip on Ray's leg and had bitten him on the crotch for good measure. In one fluid motion that seemed like five minutes but was probably a nanosecond, Floyd ran over to Ray and froze on the spot and when he looked up,

Skip had Ray's pistol pointed at him.

Floyd flinched as if to go for his own gun.

Skip cocked the revolver.

"Go ahead…make my swamp."

Skip wanted to shoot Ray and Floyd, but, even though they deserved it, we talked him out of it. We did make Floyd strip and left Ray in the clutches of Samson, who looked like he wasn't going to release Ray anytime soon. So we left them there, Ray struggling with the snake and Floyd buck naked. We figured being thirty miles deep in the swamp, one naked, the other wearing a live python, would definitely cut into their potential as hitchhiker material. Their karma would take care of the rest.

As we got ready to leave, Skip handed Floyd his cell phone, walked several paces and spun around.

"Pull!"

Floyd stood there naked and bewildered, uncomprehending, and then realized what was going to happen. After frowning and shaking his head, he tossed the phone straight up. Skip extended his arm with the pistol and fired. He hit it on the first shot and it splintered into dozens of pieces.

"That's your disconnect fee, you son-of-a-bitch."

We drove off, and I couldn't resist looking back. Ray had his hands cupped over his dangling vulnerability and he and Floyd were arguing.

The events of the last twenty-four hours had taken their toll on Skip's 1963 Cadillac and us. It took us a while to find our way out of the woods, and when we finally turned onto the main road, the sun was blazing and we were hopped up on fear and adrenaline. The Caddy was running hot and we tried to make it as far as we could. By the time we pulled into a small town called Frisette, the engine was smoking. Although we wanted to put as much distance between us and Ray and Floyd as possible, we reluctantly pulled into a service station.

There was a mechanic on duty and he came out sweating and covered with grease. The cigarette hanging out of his mouth was black where he had been holding it and the name above his pocket said, "Floyd." We wanted to leave but couldn't.

"Radiator," he said. "Gotta hole. I wouldn't drive on it. We can plug it for you."

Skip was pissed, but, considering we could have been at the bottom of a lonely slough being torn apart by prehistoric garfish, this was news he could handle.

"How long," I asked.

"Noon tomorrow," Floyd said, black sweat rolling down his cheek.

"No way," Skip bellowed. "We got to get out of here. You don't know what's behind us."

Floyd was nonplussed, and why shouldn't he be? He had us. The car was incapacitated; we were in his shop. We could squawk or walk.

We left the car with Floyd and walked down the highway to a motel he suggested where we would just have to wait it out. The three of us walking down the highway must have looked like escapees from a nightmare, which, of course, is exactly what we were. None of us had slept, we'd been severely traumatized and had a harrowing brush with becoming a lead sandwich. Indeed we were akin to fish who'd thrown the hook.

We'd walked about a mile when the motel finally came into view. Skip lit a cigarette.

"Fellows, I appreciate y'all coming down to fish. I'm sorry it turned out like this."

"Aw, Skip, don't worry about it," Truck said. "I'm just glad it worked out like it did. I never been so glad to see a snake."

"Yeah," I said grimacing, "I just need some new pants."

We arrived at the motel called Nook and Granny's. It appeared to be one of the last of a dying breed: a nonchain, mom-and-pop operation run by an older couple and their daughter, who cleaned the rooms and tended flowers in the front windowsills. There was another oddity. About every other room had a church pew in front of it.

Nook was standing out in the parking lot when we walked up. He had obviously dealt with some desperate characters in his motel career because he didn't blink when the three of us, the very picture of walking desperation, asked for a room.

"Come on in, let's sign you up."

We let Skip do the honors, and Truck and I cooled our heels on the pew in front of the office. Every time we looked, Nook was talking and Skip was nodding.

"Well," Truck sighed, "We fishin', ain't we?"

The door to one of the rooms opened and an old woman we assumed to be Granny stepped out with a housekeeping cart followed by her daughter. Truck and I looked at each other. The daughter was a strikingly beautiful young woman in her midtwenties, with long sun-bleached brown hair and wearing a T-shirt and cutoffs the way they were meant to be worn.

"I'm awake now," I said.

Finally Skip came out and unlocked our room.

As we walked past Granny, the young woman said, "Enjoy your stay. Give us a ring if you need anything. I'm Glenda."

"Thanks, Glenda."

As we filed past, I noticed our room had a pew in front of it.

"How'd you swing the pew, Skip?"

"He asked if we were Christians and I figured we needed all the help we could get, so I told him, 'Hell, yeah.'"

Good move. It's always a comfort to walk into a clean, cool motel room, but this time was especially so. The cheerful presence of Glenda offset the parade of horrors we'd endured; mainly a swamp full of spooks. Who knew, maybe the pew would help. Even though we left Ray and Floyd somewhat occupied, they were still out there somewhere.

*

This hocus-pocus succeeded and we buried death in a shroud of glory.
—Sartre

We walked into our room and all I could think about was a shower, a cold beer, and jumping between overly starched sheets. Skip ordered in pizzas and was well into his second six-pack by the time I crashed. He and Truck took their solace in a late West Coast Braves game. I awoke in the middle of the night to find Skip asleep in front of the TV, which was blaring an old beach movie starring Frankie Avalon and Annette Funicello. Truck, it seemed, had disappeared.

I grabbed a beer and went outside to sit on the pew and check the stars and reflect on being alive and how close we had come to the slimy alternative. Even though we were back in "civilization," there was still something unsettling about it all. Despite the cozy room and the cold beer, I sensed we weren't out of the woods yet.

It was when I attempted to go back inside that I discovered I was locked out. Banging on the window and door was futile. After a case of Natural Lights and the three pizzas we had devoured, Skip would doze through the apocalypse. Now he snored like the Concord while Frankie and Annette did the watusi with Cesar Romero.

Damn. I found myself wandering, looking around Nook and Granny's, when I heard a noise and noticed a couple sitting out on their pew.

I walked over and we exchanged pleasantries, but the two of them seemed a bit far away. Either drug casualties, I thought, or dimmed from years of some other abuse. There was music coming from the room and laughter. I described Truck and they chuckled.

"Go on in, dude," one said. "He's in there."

I pushed open the door and had to adjust my eyes to the smoke and fuzzy light. There were about six people in the room, laughing; some fondling each other. I moved closer to the bed and there was Truck. He was gagged, handcuffed to the bedpost, and wearing a dog collar with a long chain. Glenda was about to connect the chain from the dog collar to a leash. The wild look in his eyes made it apparent this was not consensual sex.

Two thoughts whipped into my mind: One, I hated that we were fresh out of snakes, and two, how did these people get a room with a pew?

Glenda and her crew offered no resistance to my liberating Truck.

Apparently my blundering into the room had cooled the passion and blown the discipline. Glenda disgustedly moved over to a chair and lit a cigarette while one of her love slaves looked for the key to the cuffs. Despite her kink, I had to admit she looked right fetching in her black leather. There's something about stiletto heels.

Truck worked and wiggled his mouth as the gag came off.

"'Preciate cha, man," he said, sitting up while his right hand was still cuffed to the bedpost. "What I get for wandering around, I guess."

I walked over to Glenda. "Damn girl, where'd you pick up all this S&M shtick out here in the countryside?"

"Look, just take your little buddy and go."

"I hate to think what your folks would say about this."

She rolled her eyes and walked over to the closet and flung the door open. There were Nook and Granny manning a video camera. They were filming everything and smiled at me sheepishly. That did it.

"All right Truck," I said, "I know you hate to leave all this, but I promise to spank you later."

Two of Glenda's lackeys were fumbling around looking for the keys to the handcuffs, but not fast enough to suit me. They were unable to come up with them and I began eyeing the bedpost. Then the door opened and the back of my neck burned. I looked around and someone wearing a black leather mask was standing there holding a very nervous billy goat on a leash.

Glenda sprang up and tamped out her cigarette and Nook and Granny scrambled back into the closet. The goat appeared to be the main event and I shuddered to think what they had planned for Truck.

"Okay, that's it!" I screamed, using my wildest wide-eyed look. "Everybody out of the pool!"

Apparently sensing his chance, the goat broke free and ran around the room, baaing and bawling. Someone grabbed him and worked to get the leash back on, but not before the goat jumped on the bed and took a massive dump.

"Whoa!" the one with the leash roared. He grimaced beneath his mask.

Amid the feces melee, I kicked the bedpost. On the fourth or fifth kick, it loosened and I pulled it apart and worked the cuff over it.

Truck gagged and looked relieved and vengeful all at once, but we both knew better than to push our luck. We headed out the door.

"Thanks for the bracelet, Glenda," Truck said as we stepped over the goat and the disciples and jumped out of the room. Laughter and squealing rang out behind us as we ran across the parking lot to our room. We banged on the door and looked in the window. Skip was snoring contentedly and sleeping hard, well into the rapid eye movement that generally results from rapid beer movement.

I covered my fist with my shirt, broke the window, reached in, and opened the door. We ran in sweating and panting, and slammed the door behind us. Truck looked disgustedly at the handcuff dangling from his wrist. Skip barely stirred and opened one eye.

"Where you boys been?" he asked turning over.

Truck and I looked at each other.

"Room service," I said.

We scattered first thing in the morning so as not to confront Glenda. Truck and I hiked up the road to deal with Floyd, the shyster radiator man, who cut the cuff off of Truck. He freed Truck's hand and charged us an arm and a leg.

Meanwhile, Skip negotiated with Nook.

He told us later that Nook had "talked a loon streak." Said Nook "didn't know what the world was coming to." He railed on about how kids had no respect for property or family, that he had "built his business with my bare hands from the ground up and people these days got no backbone."

Right. His sweet daughter Glenda seemed to be making a pretty good living off hers.

Luckily Skip could keep a straight face. He had slept through the orgy. He hadn't witnessed young Glenda—a long, lanky, sunny picture of Southern womanhood, exhibiting, shall we say, her "dark side." Fortunately Skip was oblivious to the cold fact that when the lights got low, Good Witch Glenda turned into Trailer Trash Glenda,

Motel Slut, whose nightly repertoire included billy goats, masked men, and squealing like a pig while her daddy videotaped the whole thing.

Just before dark we finally made our escape. Floyd, the radiator man with a heart of oil, had taken us for twice what the work was worth. By the time we climbed into the Caddy for the two-hour trip to Vicksburg, we had what we were wearing, a full tank of gas, six lukecold beers, and goat fumes. The windows were down, and the rushing warm wind made conversation impossible, and it was just as well. Each of us was lost in our faults. By any reckoning the weekend had turned into a low-down litany of peckerwood horrors:

I had folded under pressure, messing my pants. Truck had stumbled a hoof away from bestiality, and Skip had basically caused it all by his crass gaming impulses. You drive down for a little fishing and you wind up fending off casino highwaymen packing heat, snakes in the glove compartment, busted radiators, near death, romantic goats...

Despite our escape, we were left with the hair-raising thought that somewhere out there, in the great evil blackness of a fetid swamp, there were two grown men who fully intended to kill us. That kind of nagging knowledge can change the way you manage your life. Change the way you get dressed in the morning. Definitely make starting your car an adventure.

I put it out of my mind. We just set our sights on getting to Laidlaw's. It was the first outpost of sympathetic shelter we would reach, and after an eternity of interstate, we arrived. Stunned with fatigue, hardly able to pull ourselves out of the car, we staggered up to the door. We walked with spent stiffness, like astronauts crossing the deck of an aircraft carrier. George Jones was playing in the garage, and we smiled at each other. Did we have a story for Laidlaw or what?

Laidlaw answered our knock by looking through his peephole, then opening the door. We walked into his garage, and, well, it wasn't exactly the homecoming we had in mind. There was Floyd sitting in front of a Monopoly board, while Ray fed a mouse to one of the snakes.

Laidlaw drew his pistol.

It was over, and it was just as well, I thought. As I walked into that garage and saw those two cannibals sitting there, apparently in cahoots with Laidlaw, I knew the jig was up and the worm had turned. Luck is like fishing line; when it runs out...you're out.

"Well, well, well," Laidlaw said, waving the gun around too freely for my taste. The group of us regarded each other warily, shuffling our feet like circling bulls. But Laidlaw was completely in charge.

"Look's like we got ourselves a real dipshit contest going on here...Okay, here's the deal," he said twitching a match around in his mouth.

"These scumbags," he said motioning with the pistol toward Ray and Floyd, "killed Samson, so I'd just as soon shoot both of them..."

I smiled.

"In fact, I think I will." And with no further warning he fired two shots that punctured the back of the garage. The shells buzzed past Ray and Floyd William Tell–style.

"And you three!" he said whirling on us. "I want to shoot you too. Hadn't been for y'all going over to that damn casino, Samson would still be alive. But here's what I'm going to do. You!" he said pointing the gun at us, "Y'all haul ass. Skip, I'll talk to you about this later."

"And you," he said motioning to Ray and Floyd, "If I told the rest of the boys about y'all's little nickel-and-dime stick-up scheme, they'd shoot you. So y'all are going to chill for a minute, let Skip and them get on down the road, and I'll deal with you after that," he said, spitting.

Then back to us.

"Vamoose dammit!"

"'Preciate cha, Laidlaw," Skip said putting on his hat and giving us the signal. "Don't reckon we'll let the door hit us in the ass."

It was a reprieve of biblical proportions. Laidlaw was Ray and Floyd's boss? Was Gulf Coast crystal meth another one of his sidelines? And another question I beg to ask: How had Ray escaped Samson? As we filed out, I clapped Ray on the shoulder. In my euphoria, I had a sudden perverted respect for him, or kinship with him, maybe like the Stockholm syndrome. Like me, he depended on his homeys. Plus, he had somehow gotten a determined python off his leg and had gone through as much hell as we had. He looked up at me with reptilian regard.

"I never want to see you again," he hissed.

"Call if you get in a tight," I said.

*

The path of the righteous man is beset on all sides by
the inequities of the selfish and the tyranny of evil men.

Ezekiel 25:17

Awakening at Skip's compound, it was disorienting but comforting to look out and see the shimmering Pearl River. It took several minutes before I could focus on the Pearl River and realize where we were and what we had done. I reached for the remote control and flipped on CNN in time to see one of Skip's favorites, the fashion report with Elysa Gardner. I knew Skip had an unusual fascination with fashion TV, so I left it on and it piped loudly all through the compound. Skip's cats, Ricky and Lucy, stirred and stretched. Back to business as unusual. Skip heard me rustling up coffee and gasped in his bunk.

"My head feels like it's going to explode…somebody needs to cut it off at the neck."

"You all right?"

"Nothing a little stale casino air won't fix. Y'all want to drive over today?"

I couldn't believe it. Then again I could.

"I'll ask Truck," I said shaking my head. "If he wants to go, I'll kill him."

Looking out the window I spotted Truck, and he was finally fishing; watching a line off the pier. I hated to call him in, but it was that time. I packed our bags and helped Skip brew up another pot of his chicory coffee. Skip was glued to a Karl Lagenfeld interview.

"What's most important?" Karl asked into the camera. "Color? Size?

Shape? No. Attitude...A new way to walk, a new way to be...that's what I'm looking for with this fall collection..." Skip nodded his head. "Damn right."

Truck stared at his line and then reluctantly walked up the hill like a child coming in from recess. We'd been gone seventy-two hours and he finally gets a line out and we have to split.

"No bait on it, anyway," he said. "I just strung together old worm parts and then crumbled up some leaves and threw that out."

"Reckon that will work?"

"I don't know, but it's all part of my new attitude," he said, "my new way to be."

Truck and I didn't talk much on the ride back, we didn't have to. What more could be said? I had to agree with Karl Lagenfeld, of all people. It was all in the attitude, and I had certainly had an implant. Magic, mojo, moxie...however you spell it, the light is there if you know where to look. Fishing with Skip is as close to combat as I'll ever come, and he and Truck are my Bass of Brothers.

And one more thing: Skip called later that night to make sure we'd gotten in and to ask Truck what he had used for bait that morning. Truck told him it was basically leaves and miscellaneous debris. Skip laughed.

He told us when he had walked out onto the pier, he was just in time to see the line snap with a huge fish—"Maybe a twenty-pounder!"—the cork submerged and all the tackle moving up the channel, he said, headed to the river and slowly but majestically out to sea.

TAKING OFF FROM WELTY

Ellen Douglas

One day some years ago when I was thinking about what to say at a symposium on Southern women writers that would be honoring Eudora Welty, I fell into a transom—as a neighbor of mine was wont to say—and came up with the word *witnessing* on my lips, not knowing precisely why. But the why of it came clear shortly, as I began to think about how people in the South—men and women, blacks and whites, who follow divergent paths through our common world—tell each other stories about the perils and joys of our passage, teaching each other without saying we're teaching, offering our experience to each other for what it's worth, being reliable or unreliable witnesses and then bearing witness to each other.

I thought of Welty's story "A Memory," of the young girl who said of herself, "Ever since I had begun taking painting lessons, I had made small frames with my fingers, to look out at everything," and "I do not know even now what it was that I was waiting to see; but in those days I was convinced that I almost saw it at every turn. To watch everything about me I regarded grimly...as a *need.*"

To be a witness, that is, to be someone outside the action, waiting to see—seeing. And then? Shaping, limiting, putting into a frame.

The character Anna in a short story of mine called "Jesse" says, "I have a passion for talking over old times, for hearing from old people how it was at such and such a time in such and such a place...I like to hear my father tell how his father used to wad his old muzzle-loading shotgun with Spanish moss, aim it up into the holly tree in the front yard ('Right there—that's the tree') and bring down enough robins to have robin pie for dinner. More than anything I want to know *how it was*...and then to *understand.*"

We want to see, to know, not just how it is, but how it was. We want our stories to bring to bear the past on the present.

Thinking of the witness as one outside the action, I recall the psychology class demonstration of the unreliability of witness: the student who is in on the plot flings open the classroom door, bursts in, shouts threats, attacks the teacher, and then before everyone's startled eyes, storms out and vanishes. The class, called on to say what happened, gives as many versions of the sequence of events as there are students. What's involved is not only inadvertent inaccuracy, inattention, and physical limitations, but also, perhaps, sometimes, bad faith, vanity, and cowardice, or, at the least, intellectual limitations or limitations of character.

And here I think of the deconstructionist critics who say we writers are such unreliable witnesses that readers are required to decide for themselves what we *really* saw. But that's a subject for another day. In any case, it's true that we—not just writers but all of us—are sometimes unreliable witnesses.

But: "I had made small frames with my fingers, to look out at everything," Welty wrote. That is, in order to understand what we see, to be reliable witnesses, we must learn to *frame*, to give what we observe a form.

Here's a story from the personal and financial annals—not to say gossip—of a parish in south Louisiana, which one can use to explore the nature of witnessing, a story that Welty might have sought a frame for. There was a gentleman farmer (we'll call him Mr. Bourgeois, a common name in that part of the country), father and grandfather, owner of land, speculator in markets, whose interests were in serious trouble one winter in the early part of the twentieth century. Foreclosures were taking place. He was going to be forced into bankruptcy, to be *ruined*. The last possible day to retrieve his fortunes had arrived, every avenue frantically explored. He drove from his farm to the nearby town where his lawyer lived and, in a state bordering on despair, went to his office. What passed between him and his lawyer was, of course, privileged, and no one will ever know what they said. But after an hour or so this elderly gentleman went to the hotel (there was a particularly elegant and luxurious hotel in the town) and checked in. He walked across the lobby, looking neither right nor left, ignoring the greetings of several acquaintances who were smoking their cigars in the lobby or loafing over a whiskey in the bar that opened onto the lobby. He did not even take off his hat, although there were several ladies passing through the lobby. As he climbed the wide marble stairs leading to the second floor where he had his room, his lips moved and he seemed to be talking to himself.

After a short time, perhaps no more than ten or fifteen minutes, Mr. Bourgeois appeared again, strolling down the marble stairs, his hat still on his head. He was smoking a cigar. He was stark naked.

Horrified shrieks from the ladies, who fled in all directions. Oaths from the gentlemen. After a paralyzed minute or two, someone grabbed an overcoat and forcibly thrust his arms into the sleeves and buttoned him into it. It may have taken several men to subdue him— that's how the story goes—still muttering and mumbling. "They're going to strip me bare tomorrow," he was heard to say. "Why not today?"

His lawyer, *happening* into the hotel as all this was going on, observed the scene for a while and at last suggested that perhaps Mr. Bourgeois should be taken to the local hospital. He was borne off, struggling.

Clearly, the doctors at the hospital agreed, he was out of his head. Perhaps, though, only temporarily. But his behavior was so boisterous that he couldn't be kept in the hospital. Posthaste he was taken across the river to a state asylum for the insane, conveniently located in the same parish. Papers were signed for a temporary commitment, all the while Mr. Bourgeois shouting, "Let me out, dammit," and "Stripped bare. Naked as the day I was born. Whose overcoat is this?" he cried. "It's not mine. I don't *have* an overcoat."

The lawyer, without delay, called the judge of the bankruptcy court, explained his client's tragic collapse, and succeeded in delaying the proceedings for thirty days. The entire legal situation would be changed, obviously, if he was, in fact, proven incompetent. During the month there was time for his agents, assisted by his lawyer, to explore other channels, to make other arrangements, to borrow money from faraway banks. Indeed, several proceedings were transferred to another court, where, as sometimes happens, especially in Louisiana, but sometimes even in Tennessee and Mississippi, the judge was more sympathetic to his difficulties.

And progressively, Mr. Bourgeois grew better. His family came to visit and reason with him. He stopped muttering and shouting. He began to look around him and take an interest in the world and to speak more reasonably. By the end of the month the doctors were able to say that it had been only a temporary attack, brought on by the strain of financial worries and anxiety about his family. His clothes were brought round and he returned to his home and took charge of his affairs again. Fortunately, there was never a return of the illness.

Now, although it's very likely true that the score or so of people who witnessed this incident might have given varying accounts of what they saw and heard, and that members of his family might have interpreted the events—borne witness to them—in a different way, and that the lawyer, who kept his own counsel, had his version, it is also true that among those who went home to their families and who in later years passed the story down to their children there was a clear consensus regarding what the story meant. And I, many years later, after everyone involved is dead, hearing the story from my brother, who remembered hearing it from our grandmother, I recognize that unmistakable consensus and frame my story to bear witness to it today. My story is about wit and resourcefulness, about a desperate in-souciance, a half-admirable, half-disgraceful unscrupulousness, about survival—about how the world works.

And perhaps for women of my generation and of earlier generations this witness loomed larger than it looms now. We had less—not less stake in—access to the world of action where our fathers' friends might strip themselves naked and outwit their enemies. But we observed the scene, we heard the stories and repeated them. If we were writers, we framed what we saw and turned our observations into fiction.

The fiction writer strives for accuracy of feeling and meaning arising from the slanted witness of characters and narrators. The historian strives for accuracy of fact, understanding of cause and effect. My friend the historian Shelby Foote has said to me more than once that he never describes a day's weather or a flowering orchard on a battlefield, never quotes a historical figure—a real person—without being able to account for his words in a primary source. This (I can tell by his tone of voice) gives him satisfaction, is one of the pillars that support his work.

Primary sources? Primary sources slip away like sand between my fingers. I'm a primary source for all I have seen and known and heard and felt. And, believe me, I tell you now I am unreliable. I have been molded, branded, buried in "facts" that other primary sources—my parents and grandparents, historians, politicians, journalists, preachers—have imprinted on me, as they in turn were imprinted before me. We are always pawns in someone else's game.

And Shelby? Did his flowering orchard at Shiloh ever exist in the world, any more than Faulkner's pear tree in "Spotted Horses"? Aren't those trees the words put down by some dead diarist, filtered later through Shelby's rigorously demanding mind, put just where he wants them for a particular effect? Ah, there's a question for another day. What's true is that the historian, too, uses words to bear witness to the world—as he sees it.

Merely words. Like the words Thucydides puts in the mouth of Pericles? And like, for us fallen-away Presbyterians, the Bible. Who wrote the Bible? Holy men, my Shorter Catechism tells me, who were taught by the Holy Ghost. Doubtless I could find in any theological school someone who might want to put this in another way.

In recent years I've gotten more and more interested in what I suppose you might call dubious history: tales, events, I remember, accurately or inaccurately, like the story of Mr. Bourgeois. Thinking about my own knowledge of the past of my grandparents' generation led me to a mysterious "true" love story told me in bits and pieces by people who were old when I was young. Nothing I've been able to discover has brought me to the truth of what happened. I keep coming up against the rock of our disgraceful unreliability. I'm like the observer in the physics experiment who can't help influencing what is observed. Nevertheless, I wrote a story, "Julia and Nellie," and another story about my uncle-in-law, Ralph, whom I renamed Grant. Like the child in "Jesse," *I've listened*. Like the child in Welty's "A Memory," I've looked at, framed with my fingers, witnessed, put down. What I hope is that, regardless of what came from the corrupt primary source (me, Josephine Haxton) and what from the corrupt imagination of me, Ellen Douglas, I have perhaps evoked with my words the throbbing, life-and-death and passion-filled worlds of those long-ago times.

Here is another story (this one I heard from my father). In the nineteenth century, my great-grandfather was superintendent of schools in Adams County, Mississippi. He was a devoted Presbyterian, an elder and a lay preacher who bore witness to this faith at every opportunity. The schools in the rural parts of the county, black and white, were wherever anyone could be found who was literate and who would agree to gather the children in her neighborhood together (and of course I emphasize *her*, for the lives and education of children were always in the hands of women) and teach them reading and writing and geography and arithmetic—in the cabins and churches of black people and in the living rooms of white people. My grandmother conducted one of these schools in her living room. The superintendent practiced his profession mostly by riding around the county in his buggy, day in, day out, good weather and bad, checking on what was going on in his schools. He always carried a stack of New Testaments in the back of the buggy, my father said. At every school (shades of the ACLU and First Amendment rights) he gave away Testaments to the children who didn't have them. My father, who loved his grandfather and had been raised tumbling about his feet, so to speak, said this to me: "I have always attributed the good race relations in Adams County in considerable part to Grandpa's Testaments." In his devotion, in his innocence, he told me this early in the 1950s, shortly before the gathering storm of the civil rights movement broke over our world, before the later, the ongoing battles over prayer in the schools. Now I tell it. What sense can you and I make of it? A story, a frame, might show us.

There is another side of tale-telling—of witnessing and then bearing witness—that has loomed large in the lives of Southern women, and this is the effort of black women and white women to understand each other through watching and talking and listening to each other. In earlier times, when I was young and even up into my middle age, it was unfortunately—bitterly—true that black women and white women met only on the white woman's terms in her house. The watching was done by the black woman, who had spread out before her the whole intimate life of the white family. Most of the telling, too, was done by the black woman, who revealed to her white employer whatever she chose to about her own life. Often, though, the white woman, troubled, angry, amused, also told what she chose to tell. Sitting in the kitchen over the never-ending rites of silver polishing and preserve making, they explored their lives. This, then, was the way we came to know each other—regardless of whether that understanding, that knowledge led to hatred and betrayal or to loyalty and love on either side.

These days our lives converge in other ways. We still look out at each other across the old walls, but we meet in the classroom, the committee room, in the dormitory and the workplace. Discouraged, angry, still we deeply know that we must continue to tell each other our stories, if we are to be what we should be, equal travelers through our tragic, joyous, difficult, exciting, baffling world.

I have based stories, a whole novel, on my experiences of this telling, this listening. In my time and place, tales have been one of the richest resources upon which the writer, particularly the female writer, who has lived so intimately and so distantly with women who are not of her race, can bring to bear the eye of the imagination. These are the materials that have called out to me for transformation into fiction, into artwork. See us. Listen to our stories, these women have said, and put them down. Record our witness and bring to bear your own, so that others can experience the world we've lived in, in all its complex and fascinating mystery.

Years ago, immediately after he had read my work for the first time—the galleys of my first novel, which took off from and transformed into fiction scenes from the world of family life I had known as I was growing up—my father, who was a reader chiefly of the newspaper (three every day) and of Matthew Henry's Commentaries on the Bible and of the Bible itself, seldom a reader, after his school days, of fiction, said to my mother about my book, and she afterward repeated his words to me: "I had not thought of it that way, Laura, but our lives, in some sense I see that our lives have been like—like—a play—a tragedy."

He had heard my witness.

SPLEEN

Ole Miss, Late August

Ann Fisher-Wirth

But I don't despise the cheerleaders
at practice in the Grove,
who leap and balance
on their partners' upturned palms,
calf muscles trembling, lifting up,
up, on tiptoe. Nor the kids
driving by, I like how they signal *hi*,
one finger lifted from the steering wheels
of gas-guzzlers loaded
with the summer's boxes.
Nor the girls on Sorority Row
running from one of the houses,
waving their arms like Bacchantes
in a badly acted play—
they jump and scream
and clap their hands in a big
orchestrated semicircle,
because aunts and mothers and teachers,
grandmas and nanas and preachers
told them this
is what happiness looks like.

This summer, unannounced,
the Army Corps of Engineers
drained and paved
the bayou at the end of College Hill,
expanding the airport for football weekends.
They lost the herons, destroyed the places
where turtles could slither

down cool, piney banks
past crayfish towers and cypress stobs
into a murky lake where in spring
their babies would sit on fallen branches
like capgun caps,
nubbins nearly invisible
until *pop pop pop pop pop*
slow then faster they hit the lake
as they hear you coming.

Oh yeah? Bummer, I hear these students say.

As I pass the crowd of girls
I look for one
who knows she's faking it,
who's counting the days
till she quits.
She already longs
for the vanishing places
where, speckled with light, she can wait,
alive in every cell to solitude,
completely attentive to the water.

WHERE, BENEATH THE MAGNOLIA

Ann Fisher-Wirth

Wind shakes
the shabby cedars,
gusts and torments blowing up
harder and harder
over the mosses of Rowan Oak—
where the brick-laid maze,
derelict now, beautiful,
circled the ancient magnolia,
eaten and hollowed
and finally last year
storm-stricken,
now only a pile of black shards
and leafmeal—where once
Teresa stood
in sweat-shimmering August,
in a bower of whispering
branches,
and spoke with Caroline Barr
in tongues and rattles
and honeyed
groanings. Fern-furred
branches bowed
above the burnished
river their voices
conjured,
Teresa deep
in her Ifá trance
speaking with Caroline,
dead since 1940—with the woman
behind the book,

the woman
behind the word,
whom Teresa, unafraid,
could spell
from the monstrous
shadows. Tongues
and echoes, blue buzzings
in the honeysuckle,
snail-shine and humus
beneath them...bracken,
bloodroot, mutterings
in the air—they spoke
and were not
as they'd been spoken.
How can I say
what passed between them
in the rising wind?
What blossoms
has no name.

Rowan Oak is Faulkner's home in Oxford, Mississippi. Teresa Wash-ington was my student, writing her thesis on the West African religion Ifá. Caroline Barr was Faulkner's "mammy," to whom Go Down, Moses *is dedicated.*

STRAWBERRY FIZZLE

Kristin Grant

Mama told me Martin's Soda Fountain was spillin' over with kids last night. Mr. Martin invented somethin'! Mama says that inventin' somethin' means that God's Holy hand came down from Heaven and touched Mr. Martin upon the shoulder. And through that hand came an idea into Mr. Martin's head. When Mama told me of the invention, I knew indeed that God had worked a miracle right through Mr. Martin.

"And he calls it," Mama paused and I could barely keep from movin' around in the chair, "The Ster-aw-Berry Fizzle." Her voice rose up proudly on "Ster" and settled like the dust after a car passes on Main Street on "Fizzle." I think my heart skipped two beats: one because God personally talked to someone here in Redbud, Alabama, and two because I could already taste the sweet berry flavor ripplin' down my throat.

Strawberry Fizzle, I repeated under my breath. *Strawberry Fizzle*.

"Now, don't you go gettin' no ideas," said Mama. "You are not going to the soda fountain." One of her eyebrows raised up and I quit mumblin'.

I waited 'til Mama had been gone exactly twenty minutes before I slipped my best blue-and-green striped dress over my head, grabbed my bike, and peddled like lightnin' up Main Street to Johnny's house. Our wooden cottage was just south of town and Johnny's just north. Five minutes and I was there.

I rapped on the door three times before Johnny's mama answered, "Hi, darlin' Sarah," she said. I liked the way Mrs. Johnson always put *darlin'* and *sugar* and *sweetie* before my name. I felt important with such a title and didn't mind 't'all. I smiled as wide as I could and asked if Johnny could come with me on a bike ride.

"Why, shore," she smiled, the tips of her brown hair lightly touching the green gingham dress covering her shoulders. "Johnny," she called and I heard some rustlin' comin' from the kitchen.

"Johnny," she yelled again and I looked up at her and she smiled at me.

And then my best friend came swingin' around the corner with his hands cupped like he was 'bout to take communion. He walked up to me and through a small sliver-crack 'tween his hands, I saw one big eye starin' at me.

"What's it?" I asked.

He stepped outside, knelt in the dirt by the front door, and he looked like he was 'bout to pray.

"What you doin'?"

When he opened his hands, the hugest toad I'd ever seen came jumpin' out like he was freed from the Alamo! I knew he wasn't a frog because he had warts and Papa says that toads have warts and frogs are smooth. I jumped in fast as I could and scooped him up and held him close to my chest. Johnny looked at me with a question in his eyes. I swayed back and forth like I was rockin' a baby and then slipped the critter into the pocket of my dress. From now on, this toad was not any ordinary toad, but was Earl, my favorite pet.

"Guess what," I stated like Ms. Scarlett O'Hara herself.

"What?" asked Johnny coolly and I could tell that he really wanted to know much more than he let on by the way his feet shuffled back and forth.

"My mama says that Mr. Martin invented the Strawberry Fizzle and that God Himself has put this idea into Mr. Martin's head."

We stared at each other for 'bout five seconds, and at the same time, we relieved our kickstands of supportin' our bikes and we was on our way.

Martin's Soda Fountain was simply Heaven for me. Every time I heard the name, I imagined soda pop sprayin' out of the mouths of the five big fish balanced on the pedestal in the center of the fountain in the town square. "Fountains" of soda. Unlimited, sparkling, cool soda. On that August day in Redbud, streams of Strawberry Fizzle practically slipped down my throat with the very thought.

We rode past the bank and the movies. *Guess Who's Coming to Dinner* was playin' on that day. But Mama said I was too young to see that one. I told her that I was eleven years old now and certainly adult enough to see any movie, but she whupped me and I went to my room instead.

And then we saw it. Martin's Soda Fountain rose above us like salvation on a Sunday mornin'. (At least that's how Mama described it since she'd been workin' there.)

And Mama was right. Kids were fillin' the place, and even their parents couldn't resist the Strawberry Fizzle. We had to leave our bikes two doors down at Norma's Seamstress Shop!

Me and Johnny waited as patient as possible outside before we saw our chance—two shiny, red-topped stools opened up at the counter. And we were next. My heart pattered so that I thought that Earl was kickin' in my pocket and I had to reach in and scold him. But it turned out to just be my heart.

We hopped on the stools and swung them around so that we were facin' each other and our knees were touchin'.

"What will you be having this evening, sir," I said in my most serious English accent.

"The Strawberry Fizzle, madame," said Johnny gravely.

And then Mr. Martin himself came over to us, even though he had seven other workers there that day that we could count.

"I'll have a Strawberry Fizzle," I ordered confidently.

"Me too," said Johnny.

"One Strawberry Fizzle comin' up," said Mr. Martin.

"That's two," said Johnny in as polite a tone as he could muster.

"That's one," said Mr. Martin as he glanced over at me.

I looked around and did not know of what Mr. Martin spoke. He left and I saw him pourin' soda and juice and ice cream all into one cup. And for some reason, I knew the cup was for Johnny and not me.

He mixed it all up with his malt machine and then set the glass, pink and foamy, in front of Johnny.

"Here's your Strawberry Fizzle," he said.

"What 'bout Sarah's Fizzle?" asked Johnny.

"Now, a white kid like you oughtta know better than to ask a question like that. Now git out of here, boy!" His arm swept toward the door and we knew he wanted us to leave. And right quick.

I understood and was embarrassed and grabbed Johnny's arm. His white arm made my black hand stand out and I was very upset that all the people in Mr. Martin's shop was starin' at me.

I looked around and saw nothin' but white faces at the tables. As I scanned the room, I saw the window between the counter and the cook's area. Through it I saw Mama lookin' at me like she never had before. She had a hairnet on and was holding a white plate in her hand that she was scrubbin' until the moment she saw me.

"Mama," I yelled, and my words pierced the silent room. I wondered how God could allow such a blessed man to speak of me in such a manner. I knew my Mama would put Mr. Martin right where he belonged.

"Go, Sarah," her voice rang through the order window and over the Strawberry Fizzle mixer. "Go now."

I looked at Johnny and he looked puzzled that my Mama was tellin' me to leave. I know I was.

He grabbed my hand and we ran out. Johnny's Strawberry Fizzle sat on the counter, untouched.

He kept up with me as I biked to my house. He was right behind me as I ran in the backyard tool shed and cried. I collapsed onto the dirt floor and pulled Earl from my pocket.

"Earl," I said through sobs, "I can't have a Strawberry Fizzle." Earl looked up at me knowingly—many times he'd wished he were a frog instead of a warty toad so that he could be loved by princesses, or at least that's what I thought. I stroked his back and kissed him on the head. Johnny had already entered the room, and he just stood there, watchin' me 'n Earl.

Mama came home that night and her hair was not in a net as usual. The tight curls stood out like an untamed cloud. She plopped on the plaid sofa.

"Mama," I said.

"Yes, Baby," she replied.

"How come you can be there and I can't?"

She didn't say a word.

"I don't want to be colored! I hate bein' colored," I shouted. Mama just looked at me that evenin', her eyes lookin' swollen and the whites now red.

She never did answer my question.

I heard Mama and Papa fightin' that evenin'. I thinks it was because Mama lost her job because she didn't go back the next mornin'.

Two weeks to the day later, my Papa looked at me and said, "Come on."

I grabbed his hand and we headed down Main Street.

I could see Mr. Martin's Soda Fountain gettin' closer and closer and my stomach was tied up in knots.

"Papa?" I asked.

"Yes, sugar," he replied. He was wearing his Sunday best and today was Wednesday. He had on a navy blue coat and the pants even matched.

"Where we goin'?"

"We're goin' to get you a Strawberry Fizzle, Baby," he said. He smiled down at me and the warmth of his hand enveloped mine. I felt safe and proud.

There wasn't much of a line, since it had died down the week after the Strawberry Fizzle was announced. We took two of the many open seats at the counter. I could see Mr. Martin watching us from the moment we entered through the double-paned glass door. I shifted in my chair.

"Two Strawberry Fizzles," my papa said.

"Make that one Strawberry Fizzle," Mr. Martin said. I looked over at Papa and he was starin' right at Mr. Martin like they had some type of understandin'.

I was confused because the night before, Papa said that Mr. Martin was bound by law to give me my Strawberry Fizzle ever since

Mr. Kennedy passed somethin' called a bill a couple years back. Mr. Martin couldn't skip me this time, Papa said.

"I said," Papa repeated slowly, "two Strawberry Fizzles." His eyes met mine for a moment then he added, "Please." Papa looked handsome and I could smell his cologne and I knew he really wanted to taste Mr. Martin's invention.

"And I said, you know better than that, Nigger. Only one of you gonna be needin' a drink," Mr. Martin said, his face all crinkled. Next thing I knew, he was rootin' around under the counter. Before I could grab a straw from the jar, Mr. Martin popped up with a gun in his hands.

And it was aimed at my father. Before I had a chance to tell Papa, I saw it comin', the shot rang out like a firecracker. My father slumped on the stool. Red liquid spread across his shirt.

"Papa!" I screamed as loud as I could. I screamed for my father and for Johnny to come and get me and for my Mama to come back to work. I screamed for Earl to be back in my pocket and Mrs. Johnson to call me "darlin'" again. I screamed and I screamed.

Four nights later, my Mama said, "So, you said you wish you weren't colored."

"Why would I want to be?" I asked.

"Maybe you should ask your papa."

"But Papa's gone."

"I know, Baby, I know."

WHEN THE FISH DON'T BITE

Jason Headley

The water was cold. He could feel it against his legs, even through the waders. Fuckin' fish weren't biting worth a shit today. That's what he'd heard his pappaw say earlier. It didn't seem to matter much to him one way or the other. It wasn't fair that he was no good at something so simple. You just put your line in the water and stand there. But he couldn't make a fish take to his hook. Wouldn't have bothered him so much if it wasn't the most important thing in the world to everyone around him. Including his pappaw.

He'd forget fishing was important. Sometimes he liked to just stand by the water. Watch it carry itself down the channel. He used to like to skip rocks, but his pap gave him a good talking to about that. "Scares the fish," he'd say. So he had to just stand there and watch his bobber.

Even then there were problems. He'd get snags. Catch his hook on the bottom of the creek and have to tug and pull to get it out. Most of the time he'd snap the line. Which meant he needed help putting another hook on, so somebody else had to stop fishing. And he was in trouble. Again.

His last snag did it. He'd cast the rod back behind his head, catching the line in a tree just above him. It brought his pappaw over. And it earned him a pair of hip waders and a spot fishing out in the middle of the creek.

If they made hip waders for kids, his pap sure didn't own any. The only thing he knew about waders was that people died in them. Every year or so you'd hear a story about someone walking out too deep, their waders filling up with water and the current pulling them downstream and under the blue. Now here he was, in grown-up waders— their rubber soles searching for traction on the mossy rocks of the creek bed—trying to fish.

His brother was only a couple of years older than him, but he could fish. Pull fish out of the water like they were on his line at the start. But his brother didn't like to touch the worms. The two of them had a deal. He'd put the worms on the hook, and his brother would take off the fish.

Standing hip-deep in the water, he was in better shape. His brother had just caught another fish back on the bank, with no one to put another worm on the hook for him. But out there in the middle of the creek, the boy had worm-hooking skills and no real fear of catching any fish.

The worm had come off the hook on his last cast. So he dug out a big night crawler and folded its wriggling body in half. It squirmed as he brought the hook to it. The creek seemed to squirm a bit too. Just enough to make him shift his rubbery feet on the rocks. He thought he felt water begin to pour into his waders, and the panic made him shift his weight even more. His arms flailed as his face went hot, waiting for the cold rush of water to pull him under. But just as quickly, he regained his balance. And he realized. His waders were still well above water. He'd dropped his fishing rod. And the hook was in his thumb.

The rush of the current was pulling the rod downstream, digging the hook deep toward the bone of his thumb. He grabbed the fishing line with both hands and tried to pull the rod back toward him. The line kept coming in fistfuls, unraveling from the reel, but the rod was nowhere. Blood and line filled his hand as the pain crept from his thumb into his wrist. Finally he felt the line catch. He pulled and watched his skin go white on either side of the filament. He imagined the fish underwater pulling the rod away from him. Prey no longer, joining to defeat the mighty fisherman. Unknowing that the other end of the line held a fellow victim of the fishing trade.

He jerked the line hard to the right, then to the left, just like he'd seen his pappaw do to get loose of a snag. His head was hot with confusion as he tugged and pulled at the line. Finally, something gave. The line came toward him brisk and easy, and a force built behind his eyes. The line was too light. The severed end of line pulled free of the water and turned from clear to red in his hand. The force behind his eyes broke through.

Tears blurred his vision and his head spun. He stuck his hands into the cold water to wash the blood away. It felt good for a second before the pain eased back. Choking back sobs was making him sick to his stomach, so he opened his mouth to release some of the hurt. As he brought his hand to his mouth to bite off the line attached to the hook, he realized he was crying loud enough for anyone to hear.

"What the hell's the matter, Jeb?" he heard his pap yell from up on the bank. He didn't know where to start. His pap's fishing rod. The hook in his thumb. His hatred of fishing. He wanted to hunker down and let the waders fill with the creek.

"Nothing," he managed to shout back between sobs. He pulled at the hook, but it was caught deep. The more he pulled, the more he could feel it hooking into the meat of his thumb.

"Then what are you cryin' at?" His pap's voice was thunder. The pain in his thumb was more than his nine-year-old body could handle and his head was pounding from trying not to cry. Suddenly he seemed to really only know one thing.

"I just want to go home," he cried out to whoever would listen. "Just take me home. I don't want—" he heaved in a gasp of air to fuel more crying. "I just want to go home!"

"Aw goddamn it, Jeb! Get over here!"

His pap was standing on the bank just in front of him now. His giant frame cut a looming silhouette against the horizon, and nothing about his stance made the boy want to go to him. But he knew there was nothing to do now but receive the brunt of his annoyance. He pulled the top of the waders close to him with his good hand and walked carefully toward the bank. When he got near his grandpa, he heard him ask it.

"Where the hell's your pole?"

He looked up at him with swollen eyes. "I dropped it, Pap," he whimpered. "I slipped and the hook stuck me and I guess I dropped it."

"You *guess* you did? Well, it ain't in your hand so you must have fuckin' dropped it all right." His pap tilted his head and dropped a brown mess of spit from the chaw in his mouth. "I figure I should be the one cryin' here, Jeb. Don't you think? I mean, it was my fishin' pole. You suppose I should just start crying right now too? Why don't you show me how it's done."

More than anything else he wanted not to cry just then. He bit his lip and looked up at his pappaw with red anger in his eyes. Tears kept coming, but he swallowed every sob. His moment of strength was short-lived when he realized his pap was mimicking his own face.

"Is that how you do it?" he asked, his face contorted in an exaggeration of the boy's. "That's not the crying I heard you doing out there. I want the real thing. Show me how that goes."

He put his hands to eyes and cried as hard as he could. He didn't know anything anymore. Fishing was supposed to be fun. His pap was supposed to take care of him. But there was no explaining this. Crying seemed to be the only thing to do. So he was going to go ahead and do it until he was finished.

His pap's voice broke through his bedlam. "What in shit's sake'd'ya do to your hand?"

When he'd put his hands to his face to hide one shame, he'd exposed another. He held his bloody hand out for his pap to see. The hook stuck out from his thumb, catawampus. A shining testament to his ability to ruin a fishing trip. For a moment his pap's expression turned from disgust to pity. And it made the boy cry even more to find relief in that.

The old man grabbed the boy's hand between his own thumb and forefingers. He gave the hooked thumb a glance as he muttered some indignity to no one in particular. His other hand grabbed the hook and pushed it farther into the boy's flesh in a swooping motion. A cry hit the air as the jagged end of the hook popped through the boy's skin, right next to where it had gone in. He reached into his vest, pulled out a pair of wire cutters, and clipped the notch off the end of the hook. Then with one reverse swoop, he pulled the hook back through the boy's thumb.

Blood flowed freely from the two holes in his thumb, but it felt better now. His pap held up the reddened bit of metal, turned it over once in his hand then looked at the boy.

"Looks like I'm out a fishing rod and a hook now, huh?" He tossed the hook onto the ground and looked out onto the creek as he spoke to the boy, "Get on into the trailer there and clean up that thumb real good. Your mom'll have my ass if it gets all rotten. Then you can just stay in there and lay down or something until we're done out here. It won't be too long now. And if you stay out of the way, we might just have some trout for dinner." He turned and looked at the boy to be sure he was paying attention. "Hear me?"

He nodded as he slipped the wader suspenders off his shoulders. They slapped to the ground. He stepped out of them and walked toward the trailer. It was stuffy with all the heat of the day trapped inside, and he wished he could just lie down outside in the shade and watch the water. His whole head was tired from crying and the swelter of the trailer didn't help.

Cold water rushed out of the faucet in the bathroom. He held his thumb underneath and watched the blood carry away with the water as quickly as it came to the surface. He squeezed his thumb with his other hand to force more blood from the holes. Then he rubbed his two fingers against the bar of soap on the sink and smoothed some soap onto the surface of his wound. The stinging wasn't so bad. Not as bad as when he'd skin his knee on his bike and his mom would go at it with soap and peroxide. This was more tame.

He rinsed his hands clean then brought a handful of water to his face. It felt good against his lips, so he bent his head under the faucet to get a drink. When he was done drinking, he left his face there, uncomfortably crammed under the spigot, letting the cool water run across his mouth and chin. As he toweled off, he caught a glance of himself in the mirror. His eyes were swollen and red, and his face seemed bigger than usual. The sight of it made him want to cry again, so he turned away and walked out of the bathroom.

Some bits of canned sausage were sitting on the countertop in the kitchen. Left over from breakfast, they'd soaked the paper towel through with grease. He absently picked up a chunk of the dry meat as he walked toward the sofa bed, chewing and listening to the whir of fishing rods out by the creek. Listening harder, he could hear the water running in the creek bed and some birds calling to one another. He closed his eyes and imagined he was outside, lying in the shade of a tree with the water running right beside him. He heard his grandpa and his brother laughing together. And he imagined he was laughing with them.

A breeze found its way through the screen door as sleep settled over him. On the front of his shirt, a tiny bloodstain formed where his hand rested. And his mind settled as he remembered. Tomorrow they would go home.

THE BEAUTY SEAT

Ingrid Hill

Everyone calls it a "fishing camp," this barebones excuse for a house set on pilings out into the lake, but no one in anyone's memory has ever fished from it. Knocking against one of the pilings beneath the house is a white rowboat, but no one has ever been known to use it.

Poised on the ladder down into the lake, seeming to hesitate in her decision whether to swim, is Amalie Pavageau, brown with the sun, barely ten. Her arms and legs are just a bit longer than feels comfortable, wobbly and double-jointed as a newborn foal's. Her legs are wet, all the way up to the Lastex cuffs of her bathing suit, and the water beads up on the suntan oil, catching the overbright sunlight. Obviously she has already been in the water, so clearly we are mistaken in thinking she's on her way into it.

The water is a murky poison-jade hue, sloshing slow and thick. Amalie has stepped off the bottom of the ladder, into the sucking sand bottom, for only a second, and in that instant brushed against something heavy, the weight of a sleek fat dog, a moving thing, unyielding, unreal, alive. Her movement as smooth as a gymnast's, she backs up the ladder three rungs and clings there immobile.

It could not have been a shark, she tells herself, because sharks eat other people, whose names have appeared in the newspaper. They do not eat Amalie Pavageau.

This very summer three people have been attacked in Lake Pontchartrain by sand sharks, one dying, two losing limbs, but each time everyone seems to decide that it was a freak occurrence, unique, will not happen again. No one is staying out of the lake.

The sand at Pontchartrain Beach is full of sunbathers whose children pick up their pails and mosey out to the water's edge to build sand castles and then, forgetting themselves, drop the shovels and, mesmerized, mosey out into the slosh. The lifeguard, a canvas hat slouched forward over his forehead, poses up in his high lifeguard seat

111

on its slim legs, his lips pooching out sexy and sullen, as if he were that new white-trash singer Elvis Presley.

A man from Mobile who was visiting his brother lost a foot; his name was Herbert Bloom. "A Jew," Turk opines, out of the corner of his mouth, around the ivory-colored cigar holder. He seems to be saying: if Herbert Bloom had chosen to be something other than a Jew, he would have been safer from sand sharks. Turk raises his left eyebrow as if to say, Didn't Dachau teach these people anything?

A three-year-old named Barbianne Bourgeois has been mangled to death. Amalie has seen her picture in the *Picayune*, taken on her birthday three months before her death. She is wearing a party hat, and the credit says, "Lee Tilton Studios." Amalie finds that so strange.

Lee Tilton is the father of one of her classmates. How can a person who had her picture taken at that studio across the street from the blue-mirror-tile–fronted drugstore be dead now?

A twelve-year-old boy from Hammond who was playing in water up to his shoulders has lost an arm and an eye. Amalie does not remember his name. She remembers the bandages in the photo. No one, however, has brushed right smack against a shark and lived whole to tell about it. And no one has told Amalie Pavageau that she should not go in the water.

The sand-shark phenomenon seems much like the local approach to hurricanes, hitting and wiping out everything, and everyone except those who died coming back sighing and smiling weakly, immediately, to rebuild.

Amalie recalls the last hurricane, which threatened but did not hit them, though it did wipe out two small towns down near the mouth of the river, where most of the houses had corrugated tin roofs. She had watched her uncle and aunt sitting out on the front porch laughing, watching the gathering darkness and whipping wind. Turk and Ruby drinking what they call a hurricane punch, from a glass pitcher with pictures of lemons and oranges circling it like a merry-go-round. "Nothing much you can do," they'd said a couple of times, laughing almost hysterically, as if, on the one hand, the hurricane were an abstract test of their nerve, and on the other hand as if it were unstoppable.

Amalie had wished that their house had a basement to hide in—she'd heard in the North people had them and hid there when storms came—but on drained-cypress-swamp land as in New Orleans, no one has a basement.

Amalie curls her toes around the dried-out wood of the ladder rung and looks down at the water. Slosh. Murky slap against pilings. Green opacity. No signs of sharks she can see. On her right calf, the outside of it, she imagines, up here in the air on the ladder, the shark pressing again, its full weight, reconstituted. Pulling away, then pressing. Pulling away, pressing.

Three years before, in 1952, there had been a big polio epidemic: all over the country children got sick and died. The Audubon Park Natatorium, vast and teeming, stayed open all summer, and several children came down with the dread disease. Ruby had never told Amalie to stay home—Amalie could come and go as she pleased—and Amalie swam and did not contract polio, though other people did.

Two people from her second grade class at the time, in fact: one in an iron lung now, forever; the other wearing black orthopedic shoes, one of them built up, the other normal and flat-soled, and a leg brace with terrible squeaky screws for the shriveled leg. She looks down at the water again. Her swimsuit, across her flat little-girl belly, is the green of chlorophyll toothpaste. The wood of the fishing camp is painted pale mint green, the color of walls in the grade school bathroom. Every time Amalie looks at the fishing camp, she smells grade-schoolers' fermented urine deep in the bones of her head.

She cannot see through the dark of the screen porch, but she knows that inside the house her uncle and aunt, Turk and Ruby, are doing some business with Mr. Gemelli, the man who owns slot machines out in Jefferson Parish or collects money from them or she cannot exactly say what, but Ruby and Turk are in business with him. They are off in the back bedroom to the right.

In the other bedroom, to the left, is Dimitria, old inherited mother of Ruby's dead first husband, sitting and rocking, her dark widow's dress with the brooch at the neck so strange in this heat. She is saying her rosary, rocking, her lips moving. She fans herself with a cardboard paddle-shaped fan whose front bears a picture of Saint Michael the Archangel slaying the dragon, whose back says, "Reebie's Fine Produce" and a motto: "Nature's Best and You Know It," and gives an address on Colapissa Street.

In the big middle room—from her perch out here Amalie imagines it as huge as the marble-floored waiting room at Union Terminal, but it is not—there are a couple of old Mission sofas, hard-armed, with useless seat cushions limp as rice sacks. In the middle of the floor, as if guarding it all, is Dimitria's boxer dog, Beauty, posed majestic as a concrete library lion.

From half a dozen pilings of the pier dangle broad crab nets baited with rooster combs, undulating pinkly, obscenely, as lures. This evening, while Turk and Mr. Gemelli smoke cigars on the porch looking out to the lake, Ruby will gather up the traps and boil the crabs in the huge barrel-boiler on the side porch with packets of spices. Amalie hates the thick yellow-green fat that she has to scrape away to find the pure white meat, and when Turk is not looking she takes each half-picked crab indoors to wash it clean under the faucet. The crabmeat itself is exquisite.

Amalie has often wondered about Ruby's first husband. A Greek, she knows, straight from the Old Country, and connected with Reebie, who also comes over sometimes to play cards. Dimitria's son died before Amalie could remember, before Amalie came to live with them, but there are pictures of him in the footstool with its padded lift-up cover.

He smiles in a grade school graduation-class shot on the steps of a church. He stands with his arm around Mel Ott, the baseball player, at Pelican Stadium, both of them nearly regressed to boys, in a day that seems long past. He died of a bullet wound, Amalie knows, but she knows no more. Ruby took care of Dimitria after he died, because

Dimitria was very old and had no other sons in America. Ruby married Turk not too long after Dimitria's son died, and they both take care of her now, because it is Dimitria's money, Ruby says, that bought the big house they all live in, as well as paying for Amalie's tuition at Immaculate Heart convent boarding school across the lake in Covington.

Amalie is hardly ever "home" at Turk and Ruby's. There are three sessions of camp in the summertime that she attends, and in the shorter school vacations she visits other girls' families because she is well liked by everyone and also Turk will send money and gifts to the families.

Everyone anticipates with a kind of morbid delight the surprise of what Turk will send next. At Easter she'd gone to Ghislaine Verdelle's family in Grand Coteau. Turk had sent them a Muntz console TV with fat knobs of ivory plastic and a cabinet of real pecan wood. Mrs. Verdelle liked to watch *I Love Lucy* now in their bedroom, which was big enough to have an armchair for the purpose. Mr. Verdelle's hair was dark, slick, and wavy like Desi Arnaz's, and Mr. Verdelle waved his arms around a lot when he talked and raised his voice in a silly way, also like Desi Arnaz.

Amalie loves the dark mystery of old Dimitria and wishes she could understand how all of these people relate to her. Ruby and Turk are her uncle and aunt in some technical sense, or, more properly, Ruby is the cousin of her mother, who died when Amalie was four years old, of a hemorrhage, and Amalie's father had died not so long before, or maybe afterward, when he was hit by a truck crossing Poydras Street, but there are no pictures of them, except Ruby says, when Amalie asks now and again, that they are somewhere in storage, maybe they'll get them the next time they go. Go where, Amalie doesn't know. She has a feeling that Ruby means the warehouse down near the docks where Amalie sits in the car inside the closed garage door of the building in the dark—except for one lightbulb so high up on the ceiling that she can't read the book she has brought—waiting while they do something upstairs.

Amalie's father had been a bass player at a lounge on Bourbon

Street. "And damn good, too," Turk says, as if someone has challenged him. He bites on his ivory plastic cigar holder, which matches the Verdelles' TV knobs, when he says it, and then turns back to whatever he was doing before he got distracted. Amalie knows that there is another bass player named Pavageau, very famous, but he is black. "Right," says Turk. "Ha! No relation!"

But Amalie thinks that she knows the connection. Sister Anne Jeannette was her fourth-grade teacher, a pale, fiery-eyed girl of a nun whose wimple pulled tight at her temples in such a way that Amalie thought she could see tufts of white-blond hair there, but everyone knew nuns were bald.

Sister Anne Jeannette taught them, among other things, for instance, about circumcision in the Old Testament, especially a passage about Moses' wife Zipporah flinging their baby's foreskin at him across the room, "Like a bloody worm!" expostulated Sister Anne Jeannette. "Flying through the air!" said Sister Anne Jeannette. "Because Moses, for all he was God's chosen one, had neglected this one little thing."

The boys in the class snickered, and the girls looked at each other with their eyes crossed. She went on about some law called the Riot Act, about the French Revolution and the guillotine, about a number of interesting slave rebellions in various places.

Sister Anne Jeannette had said that in 1803, right about the same time as the Louisiana Purchase, there had been a slave uprising in Saint Domingue in the West Indies, which was now Haiti, and many French plantation owners had fled to Louisiana. She said many slaves took on their masters' names, which explained black people's showing up with Irish names like Inniss and Murphy and Jamison and also, Amalie assumed, French names like Pavageau.

Probably that black bass player's ancestors had been slaves on the plantation of her own ancestors, and she was terribly sad about that. "Sad! Jesus Christ!" Turk said quizzically, with an alien look on his face, when she told him that, as if she had made a horribly rich and complex joke. And then, as always, Turk turned quickly back to what he had been doing, which always involved piles of numbers and small slips of paper, or sometimes, if there was a card game in progress, two-inch-high piles of quarters.

Ruby seemed to have been Amalie's mother's first cousin, if Amalie had the thing right. And when Amalie's mother just bled to death with a new pregnancy and there was no one else to take Amalie, Ruby had taken her, and two months later she had married Turk.

So Dimitria has no direct connection to Amalie, but Amalie sees her nonetheless as her own grandmother, filled with dark mystery. The rocking chair in which Dimitria rocks has hard dark arms like the living room sofas. Its rockers are shallow and clumsy, and rocking seems to take more effort than it is worth. Yet Dimitria keeps rocking. Through the open door into the main room she keeps eye contact with the boxer dog, Beauty, who sits like a guard.

Amalie remembers the day Turk brought Beauty home, telling Dimitria this dog would be her protection while no one was home. The dog was young but full-grown. Two men had come to the door the previous week demanding entrance, pounding their fists on the doorjamb and shaking the walls, and Dimitria had been frightened.

Turk told Dimitria the dog's name, something ferocious, and Dimitria shook her head no. "The dog's name," Dimitria said solemnly, "is Beauty."

Turk scowled. Dimitria seemed to Amalie to be praying for protection in general a lot of the time, from the look on her face. The lightweight beads of her dark rosary slipped through her fingers, her lips framing Hail Mary after Hail Mary.

In summer the dog likes to sleep underneath the green shade of the tall fig bush in the backyard at Turk and Ruby's. Amalie stands on a short ladder to pick the figs. She loves the sensuous feel of their fur and the challenge of plucking them off without breaking their tender, almost-human stems. Dimitra cooks them in syrup and cans them in mason jars.

Amalie is mesmerized, caught on this rung of the ladder, heading neither down nor up. She thinks of a picture she saw in the paper this morning: Zev Lukassen, a Danish concert pianist, is in New Orleans on a tour of the country to give a performance.

He seemed so exotic in his wholesomeness. The interviewer questioned him about his father's involvement in the Danish Resistance during the war, and Zev Lukassen had said, yes, his father had done that, and not much more on the subject. Amalie could feel the conversation fall through, like a deflating volleyball, even on the page.

The interviewer then prodded Zev Lukassen: just how had his father been brave, what had he done? Zev Lukassen said, "The Nazis in Denmark knew the Allied invasion was coming. They conscripted many Danes to build gun emplacements. My father was one of these. He and the other workers poured sugar into the concrete so that when it set up, it stayed in place only a short time, then crumbled." The interviewer said he had never heard anything like this.

Zev Lukassen said, "Well, it happened. Again and again. And each time the Germans would come in and line up the workers and make a random example of someone." He said that his uncle Torsten had died this way, shot, and his father, Tage, had not. He said there was not much to say except that his father had been brave and now was dead of a farming accident.

He wanted to talk about other things. His performance, he said, was organized around musical pieces whose titles all had something to do with the beauties of nature, on both the intimate and the Grand Canyon ends of the scale. He said he would begin with Edward Mac-Dowell's "To a Wild Rose."

Amalie did not know the song but made a mental note to find out how it sounded. She had fallen in love with Zev Lukassen the minute she saw his face. It was a face she would see in the Kennedy family, in the news, several years later: the freckles, the Irishness. A Danish Jew.

Hanging there on her ladder rung, Amalie imagines Zev Lukassen climbing now out of a sleek, muscled Buick on the road that runs along the lake's edge. His chauffeur is waiting for him, wearing a chauffeur's cap and with his hands on the ivory steering wheel. Zev Lukassen walks purposefully to the pier. He sees her and heads in her direction. He will explain the order of all of this disorder to her, perhaps. Perhaps he will play it on his piano.

This absolute stasis, this feeling of being caught like a fly or a ladybug in a spider's web, is what trips me out of this story each time I try to tell it. I have told it so far as if it were someone else's story, but the problem is that it is not, and my artifice skewers me.

I am Amalie Pavageau, of course, and the matted complex of the relationships that surrounded me is indecipherable, even in retrospect.

That summer's end, when we went back to school, Sister Jeanne D'Arc folded her hands in front of her round black-serge midriff, fingertips pointing straight up, as if calling down angels, and said she would like us to write about our summer vacations.

I turned to look at the girl who sat next to me, Bibi Nunez, because for some reason I thought she would think that as funny in its predictability as I did. Sister Jeanne D'Arc had a look on her face as if she had invented the idea. Bibi Nunez was staring at the inkwell on her desk and not listening to Sister Jeanne D'Arc at all. I realized that actually no teacher had ever asked us to write on this topic before.

That was the first time I tried to make sense of my family in writing. I had a retractable ball-point pen, my first, and I used up half a coarse-papered penmanship tablet with pale blue lines, trying to include the spindly legs of the fishing camp and the sand sharks and the fig preserves and the dog and the way the dog lay under the fig bush. I tried to include Zev Lukassen and his chauffeur (who in my fantasy had an effete but attractive way of flaring his nostrils) and the song, "To a Wild Rose."

I tried to line up the cross-section panorama of the three rooms of the fishing camp: Dimitria rocking in the room to the left; Beauty the boxer dog sitting majestic, head erect, panting, tongue pink and quivering in the middle room; and to the right, Turk with Mr. Gemelli counting out money while Ruby made drinks in a silver aluminum drink shaker. I tried to include the way Turk called the drink shaker al-you-MINI-um. I failed.

Instead I wrote a piece for Sister Jeanne D'Arc that said:

This summer I was sent to Florida for two weeks to stay with my aunt at her beach house. It had a lovely sign out front, "Wild Rose Cottage," with a hand-painted picture of a wild rose that was the color called Brick Red in my Crayola crayons. This was at Destin Beach, where the water is clear as the stone in my birthstone ring, and the same color, which is aquamarine. My mother left me that birthstone ring when she died, along with a letter telling me that she would always be with me.

Each day my aunt made me pancakes in late morning for breakfast. Each morning I went out early before anyone else was up, to walk along the beach. The sand was very white, almost like sugar. One morning I made a pretty good sculpture in the sand, a woman's body lying on her back looking peaceful. She was not dead, only sleeping. I knew that the next tide would wash her away but I made her complete and detailed anyway, the very best I could.

Another morning, when there was no one else on the beach, I took out my tire tube and got into it. I paddled out quite a distance. I closed my eyes and let my head flop back. The sun felt good even though it was early. I let my hands hang over the sides of the tire tube in the clear water.

Suddenly one of my hands touched something. I was frightened. I opened my eyes and I was startled to find I was in the midst of a big school of small silvery fish, and I started paddling madly. I had been caught in the current and washed out so far from shore that it seemed that if the fish hadn't startled me I might have been taken too far out to get back.

My hands caught the fish and tossed them in the air as I tried to paddle. I was terrified. I made progress and within minutes was out of the current that I had been caught in. I made it to shore. I will go back to Wild Rose Cottage over

Thanksgiving vacation but it will be too cold to swim. I hope you had a lovely vacation too, Sister Jeanne D'Arc.

I imagined her in the dark convent, whose center hall and closed doors everywhere were claustrophobic, doing the same things all summer that she did all winter, except perspiring more while she was doing them, under her layers of black serge and unearthly flannel slips and long drawers. In my mind what she did involved trimming the beeswax altar candles and ironing the altar linens, both fragrant tasks. I envied the sweet-smelling order—or what I imagined to be the sweet-smelling order—of convent life.

The following September, in a classroom right above Sister Jeanne D'Arc's. I submitted the same essay, unchanged, for Sister Miriam Richard. There seemed no point in changing it, and it was a lie regardless. Sister Miriam Richard had a slight dark mustache. Her dark hair appeared at the corners of her coif, almost as obscene to me as pubic hair. This disconcerted me: nature reasserting itself in the face of attempts to tame it out of existence, in the name of holiness. This also did in our theories of nunly baldness.

The next year we were not asked for a summer vacation essay at all. I had grown quite tall over that summer, and Dimitria had shrunk, as old people do. Since I had no experience of this—I was only eleven—I found her diminution infinitely fascinating. She began sitting out in the back patio in the evening with the dog beside her rocking chair. Every evening Turk brought in the rocking chair and the next evening carried it out again.

One weekend when I was in from school, I took the Saint Charles streetcar downtown. I had no particular destination. The ride itself was the point. I had taken a transfer from the conductor but had no idea where I might be headed with it. There were probably connecting streetcar lines I had never even heard of, and that would be good. I sat in one of the long hard wooden seats along the front end of the trolley car, facing in to the center.

Ruby called this the Beauty Seat. She said that was Dimitria's name for it. She said this was because only vain people sat there, wanting everyone to look at them. On the trolley Dimitria sat in the front facing seats whose backs, at the end of the line, the conductor flipped in the other direction. The car did not have to turn around. Dimitria carried her rosary and ran the beads silently through her fingers.

The only time she rode the trolley was when Ruby took her to the doctor's or, once, to a funeral at Jesuit Church for a man she had known when she was younger. Ruby said she thought this man had been a beau of Dimitria's, in early middle age, after she was widowed. I found that idea amazing.

At a king cake party that year given by a girl whose father owned a chain of bakeries around town that specialized in making chocolate-topped cookies called "turtles," I met a boy who played the piano, and who looked like a Kennedy, though of course that thought would not occur to me until several years later, when the Kennedys burst upon the scene. He was also Jewish. The combination was amazing to me: I became fascinated with him.

His name was Maxwell Stern, and he was several inches shorter than I was. I asked him once at the third king cake party, which was held at a house on Audubon Place that had a huge white grand piano, if he would play "To a Wild Rose" for me. He knew the song, and he played it. This was a strange moment. I didn't expect he would know it.

For several minutes after he finished it, I stood next to the piano taking in the entire room: the brocade drapes, the high chandelier, the tall windows. Then I turned to look at Maxwell Stern, and he was looking at me as if I belonged in the Beauty Seat. I was only twelve, and I was not pretty. I cleared my throat and turned and walked back to the party, and Max Stern followed me.

I knew he was only playing Zev Lukassen in my mind, but I let him do that. I had no idea who I was playing. The following year Maxwell Stern took me to my first dance, and he was as leaden-footed on the dance floor as he was light-fingered on the keys. Ten years later I married a Jewish pianist, though he was not Maxwell Stern.

I had sat in the Beauty Seat before, in fact sat there every time I could. I was hardly vain, though. I knew I was gangly and awkward. I had been diagnosed with a lazy eye by the optometrist that winter and ordered to wear a repulsive flesh-colored eye-patch, with a suction cup stuck to the lens of my glasses, over my left eye to strengthen my right. It tired my right eye and made it bloodshot.

From my perch in the Beauty Seat, I watched the other riders with my single unpatched eye, thinking that if I watched closely enough, I'd discover something important. I watched people's lips as they talked and imagined from their gestures that I could understand what they were saying. I assumed that after a while little snippets of overheard truth would mount up to something and the scales would tip suddenly. In my mind's eye, the scales were a wonderful bronze color and the truths were transparent, like jellyfish.

The Saint Charles streetcar passed several huge, gray stone Jewish mansions, from the days when Judah Touro and other historic Jews did wondrous things in New Orleans. We passed Dominican College with its stately treed courts out front, and Audubon Park with its moss-hung live oaks. The conductor clanged the warning bell when a woodie station wagon impetuously crossed the tracks in front of us, chancing a collision.

The streetcar headed on to Lee Circle, and as we rounded the triumphal statue of General Lee there, on a pedestal so high—sixty feet—that no one could quite see him, I looked up at General Lee, facing north, with his arms folded somehow the way that Turk folded his arms when he was being stubborn with Ruby, and he looked to me as if he didn't realize that he had lost the war.

THE THING WITH FEATHERS

Suzanne Hudson

Inspired by the sculpture Lilith, *by Rachel Wright*

She didn't meet her stepfather until she was five, having lived with a cousin of her mother's in Beaumont, Texas, since she was born, having been ensconced in the womb during the marriage ceremony. An apathetic judge of probate oversaw the wedding, a hasty, desperate ritual her mother rushed at, in order to find legitimacy for herself and, by default, her daughter. In 1950, the world of small-town Alabama did not look kindly upon unwed mothers, and her own mother thought it best to spend some time alone with this man who was now a husband, would be a husband for the next thirteen years, until he shot himself in the head on a creek bank—accidentally, some said; on purpose, said others.

The relative who brought her up to the age of five was sometimes affectionate but many times harsh, tugging at the child's clothing in frustration as she dressed her, brushing, too hard, at the tangles in the child's hair, impatient and full of spat-out sighs, like the sounds of an angry cat. Still, there were storybooks read, in drowsy snuggles on the relative's bed, when it was time for a nap. There were stories the relative told for truth, about God and Jesus and arks and healings; but mostly there were fairy tales: "Snow White and Rose Red," "Jack and the Beanstalk," "Rapunzel." The toddler, the child, did not understand all the words, the intricacies of plot, but the soothing sound of her surrogate mother's voice spun silky tendrils of hope, though she couldn't name it at the time, around her unclaimed heart.

Her mother visited her on her birthdays, sent her packages at Christmas time, doll babies in shiny wrapping paper tied up in fumbled ribbon, shipped in boxes all bumpled and scarred by errant postmasters. The child played with the dolls in the floor of the relative's kitchen while boiling cabbage eked its humid, acrid scent into the walls, the curtains, cheap furniture disemboweling brown-flecked stuffings across the linoleum. Then one day she was told it was time to go and meet her stepfather.

She remembered hanging back, there in the doorway of her new parents' house, dropping her eyes from his overpowering form. He was all plaid flannel shirts, khaki work pants, and heavy boots that seemed to shake the earth, like the giant in "Jack and the Beanstalk." And he worked to win her over, his fingers nibbling at her ribs, games played until he drew her into the fun he concocted, though she always glanced away, holding back a bit of herself. "She's shy," her mother said, but she wasn't. So he called her "Sugar Bugger" and "Baby Doll" and "Dipsey Doodle." When he came in from work he would throw her in the air and the world would blur and the colors would bleed into each other and she would shriek with delighted laughter, even though there was that quick moment of terror, breath sucked back and where was Jesus?

He had a shotgun for killing deer, limp brown forms laid blood-spotted in the bed of his truck on autumn evenings. He had a thick-handled, thin-bladed silver knife for slitting through the skins of squirrels and catfish, or carving through the meat of an apple to offer her a small slice: "Eat it down, Sugar Bugger. An apple a day keeps the doctor away." He had a pistol he would use sometimes at night, to shoot at the raccoons that dug in the garbage, crashing her awake, sending her screaming and crying to her mother, who would say, "Don't be a silly girl. Go back to sleep. Your mama's tired as the devil."

He had a collection of fishing lures—rubber worms in purple and orange, golden spinners shimmering, enticing her—a kaleidoscope's colors, some like feathered jewels in the hinged, top-handled treasure chest he carried.

"Show me the thing with feathers, Daddy," she would say, for he had insisted, insisted that she call him "Daddy," and she, who had never had one, tried the word on and enjoyed the way the sound of it wrapped her in the feel of a safe-layered warmth.

"They ain't feathers," he would say, pulling out the shyster lure, letting her tickle it with the soft tips of her fingers. "Fish don't eat nothing with feathers."

He drank beer most of the time—like water, her mama said—and whiskey of an evening, and if the child was up too late, or lucky enough to be invited to sleep in the big bed next to her mama, she would sometimes see the other man emerge, the one who was much more unpredictable, the stumbling one, who mumbled curses and kicked her mother's bedroom door when she shut him out.

"Don't want no drunk slobbering over me," her mother would say.

He finally took her fishing when she was six, a special day, just the two of them, to a pond that pooled a blue stain in the woods, where he cast into the weeds, building a mound of empty cans, with each toss of a can, a glance at her, going from strange into threatening into frightening and where was Jesus? Then, the pile of cans grown to maturity, when the sun caved in to the horizon, he twirled her hair around his fingers, stroked her face, her little arms without recourse because she didn't understand. And when he put his hand to her panties, the soft white cotton ones her mother hung out on the line each week to dry, the ones he would throw into the blue pond going all deep-colored as the sun withdrew, tears streaked trails of salt down her cheeks because it hurt and she wanted her mama.

In elementary school the child was not especially noticeable, moving at an average pace, producing average work, sometimes pushing at the rules, as children will do, seeming good-natured, even charming at times. She raised her hand, walked single file, clattered her green plastic tray along stainless steel bars in the lunch line, flew in circles around the metal-chained maypole, ran in games of tag on a playground dusted with dirt. But at home she had grown tense and vigilant, keeping alert, watching doorknobs, listening for the pad of feet down the hall, in the night, while her mama slept. She had to be aware, stay keen to the barometric changes in the atmosphere of the little house, because she knew that darkness held the thick, syrupy smell of whiskey riding warm breaths across the slurred dreams of a girl now eight years old—when her only father would stand beside her bed and put her small palm to the thing that lived there beneath the hairy curve of his belly.

She would try to shove pictures into the grainy dark, try not to see him, not feel the mash of her tiny hand into his, but she could not pretend his looming form away or conjure anything that would color the dim shadows of her bedroom, not while she looked into the dark. So she shut her eyes tight, so tight it hurt, sending bursts of light against her clenched lids. And all the while, as he moved her palm along the creature he coaxed with his own, she would see nothing but the black-eyed Susans growing along the highway, or yellow butter-cups at Easter, or her mother's azalea bushes, hot pink and white against green. She would bathe herself in floral colors, fending off the dark and the molding of her fingers to the creature taking shape there, boozy breaths—all laced with the harsh, hot scent of the Camels he smoked—bearing down on her small body. She strung the flowers into garlands spiraling out around the little bed until his breaths hit hard and the thing spat venom across the pistils and velvet petals she had laced through the thick layers of the night.

When she was nine, ten, eleven, he would take her on long rides in the game preserve, slits in the rough-trunked horizon strobing sun-light into the periphery of her vision, where he lived, on the edge of a look, a quick cut of an eye, never full-on and vulnerable, never a challenging stare. She would lean her chin on her hand and hang her arm out the open window, trying to catch and hold the air, pushing her palm against the gale. Just the two of them, away from the house, furtive, like lovers trysting and traveling across the borders of contexts and closed-off emotions. He would find hidden, high-walled creek banks, where he would fire his pistol at the empty beer cans that for-ever clattered across the bed of his pickup. He taught her how to shoot, wrapped her small fingers around the butt of the Ruger and helped her support the weight of it, showed her how to hold it, palm cupping wrist, breathe in, let out slowly, and as shoulders drop, squeeze—no, no, squeeze, real slow, Baby Doll. That's it, that's it.

The noise of it, set off from her own thin fingers, crashed booming into the wild silence of the forest, an ear-ringing power of more dimension than she could have ever imagined, and its echo cracked and cracked its fade into a silence. And she liked it. So she practiced, asked him to teach her how to load, clean, and care for the thing, squealed with the thrill of firing it, exhilarated by its deafening blasts, those sounds that had more than once chased her from her little bed. She made secret dares, vows to herself to get better, be the best, know it like an intimate friend, a confidant. In time she began to practice with even more determination, with the grim focus of a guerrilla warrior, whenever he took her out for one of their rides down the red clay roads curling through the wooded, forested walls that hid them. She took aim at beer cans and milk cartons and squares of cardboard with bull's-eyes drawn on them. She exploded an olive-green wine bottle she had found under her mother's bed, sending a spray of glass bits sparkling like emeralds scattered to the sky.

"Got him!" her stepfather grunted.

And she smiled at him, a coy smile, the one she had learned to use early on, to maneuver him there in the unpopulated margins of her life. She could force an advantage, she had gradually discovered, could write a tune without words and suspend him in a dance. A lift of her chin, a pout of her lip, an inflection, a glance—she had found where the lines could be, if she wanted them there. She could change the course of a day with the bat of a lash, the turn of a wrist, the knowledge she had gathered and filed away during those solitary moments at his side. She could finally see who might really hold the cards, and where his weaknesses resided, and get the true lay of the land he had hidden for so many years without her ever suspecting. She squeezed the trigger.

"Got him!"

And she knew she had. Even at the age of eleven, twelve, and then, thirteen, she knew she had "got him," would get him, eventually, Jesus or no. She would take it upon herself, still a child but not a child—never, really, a child. She would take herself up on her secret dare and look at him directly, for once, eyes focused hard down the barrel of a gun, silver and straight, its lines looming outward from her fixed gaze like railroad tracks, parallel until she inched it down, real slow, breathing out, the squares of the sights put to the target at the end of her vision. She would get him and reclaim herself, take herself by her little girl's hand, dimpled and unscarred, to the place where her soul was hidden. And then, finally, the two of them would blend into each other, into the notes of the music, notes in chromatic half steps and notes of modulation, staves winding around and nestling against the warm skin of the relative in Beaumont, Texas, where the thing with feathers could sit unabashed on its perch, and reach into its sweet, sweet depths, and sing.

CICADAS

Cecilia Johnson

My sister and I found their empty husks clinging to the side of our garage, to the plastic straps of our lawn chairs, to the thorny stems of our mother's roses. The small translucent shells, the perfect amber skins that held the shape of folded wings and bulging eyes and tiny legs, were more miraculous to us than our mother's flowers. The discarded skins were evidence of magic; they were ghosts and they were jewels.

In Houston, summer was a weight, a heavy thing my sister and I wore thickly painted to our flesh. I was nine, pigtailed, still round with baby fat. Allison was thirteen, gorgeous, and in love with a high school boy named Mike who lived next door and played the trumpet.

A six-foot-high privacy fence separated our backyard from his, but we would take turns watching him through a knotted hole in one of the boards. He played "The Eyes of Texas" and "The Donkey Serenade" with his shirt off, sweat dripping off his chest and arms like falling stars.

One day he caught my sister spying, saw the flash of her eye gleaming through the wood. "Come here," he said, his lips to the hole. Allison crouched down, her ear and body pressed against the fence. I tried to hear what he was saying to her, and what she whispered back, but the buzz of the cicadas was a blanket of sound that covered everything. My sister kept her eyes away from mine as she stood up and brushed the dirt from her knees.

"What did he say?" I asked, eager for her secrets.

"Nothing," she said, her face as serious as stone.

The cicadas throbbed in the trees—half roar, half whine. Allison met my eyes again, pointed at the base of our favorite tree, the one where my father had tied a rope for us to swing. "See," she said, poking at the torn earth with a stick. The tiny holes were everywhere, like open mouths in the dirt. "This is where the cicadas come out at night. They spend their whole life waiting underground for the right time to climb out and shed their skins and fly up into the trees." She tossed the stick into the grass, glanced at the fence, and then at me.

"It's the boy cicadas who make all the noise," she said. "They're calling for their mates." That buzzing was the sound of desire. The racket of their wanting. Mike began to play his trumpet on the other side of the fence, the golden notes like twirling yellow ribbons un-curling in the sky.

That night, I woke up just in time to see Allison climbing out the window. "Hey," I said. She put her finger up to her mouth. She was halfway in and halfway out. I could see her lips were wet and painted. "I want to go," I said. She shook her head and dropped to the earth outside our window. By the time I could scramble out to follow, she was gone. I peered through the hole in the backyard fence, but all I saw were empty lawn chairs and a clothesline hung with sheets.

I waited on the rope swing, sitting my chubby bottom down on the plank of wood. "Where is she?" I thought, straining my ears so that I might catch the murmur of her voice. All that came back to me was the pulsing drone of the cicadas. I saw one struggling up from the dark ground, its body luminous against the black roots of the tree. I closed my eyes, pushed backwards in the swing, and pumped my legs to build momentum. My nightgown billowed in the air and I flew above the earth.

Allison did not come back until sunrise, when our yard was jew-eled again with the husks of new cicadas. She hauled herself up through the bedroom window and didn't say a word. Her face was smudged, a blur of makeup and swollen skin. She pulled a hard pack of Camels from her pocket and thumbed open the lid. Inside, a live cicada fluttered its wings against the cardboard, and she dumped his fat green body onto the bed. He sputtered on the sheets a moment, and then rose up in confused flight.

As he floated near the ceiling, I saw he had been tied with a thread. "Mike turned it into a little kite for me. See?" Allison grabbed the end of the thread, guiding the cicada back and forth—an airplane, a balloon. "You want to try?" she asked.

I took the thread from my sister's hand, and I could feel the tremble of the cicada on the other end of the string—all energy and clamor. I tried to guide him back and forth along the ceiling but I pulled too hard. I felt the string lose its resistance and the cicada plummeted to the carpet, a sudden stone.

"Silly!" Allison laughed, but I could hear tears in her throat. The cicada lay in two pieces. "You pulled his head off. Now we'll have to have a funeral."

In the backyard, we burned the pieces in a Maxwell House coffee tin. "You're supposed to cry at funerals," she said.

"I'm sorry," I said. "I didn't mean to." The smoke rose up from the coffee can, a dark smear against the dawn.

In the Tall Grass

Bret Anthony Johnston

My father is removing his rings. We are outside of Corpus Christi, Texas, on a ranch owned by a man named Edwin Butler. A busted gate hangs open behind us, and the odor of mud and horses seeps into the cab of our small truck. This is 1979, a year when my mother's spirits remained low and I was fourteen and my father wore three rings. He has not been arrested yet, and while that comes soon enough, he is already gone from me, as distant as the ice-blue snow of my dreams.

George Kelley, my father, had slender hands; on another man, his trimmed nails and long fingers might have been good for playing the piano. He worked at the Naval Air Station, building ship engines, and although most men in his shop were enlisted, his was a civilian job that he'd lucked into after serving in the Coast Guard down in Mississippi, where he was born. My father left for work early, when our floors were cold and the house and morning were without light. Often the sounds of his rising woke me too, though I soon slipped back to sleep, hearing him shave and dress and say "I love you" to my mother.

They'd met in 1964. My mother was waitressing at the Esquire Club, where my father enjoyed eating dinner and playing cards. Her name was Price then, Marie Price, because she was waiting for a man in Boston to sign annulment papers—his name was also George. My father was twenty-five, himself divorced from a woman in Mississippi; my mother was nineteen. Within a month she'd moved into his apartment and a year later a judge married them and they honeymooned in Mexico. A black-and-white photo someone had taken of her hung on their bedroom wall, my mother wading in the Gulf, looking young and delicate and happy.

But my mother also suffered from depression and often refused to leave her room for days at a time. She took pills to raise her moods, but sometimes those failed and my father called her boss and she stayed in bed. Occasionally, my parents spoke of an operation, a hysterectomy, which a doctor had suggested, but they distrusted that procedure and talked of it only, I thought, to reassure themselves that they agreed about not having it. During these days my mother lived on Cokes and cigarettes and chocolate, and she liked me to sit beside her and talk. The lights in her room remained off, and always, before I entered, I knocked to warn her, to allow her time to compose herself or cover her head with the pillow.

We discussed programs she'd watched on television. Or my days at school. Or she examined me in the dim light and noted how I had my father's posture, but her skin and eyes, attributes girls would eventually find beautiful. Sometimes I answered questions she'd thought up earlier in the day. How did I picture myself in ten years? Twenty? Had I kissed girls? Had I drunk alcohol or smoked cigarettes? Usually I spoke honestly, but sometimes I embellished or contrived answers to make her smile or, with luck, laugh.

In the spring of 1979 my father was a shift supervisor, and wore ties and slacks instead of coveralls. My mother worked at the high school I would attend that fall; she was the principal's secretary. The previous year someone from my father's shop had given us two horses because he needed space on his property and didn't want the hassle of selling them. My father had handled horses before and knew my mother had enjoyed riding lessons as a girl, so he arranged for two stalls at Edwin Butler's ranch and drove four hours south to Mexico for cheap blankets and saddles.

My mother's horse was named Lady, a black thoroughbred, well over sixteen hands high and too big for her to ride with any control. On Lady's back, my mother looked like a child. Mine was a brown-and-white gelding that I named Colonel because of a white star on his shoulder. He'd won trophies for running barrels in the past and that excited me because I longed for a trophy then and lacked any skills to earn one.

Because my father arrived at the naval base early, most afternoons he left in time to take me from school and drive to the stables. We arrived earlier than the other owners—a privacy that comforted me—and sometimes in those hours before my mother met us there or before Edwin Butler unlocked the steel gate to give trucks access to the stable area, my father saddled Lady and we rode together. Horses responded to my father, obeyed his commands in ways I'd not seen them do for other men. Although his belly rolled over his belt, my father could swing himself onto a horse in a single swift, graceful motion. He rode fast and hard. When he dug his heels into Lady's sides and hollered for her to come on, she exploded into a run so loud and strong and gorgeous that it made you gasp. Leaning close to her mane, he held the reins with one hand and clapped her backside with the other; they were nothing but run. Colonel struggled to follow, but Lady's legs powered ahead until we fell back and could only listen to them ride.

It was on a day when I hoped we might ride together that trouble came about. We'd not ridden much that week; a storm in the Gulf had soaked Edwin Butler's corral. And my mother's spirits had been low—her mood usually suffered in bad weather. Men from my father's shop were being laid off, friends of his who had worked there longer than him, and he'd been taking overtime, having me catch the bus from school. So it surprised me to see him that afternoon, parked outside in his little Toyota truck. But I liked finding him there, and remember thinking he looked pleased.

"Was today a good day?" he asked as I ducked into the cab. He wore a lavender tie and gray slacks and musky cologne. His boots were shined, though I don't know if I noticed that in the truck or later. His lunchbox sat on the floorboard, a thermos rattling as the engine idled. My father smiled. He was growing a beard. "Are you smarter than you were yesterday?"

"Maybe," I said. "It was okay."

"And math? How was that old bear?"

Math had troubled me that year, and every evening after returning from the stables, my father worked equations with me, hoping

I wouldn't repeat the course in the fall. "Better," I said. "We review on Fridays."

"Say, Benny, did I ever tell you what my favorite math problem was when I attended school?" We were waiting to exit the parking lot and he was watching traffic, staring away from me. "Seven times seven," he said, accelerating onto the street. "I remembered that today. It's a unique thing to recall, I guess. Maybe I liked the symmetry of it."

And although he was talking in an unusual way, using too many words, I understood him. My father enjoyed numbers because they were absolute, and linked with money and credit, words that in our family carried the weight of religion.

We turned into South Shore Estates, a neighborhood of two- and three-story homes, all surrounded by a brick wall. It was a route we'd not taken before. Sailboats occupied many of the driveways and a golf course fanned out behind the houses. I could smell the ocean.

"Do you wish you lived in a house like these?" he asked.

I did wish that, and wished it often, but I said, "No," and when my father made no response, I added, "Not at all." We lived in a two-bedroom wood-framed house on the corner of Longcommon Road, across from a mechanic's garage.

"Your mother used to live this way." He ran his fingers through his hair, which was dark and combed straight back. "I'm sure she misses it too."

My father eased off the gas and slowed enough that I thought he was listening for something in the engine. He lowered his window and craned his neck outside. All of the girls I liked from school lived in South Shore, and although I felt guilty for it, I hoped they wouldn't see me with my father in their neighborhood. He steered with one hand and the truck veered to the wrong side of the street.

Then he raised his window and gave the engine some gas. "There's a small problem at the stables." My father opened his hands and stretched his fingers so only his palms rested on the steering wheel, then he tightened his grip. "Not with the horses, don't worry on that. It's a misunderstanding with our man Butler." He pushed the clutch and went to shift gears, but the transmission was already in fourth, so he had nowhere to go and let it alone. "He called your mother today, claimed we missed this month's rent. She says she paid it, but we'll hear him out. There's time for that."

We curved onto Yorktown Road, which would take us to Edwin Butler's ranch, and began heading south. My father passed cars traveling slower than us. An unfinished house, just a skeleton of studs on a foundation, stood in a hayfield to our left, a snarl of mesquite branches stacked by the road.

"Do you know," my father said suddenly, "what I've seen your mother doing these last few nights?"

"No," I said. "What?"

"Feeding ants." He chuckled and shifted his eyes to me, shaking his head. "They're rebuilding their mound beside the house, but the rain keeps catching them. She slips out there and sprinkles popcorn over them."

I remembered seeing the anthill and could picture my mother crouching beside it. "Was she sad?"

"No." He straightened himself on the seat. "No, she smiles and is content to feed those ants. It's a relief to her, I guess."

A sign marking the city limits stood to our left and my father snapped his fingers and pointed at it. "We're free men." His voice came out flat, though it sounded like a joke to me.

The road narrowed to two lanes and ran alongside shallow ditches, where weeds extended from brackish water. My father loosened his tie, removed it, and folded it on the seat between us. "We should buckle our seatbelts," he said, so we did that. We rode beside a cornfield and I watched the rows of soil tick by, trying to focus on the point where they converged at the horizon. My father rolled his window down again and extended his arm outside, the air slicing around it, creating the illusion of wind.

"A person can care too much." He raised his voice. "Does that make sense to you right now?"

"Yes," I said. "It does."

"You're smarter than me," he said, then laughed. I faced him and laughed too, because he did. He squeezed my shoulder. And I thought of my father as a boy, something I could do easily then. It was my habit to compare his youth to my own and question the ways our lives already differed. The images lacked any colors except black and white, and it seemed a time when things moved faster, not slower as you might guess, but like an old movie where the film speeds from frame to frame without sound or pause.

Edwin Butler stood, like most men, taller than my father but limped from a knee operation that kept him from working. He collected checks from the government, and when they arrived, he went to bet on the dogs in Annaville. His wife was a long-haired woman named Deidra who bred dalmatians for a living, but I'd seen other women step out of Edwin Butler's house trailer. A plywood sign stood in their little yard, a cowboy riding a whale under the words SEA-HORSE RANCH. The property was only ten miles from the ocean, maybe less than that, but out there you couldn't smell the water or know that you were close to it at all.

"No one's here yet," my father said.

In a pen beside Edwin's trailer, two dalmatians rose and watched through their fence as my father steered into the parking area. Horses and a few cows grazed in the pasture, their legs and bellies caked with mud, and Lady stood in her stall, flipping her tail at the gnats and mosquitoes that appeared after rain.

Instead of parking close to our stalls, my father cut the tires toward the house trailer and angled the truck back toward the street. He braked. I asked what was wrong, but he offered nothing and I heard the faint murmur of voices on the radio, which I hadn't realized was playing. We rolled forward, then stopped, and my father shifted gears, unbuckled his seat belt, and twisted to look through the back window. And suddenly he punched the gas. The truck gunned backwards—it felt as though we were in a freefall—and we slammed into Edwin Butler's steel gate. My safety belt locked across my chest; the gate rattled. A low, thin pitch rang in the air. I saw, or felt, horses spook in their stalls, retreat to opposite corners with their ears pinned back. The dalmatians froze, their heads cocked toward the sky. And although I was staring at my father, he never looked at me, but just shifted gears and accelerated forward, then stopped and reversed into the gate again, busting the lock and swinging it open.

Edwin Butler parted the curtains in his window and squinted at us, then he nodded and the curtains fell together. I was holding onto the seat, the muscles in my arms and ankles flexing. The trailer door opened after a moment, a long moment in which everything stood very still and the only noise was a disc jockey's laughter on the radio. When Edwin Butler stepped outside, my father cut the ignition. "Here it is," he said.

In a pink T-shirt, jeans, and ostrich-hide boots, Edwin Butler puckered his face as though it had been dark inside the trailer. A truck passing on Yorktown honked and he saluted the driver, smiling. "That's right," my father said, "Keep it up." He shifted his weight and removed his wallet, stashed it under the seat. "Don't let me forget that." I said okay, but couldn't tell if he heard my answer. His eyes stayed on Edwin Butler, who'd squatted to wipe mud from his boots. And as we sat there, waiting and not speaking, my father pulled off his rings.

He closed his fist around them, not for more than a second, but long enough for me to know he meant to hold the rings that way. Then he reached over and pressed them into my hand. His palms and fingers felt warm, as did the rings. "Keep these in your pocket," he said. "Your old man might go to jail tonight."

I answered my father by saying "Yes, sir," something I'd never said before. I felt myself breathing.

"Now go say hello to those horses," he said. "They'll want to see you today."

Edwin Butler was closer to the truck now, skirting a puddle as my father stepped outside. I looked at him then, turning and starting toward Edwin Butler, and he appeared normal. Nothing crazy burned in his eyes and he wasn't rushing, but everything else seemed unfamiliar, part of another boy's life.

"I thought I'd see you pretty soon," Edwin Butler said. "I tell you what." Then he laughed a high laugh. I opened my door and eased it closed after stepping out. Edwin Butler averted his eyes to me, looked at me as if my presence might explain something to him, but when it didn't, he turned back to my father. The dalmatians chased each other, their black-and-white tails wagging; horses whinnied.

If Edwin Butler expected anything, it was for my father to push or curse him or, at worst, to swing at him with his right fist, with a hook or a straight punch from the chest. Probably my father realized this. Earlier in his life, he'd fought a lot, I'd heard that, so what my father did to Edwin Butler shouldn't have shocked me. But I was fourteen and when it happened, my stomach clenched and I covered my face.

He kicked him in his bad leg, just lunged forward and brought his heel and all of his weight down onto Edwin Butler's kneecap. The joint popped, made a *thwack* sound, and buckled. I felt the impact in my chest, on my skin, and without meaning to, I stepped backward, away from my father. Edwin Butler staggered—he stayed upright longer than you might imagine—then collapsed without trying to break his fall and landed in the puddle he'd avoided earlier. My father leaned over him. The dalmatians were playing, rolling and growling and thrashing a muddy rag. Edwin Butler squirmed under my father, his face pale and his eyes very wide, the back of his pink shirt soaked in mud. He tried to raise himself. But his knee was broken, bent to the side, and seeing that, he stopped struggling and lay backward, his hair sopped in the puddle. Then he began screaming. Just opening his mouth and letting out whatever shrill, jagged noises he could, and when that started, my father turned and fled toward our stables, where I was supposed to be.

The dalmatians howled at the ambulance's sirens. We were loading the tack and horses into our trailer, and my father remained quiet except to tell me what to leave behind. The paramedics' voices and the rattle of a gurney made their way to our stalls, and Deidra

Butler sobbed and kept saying, "Still here. He is still here." Edwin Butler cried out when they lifted him into the ambulance, again just some guttural noise, then came the sound of doors slamming and tires spinning in the mud and onto asphalt, then finally away. During all of this, my father worked as though the spectacle didn't concern us and everyone would benefit if we kept clear of the trouble.

We drove to a ranch farther outside the city, one nicer than Edwin Butler's and owned, I learned later, by the man who'd originally given my father the horses. A sign reading OLEANDER CREEK, HUNTERS AND JUMPERS hung over the entrance. My father left the truck idling while he negotiated with the owner inside the office. I climbed out and slipped sugar cubes to the horses, whispered to them through the trailer. White fences ran around the ranch, and the name of each horse was engraved on its stall, Fancy, Texas Tuff Stuff, Madeline, Coffee Break. A covered arena loomed behind the stables and a small girl was taking a lesson, giggling in her riding cap and boots.

Twenty minutes passed before my father returned. An electric gate opened and I sat on the tailgate to ride into the stables. He could only secure one stall that night, but another would open tomorrow, which suited him fine. He commented on how my mother could ride English-style in the corral—something she'd never done at the Seahorse, and I couldn't recall her wanting to ride that way. My father asked if I liked the property and I said yes, because that's what he wanted to hear. Dusk blurred the sky as we unloaded and a lamp brightened near the stall, illuminating dust and other imperfections in the moist air.

"My thoughts feel focused now," said my father. We were driving home, and he started talking in the dark. "How are you doing?"

"I feel worried," I said. Then, a moment later, "Aren't you scared?"

My father chuckled and looked at me fondly, light in his eyes. "Boy, the only thing in this whole woolly world that scares me is losing you and your mother. I'd be in the tall grass without the two of you. I'd be in the weeds."

I didn't answer him. Outside my window the stubble fields looked like black water. My father braked at a stop sign, and the telephone lines buzzed above us. He cleared his throat, moistened his lips, then looked at me. "I lost my job today, Benny."

"Oh," I said. "I'm sorry."

We remained at the intersection, though for how long I don't know. There were no other vehicles around, and I began wishing my father would turn the corner.

"It's political, of course. It'll blow over soon enough." He rippled his fingers on the steering wheel, and lifted his eyes to the rearview mirror. Then finally he checked over his shoulder, and accelerated. "You're not supposed to know any of that."

"Okay. Does Mom know?"

My father shook his head, and after a moment, inhaled.

"About Edwin," he said. "It was reckless, I'm smart enough to know that. But the trouble's behind us now." For a moment, my father fixed me with his eyes—I felt him do it—though I didn't look back, but stared straight ahead, watching our headlights shine through the night.

I said, "He didn't know what happened."

"He's no Johnny Straightarrow, remember that," my father said. He leaned forward, angled his head to look at the sky. I thought he would say something more, comment on the night or why he was out of work, but we did not speak again. Maybe he was allowing his mind to continue focusing, or maybe he felt he'd already said too much. He clicked on the radio to a man singing opera and although neither of us liked that style of music, we listened. I wanted to say something, though I didn't know what and so stayed quiet. My father seemed caught in his own thoughts, maybe absorbing the music or worrying about my mother or concentrating on something else I couldn't know. Or maybe he was realizing that he'd crippled a man and that trouble was not at all behind us, but would be waiting when we rounded the curve of Longcommon Road and the lights of our small house came into view.

When he saw the police cruiser in front of the house, my father said, "Okay then. All right." He wasn't speaking to me, but just collecting himself before he parked near the curb and stepped out into the night.

My mother sat on the porch, smoking. She was wearing a robe, an old one I'd not seen in some time, and her hair looked wet and recently brushed, tucked behind her ears. Our floodlights beamed down on her, making her look far away. Two policemen stood near her, one leaning against her Chevy and another, shorter one in the grass, but when my father opened the door, they clicked on their flashlights and started toward him.

"Mr. Kelley? Mr. George Kelley?" the short policeman said. "I'm Officer Barrera."

"Are you fine, Marie?" my father called. "Are you feeling better?" The policemen and my father were nearing each other, but he was eyeing my mother on the porch.

"I don't know what's happening now, George," she said. "I was in the shower." She shielded her eyes from the floodlight and leaned forward, tiptoed to see us better. Her voice sounded strong. A line of cars rumbled by on Longcommon and my mother waited for their noise to fade before she spoke again. "Is Benny with you?"

"I'm here," I said. The taller policeman shined his light in my face. I was on the passenger side of the truck, standing in the dark street.

"Come here, Benny," my mother called, then in a lower voice, "Is that okay? Can my son sit beside his mother?"

"Sure," my father said. He was sliding his wallet into his pocket. "He'll do that just fine."

The three men stopped under our chinaberry tree, close to each other, as I walked to the porch. A wind blew that night, strong enough to rustle the leaves and make a set of chimes tinkle down the street. My mother grabbed my hand and squeezed it, then patted my thigh when I sat.

"I'll be with you soon." My father flashed a smile at us. "We'll clear this up in a hurry." Then Officer Barrera motioned my father toward the cruiser, while the other officer followed. And after that, they conversed in voices too low to hear.

Several of our neighbors had gathered outside, clustered on their porches. Occasionally a man's voice rose or a woman giggled or someone popped open a beer can, then everything would fall silent again and I felt people studying us in the dark. Through a window across the street, I saw a woman dancing on a television screen. My mother whispered that she recognized her, but couldn't recall the dancer's name. I expected her to ask me what had happened, but after a door slammed down the street, she tightened her terrycloth belt and disappeared into the house.

My father spoke with the officers for some time. They frisked him. My mother hadn't returned and I appreciated her not seeing him bent over the cruiser's hood, his arms and legs spread. As Barrera patted him down, my father said something and the three men laughed. They'll let him go, I thought. But the taller officer crossed my father's hands behind his back and clasped the handcuffs on his wrists; there were no cars just then and the click of the locks snapped like a ratchet. He continued grinning, as did the other officer, while they placed him in the backseat and closed the heavy door. Across the street, the camera zoomed in on another woman's face, a singer, and inside our house, I heard my mother pouring a drink.

Soon Officer Barrera came up our driveway and smiled a smile to say he was sorry. The taller officer lowered himself into the cruiser— the interior light illuminated when the door opened and I saw my father in the backseat, adjusting himself so he wouldn't be sitting on his hands or hurting his elbows. The officer in the car said something to him, gestured with a pen, and for some reason I thought they were discussing me, maybe my riding or grades or my being an only child. Everything seemed very loud to me just then, each sound magnified— a dog barking on another block, the rope clanking against the flagpole beside the mechanic's garage, the crickets trilling in my mother's flower bed.

"Ben, this is hard. I know." Officer Barrera flipped his tablet over.

"But will you, please, to the best of your ability, describe the altercation between your father and Mr. Butler."

I watched my father in the car; he was staring toward the mechanic's garage across the street. It occurred to me that whatever I said would influence what happened to him, that right then the responsibility for our family lay with me, and he would want me to think in those terms—what became of us in the future depended on this moment in my life that felt like a dream.

I said I'd been feeding Colonel and hadn't seen anything. Barrera told me to estimate the distance from our stalls to Edwin Butler's trailer, so I guessed the length of a football field, maybe two. He positioned himself between me and the cruiser so I could no longer view my father, and I wondered about his family, if he was thinking about his own son as he spoke with me. Barrera resembled a fire hydrant, with a black mustache covering much of his upper lip, and I thought he could beat my father. He asked me where the horses were right then, and I admitted they were at Oleander Creek but added that my parents had been considering the move for some time. He jotted my answers onto his tablet and with each one he glared at me as though he didn't believe me, which, of course, he shouldn't have.

My mother returned then, dressed in shorts and a blouse. She covered her mouth upon seeing my father in the cruiser. Officer Barrera handed her his card and said my father would spend the night in jail, but a clerk would call in the morning with more information. She asked if they served dinner there because he hadn't eaten since lunch, and Barrera promised to arrange a meal later that evening. Then my mother asked to speak with my father before they left and Barrera okayed that too. It was around nine o'clock then, the night sky streaked with gray cirrus clouds, and most everyone had abandoned their porches and dimmed their lights. I guessed they'd seen my father get into the cruiser and could imagine for themselves what would happen next.

Sleep came easily to me that night and that still surprises me. After the police took my father, my mother followed me inside and warmed the dinner she'd cooked that afternoon. We sat at our small table together, my mother and I, and talked not about the stables or Edwin Butler, but about regular topics, as though my father was working late and would soon waltz through the front door and our lives would resume. "Go to bed, Benny," my mother said as she cleared the dishes. "The sun will rise tomorrow."

She called someone while I readied myself for bed—I heard her dial the phone and say, "Hello. Okay. It's Marie," and the sound of a cigarette pack tearing open, followed by my mother's cough. Soon, though, she spoke in a soft, private voice and my thoughts drifted to Edwin Butler. I wondered where he was at that moment. My best guess placed him in surgery or possibly in the recovery room with his wife, who would be waiting for him to regain consciousness and ask what had happened. I sympathized with him. I thought of my father, awake in the night and in jail, punishing himself with words like *patience* and *restraint*. Then I fell asleep, and if I dreamed, I don't remember it, except that I slept well, so they couldn't have been nightmares, just the uneventful dreams of a boy my age.

The hinges of our front door woke me. My first thought was that my father had returned, either legally or he had escaped, which made my heart pound. I dressed myself—just my jeans and shirt from the day before, no shoes—and crept into the kitchen. The lights were on, the radio played at a low volume. I checked my parents' room for my mother, and the bed was made, but when I called her, she didn't answer. It was six o'clock, the time my father left for work on weekdays, so outside the air felt cool.

"They love popcorn," my mother said. She was kneeling beside the anthill. "I once owned a dog who liked it too. Maybe we should offer some to the horses."

I only responded by nodding and putting my hands in my pockets, though my mother didn't seem to want a response. She had changed clothes since the night before, and wore now a gingham dress with her hair pulled back. I smelled a citrusy perfume.

"I used to kick their little piles and make them run around where

I could see them, but not anymore." She raised her eyes to me, smiled, then looked back at the ants. "It's a change I've made in myself."

"That sounds good," I said. A van towing a trailer careened past.

"If you could change anything about yourself, what would it be? That's an important question." My mother crushed some popcorn in her hand, then sprinkled it over the ants. The concrete felt rough beneath my feet, cold. "And it needs to be something you *can* change, nothing like your height or the color of your eyes."

My response came quickly, as if I'd considered it often and had only been awaiting the question. "I'd like to be braver. I'd like to be less afraid of things."

"What a wonderful answer," my mother said, nodding. "I suppose that's inspired by your father." She stood and dusted the last of the crumbs to the ants, then clapped her hands together. Cars passed on Longcommon, their tires swishing over the asphalt, as though it were wet. My mother leaned over the ants again, then shouldered past me and sat on the porch. She lit a cigarette and sent the smoke through her nostrils. "I don't want to know what happened yesterday. Is that fine?"

"Yes," I said. "That's fine."

"Edwin's hurt, I know that. Your father is to blame for it, I know that too." She closed her eyes and drew on her cigarette, held the smoke in her lungs before blowing it out. "The officer called about an hour ago and said they'd release him shortly."

"That's good," I said.

"Of course it is." My mother flicked her cigarette into our yard. Someone cranked a car's ignition down the street.

"These last few days," she said and stopped. She shook out another cigarette and lit it. "I haven't been upset over money. Or not having money. Your father can't believe that, but it's true."

"Okay," I said. "I believe you."

"I'm worried that when I die, people will only remember me for my mistakes." The air in front of my mother became clouded with blue smoke, then it spread and its scent wafted toward me. "Maybe I didn't pay Edwin. Maybe all of this is my fault."

"I don't think so," I said. My mother sniffled and touched the back of her hand to her eyes, then she looked at the sky, which wasn't special that morning, just hazy and slate-colored. Longcommon was quiet; the morning lacked the noise of wind or dogs or people whispering on dark porches.

"It's hard to know your parents. Both of mine had affairs." She glanced at me. "Can I say that in front of you?"

I nodded. It crossed my mind to tell her about my father being fired, but I said nothing. I wanted to protect my mother, but it was also easier to keep quiet.

"I knew my mother's boyfriend. He was their handyman, but he boxed on the weekends. A pugilist. She loved it, the fighting, and sometimes he showed her different punches or how to breathe through her nose. It was an art to her. My father hated it, though, said boxing was just violence, nothing deeper. Basic brutality."

"I didn't know any of that," I said.

"I wonder what you don't know about me." My mother smiled. "Who knows what we don't know? I wish I could remember the things I've forgotten." She pressed herself from the porch and dropped her cigarette, toed it out. My mother looked pretty with the sun starting to rise behind her and I liked being awake at that early hour. "Benny," she said, adjusting her dress, "think of all this as just violence. Maybe it's nothing more and everything will improve."

Then she stepped inside and left me alone.

What I remember of the morning when we drove to take my father from the police station is only the sensation that we were loose from our regular lives, floating and spiraling away from where we had been the day before.

He just spent the one night in jail. Edwin Butler refused to press assault charges against him, so the police held my father for disturbing the peace and released him the following morning. They let him go without posting bond, just opened the doors and set him free. All of that confused me at the time, though it no longer does.

My father fixed breakfast for us after we arrived home from the police station, chorizo omelettes and pecan pancakes, the way he did on holidays. For much of the meal the only sounds were our forks scraping against the plates, or glasses being raised then replaced on the table. Gradually, though, my parents surrendered to conversation and by the time my father took our plates, he was making jokes and saying how he looked forward to bathing and washing the jail off his skin. My mother ran him a bath.

While she was out of the kitchen, he said, "Tonight a man asked me how old I was." He was staring through the window behind our table. "And do you know what I almost said? Twenty-two. I had to stop myself. It's not something that has happened to me before."

I thought to tell him what my mother had said or to ask him about being arrested, but finally I moved to the sink and started soaping the dishes.

"The house feels bigger," he said. In the bathroom, my mother opened a cabinet, then she shut the door. "How was the old girl last night?"

"Not so bad," I said.

"Good," he said. He put his hands on each side of the window, leaned his weight against the wall. He exhaled. "Oh, Benny, there's a life ahead. We just make our way by the best light we have."

Then my mother called that the tub was full, and my father brushed past me. He thanked her for running the water and I heard them kiss, heard the floor creak as he stepped into the bathroom. I expected my mother to return to the kitchen, to sit at the table and smoke or drink coffee, though when I finished the dishes, she hadn't emerged from the hall.

The bathroom door was closed, but through it I heard the murmur of my parents' voices. My mother said, "That dirty Mexican," in a tight, hushed tone, and after leaning close to the wall, I suspected they were talking about my father having not eaten in jail, despite Barrera's promise. I pictured my mother sitting on the toilet, her legs crossed, while my father lay submerged to his shoulders in gray, sudsy water. And for a time, they were silent and I listened to cars swooshing by on Longcommon.

Then my mother said, "Oh, baby, that's okay. No, no, now. George, baby." Her words came quickly, but calmly, and although a minute passed before his sobs grew loud enough to carry from the bathroom, I realized my father was crying. I'd never heard that sound before. Maybe he'd told her about losing his job or about Edwin Butler, or both, or maybe he'd kept silent and his face just bloated and crumpled with tears. I imagined my mother leaning over the tub and embracing my father, pressing his wet hair to her breast, trying to still the heavy shudder of his weeping. It made me feel very young, younger than I'd ever felt in my life.

Memory is made of loss, and sometimes your only hope is to recall that you've forgotten something you once knew, or thought you knew. If I ever knew why my father took me to the stables that afternoon, I no longer do. Maybe he thought he'd teach me something viable, maybe he only intended to talk with Butler and he believed his young son's future might benefit from watching two grown men negotiate a misunderstanding. Such considerations would have been within his character, but I distrust them. They come twenty years later, from a happily married, college-educated man who's never known violence. What I think, simply, finally, is that my father made a mistake.

We moved the horses into neighboring stalls at Oleander Creek the day my father came back from jail. My mother stayed home, napping. Setting up the tack rooms, I worried that my father would bring up Butler or Officer Barrera, but I also worried that he wouldn't. I wanted him to know what I'd told the police, wanted him to say that I'd done right by him and he was proud; I wanted him to thank me.

But he was quiet that muggy afternoon, quieter than usual. I asked him if he thought we'd keep the horses here for more than the month he'd paid for and he said, "If it feathers our nest." He was kneeling in the dirt, cleaning Lady's hooves, then he stood and started combing out her tail, then her mane. He gave me chores to complete—carry over the salt blocks, find nails whose heads or spikes stuck through the stable fences and knock them in with his hammer—but he said little else. He seemed wrung out to me, as if he'd been laid up in bed for weeks with an injury or illness, and now that he was back in the world, every small task exhausted his strength. Yet when the other owners started to arrive and walk over to introduce themselves, he rallied. His laugh was loud and generous, his handshake looked firm, his posture straight as a post; I'd never felt worse for him.

These were not the people from Edwin Butler's ranch. Their shirts were starched and bright, the rims of their hats were not crooked or lined with dust or sweat. They wouldn't think of digging a pit beside the corral and roasting a hog; they wouldn't come out to play all-night poker and watch over a colicky foal, and they would never let their horses hit more than a stiff gallop in the pasture. And although the men and women meeting my father seemed unaware of the differences between their lives and his, I think he noticed them acutely. I think their saucer-sized belt buckles were like mirrors for him, and he saw that he'd led his family into a different life, saw that we'd crossed a river and were wandering in an open field where we were as vulnerable as mice. Suddenly he knew he'd surrounded himself with people who could never conceive of doing what he'd done and not one person there would spend a night in jail. I tried to imagine myself being fingerprinted or raising my fist to another man, but I couldn't do it, and neither, I fear, could he.

But I wanted not to think of the future just then, only to hold tight that afternoon with my father and to stand between him and the life that would soon overtake us like a storm. I wanted to throw the saddles on the horses and ride, to prove to him that I was still there and all was not yet lost.

"Here you go," I said once he and I were alone in the stable again. Other owners would show themselves soon, so I wanted to seize the opportunity while I could.

I extended my hand where his rings were warm in my palm. They'd been in my pocket since the day before, and I had slipped them on and off my fingers countless times and I had been bothered by how even the smallest was too big for me, even on my thumb. My father seemed surprised, though not necessarily happily surprised, to see them. He'd given the rings to me when he had known he'd wind up in jail, but I suspected he'd not thought about when they'd be returned. Maybe depending on his son in this way was insulting or humbling or liberating or confusing. Of course he eventually took them back, but he didn't do it right away. I said, "You forgot about them." He laughed a little then, which made me feel that I'd betrayed something about myself, my youth or optimism or how little I knew of him. We stood in the hot stable for a long, long moment, my arm growing tired of holding out the rings and him looking at me suspiciously, as if I might be tricking or trapping him, luring him to reach for something that I'd only take back at the last second.

THE MIDWIFE'S SON

Suzanne Kingsbury

During the winter of my neglect, a strong wind blew in from the frozen tundras of the northeast, beating us indoors. Nineteen forty-three, the great war, men gambled their lives for our country, humiliated themselves, dying in spent feces, their bright red entrails staining fields in Germany, the hillsides echoing death cries, and I was born.

My father was a lumberman with one green eye, one blue, a massive man with hands like slabs of meat. The midwife was a compact dark woman from across the river, swathed in scarves, canvas skirts, scarlet turbans, rings on her fingers, tinctures tucked in sacks tied with rope and fastened with pins to her brassiere. She pulled me out of my howling mother, who died.

My father paced outside and, when he heard the silence of his wife's cries, entered the still, wood cabin and beat the midwife unconscious while my grandma watched; then he dragged the midwife to the lake to bury her. When she woke, she fought. They battled. The river, steaming with frost and dawn, broke and bubbled, swallowed them both, my father in his logger boots, his wool jacket inhaling water, his mouth a gaping hole. My grandma, at the house, took me in her arms and wept.

She raised me, my mother's mother, a woman with braided onyx hair and copper eyes and deep ebony lashes like fans. She kept me home, told me stories. There's a river goddess, she said, who captures the rivergoers in her lair and makes of the drowned dead, her concubines and lovers.

Days of emptiness defined my rearing, summers of scorching, wounding heat, springs of brilliant green, autumns when the ocean brought weeping, angry winds and rain and the houses leveled and the men raised their hands to the sky and asked, Why us, God?

The soldiers came back half-men, amputated, their eyes terrible, lonely, waists slender, ribs protruding and hair thinning. One was the midwife's husband. He had volunteered. His youngest son wheeled him in a wood wicker chair. I saw them in town and the son stared at me with hazel, ghost-sad eyes. My grandma pushed me forward, Don't look, she'd say. Evil lies there, hate.

I grew a whore to that river, obsessed with it. My father had a dugout canoe he had fished off in earlier times, and I rowed out to the middle and sat chanting words grandma had taught me, thick, guttural tones of which I did not know the meaning.

Grandma was a Native mix of all the southern tribes, and she was Christian too. She said, If you must go to the river to tempt her, wear this, and gave me a thick pewter cross to hang around my neck with a serpent wrapped around it, the beady eyes half-lidded and slovenly, watching my viewer.

Even in winter I rowed. My muted blue breath shown in clouds. Sometimes I had to feel my way back through misty fog, the shapes frightening. I spoke to the goddess about my life, told her I understood the loneliness that made her take victims hostage.

Grandma hadn't ever cut my hair, she said it would thwart and strangle the river goddess if she came for me. At sixteen, it fell raven black down my back. At night grandma fed me brews of roots and conjures she believed kept spirits away. When she brushed my mane, she said, Dark Rapunzel, let down your hair. I thought about that prince climbing Rapunzel's hair. Always I came back to the pain the princess must have endured. Grandma told me my spirit was too lonely to let a lover climb up. She said, Let a man inside, he'll steal your soul away, just like your mother. Just like me.

Her husband had tried to kill her in the upper Mississippi hill country. She'd beat him senseless with a brick until it crumbled. She said, When you kill, the victim haunts your every move, makes love to you at night while you sleep. In the morning you are drugged, pinned to the afterworld, paralyzed until the day becomes light.

At school, the girls wore shiny ribbons in their hair, fresh-pressed cotton skirts. They carried silk purses and whispered behind their hands when they saw me. I stopped going. Grandma's stories were my education. She hiked me through the vined Alabama landscape, reading books aloud while we went, carrying a warped, knotted hickory stick, pointing out birds of prey, plants, the tracks of rabbit and possum. She told me to close my eyes and be very still. I heard the call of geese and owls and the response of their mates.

I had been rowing every day of my adolescent and teenage life save the rainy ones or the ones too brutal with cold to venture out. In February of my sixteenth year, I felt him standing in the break of pines on the west bank. The midwife's youngest son. I looked at him brazenly and he looked back. In my mind, I said, Hate me if you will. My only fault was being born. There was emptiness in his stance. I told him silently that I could fill it up.

On a night when feathery fog hemmed the trees, and their limbs were black lace against the sapphire sky, he called out, You want me to row for you? Half I feared he was the phantom incarnation of his mamma, who perhaps believed my daddy lived in me. I wanted to show him the truth, I was nothing but a beating heart, blood coursing innocently through my veins. Grandma said the plant is not always its seed, I had come from the sun, the honey of bee's nests, wind picking up sweet-scented brambled wisteria and silver rain falling, softening the land.

He was Jacob Sterling, the last of seven sons, their surname far richer than the family. He pushed his right ear toward me when I spoke. He said he was deaf in the left ear after listening to bad news when he was three. He was nineteen now and I did the math, knew what words had killed the hearing.

He watched me while he rowed and sometimes we'd sit in the middle and stare at one another. I'd sing songs I'd conjured from Bible stories; each name rang rhyming on my tongue. The mountains and seas and plagues and floods and battles, making webbed lyrics and echoing out into the stands of pine, over giant catalpa roots, snaking towards the water. He said he hewed trees during his days, felled hardwood till his palms bled. He breathed pine-scented air. One night in May, when the whip-poor-wills sounded and the forest was racketed with deep buzzing and fireflies lit up the sky, he finally said it aloud: My mamma was the woman came to an end in this river, bludgeoned by a heartsick madman, and they never did revive her.

I was part of my mama's umbilical chord, I told him. And that's the only kin I know except for Grandma.

Well, I come to make sweet with the girl in you, lost the mamma, and the boy in me lost mine, he said.

In his arms I was a rocking infant of the womb. Chestnut haired and hazel eyed, he licked my skin like a deer would her fawn. He said, Turn over and he licked the other side. There I was, cool next to him, my skin warm where he lay beside me. In the places the lumberyard never saw, his flesh was alabaster and soft.

After my breasts grew and my blood stopped, I asked him if he were Abraham, would he sacrifice his son? He thought for a while and said the Bible writer got it wrong, it was the devil who spoke first and God who put the goat there. I saw he might make a good daddy. He carried in his belt a knife of thick, shined, and sharpened blade. He took it out to cut a strand of my hair, holding it in his hand while he rowed. That day onwards, he always wore it in a wood box he hand-made and screwed a hole through with a string. He kissed the box when we were done loving, a worshipper after prayer with crucifix.

He was killed out in the forest by a hardwood in mid-September. I heard of it in town. It was a lumberman, drunk on the job, who held the guilt. I knew from Grandma why not to drink. They call it spirits because a man, like my daddy, can enter into another's heart, make him perform evil the ghosts can't do for themselves. They didn't bother to have a proper funeral for a poor family such as that. He was buried on his land with the preacher from the one-room Baptist. I was tired with grief. In dreams he came to me and spoke, holding me. I wanted to be dreaming, always.

The baby came six months later.

Grandma did not ask me who the father was. She was granite and denial when it came to telling her. I saw this before she ever gave me the chance to say the truth. She called my boy a barn swallow baby.

Girls go into the barn sometimes to daydream, she said, standing over me in the hospital bed, her eyelashes beating silver, the lines around her eyes and mouth twitching. And come out pregnant, she told me.

He wasn't born right in the head. I believe this is due to Grandma's potions. My son has equine eyes, spaced far apart. They have a habit of tumbling backward. His smile is perpetual. He came out un-screaming, just a soft hollow yell like somebody about done mourning. Each nurse, with her jittering eyes back and forth, from mama to baby, tried to smile. My smile was not make-believe. Him, born an eternal child, and me, always a mother, was scripted.

I rowboat him around. Sometimes I pail the rainwater out with a collapsible tin cup Jacob Sterling gave me. He thought I'd need it after storm on a night when he couldn't come.

I sing songs of Jacob to the baby, telling him about the dreams his father's biblical namesake had, of angels running up and down the ladder, to heaven, and back again.

GHOST DANCE

Chip Livingston

I think I'm going crazy when I see my reflection in the camera's lens. I'm surrounded by the dead. Jimi, Marilyn, Joan—face covered in cold cream, hand holding wire hanger high above her head. The Halloween Parade has paused for television crews in front of the Revolver on Duvall Street in New Orleans. I duck inside for a drink, take the elevator to the thirteenth floor.

I walk inside the club without ID. Tonight I don't need it. Tonight I'm invisible. I pass witches, goblins, boys dressed like ghouls. Once I was one of them. Once we both joined the annual masquerade. But tonight is different. Tonight I don a plain white sheet with ink. Circles traced around holes cut out to see through. Another hole through which I drink, from which I breathe.

I wasn't coming out tonight. Didn't plan or purchase a costume. Wouldn't wear one hanging in your closet. What led me to the linens then, to quickly cut a cotton sheet into a kid's uniform? What drove me to this?

Beneath this sheet, your medicine bag hangs around my neck, the tanned leather pouch you made me promise never to open. This is the first time I've worn it. But no one can see it. No one can see me.

I finish my drink, Scotch, neat, with a gulp, sing the invisible song you taught me, set the glass on the black wood rail, and, still singing, step onto the crowded dance floor.

Beneath this sheet, I imitate you dancing. My feet, awkward at first, soon find your rhythm, and my legs bounce powwow style in the steps we both learned as kids. The steps that never left you. I dip and turn between, around, the fancy dancers in their sequin shawls and feather boas. I shake my head like you did when your hair was long, the way you flipped it, black and shining, to the heavy beat of house music. The music hasn't changed much in case you're wondering. I dance in your footsteps; sing the invisible song; close my eyes.

When I open my eyes, I swear I see Carlo. Impossible, right, but he's stuffed inside that Nancy Reagan red dress and he's waving at me, sipping his cocktail and smiling. He's talking to Randy, who's sticking out his tongue that way he always did whenever he caught someone staring at him. I start to walk over but I bump into Joan.

She's glaring at me. Or it may just be the eyebrows, slanted back with pencil to make it look like she's glaring at me. She reaches past me and grabs Marilyn by her skinny wrist and pulls her away, but Carlo and Randy are gone. Where they stood are faces I don't recognize. Faces dancing. Masks I realize. Faces behind masks.

The DJ bobs furiously with pursed lips, headphones over fiendish disguise in the booth above the floor. He introduces a new melody into the same harping beat, and I remember to dance. I remember you dancing. My fingers sliding across your sweaty chest, I find the necklace. The sheet clings to my body in places. The new song sounds just like the last song but I'm being crowded together with strangers. I can no longer lift my legs as high as I want to, so I sway in place, shuffle with the mortals on the floor.

Behind me someone grabs me, accidentally perhaps, but I turn violently, jealously. There are too many people in this equation. Two become one again and again, and ones become twos. All around me real numbers add up to future possibilities. Imaginary numbers. It's why we're here dancing.

A cowboy nods his hat in my direction. But he can't be nodding at us. We're invisible. I think maybe he is a real ghost; he's peering intently into the holes cut out for my eyes. He looks like Randolph Scott, blond and dusty, so I look around for Cary Grant as Jimi lifts the guitar from his lips and wails. Randolph Scott is coming this way and I turn my back and dance.

I want you back, Elan. I want you back dancing beside me. I start chanting this over and over to myself. *I want you back. I want you back.*

You taught me the power of words. I believe you. I can even smell you now. Sandalwood oil and sweat. I turn and expect to see you.

Not you behind me.

Not you beside me.

Not you in front of me.

Not you anywhere around me.

I make my way to the bar, but the bar is too crowded. The barman's face grimaces over hands holding up folded dollars as he tries to keep the glasses filled. The air is thick with bitter smoke. It's hard to breathe. I make my way for the door, notice the cowboy trailing me. In the elevator, I go down alone.

Into the rain on Duvall Street, we walk out together. One set of footprints splashes our muddy way toward home, then, turning, I realize we are not going home, but passing more pagan tricksters decked out in holiday spirits.

The bells in the clock tower tell me it is midnight. Squeaking from its hinges, the door to morning slowly opens and it's All Saints Day, the Day of the Dead, and I am walking toward Boot Hill, to where you are buried.

We're alone in the cemetery. And the wind lifts the rain in a mist rising up from the wet earth that is claiming me. I remove my sheet in front of the cement memorial that holds your body up above the boggy ground. I remove my shoes. I strip off everything except your leather pouch around my neck, and I dance for you. My legs are free and I whirl and sing.

I'm dancing for you now, because you loved to dance. I want you back dancing. I want you dancing now.

I'm dancing for you now, because you loved to dance. I want you back dancing. I want you dancing now.

I'm dancing for you now, because you loved to dance. I want you back dancing. I want you dancing now.

I'm dancing for you now, because you loved to dance. I want you back dancing. I want you dancing now.

LOST, NOT LOST

Humphreys McGee

The midget Darby played a confounding game of golf. He carried his thousand-dollar set of irons, which he cut down to half-length, in a long burlap tool case that belonged to his inventor grandfather, also a midget, from whom Darby inherited exclusive patent rights and the recessive midget gene. Darby called his hacked-down irons "my wrenches," and he swung them like a matador his cape, tight and subtle. He could pinch the ball from any kind of lie and send it on a low, knifing flight that traced in on the flagstick, every time a small, square divot flying up behind the ball like the shadow of his precision. He was used to hearing someone in his group clap for him at least once a round. The applause was never too precious though—which is to say it never suggested his game was just pretty good for a midget. And he knew how to act. People in the town respected him for his dignified carriage and his elegant play.

Darby's irons, wedges, and putter were all half-size, but his driver was regular, an inch taller than Darby himself. He leaned against it when he watched his partners tee off, his meaty hand pressed on the grip-end next to his head. When it came his turn, he cut a crazed, shut-eyed slash at the ball: front foot reared up on the backswing and planted back down right before impact, Darby impossibly hanging on at the other end of the club in a desperate unwinding of muscle through the swing, the midget's only expression of malice and aggression at the world; then, the ball on its way, the driver's momentum yanked him backward and he spun on his heels away from the tee, the little man peering over his shoulder for a glimpse of his shot arcing over the fairway. Usually the whole stunt was too much and Darby would not see it. But he had a loyal group of partners who watched the ball for him. They envied his iron game and for twenty years howled themselves blood-faced every time Darby leveraged his body into getting the last inch out of his driver. They simply loved him for that. It was the only thing in their lives, they agreed, that had never gotten old.

Darby lived off patent royalties and winnings from his partners at the country club. They played out of electric carts on a flat, square sprawl of buckshot Delta land bounded on three sides by cotton and soybeans and on the fourth by a two-lane highway. Narrow ditches matted with Johnson grass and water moccasins served as hazards. Everybody in the group kept a .22 pistol in his bag, for snakes that took to defending an errant ball, they said. They played eight men in the group and wagered in units of fifty dollars. Every day, by the time they reached the eighteenth, each man had fashioned at least a dozen bets to negotiate among the four players he'd been pitted against.

Darby won more often than not, but his older half-brother, Conrad, who was normal height, lived in a permanent slump. He did not share a rich inventor-grandfather with Darby—that was Darby's mother's father—so he inherited neither the royalties nor the stature of the midget side of the family. No, he and Darby shared a father, a journeyman minor leaguer who was away from home the night Darby was born, playing third base against the Amarillo Armadillos. He committed exactly five errors that night, including two in the same play, got buckling drunk after the game, and returned to his motel room at four in the morning to find the following message from his inventor father-in-law: *It's a boy and a midget, I can tell.* His father-in-law hated him, and the third baseman was not too drunk—or perhaps just drunk enough—to read in the message the satisfaction of the little inventor who had always made it clear what would belong to the son-in-law and what would not. It was apparent in the message that the baby, being a midget, would not. The next morning, barreling toward nine kinds of hungover remorse in Amarillo, the third baseman telegraphed his wife: *I should like to name him Darby.* It was an undeniable but bloodless request: The third baseman was also named Darby, and he made the midget his namesake knowing that he was never going back.

So Conrad, who was six when Darby was born, grew up with a

midget half-brother carrying his gone father's name and a rich midget step-grandfather who saw to it that Conrad would survive his childhood but would have no guarantees after that. Still, Conrad never, not once, held Darby's name against him. He considered it both a badge and a stain and his half-brother, as a result, just a walking contradiction. Through his youth, Conrad fantasized about what kind of game their father had played that night, conceiving only that the birth of the midget must have crashed the third baseman down from the buzz of some soaring performance at the plate and the hot corner. These were not wistful fantasies, though, for Conrad always believed he would be the fullness of his father's thwarted promise on the field. At eighteen, he left for the game on the road expecting finally to get his rightful due, to *inherit*. He did not know, of course, that he was heir to five errors in one game, including two in the same play.

Conrad began and ended his career damned in the Texas and Louisiana minors, never advancing above single-A. At first he took his struggle as even heavier motivation to perform—play for redemption, not restoration—but one night at a bar, after one of his own late errors in Amarillo cost the game, some of the Armadillo faithful approached and asked if he wasn't related to another Mississippi man with the same last name at third, the one with two errors in the same play. Conrad denied it, and that was it. The next morning, he ruined a killer blue spring day by surrendering to his nontalent and heading home to Darby and the group, none of whom had ever tested their skills off their home course.

Quitting professional ball was a wrenching physical act for Conrad; he did not fully let go. He wore thick baseball goggles when he played golf and waggled his driver horizontally over the tee before he addressed the ball—as though, it was perfectly clear, he was stepping into the batter's box. The group found all of this pretentious and embarrassing. But worse was the mental display: He had skills enough at the game to keep up with most of the group—though never with Darby—until the money got high, at which point he folded into a tremendous choker. Conrad blew his matches with such a dead, rank style that losing became something Calvinist with him: It was hard but it was also predestined. Soon the burden of being consigned his partner grew into a serious wager itself, and Conrad became his own currency. When the group hedged and bartered with each other before a round, it was not financial. It was over the high annoyance of having to put up with him.

Conrad knew of the group's transactions, and they did not cushion his return. He was emboldened only by the stories he brought back from the road, of gambling in Lake Charles and whoring across the border, but stark nights in Monroe, Nacogdoches, and San Angelo—and Christ, that last night in Amarillo—were the canvas of his most vivid, sweat-drenched dreams. Darby's eyes flashed at his brother's stories like a child watching a magician for the first time. The group disbelieved most of them and wanted Conrad to get a job—a standard they did not hold over Darby, whose inherited pile of patents they considered just compensation for the unlucky gene they believed held their fearless and talented friend back from world fame.

*

By August Conrad had more losses on the course than he could pay for. He could have squeezed a loan from Darby by barely asking, but he was too proud for it: He would lose the shabby prestige of his long days in pro ball if he took his midget half-brother's money to pay off bets lost in competition. It would be a relinquishment, his last concession, and the thought of it made him shudder. So he persuaded Darby to come with him on the road for bigger money. Darby's game could travel, Conrad told him, he knew it could—and just think of winning on the road! It took some talking, but finally Darby believed in it. They left before sunrise for Mercy Oaks, a hilly course northeast of Jackson and venue of the biggest money game in the state. Membership at Mercy Oaks was not prestigious. The club consisted mainly of hustlers and failed athletes, some of whom had tolerated Conrad in single-A. The game there was mean and nervous. Payment of losses was expected immediately; nonpayment could drive a man straight out of the state.

The Delta group was ignorant of Darby's trip to Mercy Oaks and put off by his strange absence that day. They had never played without him, and they found their game bland and coarse without the midget's show of alternating wildness and precision. Left to themselves they had no reason to howl. One of them tried to imitate Darby by teeing off from his knees. It was crass; no one laughed; the man was lucky not to have hurt himself. They quit the game after the front nine, announced all losses waived and settled for disgruntled drinking by the bay window in the clubhouse.

The bartender had heard about Darby and Conrad's trip to Mercy Oaks and told the men what he knew. They grumbled in disgust and swore to force their payment from the no-good Conrad or else—out of the group forever! Some said they hoped Conrad would *not* pay, just so they could throw him out, it would be worth it. Everyone nodded and they sat drinking, sated with this fantasy of exclusion. Beyond the bay window the August heat collected over the course like a fume until dusk struck everything with its redness.

In the day's last light they saw a figure walking down the eighteenth fairway. He carried no clubs and stalked over the green for the clubhouse, head down, a man driven by something beyond himself. It was Conrad, alone.

Conrad burst through the clubhouse door and collapsed into a chair. He reached into his back pocket and took a pull off a pint of Old Charter. He was drunk already, but his face was gray, stricken. He closed his eyes and did not acknowledge the men across the room. This infuriated them. One of them hurled an unopened beer can at Conrad. It glanced off the top of his head, crashed into a brass listing of club champions on the wall and hissed on the floor, spewing white, warm suds of alcohol at Conrad obscenely.

"Where's Darby?" someone demanded.

"What'd you do with the midget?" blurted another.

Conrad sat up and pulled again from the bottle of Charter. "I lost him," he said, still not looking at the men.

"Lost him? Like what, you looked up and he was gone? You don't know what happened to him?"

"No, I know what happened to him. I know exactly what happened, and what happened is I *lost* him." Conrad looked at the group for the first time, cocked his head down a bit and peered over his glasses at them. "Not lost." He raised his eyebrows. "*Lost*."

"Well where do you expect he might be?"

"I expect he's somewhere in the Mercy Oaks clubhouse. A hostage." He began to untie his shoes and chuckled to himself. "Ha— Mercy Oaks. Man, that fucking place. Nothing merciful about it."

A few of the men cut their eyes at each other when they heard "hostage." Then one of them pointed a putter like a long-barreled pistol at Conrad and said, "Son of a bitch, ain't nobody going to listen to talk about Darby being lost, not lost. Now, you owned up about Mercy Oaks, which we already knew you took him to. You just tell us where the midget's *at*."

Conrad's face turned from gray to red, and he closed his eyes again. The room fell quiet as the men looked at him. They saw that this man was beset by memories of something very close in time. They could nearly hear the visions of Conrad's day at Mercy Oaks run through his head like a river off a cliff.

"The hills, it was the hills," Conrad blurted, on the brink of crying. "It was the hills that got him. I took him up there to win money to pay you sumbitches back. But the hills ate his drives up like Satan himself was swelling the earth just to beat us. And those men! Their howls weren't anything like here. It was pure *derision*. Darby would haul off at his tee shot like he does, but into the steep hills his ball would scuttle sideways like a shot rabbit, and they'd howl evilly at him. Never seen a man so demoralized. If the little dude hadn't putted his ass off they'd have slit our throats, I swear. But we held on, and we pressed it all on eighteen to get even. Then this wop-looking guy, their leader, he asked me would we be able to pay off if we lost. What the hell kind of question is that to ask on the eighteenth tee? I told him: 'Hell no 'cause we ain't going to lose.' Then he said: 'Well, just in case, we'll take the midget over cash, because watching him is the funniest damn thing ever and that makes it all worth it, win or lose, don't it?' That's exactly what the wop said.

"Before I could say anything back to him Darby went on and hit. Eighteen is straight uphill, and it *tilts*. The slope snatched his ball left and it disappeared into a giant mudhole full of cattails. And that was it. All was lost. No sense playing it out—the wop and his group were all in the fairway, and I ain't any good. It was over, and they set after us like animals. I yelled, 'Run Darby!' and we took off for the car. But the hill—those goddamn hills!—they were too much for his little legs. The wop and his group caught him, threw a Titleist towel over his head and carried him off, laughing like demons. It was the worst sight ever, him kicking under that towel in their arms. And his screaming—God, God it was awful!" And with that, Conrad put his head in his hands and cried.

The men were quiet, flabbergasted. Darby, lost in a bet. Darby *as a* bet. It was past understanding, yet for the first time that summer they believed everything Conrad had said. Conrad wept into his hands while the men sat still, jolted beyond anger or sorrow, all the soul knocked out of them, like a people who had suddenly lost their nation.

*

Darby lived well for a hostage. Mercy Oaks arranged a place for him in the clubhouse locker room and set up a schedule of members to guard him after closing. He ate prime rib and got drunk on red wine most every night. Such a life is not entirely unpleasant, but he could never adjust his game to the steep hills and ravines that gathered up his low shots like dread itself. Decent play became an impossibility for Darby, and the members soon confined him to the flatter theater of the driving range, where they came to drink and watch him lunge at one ball after another, howling the evil howl that so haunted Conrad. It was a high, rebel-howl of laughter that reminded Darby of his beloved old group in the Delta, but it was absent the admiration he had taken for granted there. The Mercy Oaks men laughed in a pitch of degradation, a hideous imitation of Darby's home that tore at his heart like the eyes of a living friend lost to some merciless disease of the mind.

The Delta group knew they had no game, no life, without Darby. They told Conrad they would pay Mercy Oaks twice the total of his losses there to get his brother back. Conrad called and made the offer to one of his ex-teammates, an uncontrollable southpaw who was close to the wop, but Mercy Oaks would not take money for Darby. Mercy Oaks believed foremost in competition, in the bets and the action, and though some of them did not like the risk of losing the midget, the chance to play for a man's soul was too good to pass up. They would not take money for Darby—but they would *wager* for him. And so the game was set. Everyone on both sides insisted on a neutral site. They settled on the course at Silver City, a brown, baked-out spread split by an old levee of the Yazoo, half hills and half flat delta.

Conrad knew better than to ask into such a high-stakes game, but he prevailed upon the group to at least let him tag along. They agreed he should go, since he was the cause of the whole thing and had forced upon them the unthinkable possibility of never laughing at anything again. Yes, Conrad could come to Silver City: The ninety-minute ride offered an opportunity for each man to tell Conrad exactly what he thought of him.

The day of the match came. They convened in the club parking lot as the sun shot its first light through the still, grimy blanket of air that hung over the cotton fields. One of the men, who was both religious and of a literary bent, led the team in a prayer. He informed the group that Conrad had been sent from the hell of single-A to be their dark angel, that the time comes for every man to look into the abyss, that this late August day was it, and that, whatever the outcome, they could at least be thankful that after today they were finished putting up with the dark angel's no-playing ass forever. Conrad missed all this malice: He was fifteen minutes late.

When they arrived at Silver City they found the Mercy Oaks team tying Darby in a cart by the clubhouse, a towel over his head, his meaty arms bound behind him. No one else was around. Both teams, unbeknownst to the other, had wired the Silver City club five thousand dollars to evacuate for the day, so as not to alert the public that this captured little man was what was being played for.

The Delta group was livid when they saw Darby's bondage. They loaded up their carts in a fury and circled the Mercy Oaks men, taunting them with one last opportunity to hand over the midget without an ass-whipping. The wop laughed at this. He produced Darby's driver from his bag, showed it to the Delta men with some ceremony and slid it between Darby's arms and back, perpendicular to his spine, in the fashion of war prisoners who are marched through the jungle. That was all the Delta group had to see. They spewed profanities at Mercy Oaks and pointed at the course. Darby, bound fast in the golf cart, listened from under the towel as a dozen carts peeled off toward the first hole. The burlap tool case, full of his wrenches, lay in his lap.

Conrad watched the game begin amid more obscenities and empty threats on the tee box, which the men possessed like fine actors on a stage. Then, after the huge group disappeared around the dogleg of the first fairway, he sat next to Darby in the cart. He lifted the towel off his brother's head. Darby would not look at him.

"Darby, I'm sorry about Mercy Oaks," Conrad said. "I'm sorry I couldn't play better and that I left you." He started to untie his brother's hands, but Darby jerked away from him.

"Brother, you didn't leave me. You *lost* me." Darby stared at the pavement beneath them. "You lost me, which is what you do. You're a loser—a genius of a loser, born and bred for it. You're a loser like Lee was a general. The group fears you because of that, but don't worry. You can't lose them because they know I can't lose you." He looked closely at Conrad. "Your whole life proves something that I don't have the luxury of really even believing: That it's more impressive to lose big than to win big. To put up more than you can stand to lose, actually lose it, and live like that *every day?*" He looked away and shook his head, incredulous. He stared in the direction of the first green, which he could not see around the dogleg, where he knew his friends and enemies were already dying over putts an arm's length, dying over him. "Without even trying, just by coming back and hanging around, you've managed to make them play for more than they—more than I—can stand to lose. That's what all of this is." Then Darby looked at Conrad again, with the first disdain he'd ever shown for him. "And of course you're goddamned clueless about it." He looked away and nodded toward the course. "And I expect so are they. You belong out there with them, not back here with me. Now put the towel back on my head and go watch them play."

Conrad draped the towel over Darby's head again, but he did not leave. He walked to a beige brick patio a few yards away and took a seat there, occasionally looking at his brother who sat sweating underneath a towel in a golf cart. *A genius of a loser.* Conrad did not care for this, but he knew it to be true. He leaned forward in the iron patio chair and stared at the bricks under him, contemplated the red milkweed spreading from the cracks and admitted to himself right there that it had always been true, and he longed for it not to be. He listened for a sign of the match's progress from the course but heard nothing. For hours there was only silence.

*

The men of Darby's group never struck it better than they did that day. They nailed their drives deep down the fairway and never saw trouble. They prowled around the greens like they were stalking prey and cheered when their opponents hit an errant shot. Mercy Oaks had never seen such resolve in a group or played for so big a stake and it shook them radically, cracked open to each of them the heavy vault of their basest regrets and shames. And that, really, was the difference, for the Delta group would not be so burdened. They had more to play for. They already knew the black tedium of life without the midget.

The match ended on the remotest point of the course, the fourteenth green, set hard in the shade against a dark cypress brake. The wop missed a putt that crossed fewer inches of earth than Darby's own grave would take up. The ball slipped by the hole and the wop doubled over, groaned and twitched like he was gutting himself with his putter. Indeed every Mercy Oaks man right then winced at the sum of his own life, for there would be neither pity nor pride on the fourteenth green. The Deltans danced to the music of the wop's perfect yank. They jigged across the green dishonorably, as though, just when the wop's ball peeked insidiously past the hole, their favorite country club cover band materialized from the swampy cypress behind them, everybody gone kinetic, high-stepping, hot-footed, pot-bellied men without physical grace or social decorum or anything else that ran against taking consumptive, sucking delight in a wild, wild victory. They raced their carts back to the clubhouse, laughing as they had not since Darby left them. They let out their truest howl as they rounded the last curve of the cart path and saw him there, still tied in the cart next to the clubhouse. Darby trembled under the towel when he heard his friends coming for him, knowing only then his fate, his world won back, and he shook with the joy and vindication of hearing his soul howled for again.

And Conrad? The most relieved man in the universe—the genius loser Conrad? He raised his hands at the sky, shut his eyes tight and praised Jesus for the first time in his life, jumping up and down on the patio, looking and sounding and feeling like a man who had at last earned a victory and no longer feared the prospect of getting what he deserved.

But he was still a man apart. He stood for a minute and watched the group swarm around the cart where his bother sat and trembled. Then the group looked at Conrad, remembering he was there, the cause of all this, and they summoned him to the cart. They let Conrad untie his brother. Conrad gathered Darby on his shoulders, carried him to the first tee and pegged up three balls in a row. Darby slashed at them with inspired repetition, uncorking his three finest drives. Everyone laughed in rapt jubilation, lost in their laughter and their love for the midget, and as Darby's last drive reached the top of its arc over the fairway, Conrad stepped once, backwards, to admire it. Backwards, one step, to melt into the group howling behind him. He doubled over as they fell upon him and finally—finally—wrapped their arms around Conrad like he was a prince returned.

Against all his dreams, Conrad would disappear behind those arms forever.

JIMMY THE PLAYWRIGHT BEGAN TO SLUR

Jeff McNeil

I walk home from work so Nancy can have the car. It's not a long walk, maybe a mile, but I trim hedges and put out pine straw all day, so as soon as I get home I'm ready to strip down to my underwear and sit in front of the box fan with a cold beer.

A while back, as I turned onto our street on my way home, I saw Nancy standing in the neighbor's front yard talking to a man with thinning hair and baggy pants stained with white splotches. He listened with his arms folded across his chest. Nancy's arms flew around in the air as she talked. I walked into the house, stripped to my sweat-dampened underwear, got a can of Milwaukee's Best, and lay on the floor in front of the fan, letting the air run into the legs of my boxers.

I had probably been asleep only a few minutes when Nancy nudged me with her foot. My hand was wet from the sweaty can and the fan had almost dried my underwear.

She looked down at me with her hands on her hips.

"Your face is red."

"I'm hot."

"I mean it's really red. Redder than normal. Did you get into some poison ivy today?"

"I don't know. Are there blisters?"

Nancy knelt closer. "I don't think so."

"With the little white tips?"

"Does poison ivy blister?" Nancy cupped my chin in her hand and turned my head slowly.

"I don't know. Are there whelps? Raised ones? Or a general discoloring?"

"Maybe it's a sunburn."

"I used sunblock and a hat."

"Does it itch?"

"Well, I don't know. A little maybe."

"It looks like a general discoloring, though there may be a slight whelping just below the ear." Nancy took a sip from the beer and then held the can against my cheek. I remember thinking this is what love is. "What about bees?"

"Did I get stung by a bee?"

"That's what I'm asking."

"Do you see a stinger? A little black thing like a splinter in the center of the redness?"

"No."

"I thought you saw a stinger the way you were acting."

"No, just a general redness with the possibility of suspicious whelping, particularly below the right ear and the upper part of the right cheek."

"My cheek too?"

There was a knock at the rear screen door. Nancy got up to answer, taking the beer with her. I heard talking. I touched the spot below my ear with my fingers, gently. There was no pain, so I began pressing down a little, checking for signs of something lurking below the surface. Blood clots, splinters, little microbes swimming around eroding the cell structure.

Nancy came back, stopping on the other side of the fan. The man next door with the white splotches was with her. They each held a can of Milwaukee's Best.

"Ogden," Nancy said, "why don't you put on some pants now."

"Just cover me."

Nancy put a sofa cushion over my midsection and introduced me to Jimmy the Playwright.

I lifted my hand in a silent request for beer. Jimmy the Playwright shook it. Nancy drained her Milwaukee's Best then crumpled the can with her right hand.

"You remember where you and I met, don't you, Oggy? The Shakespeare festival? Watching the play with that crazy Roman guy and his mother?" Nancy's voice was in guest mode—more cheerful and intonated than the subdued one she reserved for me.

"Coriolanus, right?" I lifted the cushion to allow air between the scratchy fabric and my skin.

"Well here's a coincidence; it turns out Jimmy the Playwright is working on a science fiction version."

"Yeah?"

"That's right."

"Whadda you know." I lowered the cushion and closed my eyes. "Are my eyelids swelling? Bend down and check."

"Ogden's been outside all day trimming hedges and pruning," she said to our guest, ignoring my request.

"Tough job," Jimmy the Playwright said. "Looks like you got a nasty heat rash."

Jimmy the Playwright invited us over to sit in his kitchen. He claimed to have a window unit and a bag full of grapefruits, so we said yes.

The air in Jimmy the Playwright's kitchen was cold. The refrigerator made a peculiar noise, like running a fingernail back and forth across corduroy pants. After about fifteen minutes of sitting and eating ice-cold grapefruit, I found myself wishing I had worn a shirt.

There was a small sink in the kitchen littered with torn strips of newspaper. Buckets of milky water sat on the floor, papier-mâché puppet heads gathered on the shelves in small groups.

After the grapefruit, Jimmy the Playwright broke out the apricot-flavored wine. It was a dirty yellow and tasted horrible, especially right after a Milwaukee's Best and a grapefruit. He went into a long monologue about an old man named Christopher Mead who sold pecans, and then something about a speech he heard once on the radio about Hitler's art, and then he replayed an argument he had overheard near the fountain at the mall between two people about a Sesame Street T-shirt, playing both parts convincingly. By the time I was halfway through with my first glass, Jimmy the Playwright had finished three.

His voice trailed off during his last story, and he ended up staring at the glue-spattered floor in silence. Nancy and I looked at each other. She yawned and excused herself, adding that I should stay awhile and unwind.

As soon as she left, Jimmy the Playwright filled my glass and told me his wife had left him that morning.

"She thinks I'm a deadbeat. Maybe so." He finished his drink and quickly refilled, sloshing a small portion of the urine-colored liquid over the lip of his glass. I watched its shiny trail lengthen and land on the tabletop.

"I met her at the only play I've ever had produced." Jimmy the Playwright began to slur. "It was a little one act called *The Birch Twig*. You ever heard of it?" His eyes were bloodshot, and his neck muscles struggled to support his head.

"Nope." I drank the wine. The second glass wasn't as bad as the first.

"Figures."

"What's it about?"

"Well, a birch twig. At least ostensibly." He stopped and gulped more wine. "As they say. Ostensibly. You know what that means? Of course you do. You're a smart guy, aren't you?" He pointed in my general direction.

"No. Does somebody play the twig onstage?"

"That's not a bad idea, Ogden. Not bad at all. I think you may have quite a future in this business."

Jimmy the Playwright poured himself another drink and pushed the bottle in my direction. I helped myself. We were both getting very drunk.

Jimmy the Playwright went on about the twig play. It didn't make much sense to me. Two guys standing on a hill get a delivery of twigs. They hide the birch twig. They ring little bells. They talk about other deliveries. They try to make a map showing the placement of the twig. They are suspicious of other delivery persons. They try to keep the birch twig a secret. He said it was a hit in New Orleans. Donna was a stagehand. She encouraged him. You have a bright future, she said. They married. Then he started the Coriolanus adaptation. It was to be his masterpiece.

Jimmy the Playwright acted out some of the dialogue, pulling a bowler from a file cabinet drawer and wearing it during Corey's lines. I don't know why. After a while he seemed to lose interest in his own drama, struggling through the Spanish-American War references and then forgetting which planet Corey's parents had isolated in the Solar Wind Conflict of 2068. Finally, in the middle of Lizenium's speech about the possibility of stealing the vocal chords of children for use as dietary supplements back home, Jimmy the Playwright broke down, bawling until dawn over Donna and cursing the man who lived upstairs from him, referring to him as the Enemy of Good.

When the sun came up I went home for coffee before heading to work.

I worked all day in the withering heat. By sundown I was almost dead. I don't understand how the plants do it. How do they live like that? Violets. They look delicate as snowflakes, but they grow right out in the open, exposed to torrents of rain and hellish heat. Tough little guys, I guess. I skip them when I'm trimming, and if I'm on the mower I raise the blades a little when I'm about to run over a patch. I see it as sort of a tip of the hat to violets everywhere.

That night Nancy heated frozen French toast sticks in the toaster oven and we made a special punch with lime sherbet and canned pineapples. A lot of sugar, but it's good for me. Refreshing after a hard day. Nancy's a gem.

I walked into the kitchen to put some of the dishes in the sink, and Jimmy the Playwright was standing at the screen door holding a half-empty bottle of Jim Beam in one hand and a puppet head in the other.

"Ogden," he whispered.

"Jimmy the Playwright?"

"I'm here because of the Enemy of Good."

"Who?"

"He's awake."

"Ah, you've been drinking, that's all. You're upset. Come on in for some coffee if you want."

"You have to come over."

"My uncle used to hear rabbits talking to him from behind the curtains. It'll go away after some coffee."

"He only starts his noises when I'm working. Why? I always hear him walking around but never any voices. Why? Come to think of it I never hear water running either. Or the toilet flushing or the shower pipes heating up. Maybe it's a ghost. I don't like it. I used to be mad but now I'm creeped out. What do you think, Ogden? A ghost? You believe in ghosts?"

"Maybe you should just knock on his door and ask him to keep it down."

"What if he's dangerous?"

"What makes you think he's dangerous?"

"You think he's dangerous?"

"I didn't say he was dangerous, you did."

"No I didn't. But it's possible."

"Look, what if I come with you? We'll knock on his door together."

Jimmy the Playwright took a swig from the bottle and thought about it, glancing over each shoulder into the darkness. "What if we just listen? If you're willing to knock, you should at least be willing to listen."

The noise was unlike anything I'd ever heard. A strange flapping, followed by a scraping, then a pounding, then silence. After about two minutes the noises started again. A high-pitched whistle, a rolling ball, fabric being ripped, then silence. Two minutes later it started again. This went on for several hours, and each time it was a different set of noises.

Jimmy the Playwright crossed his arms, satisfied at my amazement. "You still want to knock on his door, mister 'my uncle hears rabbits'?"

"No."

"I didn't think so."

"Maybe it's just animals playing," I said. "You know, squirrels or something. They climb in windows and wreak havoc. I've read about it. Yeah, that's what it is. I see them do it at work all the time."

"Well if you're so sure, Mr. Smar-tee, why don't you go knock? Go ahead. Walk right up the stairs and knock. I'll wait here." He stood with his arms crossed looking at me.

"What for?" I said. "It's just squirrels."

I went home and told Nancy about the noises. She laughed and said we were acting like a couple of girls. I drifted off to sleep as she made strange noises in the dark, thinking she was funny.

I woke up a little after two A.M. It was raining pretty hard, which meant I probably wouldn't have to go to work as early as usual. I walked into the kitchen for water and stood at the back door. There were large puddles in the parking lot and some of the drains on the opposite side of the street were overflowing onto the sidewalk. A few minutes passed. Rain spilled over the lip of the gutter and dripped into a ceramic pot full of water. Little expanding circles like the radar screen in an old war movie appeared and disappeared, merged with others or lost their energy against the side of the pot. I watched and drank my water and the rain kept coming. By then I knew I probably wouldn't have to work at all the next day.

And then I noticed the car windows. Between the rain, the glare of the streetlight, and the water splattered against the screen I couldn't tell if they were up or down. I opened the door and stuck my head out to check. I still couldn't tell, so I had to make a quick run there and back.

It was the kind of rain that soaks a person just from the back door to the car. Large drops of rain like they have in the Amazon jungles, the kind that make a noise like a drum when they hit metal or hollow plastic. And I got extra soaked because I had to stop on the way back to the kitchen to look up at the Enemy of Good's apartment.

Strange shapes flitted across the drawn shades in a seemingly chaotic pattern. Some of them were human, others animal, still others inanimate (a feather, a stick, a lamp). It was obviously not an apartment full of squirrels. After a minute or two I was too soaked and cold to stand there any longer.

I changed clothes in the bathroom and checked my rash in the mirror. It was still there. A bright red streak under the right lobe that ran down toward the jaw like a shooting star and the little red zero on the right cheek that seemed to be oozing outward in every direction.

Nancy brought me coffee in bed about nine o'clock. She put it in a ceramic mug her niece had painted and given to her as a Christmas present. A giant yellow sun and a tiny tree and a chicken against a blue background. I sat up and warmed my hands by wrapping them around the cup.

"Thanks," I said.

"No sweat. You were up last night."

"Checking out the rain." The coffee was strong and sweet. Perfect.

"There's wet clothes in the bathroom."

"I went out to check the car windows."

"I guess you're not working."

"Nope."

Nancy sat on the edge of the bed as I sipped my coffee. She told me about a dream she had that involved a snake and an old dirt road and a car.

I stared out the window at the rain as she talked. When she stopped I turned and noticed her staring out the window. I watched her straight black hair and her round, clear eyes in the gray light. Then she smiled at me and I could see the little gap I like in her front teeth. Beautiful.

"Maybe we can do without a car one day," she said.

"How's that?"

"Well, when they finish that store around the corner, maybe I could get a job there and I could walk to work. Then we'd both be walking to work. You could walk me there in the morning and pick me up in the afternoon."

"Yeah, that sounds okay."

She curled up next to me and put her head on my shoulder. "And we'll do that until we get old and we'll never have to buy a car. Ever.

I hate them. They're worse than TV. Not only do they keep people from looking at each other, they're designed to actually separate people. They're evil."

"You might change your mind if we could afford a nice one."

"Never." She smashed herself harder against me and sighed. "Never. Let's just lay here all day."

I set my coffee on the windowsill, closed my eyes and rested my head against Nancy's and fell asleep. When I woke up it was eleven o'clock. Nancy was gone, it was still raining, and the coffee was cold.

I walked into the kitchen and there was Jimmy the Playwright, sitting at the table across from an older man wearing a fuzzy red robe. They were both holding a can of Milwaukee's Best.

"Hey, man," Jimmy the Playwright said. "Look who's here. Sleeper Beauty." He laughed and drank his beer.

The man in the fuzzy robe lifted his can above his head and began a combination of singing and rapping. "I was standing on the street in my oversized feet, checking out the junk mail and wondering 'bout my homies in the crib and how they bailed me out of jail, last thirtieth of May on a very sunny day." He finished his tune and lowered the beer can, but continued bobbing to the imagined rhythm.

"Does this guy rock or what? Ogden, I'd like to introduce the former Enemy of Good, Lester Endicott Fain."

"Please, Ogden, my friends call me Clutch. And as I expect you to be my friend, an expectation fortified by a brief survey of your canned goods, I expect you to call me Clutch as well."

Clutch looked to be about eighty, wiry-limbed, with big watery eyes and tiny blood-red lips that stood out against his pale wrinkled face.

"It's the canned goods that give it away every time. Some order, but not too much. The hint of a system, but without the obsessive bent that has been the ruin of so many. My late father, Thaddeus Gregory Fain, God rest his soul, a saxophone man, good one too, played with some of the best studio musicians of his time."

Clutch abruptly stood up, placed his empty beer can between the robe and its belt and tightened the belt until the can was crushed against his belly. He was content to have it remain there as he walked to the back door and stared out at the rain, hands clasped behind his back, rocking on the balls of his feet.

"Jellyman, Big Leg, Sonny, Blind Boy—all those guys. Giants of the music industry. And then there's my father, near the bottom of the list and I'll tell you why—canned goods. Fruit mainly. So many kinds, you see. The nature of the canned fruit industry was, and is, such that it provided him with limitless possibilities for arrangement. It slowly consumed him, like a cancer, or a giant beast of some kind."

Clutch spun around suddenly. The energy of the turn was enough to part the robe down the front, exposing a pair of boxer shorts with the flag of Switzerland in the center, underneath which were the words "Neutral, Hell!"

"I can still see him." Clutch closed his eyes and waved his hands in front of him as he walked in a small circle. "In my mind's eye I'm being transported back to a small Nebraska-shaped house in Hoboken. The home of my youth. My father stands at the cupboard in his undershirt and bathrobe making slight adjustments, clearing out space, turning and stacking, over and over."

Clutch frantically acted out all the motions of his father, pulling several cans out of the cabinet and then quickly replacing them, as if he were trying to perform a magic trick. The sleeves of the red fuzzy robe rode up his arms in the process, revealing a seashell bracelet and something written on his wrist in red magic marker.

"He mumbles little songs, show tunes and the like, the popular stuff of the thirties and forties, bites his nails, wrings his hands." Clutch put his fingers in his mouth and tore at his nails like a wolf. "But I can only see his back. He has devoted his entire attention to the canned goods!" Clutch raised his arms in exhortation. "Thaddeus Gregory Fain has literally turned his back on his family!"

A few seconds passed. Clutch dropped his hands, then his head. He let out a long sigh followed by muffled weeping. Jimmy the Playwright looked at me. I looked back. Jimmy the Playwright smiled. We waited for the next thing to happen. Nothing happened. Clutch remained in front of the cabinets sulking.

"Is this guy great or what, Ogden? Shouldn't we form a club? I think we should form a club or something and go around putting on shows for kids. You know, schoolchildren. Those kinds of kids. I think it's educational and all, don't you? It's about acting and life. I don't think parents would mind. Or not too much. And we could get paid for it too. And then we'd all have good jobs. And we'd make sure we got paid up front too, and in cash if possible, so they can't back out on us. You know how the government is. And that way we could back out on them if we wanted and there'd be nothing they could do about it. You know what I'm talking about, right? I'm gonna get another beer."

Jimmy the Playwright walked toward the refrigerator, slapping Clutch on the back along the way. "You want another, Clutch?" Jimmy the Playwright didn't wait for an answer as he opened the door and retrieved a Milwaukee's Best.

Clutch turned toward me and said, "Another what?"

Jimmy the Playwright answered. "Another beer, man. Just say the word. Plenty left."

"Ogden," Clutch said, taking a step away from the counter. "I know you're aware of what I'm talking about. Perhaps all too aware. Perhaps you have a collection of coffee mugs stashed away in some dark corner, like the guest bedroom closet or the attic-relegated hatbox of some dead aunt. Coffee mugs with pictures of cats, or puppies, all labeled with the date and where purchased scribbled onto little pieces of masking tape stuck to the bottom. You arrange them by date or breed or color. Am I right? When no one's around, perhaps on a rainy day such as this."

Clutch looked at me like he was trying to make his eyes move in opposite circles, like a cartoon character who's just been hit over the head. "Are you trying to hypnotize me?" I asked.

"And even if it's not coffee mugs it's something else. There's something, right? Something you do that could easily consume you?"

Clutch adjusted his ascot, a pale blue shimmering thing dotted with silver stars.

"We're all potential victims of something. That's nothing to be ashamed of. If we keep it in check, that is."

"I think I make too many puppet heads." Jimmy the Playwright was drunk.

"Balance is what we're after in this life. A little fun, a little work, etc. I think you get the picture. Serial killers who keep their victims buried in the basement, or their body parts in the freezer, what do you think that is? It's a collection and then an arrangement of the collection, that's what. Fundamentally there's no difference between that and collecting and arranging canned goods. The latter is a pathology, what the serial killer does is a pathology of a pathology. His imbalance is itself imbalanced."

"You know," Jimmy the Playwright said, pointing his finger at me like a gun, his eye lined up behind it like he was aiming. "Clutch is right. I don't have to mention my puppet heads, cause I'm sure that's what you all were thinking anyway." Jimmy the Playwright lowered his finger, formed a fist, and crushed his empty beer can on the table. "I'm gonna work harder at controlling my desire to make more and more, Clutch. Just a few now and then. Gonna stop aiming for perfection, which is ultimately elusive, which is what I think you were getting at earlier. And I wanna change my name too. I don't wanna be called Jimmy the Playwright anymore, Ogden. From now on I want to be called...Wheel."

"Wheel?" I asked.

"No. Big Wheel. That's what I meant."

"Take me for example," Clutch said. "I once worked for an oil company, a big one. In charge of distribution for the whole of southern Oklahoma." Clutch moved his hand across a very large imaginary map of Oklahoma. "That is until I realized it was getting the better of me. I won't go into details. Gusher and Slick were the name of my cats. Derrick-shaped salt and pepper shakers sat next to oil-barrel napkin rings on my kitchen table. Such is the insidious nature of the oil business. So I stopped. Cold turkey. Refused to speak to anyone about the industry or even drive a car for three years. I cashed in my retirement and stock and took an Amtrak to St. Louis, where I dabbled in journalism for a few years before coming here. Now I teach acting, almost exclusively at night. In fact, I'm usually abed at this very hour.

"You see, I believe the night is magic. If you're in it correctly. That is, with the right attitude. Don't ask me to explain. The wee hours are the delicate fabric in which we find our desires wrapped, like a blushing bride on honeymoon, in the summer, scampering across a wooden floor toward an open window in a negligee designed to reveal the equally delicate substance underneath—but only to the keenest of gazes. It is this gaze which I attempt to teach my students."

"Man," Jimmy the Playwright returned to his seat. "Can you bend a spoon?"

Clutch picked up a spoon, bent it with his hands then threw it down on the table triumphantly. "Never make fun of my gaze. I possess a very powerful one. I assure you that is not a brag. I can see things. People's dreams."

Clutch zoned out at this point, staring at a spot over my shoulder, like he was in a trance. His voice became soft, like a little girl's, and it creeped me out.

"I am beginning to see yours, Ogden. It is purple. Yes. It is a part of some kind—like a space or a hole. It is a deep, rich purple. It is closer now." At this point Clutch fainted.

"Man," Big Wheel said, "we should start a religion with this guy."

Through the window I could see Nancy walking toward the back door. She was carrying a fistful of violets, and she was smiling.

TALK

Diane McWhorter

A friend and I were going out for martinis, a cocktail that affects me with subtle specificity. "What are you like when you drink them?" he asked. "I'm the same," I said, "except I talk more." I paused for him to compute that and said: "Does that help you understand the definition of 'infinity'?"

Talking is the miracle life force, the social equivalent of those late-night-TV elixirs that do everything from stripping varnish to eradicating poverty. Or, to use the metaphor my friend the writer John Sedgwick prefers, "It's the great I-90, the mighty Mississippi, except it's the *source*, not merely a conduit, of everything that unites us." Yes, talking is what binds us into a people. But it also builds our individuality, welding intelligence and emotion into the infrastructure of personhood, soul. Talking is our solace in the face of extinction, as cell phone technology demonstrated on September 11, 2001.

Of course, you might protest that putting your trust in talking is like believing in eating. It's a utility, not a luxury. So herewith the disclaimer. We are not dealing with Orwell or Freud—public discourse or the psychoanalytic interchange known as the talking cure. I am speaking of conversation, the "world of sound" explored by the Jesuit intellectual Walter Ong: "the I-thou world where, through the mysterious interior resonance which sound best of all provides, persons commune with persons, reaching one another's interiors."

To be comfortable in the world is to trust one's social instincts. Talking is the laboratory in which we learn to read the covert meaning behind overt interaction. By the time we are mature scientists of the species, we are lucky if we have achieved some harmony between instinct and reason, between our animal pedigree and our civilized inheritance. My friend Carroll Bogert feels the lovely choreography between the two forces whenever a woman comes up to her and says, "Are you thinner?" She knows the comment has nothing to do with her appearance. It simply means *I like you.* "She has just plucked a nit off my body," Carroll says, "and popped it in her mouth."

That metaphor speaks to a theory that Robin Dunbar, a professor of psychology in Liverpool, England, advanced about the origins of talk in his book, *Grooming, Gossip, and the Evolution of Language* (1996). According to his charming thesis, language was the evolutionary continuation of the grooming behaviors of our primate ancestors. The social cohesion essential for their survival flowed from the emotional bonds established by the obsessive physical intimacy of nitpicking and fur-raking. As the size of animal groupings grew, however, social management became trickier, and the investment of physical attention necessary to grease the system (up to 50 percent of a primate day) began to interfere with the basic survival activities of gathering food and defending against predators. So humans evolved in such a way as to vocalize the rituals of emotional maintenance, which freed them to attend to other business simultaneously. And *voila!*— multitasking. Thus, through talk, are we *H. sapiens* able to massage the body politic while shelling peas on the porch.

Every member of the species undergoes her personal evolution as a talker. (The alternative, according to Ong, is this: "Persons who do not…learn to talk remain imbeciles, unable to enter fully into themselves.") Here I offer my own Life as a Motormouth, a quest for truth and connection. It is also a tribute to nitpicking, itself an enterprise of discovery as much as of comfort.

TALKER IN TRAINING

Not long ago, as I was leaving a party, the host looked at his watch, noticed it was not yet midnight, and said, aghast, "What, you didn't have a good time?" I'm not proud of my reputation for closing down parties, but I do know I am an asset to any 2 A.M. postmortem. My social stamina is impressive, honed at the spend-the-night parties of childhood. I was always one of the last two girls awake. Usually, the fellow night owl in the facing sleeping bag was my lifelong friend Jane, who had the gift of morbid fascination. She told story after story of ruination—plane crashes, alcoholic parents, electrocuted children, and, primarily, suicides. At an hour synonymous with the dark night of the soul, I would become despondent, convinced that I along with everyone dear to me would succumb to some item on Jane's menu of doom. The perspective restored by the morning sun (suicide was not inevitable after all!) was my first inkling that the spoken word had some mad vagrant power behind its content—a lesson that has to be learned over and over throughout life during middle-of-the-night lovers' quarrels.

Here I feel obliged to roll out a little Freudian boilerplate about "orality." Of course, our first connection with "the world"—read "a breast"—is through the mouth, and the tongue is a sort of bridge from the budding new person's total self-absorption to the exterior world. *Tongue* is a synonym for spoken language. Hence, my talking jones was a desire to swallow the world. At least that's how I interpreted my last-to-bed party record. I just didn't want to miss anything.

Robin Dunbar would counterpropose that my actions belonged as much to Darwin as to Freud. He might say I was exhibiting "coalitionary behavior": the clique-making that primates engage in through the back-scratching antecedents of language. Small grooming partnerships make it easier to cope with the stress endemic to larger animal groupings—what Dunbar calls the "havoc of harassment and competition." Maybe what I was doing in my alliance with Jane was disarming the person whose precocious sense of tragedy had potential for upsetting our still innocent subspecies. Also, staying up till the bitter end ensured that the other girls would not gang up on me.

Even though my conversations with Jane sometimes led to anxiety, Dunbar's findings suggest that there may be physiological benefits to the total talk orientation of teenage girls. In primates, the repetitive protocols of grooming trigger the release of endorphins, the body's natural opiates. The elation brought on by monotonous activity—the runner's high, say—also accounts for the obsessive pacing of caged zoo animals (which may be a better analogy for teenagers). Overhearing my thirteen-year-old daughter's phone conversations, I am struck by the single-mindedness with which she picks over every last square inch of the conversational beast ("Oh, lookie, another zit on Chloe!") through the reiteration of detail and conviction ("She had an *obligation...*"). With its emphasis on hair, self-tanning cream, shopping, and other grooming formalities, the endless teenage chat could be nature's way of medicating one against the angst of adolescence, that period when instinct drives one *to* rather than *from* self-destructive choices.

By high school I was in the social Darwinist major leagues, as a sorority girl in command of a vast teenage network in Birmingham, Alabama. I had made the connections, at least in the cheapest social definition of the word. My personal evolution seemed to be careering down a dead-end path of preening and popularity, when along came *The Stranger*. Albert Camus's "Lay Trawn Zhay," assigned in eleventh-grade French, corrected the course. Existentialism was just the right cold-water-in-the-face for a sixteen-year-old who had made too much sense of everything. It was a big world out there. Nothing made sense! There was no meaning to anything. I was not in charge of my destiny. There was no destiny! For me, the canned conversation was over. It was time to mint a real voice.

But first a college interlude in pursuit of the peak experience. With Kerouac as my Virgil, I embarked on the standard post-adolescent tour—Grateful Dead concerts, moody walks in Paris's Père-Lachaise Cemetery, and all-nighters to write papers on man's inhumanity to man. Then it was on to the next destination, a world in which experience and talk were inseparable.

The Talking Racket

The career I chose, journalism, has only one discernible qualification: the ability to talk. Or more pointedly, the ability to converse. The newsroom itself can be the verbal equivalent of what anthropologists call a *lek*—an arena where males of the species engage in a booty-shaking competition. But in the actual practice of journalism, talk between reporter and source becomes a sacrament of trust, though one that may ultimately be upended by the reporter's instincts.

Part of what makes journalists good interviewers is that they are obsessive groomers, compulsive about the minute specks. These must be labeled, sorted, and categorized by phylum. The intensity of focus produces something like endorphins. That is why most journalists feel a painful letdown when they must abandon the fullness of the conversation—"Hey, I can ask this person anything I want!"—for the linear two dimensions of the written word. Without that talk high, I doubt many of us would risk the most dangerous requirement of the trade: committing our instincts to print and signing our name. In the process, we sometimes must betray the intimacy we have established with our grooming partners—sources—and serve harsh intuitions that revolt against our conscious beliefs. Writing is often the opposite of grooming: ruffling feathers.

Talk expedites truth, but I did not fully appreciate this equation until I entered a world that did not appreciate it at all. When I began to write a book-length history of my hometown many years ago, I had to leave the immediacy of journalism and venture way back into the archives. Many of the academic historians who live there, I learned, have a bias against "oral histories"—interviews to you and me. Elevating one form of nitpicking over another, they prefer to commune with the silent documents—letters, newspapers, public records—on the grounds that the memory of live humans is less reliable than contemporaneous written sources (notwithstanding the inhibitions inherent in "putting it in writing").

The challenge for anyone who contends with alien periods or environments for a living—whether journalist, historian, or spy—is to break the code of the realm. During my early months in the archives, however, the secret history of Birmingham was not revealing itself through the proper written channels. It was incomprehensible to me, for example, how Hugo Black, the liberal senator out of Birmingham, an architect of the New Deal who went on to be the most uncompromising civil libertarian on the Supreme Court, could have been launched politically by the Ku Klux Klan. What finally cracked the code was not the microfiche but plain old gossip.

Early in my research, my grandmother, an acquaintance of Black's, had remarked offhandedly to me, "Of course Hugo was an ambulance chaser and that would always be his mentality." At first I thought she was just haughty and uninformed, but I came to see the cunning of her statement. Black had indeed been a legend of Birmingham's plaintiff bar. But at that time, I discovered, personal injury lawyers were the chief defenders of the city's downtrodden against an employing class that had managed to deprive its workers of virtually every right except for the constitution's guarantee of a trial by jury. Once I figured out the personalities—why my grandmother's country club crowd had it in for Hugo—it was only a short leap to understanding that the Ku Klux Klan to which Black belonged in the 1920s was actually the insurgent populist wing of the Democratic Party, liberal on everything but (but!) race and creed.

Eventually I learned I could count on this: Any impression of an event I had formed on the basis of the gold-standard written sources would change about thirty degrees once I talked to the actual players—not because of any new factual information they offered but simply because of their complexity as human beings. The faithful country-club bartender turned out to be not the "white folks' Negro" I was expecting but a devoted voting-rights activist. On paper, a former Klansman had appeared to supply dynamite for Birmingham's house bombings of the 1940s; in conversation he turned out to be the sworn enemy of the man who was doing the bombings.

Whenever my will to write flagged over the years I worked on my book, I would indulge the need to talk. Fortunately, that drive seemed to be universal and, in the case of some of my subjects, at odds with their better judgment. Former Klansmen invited me into their living rooms, policemen told me about beating up blacks, and an aristocratic industrialist confessed to having participated in a machine gun assault on some union organizers.

C. R. "Bunny" Boyd, one-time member of the Birmingham Police Department's notorious K-9 Corps, rescued me, almost too diplomatically, from professional regret. I had called Boyd from my office in New York to get some background on one of his former K-9 colleagues, the officer who had been famously photographed during Martin Luther King's demonstrations of 1963, siccing his German police dog on a black youth. I had been told that the officer's name was Bobby Joe Danner, and since Danner had threatened to sue me if I divulged his name, I had no reason to doubt that he was the tooth-baring man in the picture. My interview with Bunny Boyd was not going well either.

"Now Bobby Joe Danner's right-handed," Boyd said when I asked him what kind of guy Danner was.

"Um, someone else told me he was sort of a sweet guy. Are you aware of any particular reputation he had?"

"Well, he was right-handed."

"Um, I was hoping to get something a little more personal, you know, to bring him to life?"

"Now, Dick Middleton is left-handed. He owns that German bakery over in Vestavia."

Since I did not know who Dick Middleton was, I wrapped up the interview. Wondering if Mr. Boyd was daft, I went to my files and pulled out the photograph. I studied the officer. His sunglasses were from Central Casting. His holster was on his left hip. He was not the right-handed Bobby Joe Danner; he was Dick Middleton.

I called Bunny Boyd back, laughed, and said, "Thank you."

"That's all right," he said, and asked me a small favor in return. "Did you say you was a writer from New York? Well, you be good to us rednecks down here, y'heah?"

The Talking Mom

When my two daughters were very small, we took a ferry late on Friday nights in the summer to a quaint beach community at the tip of Long Island. As we drove like Ma and Pa Kettle in our overflowing minivan past the local Beautiful People's hangout, the sound of laughter and clinking glasses spilled from the candlelit balcony through our open windows. And Ronald Reagan's signature movie line would pierce my soul: "Where's the rest of me?"

The toughest sacrifice levied on me by parenthood was giving up the long evenings in darkened bars, lost in a fugue of what Henry James called "the terrible fluidity of self-revelation." Counterintuitively, that adult-only hobby rehearsed me for my crowning talent as a mother. Being crafts-phobic and a hairstyling klutz, I was not cut out for the standard maternal specialties of sock-doll making and French braiding. Instead, I was the Talking Mom.

Over the Christmas holidays, my girls and I make a regular excursion to Bemelmans Bar at the Carlyle Hotel to have Shirley Temples amid the murals that the establishment's namesake, Ludwig Bemelmans, painted of his children's book character, Madeline. My first-born, Lucy, and I made the inaugural trip when she was three, and we killed a few hours over a single "cocktail" and several bowls of mixed nuts and homemade potato chips. Listening in on the conversations my girls and I had, their father would sometimes go googly-eyed at how long I could string out a discussion of, say, my first pair of earrings—silver four-leaf clovers that I never wore again after the requisite six weeks in my newly pierced ears. But I glowed to hear my daughters counseling friends who were approaching the pierced-ear birthday: Pick something "simple and elegant" so you won't get sick of it. Once Lucy explained to her best friend from first grade that our family shopped for organic chicken and milk because some people thought the hormones added to foods were causing Puerto Rican girls to get their periods at age six. Her friend seemed perplexed, and Lucy asked solicitously, "Do you know what a period is?" Then she shot me a look that was the unabashed pride of information supremacy, though I do feel I should point out that she still believed in the Easter Bunny at the time.

Last year, we were watching *Waiting for Guffman*, Christopher Guest's spoof of community theater, and Lucy drew a blank when I laughed as the Guest character extolled his new line of "My *Dinner with André* action figures." Trying to explain a 1981 cinematic artifact to a thirteen-year-old—it's a big world it is out there!—moved me to take a second look at the quintessential talk movie. Now that I am the age of the eponymous André Gregory at the time of his on-screen midlife crisis, the self-indulgence of that interminable dinner soliloquy struck me as practically onanistic. It was the opposite of real conversation: the erotic "language of the heart" that Gregory himself pines for just before the espresso: "some kind of language between people that is some kind of poetry." What he is grasping for is Walter Ong's definition of poetry: words that dip "below the range of the human process of understanding-by-reason."

Tombstone Talk

A few months ago, I began to act on the tragic recognition that the found poetry issuing from my friends' mouths—their "idiolect," as linguists refer to an individual's distinctive verbal choices—was disappearing without a Homeric trace. How sad that Gutenberg had snuffed out the cultural imperative to preserve oral language: our essence as social beings. I started writing down the words of my conversation partners that I couldn't bear to lose.

A number of the notations are knowing aphorisms typical of my literary cohort—"The only universally held principle of communism," a friend declares over a steak-frites dinner, "is that there is no private ownership of French fries." Others are life advice I get from the friends I consider my Board of Directors, like the former Master of the Universe who cautions me: "Opportunities are not constant. They come in a random distribution. The trick is to recognize the apple when it hits you on the head." Most are tinged with the poignancy of endurance. A secretive friend gives his age as "older than a goddamn mountain." A man who hopes to find middle-age love with a woman who has no "issues" explains, "And what I mean by not having 'issues' is that she's willing to be comforted." A Christian friend beginning to behave a bit like Hazel Motes instructs me, "You do not *determine* what is right or wrong; you *discover* it, inscribed in reality."

Looking back over the expanding chapbook, I see that many of the comments are stand-ins for grooming—evidence that talk is, as Jan Freeman, the language columnist for the *Boston Globe*, puts it, "the endowment that allows you to do hugging and caressing from a distance." Offhanded axioms reassure that life is supposed to be hard—"There are so many ways to go wrong," one of my board members says, soothingly. When I fall off the recovering-know-it-all wagon and impart some gratuitous wisdom, he sweetly lets me know by saying, "How else am I going to learn about the human heart except through your reportorial skills?"

Probably one of the earliest functions of grooming was that it allowed intimates to serve as mirrors for one another before the invention of glass. Likewise, the platonic goal of conversation is mutual recognition. One faces a self best that is accepted by others. When I get that recognition in words, I write it down under the heading of Tombstone Material. "You think about shit too much, I swear to God," says one of my board members. And another gives his blessing to the ongoing conversation this way: "There's plenty of time for silence. Talk away."

BROAD AND JACKSON

Carol Megathlin

When Martin Luther King walked by right in front of me, I didn't think too much about it. I was young—seventeen years old—and not particularly concerned with the civil rights movement erupting across the South. The marches and boycotts had been only black-and-white images on our television sets in Albany, Georgia, not a flesh-and-blood reality. But there he was, the man himself, strolling down the middle of Jackson Street.

The year was 1961 and the December sky was cold, hard, and blue over Albany. My friend Janet and I had spent several hours Christmas shopping downtown and were headed home.

Janet backed her mother's two-tone Buick out of the parking space in front of Crowe's drugstore and started down Broad Street. As we approached the first intersection, a policeman stepped in front of us and motioned us angrily to a stop. I was startled and confused. What had we done wrong?

Then I saw them.

A small group of Negroes were walking in an orderly line down the middle of the street, two abreast. They were dressed as if for church, the women in sober black coats and hats, the men in suits. The younger men, perhaps too poor for sport coats, braved the cold gaze of onlookers in cheap new dress shirts, long-sleeved and white. Two men walked near the back of the line, off to the side. I didn't recognize one of them, but there was no doubt about the other. It was Martin Luther King.

I watched him with the bored half-interest of the self-absorbed teenager. If I felt anything, it was a faint echo of the suspicion and re- sentment circulating in the community. Martin Luther King meant only one thing: trouble.

The people in the small procession walked silently, their pace slow but not timid. They held their heads erect, chins neither low nor high, eyes straight ahead. Some carried Bibles. There was no defiance in their faces, but there was a tension beneath their deliberateness, as if their dignity were knit together with every ounce of their courage.

The afternoon sun bounced off the shiny black straw of a woman's hat. The wind lifted a corner of Martin Luther King's raincoat, revealing a plaid zip-out lining. He walked more casually than the rest, his hands thrust into his coat pockets against the cold. There was an intensity about him, a confidence in the way he glanced around as he walked. His demeanor was what I would have expected of my father, walking down a city street from his office to lunch—as if there were no question about his right to be where he was.

As Janet and I sat in the quiet warmth of the car, I knew I was witnessing a fragment of history. But I was too young to understand the hunger for respect that drove these protesters into the street, shivering in their thin coats and shirtsleeves. I didn't know what their particular mission was that day, but I had no doubt that they had been denied a permit for their parade. They knew they would be arrested at the end of the march. Weren't they frightened?

After Janet and I were cleared to cross the intersection, our teenage priorities reclaimed our attention. But as we drove home, the thought of those quiet, decent people who would spend the night in jail lingered at the back of my mind.

As my thinking matured over the years, I remembered my encounter with that small band of marchers many times. Sometimes the memory stings my eyes with tears. When their lives brushed by mine on that cold December day, I was able to see the faces of individual protesters, to think, for the first time, about what they might be feeling. Perhaps that's when I began to understand that any group has many faces, not just one.

How could a people, having endured the generations-long cruelties of racial contempt, have resisted the temptation to violence? Yet they chose the better way—an implacable insistence on their rights presented with dignity, restraint, and a quiet perseverance. The wisdom of those December marchers was Martin Luther King's gift to our nation. That I remember them, often with tears, is his gift to me.

Rehab

Janet Nodar

We damaged people sit in a circle, in our orange plastic chairs, and imitate Heather. We make feathery little movements with our legs and arms. Those of us who are strong enough stretch long rubber bands or move weighted poles up and down. Heather never ceases to smile. Her shiny brown ponytail bobs when she moves her head. She's cheerful in the therapy rooms too, tender with the uncertain, even though we can take seconds to lift a hand to a pulley, a foot to a tread-mill. A sudden disruption in the brain and we woke to being aged in-fants, unstable and tremulous. Our faith has been undermined. She understands this, even if only in theory. She is young and strong, and can look at an arm or leg or hand and reflexively list the muscles and nerves encased within.

I saw her eyes very clearly once (as clearly as if we were lovers). We were in line at the water fountain, I itching in my chariot, and she tilted toward me and asked me if I was having a nice day. I said yes. I'm not out to cause trouble. Her eyes are bright brown, penny-col-ored. Shards of green radiate out from the pupils. The green is not evenly distributed; there is more in the right eye than the left. It means nothing, though. A trick of genetics. Our eyes met, but I didn't feel that I was seeing into her soul. It's a myth that you can see into a woman's heart by looking into her eyes. You can never see into an-other person's heart. You see only the reflection of your own. This sounds like something to regret, but I'm not convinced. Maybe it should be enough just to see her. To say, here is a woman; her eyes are beautiful.

Anyway, on that day Heather was kind enough to hand me a paper cup. We are hygienic here at Rehab. The staff is constantly vac-uuming, organizing the magazines, wiping down the treadmills with Formula 409. We don't drink straight out of the fountain, but wait in line and fill our paper cups, a step to intervene between thirst and water, to make our lives more orderly. At the end of the day there will be a row of plastic bags filled with our buoyant trash.

Heather wears a cheap engagement ring. Her boyfriend comes in late sometimes and lifts weights, waiting for her to get off work. They're in love. This in itself is not interesting, I know. Love is not rare and precious. It's thick on the ground, and there's nothing more tiresome than the newly dazzled, locked in each other's high-beams. I remember. The simplest conversation hums with covert meaning. You feel the current coursing. You think that if you can just say, just do, the true thing, she won't turn away from you. For years, well after I knew that even the right woman would not complete me, hope could still act on me like poison.

Don't think I'm a cynic. I'm not ungrateful. Fortune can still smile on me. For example, I have Doris, my attendant, who drives me to these sessions. We're not friends, but we get along. She takes me to see my doctors too, and to the library and the video store. My taste in movies always disappoints her. She frowns and shakes her head at my thrillers and westerns. She could exercise while the therapists attend to me, but she won't. The suggestion makes her laugh. It makes me laugh too, really. I know what she thinks when she looks at me. What's the point of all this busywork? I'm made of meat and blood, like everyone else, but my time is running out. I need a taxidermist, not a doctor.

My daughter Cheryl hired Doris. My Cheryl remains blond, although it is a lot of trouble for her now. She's the most fretful of my children. Her laughter never carries conviction. Her worries are like ants. They gorge diligently on any small crumb, and somehow free her from seeing the corpse lying across the path. All of my children work to hide their dismay. They don't want to hurt me. They want to be good. That's the legacy of their mother, who also wanted to be good. Her sustaining belief: sooner or later, I'd get what I deserved. And now she isn't here to see me trembling. I fought her so tenaciously for my little wants. What do I want now? A dish of ice cream. A handful of Seconal. An orgasm? Such foolishness. The honeyed trance, the idiot thrust. The woman breathing my name.

Personally, I was not prepared for adulthood. The complacent town where I grew up, the closed circuit of my father's house, my little rebellions, sufficient to shatter my mother's assumptions—these things misled me. I expected something more significant. I expected to matter more. Eventually, though, I saw that none of us are prepared. How can you get ready? I remember rising above a green jungle in a helicopter, my shattered leg wrapped in a bloody blanket (this the first time I met with mortality), floating in a sea of noise and heat and pain so intense it emptied me out, a poured cup. The sun was in the sky. It lit us, and the trees below us, and I was nothing, a pulse and a set of eyes, and yet my heart lifted, suddenly joyous. I did not question. I just thought, I'm here. I am still here.

Now, once again, I'm forced to meditate. I'm no longer a man of action. I look around me—these people don't know the name of what fuels them. The skin lies. The woman touching my arm, my leg—she doesn't love me. She's only a therapist. This is her vocation, her selected chore. If she loves me it is only in the abstract, as one admires an idea, a principle. Yet my body records her touch. I don't suspect her of affection, but I know she's alive, I know her heart beats, and she knows the same of me.

Years ago, when my children were small, the requirements of my job temporarily took me away from home. It seemed foolish, even selfish, to uproot the family from our leafy suburb, the familiar schools, the malls—and so I went alone. I lived in a new city, in a furnished apartment. It came with spoons, with cups and books, with a clock and a white bed. A few towels—that was all I added. I was exhilarated. A new life, without losing the old, without the weight of permanence. It was a gift. I was of course thinking of sex. Not love. Well, perhaps love. And certainly sex, the marrow of love.

The girl I met, the real girl, her eyes were brown also, but darker than my Heather's, so dark as to be almost black, pupil and iris merged. She was a clerk. She answered phones and filed papers. She had nothing, except youth and beauty. The very walls melted when I saw her. Naturally, I—married, older, moneyed—had the upper hand. Yet I seemed to need her, and she could not help responding to me, even though she was a clever girl. So we were together in the white bed. The skin lies, yes, but she breathed my name from her heart; that, I believe.

I had not imagined that I could be tempted, that love could suddenly seem a living thing. I hadn't imagined regret. I hadn't imagined her crying. Soon the bed, our oasis, wasn't sufficient. Why did she want so much more than I had to give? Really, she was a fool. She was too young for compromise. I had encouraged her to dream—that was the extent of my crime. She denied me the expiation of kindness. That was her cruelty. Eventually she went off to be happy with someone else, and I admit it was a relief to me.

It grieves me, here at the slack end of my life, that I don't remember her face more specifically. There was a woman; her eyes were beautiful—but the years have corroded me. I wish I'd never wanted anything from her. I wish generosity had come more easily to both of us. I remember the beat of the rotor blades, and the sun in the trees. I remember my father's house, and hear my daughter's uncertain laugh. I wish I'd been kinder to my wife. Her little wants; they were not less important than mine.

CHICKEN BONE MAN

Memphis, 1927

Anna Olswanger

The kid I hang around with is a wonder for playing the piano. So one morning I'm sitting outside under the breakfast room window listening to him gab to his sister Gertie about the Vaudeville Revue down at Loew's Palace. In between eating up quite a few slices of his old lady's toast and jelly, Berl says, "Read the part again about Princess Rajah and her snakes."

Gertie rattles the newspaper and acts like her valuable time is being wasted. "It says here that Princess Rajah, the headliner act in the Vaudeville Revue down at Loew's Palace Theater, charms her snakes by playing an old-timey rag number on the piano."

I happen to know the kid is planning a career for himself with regard to the piano. So when Gertie takes a quick breather from opening her face, I say through the screen, "Hey, kid, it just so happens I'm friendly with a frosty blond by the name of Hortense in the dancing dog act that's playing the Vaudeville Revue. You want her to get you in stout with the management? I figure she goes woofle-woofle in the right party's ear, you're a shoo-in at the next Amateur Night auditions."

"Jerry's driving me crazy with his barking," Gertie says to Berl. "I bet it's his mange. Rub him down with coal oil."

That Gertie's a pill. How am I supposed to show my mug to Hortense if I'm covered in coal oil?

Now, Fast Eddie is a mouse acquaintance of mine who makes his home in the first balcony at Loew's Palace. He tells me what comes off regarding the kid and his sisters, Gertie and Dippy, the night they bust along to the Vaudeville Revue. It goes like this.

The four of them, Fast Eddie included, get settled into their seats in the first balcony where they're sopping up the cool. The Palace has a sweetheart of an air-conditioning machine. Then the orchestra starts in on the overture. The screen rolls down for the picture part of the bill, and Dippy says, "It's a shame about vaudeville being on the downswing because of moving pictures." This crack doesn't sit too well with the kid. Like I told you, he's got his sights set on pounding the keys in vaudeville.

By and by, the noggin of John Barrymore, the famous film star, hopscotches across the screen. Dippy sighs, "Gosh, he makes the goose flesh come out all over me." The kid tells her, "It's just the refrigerating system." This puts the lid on Dippy. So does noticing Fast Eddie one seat over, because next thing, she faints.

Dippy rouses herself in time to clap an eye on Czinka Zann, Cymbal Virtuoso. Eddie, who by now is keeping a low profile under Dippy's seat, says this Czinka Zann doll sounds to him like she's dropping pots all over her kitchen floor.

The next act is the headliner's spot. Out comes Princess Rajah, the dame with the snakes. I see her sideways from where I'm standing in the alley making conversation with Hortense. The Rajah dame looks like she's stuck gold coins all over her best nightie. She lets loose a half-dozen snakes from some hat boxes, and by the end of her act, these snakes are slithering up and down her arms in time to "Moonlight on the Ganges." You ever hear "Moonlight on the Ganges" played in ragtime? Well, if anybody asks you, it's got plenty of steam.

After a pig act by the name of Paulette's Pork Chops closes the show, the kid and his sisters and me hop a ride home on a streetcar. I sit by the back step where the driver can't take a squint at me.

"I wonder what Princess Rajah feeds her snakes," the kid wonders out loud.

"Mice," says Dippy, who's clearly holding a grudge against Fast Eddie.

"Chickens," says Gertie.

So by the time we get to the turnaround at Crump's Feedstore, the kid's putting together a ragtime number about chickens for Princess Rajah to use in her act. He's pouring out words by the bucketful:

I don't like soup bones in my soup, or ham bones in my ham.
When the coffee's makin', don't fix me bacon.
I'm the chicken bone man.
I don't want rabbits in my hair, or sardines out of the can.
Gimme what'll cackle with a crunch and a crackle.
I'm the chicken bone man.

I immediately stake the kid to some valuable advice. "Kid," I tell him, "you don't want your old lady listening in on this catchy tune. She might get the idea you're having truck with ham and bacon." The kid's Jewish, in other words, which means he's not supposed to feed himself up on pork. This is all right with me because I don't like looking in my dinner plate and wondering if one of Paulette's Pork Chops is looking back at me.

The kid, who's always thinking of my welfare, tells me to put a lid on it before the driver cocks an ear. Then he announces to Gertie that he's playing his "Chicken Bone Man" number at the next Amateur Night auditions and doesn't she want to come along and be the singing half of the act.

Gertie gives him the chill. "You know I'm training with Miss Stoots to sing in opera."

Dippy puts in her two cents. "Piano players end up being bums." Now, this is coming from the mouth of a doll who spends her evenings flopped across the living room sofa while soaking up Rickenbothom's Rejuvenating Cream.

I don't say anything back, though, because the streetcar is rattling back and forth on the tracks so hard it's making my teeth rattle with it.

The next day I'm going ploppity-plop down Faxon Avenue at the kid's heels. "Kid," I say to him, "I've been doing some thinking. What if this Princess Rajah dame's snakes eat dogs? You think those bums would take a bite out of Hortense?"

The kid steps along like we're playing tag. Sometimes he doesn't see the serious side of life.

We stop at the home of Miss Irma Stoots, a dame with a music studio on the premises. This is where the kid and Gertie take their lessons. It's the kid's turn this afternoon. I sit on the back porch and listen through the screen door to the Stoots dame counting *one-two-three-one-two-three*, while the kid plays right along, not missing a note. The thing about the kid is, he can talk a blue streak and play the piano at the same time.

"I'm writing a special number for Princess Rajah to use in her snake act down at Loew's Palace," he tells Stoots. "You want to hear it?"

"Forget the snake act, will you?" I call through the screen.

The dame wants to know how she's supposed to hear anything, what with me and the kid talking nonstop.

The kid goes right on bending her ear about how it's an old-timey rag number he's writing. "Of course, what I'm really swell at turning out is the blues," he tells her. "That's because Willie, my mama's washwoman, teaches me all the latest blues numbers from the Negro vaudeville house down on Beale Street. Say, you want to hear me play 'Kate-er-oo, Kate-er-oo, You're a Big Stinkeroo?' It's a hot blues number I wrote myself."

"Berl, dear, you're talking nonsense. You know I'm training you to accompany Gertie on the opera stage." Then the dame looks the kid in the eye very cool and says, "By the way, dear, I've decided to let you accompany Gertie in our singing recital next Wednesday night."

Right away the kid starts banging out notes, none of them 100 percent. "But next Wednesday night is Amateur Night auditions down at Loew's Palace!" he tells Stoots.

"Keep your wrists up, dear."

Anybody can see how sorrowed up the kid is over this recital business. I stick my snoot against the screen and tell the dame, "Sister! It's a dirty trick you're pulling on my pal. The minute you set foot on this porch, you're dog food!"

That night I'm in the kid's front yard turning around a few times under a hydrangea bush. I'm about to plop down and call it a night when I happen to catch sight of the kid through one of the upstairs windows. I see he's opening drawers and yanking stuff out. I figure he's planning to take it on the lam, maybe soon, which gets me jumpy. I yell out, "You're not packing up to take a little vacation, are you?"

Feibush, the next-door neighbor, opens a window and says, "Somebody shut that dog up." Also, the kid's old lady pokes her noodle out the kitchen window and tells me I'm keeping the neighborhood awake.

"All right, kid, we'll talk about this later," I mutter, only I'm talking through my hat because I know in my bones later is too late.

I don't waste a minute. I step along to the side of the house where I sniff the kid's old lady through the kitchen window cooking jelly. I stake her to some of my valuable advice. "It's about the kid we both know and love dearly," I say through the screen. "He's taking a run-out powder. That is, unless you hop over to where the Stoots dame lives and tell her to lay off the opera dodge."

"Berl!" she calls up the stairs. "It's Jerry's mange again. He's going to bark all night unless you go outside and doctor on him."

I see I'm dealing with a hard-hearted dame and that I'm going to have to get the kid out of this hot spot myself. When he opens the back door, I say to him like this, "Excuse me, kid," and without so much as saying "boo" to his old lady, I'm running between his legs and grabbing an open pot of Dippy's rejuvenating cream off her dresser.

The kid comes busting in and says, "Jerry, you better scram before Dippy finds out you're in here."

My mouth being full, which saves on conversation, I mumble, "Don't worry, kid, I'm already taking the breeze."

Now, this is how I come to be copping Dippy's pot of cream off her dresser.

A while back, the kid, who knows what he's talking about in these matters, gives me the lowdown on Jewish spooks. "Jerry," he says, "you ever seen Dippy when she's got that rejuvenating stuff on her face? It makes her look like a dybbuk. That's a Jewish spook."

So I'm in the backyard rolling this tidbit of information around in my head and smearing some of the stuff across my own mug. When I see by the moon that it's coming on late, I step along to the side of the house where I catch a whiff of Gertie inside getting her forty winks. "Gertie," I call through the screen, "you awake?"

As soon as I hear her flopping around in her bed, I wish her hello from the spook world and say to her like this, "Gertie, your ever-loving brother Berl is a big topic of conversation back where me and the other spooks put up. Here's the lowdown. He's all wrong for you in the opera dodge. Now, unless you want some dybbuk, such as myself, paying you a house call every night, you better get yourself another sucker to accompany you on the piano." But before I get all this out, Gertie starts screaming her head off.

"Mama! Papa! There's a peeping Tom outside my window! I said, Maaaamaaaa!"

Well, I see right away why the Stoots dame is planning to put Gertie on the opera stage. She can hold a note, indeed. What a pair of lungs!

"Gertie," I say, "you don't have to get so busted up over it. You'll find some other sucker to take the kid's place."

Feibush, the next-door neighbor, opens a window and says, "What's going on? Can't somebody shut that dog up?" So I beat it before Dippy comes to her window and sees where her rejuvenating cream walked off to.

The next day I'm sitting on the front porch listening to the kid plunk out his "Chicken Bone Man" number on the piano. He's pouring out fresh words by the bucketful:

I don't like T-Bones in my tea, or lamb chops on the lamb.
I won't ad-lib with a barbecue rib. I'm the chicken bone man!
I don't want oysters on the shell, or frog legs in my hand.
I jut my chin and I dig right in. I'm the chicken bone man!

Dippy comes hopping into the living room. "Berl!" she shrieks. "You want to wake up the dead, not to mention Gertie? You heard what Dr. Adler said. Gertie's got a bad case of laryngitis!"

I advise Dippy to go off and pour a dose of her old lady's jelly down Gertie's throat.

"Be quiet, Jerry," she says on her way out.

Then I stick my snoot up against the screen and say to the kid like this, "Kid, it's too bad about Gertie losing her voice after all her first-rate screaming last night. It seems she's going to be out of circulation for a while. The way I figure, you won't be accompanying her in any upcoming recitals. So what do you say you cancel your vacation and the two of us form a dog-and-kid act for next week's Amateur Night auditions?"

The kid takes a squint at me through the screen.

"Picture this," I tell him. "I come popping out of a hat box like one of the Rajah dame's snakes. I slither around, thanks to a little coal oil, only not too much. I don't want Hortense giving me the chill. I sing your catchy "Chicken Bone Man" number and the next thing you know, we're both getting serious attention from all the dolls at Loew's Palace!"

By this time, the kid can't help but notice the top-notch way I'm thumping my tail to the beat of "Chicken Bone Man."

"Jerry," he says, "you're about the most talented dog I ever met. Mama says so too. She can't get over the way you scared off the fellow nosing around Gertie's window last night. She says you're a bigger hero than Rin-Tin-Tin!"

Of course, I don't dicker with the kid, or his old lady either, on this proposition. I start in singing the words to "Chicken Bone Man," the kid accompanies me on the piano, and Feibush, the next-door neighbor who's got no taste in music indeed, opens his window and yells, "Can't somebody shut that dog up!"

This is the kid's catchy tune, which I cop off his piano:

"CHICKEN BONE MAN"

Words and music by Berl Olswanger

AFTERWORD

Berl Olswanger ("the kid") was born in 1917 in Memphis. He won a Tennessee Federation of Music Clubs contest when he was eleven years old, but couldn't accept the prize, a scholarship, because the winner was supposed to be a high school senior. When he was twelve, he made his professional debut as a piano player at Dreamland Gardens, a Memphis dance hall.

Geneva Olswanger ("Gertie") was born in 1911. After high school she went to Chicago to study voice at the Bush Conservatory. A coloratura soprano, she sang several seasons with the Chicago Civic Opera Company.

Anna Olswanger is the daughter of Berl Olswanger. After her father died in 1981, she discovered "Chicken Bone Man" and thirty-five other compositions he had written in the 1950s.

THE CRYPTOGRAPH

Nic Pizzolatto

Adam left one night in April, and Sharon found a paint-dusted stencil under his bed. Everything else was as he'd left it in his room— the computer, the television, CDs, most of his clothes, his high school pictures, yearbooks. She sat on his mattress after taking the stencil from its place under the bed. She scrutinized it like a note she was meant to find. A cardboard sheet, no bigger than a file folder. The picture of a military tank had been cut out of it, with the words *Police State* cut below. Orange spray paint lined the edges of these voids. She tried to remember if she'd ever seen this picture sprayed anywhere in town.

It was September now, and she'd begun carrying the stencil in her purse. She was walking more, forgoing the bus in the mornings, taking odd routes into the city, searching alley walls and the sides of dumpsters for the orange silhouette of a tank. Her legs began acting up, and her back ached. When she got to school in the mornings, she was often hunched, too tired to properly control the children before noon. She taught fourth grade at a public school largely composed of low-income kids, most black, some Hispanic. What the state referred to as "at-risk" children. Lately she'd let them do whatever they wanted until lunch.

It was the stencil's fault. Among the trappings of adolescence her son had left behind, the stencil was the only one that possessed this hypnotic gloom. The other objects in his room had their place; though abandoned, sad, they were understandable, they belonged. The mystery of the stencil became the mystery of her son himself, his incomprehensible desertion, his anger. She never understood his anger.

"Why you gone paint stuff?"

Sharon looked down. Eaton Slavin was beside her desk, staring into her purse where the cardboard stencil stood out among the tissue, prayer books, cosmetics, and wallet. The rest of the kids were at their desks, trying to complete a coloring project.

"Excuse me?"

His shirt, crusted with stains, rose up over a small brown belly. He lifted the cardboard sheet with a tiny hand. "You paint the telephone pole?"

"That's, that's not mine. What are you doing out of your desk, Eaton?"

He held the stencil and looked at its picture. "I seen you paint-ings on the phone poles."

She snatched the stencil from his hand.

He jumped at her gesture, but his surprise immediately vanished, his face returning to its placid, slack-jawed expression of inquiry. "Can I go th'bathroom?"

"Yes, go." Sharon felt bad at the hardness with which she'd grabbed the stencil, felt that she'd frightened the boy. But she recalled his reaction–shock, followed by instant acceptance. She'd seen that before, and many times, the bovine acceptance these children had for sudden, violent gestures. Most were used to seeing hands fly at them. She watched the fuzzy top of Eaton's head pass in the hallway.

She'd never hit Adam, not once. Even when his ranting took the Blessed Mother and the Holy Church as its targets, Sharon had never struck him, only listened quietly, her mind reciting prayers that his anger might be relieved. Adam would talk about the church or the government as if some ravenous creature were standing right out in the street, waiting for them to leave the apartment so it could chew their bodies with razor-toothed jaws. He was six feet by fifteen, with thick blond hair and an improbably attractive face, gaunt, projecting. This compounded her bafflement. Adam could have been the type of effortless youth that devastates the people around him. He'd let his hair grow long and stayed skinny as he grew, but she encouraged him to lift weights to correct that. The sounds of his harangues had be-come the jumbled noise of the children in her classroom.

Mo'Nique and Yolanda were struggling over some scissors.

Looking out at the classroom, Sharon marked two of the three—Lester Tuttle, DeRay Fauk, Eaton Slavin—almost surely headed for jail in a few short years. She'd seen the boys chase a limping dog with rocks. Sometimes they all stood on the front steps when school let out, watching their classmates depart and eyeing each backpack, trying to determine who had money on them, no doubt. Behind her desk, she discreetly slid off her shoes, her feet swollen from walking.

Locked in her bottom desk drawer, she kept the stack of comic books she'd taken from the three boys a couple weeks ago.

She'd been teaching here for six years, after a professional absence of fifteen. Sharon had given up teaching once David's dental practice was established, but she'd had to start again after the divorce. Coleman PS was the only school that notified her of an opening, and it had had three. She was forty-six. In early October, Adam would be seventeen, if he was still alive. But of course he was, she knew, because someone would find him if he was dead, and because she did not feel he was dead, not at all. She felt him living so strongly that she'd wondered whether she could simply set out, with her heart's thumping as a kind of homing device, and eventually locate him.

When Adam first disappeared, Sharon had called David to see if the boy had run to him, but David said he hadn't. He reminded her that she was to contact him through his lawyer. She remembered when she'd learned about his assistant. How unmoved David's face had been when he packed the suitcase. That had been hard to endure, his face. It had shown no anger or regret, just a stoic determination to get away from her. Now he had another son.

The stencil sat flat on her desk, the wood surface coloring its inscription. She read it again. A tank. *Police State.*

She did not like puzzles, never had. The door opened and Eaton strolled back in, picking at his nose on the way to his desk.

"Eaton?" Sharon said, leaving the stencil on her desk.

He paused, looked up with dull, bored eyes. The other children stopped what they were doing to watch. Mo'Nique had won the scissors. "Huh?"

"Don't 'huh' me. Come up here, please."

The children were quiet. They observed Eaton walking languidly to the front of the class, running his fingertips over the edges of desks.

He stood before her twisting on his heel. She tapped the sheet of cardboard.

"Eaton, did you say you've seen this painted somewhere?"

He nodded his head, pulled his arm behind his back. His navel protruded like the tip of a brown thumb.

"Where?"

"I seen that on the poles at my house. An' on the walls." His eyes were wet, deep black, like the onyx in the class's rock collection.

"Where do you live?"

He pointed behind himself. "Timpan'ca."

"All right. Thank you. You may sit down now. Finish coloring your picture."

He almost sashayed back to his desk, giving one little foot a limp. His sneakers were far too big for his feet. Timpanica Gardens was a housing project near the school, about eight blocks east. Many of the children lived there, and Sharon knew it from the day she had bus duty. The building itself was a large cube of apartments with a hollow center. Gray brick, paint stains on the plaque at the end of the sidewalk, a tall wall around it, she remembered. It had been raining that day. The neighborhood had looked broken. Everything from the walls of buildings to people's legs seemed in the process of buckling, slowly, toward the ground. Aster Street, she reminded herself, had seen its better days. And the house was now coming into question.

She hadn't known about David's loans until the actual divorce. The house was not hers as she had thought; there were several liens against it, outstanding loans, half of which were now hers to pay. She'd worked it so they took something out of her paycheck every month. Her fingernails slowly moved around the sides of the stencil.

The stencil had creases down its middle, as though it had been folded around something. The children were all talking, a rumble of noise and movement in front of her desk. They were laughing and arguing, making a racket.

Without considering her own intentions, Sharon reached into her desk and produced a sheet of white typing paper. She slid it beneath the stencil, took a Sharpie pen and began shading in the picture. She didn't notice that the children all stopped, briefly and as one, to watch her. Then they were making noise again.

When she'd finished, she stared at the black sketch and the two words below it, and her eyes seemed to fall into those spaces, to descend into the ink and the bottomless shapes of letters. A few of the children were running in circles now. Someone pulled a reading poster off the wall.

Gray buildings fenced her. This area of the city did not feel safe, though she saw several other, older women hobbling about on the streets. There was a blocklong line of Arab vendors, and she wondered what the police were doing about that. A few black men stood in front of a corner store and didn't acknowledge her. Children, home from school, were tumbling into the streets shouting. To maintain her calm, she prayed a rosary silently, extending her prayers to the denizens of the chipped and patched buildings around her. Boards over those windows. Big slabs of metal warehouses in line toward the river. She saw the walls of Timpanica ahead, and had to rest at a crosswalk before going the rest of the way. The air was cool and damp, heavy in her lungs.

She saw one almost immediately, a blur of orange on a telephone pole that also had dozens of tattered flyers stapled to it. She peeled off some of the papers until the mark of the tank and the words were clear.

Her hand spread slowly and she laid it over the graffiti, pressing into the splintery wood. There was such a pitiful homecoming in this gesture, she wanted to weep at her own stupidity. But she never cried anymore. All her life, she had been easily moved to tears, but for many months she'd been unable to cry, even when she was most willing, even when Adam left.

She moved to the next pole and saw another tank. They were both at about the same height, a couple of inches above her head. She took a deep breath and began walking around the wall that surrounded Timpanica.

Another tank, this one in green, had five copies painted side by side along the gray brick wall. The stencil she'd found showed the residue of no colors but orange. Maybe that was only the most recent color he'd used. Maybe somebody else had painted these things. If that was true, someone might know where he'd gone. She wanted to move outward, to search the sides of alleys and the overpasses in this part of town. The sun was setting though, new life rising into the dimming light. She waited for the next bus and noticed that across the street, about thirty yards away, three figures were sitting on the outer wall of the housing project.

They were her students, Eaton, DeRay, and Lester. Their feet dangled down the side of the wall. She couldn't be sure that they recognized her, but they all sat unmoving, staring in her direction.

When the bus came she hurried on, feeling gratitude she couldn't account for. Odors crammed the bus, passengers close together. She stood holding one of the handles to her right. This caused her to stretch over a young man who was sitting, and he gave her a look of disdain as her arm reached above his head.

Those children that spray-painted things almost surely did so at night, and she would be unable to walk these streets at such times, so Sharon realized there was little chance of ever catching someone else using the stencil. But that feeling of recognition was still with her, and when she got home she looked in on Adam's room, studying the empty bed, the inert computer, dusty desk. For the first time in years she felt an authority over the room.

She felt a little superior, standing in the doorway, and thought to herself, *I saw you.*

The following day at school she again showed Eaton the stencil and asked if he'd ever seen anyone spraying it. He told her no, but she knew that he might be lying. She asked him if he'd seen her yesterday. He shook his head no, very slowly, the moist black of his eyes unblinking.

Today she'd tried to instigate a reading lesson, but too many of the children had become restless, refusing to follow along, and now she had them assembling animals out of construction paper and glue. It was nearly time for lunch, anyway.

When the children had gone to recess, she found herself thinking about the graffiti she'd seen the day before, wanting to revisit the picture as though in its markings she saw Adam. He had been nine when David left her. She'd worried that David would fight for custody, but he didn't have any such wishes. Adam became quiet. He had grown into a sullen reader.

You'd look up and he'd be on the couch, then across the room, then gone.

As the children ran across the grass, leaped on the climbing equipment, she remembered Adam's athleticism as a child, his speed and grace when running. It was already an old trick that she did not think of him in the present tense. She did not think of where he might be at that moment, or what he might be doing, but kept her emotions firmly tied to their past life, and she would cast those emotions as far back as she needed in order to remember a boy who was not angry, who did not see injustice in every human endeavor.

That was his most aggressive quality, his sense of justice, and it permitted no shades of gray. In his early teens, he'd begun asking questions when they went to breakfast after mass. Soon she saw him reading histories of Catholicism, then Christianity in general. She became afraid to sit down with him at dinner, stressed at the thought of what he might want to tell her.

Once he'd insisted on her staying put while he recited the history of the Crusades. He hadn't stopped until she wept, and then he scolded her for that. He asked if she knew her church's position during World War II. By the time the new war started, he was inconsolable on matters of church or state.

The worst night, he'd been dusting his roast with red pepper. "But you can't be telling me, honestly, mom, that you actually believe that, like, hell, is a place, or even heaven. Like these are real places where people live and it's good or bad depending on how well you followed one interpretation of the Bible." He was cutting his food with hard, brief strokes. Sixteen, and this is what he talks about.

"Well, I do," she said. "Of course I do."

Chewing, his mouth full, he said "Look around, would you? Think about the world for a second, the enormous expanse of matter, the shape of the universe, and you really think that an idea developed by a completely savage, uneducated people somehow explains all that?" He bit off his words, and the scowl he summoned indicated an alarming disgust. "And you're going to vote with this as your criterion?"

She'd kept her head to the roast. Why wouldn't he talk about things like other teenagers did? Why? Couldn't he look at the roof over their heads, the food on their table, and admit the essential goodness of life? Lord knew she had enough reasons to be soured, but she persisted. She persisted out of faith—nothing more.

"So how do you justify voting for an idiot, spendthrift warmonger in the name of your pacifist, nonmaterialist God?"

She placed her fork down calmly. "You know, you have made it very clear that you do not share my beliefs. I believe we should support our leaders and their decisions. You do not. But since I am the one providing us with food and shelter, I'd think that you might have the grace not to attack me because we disagree about politics."

He leaped upon her participation the way a cat would a mouse. "And that's it! It's not just a difference in opinion!" He leaned over his plate, blond hair falling in front his face a little. "It's not just a disagreement. I'm talking about fundamental issues of good and evil."

"Ah!" she said. "But you said heaven and hell don't exist. So how's there good and evil?"

He paused. She thought that was because she had him. "I'm sorry, what's that mean?"

"If you say there's no heaven and hell, then what's good and evil? Why be good at all?"

He seemed genuinely aghast. "Are you saying, Mom, that if

there's no heaven, there's no reason to be good?"

She shrugged. She hadn't thought that was what she said, but maybe she had. It sounded dumber when he said it.

"Being good means doing so without thought of reward, Mom. *You're* the one who's supposed to teach *me* that."

He was silent then, appeared satisfied. He ate the food she'd prepared, silverware clinking against the plate. The dark house settled around them once again. But she, for once, nursed a silent fury. As if he'd smashed something dear to her for no other reason than to see it break. It was the smugness she couldn't stand, his amusement with her as he chewed the roast she'd cooked.

She no longer felt willing to tolerate his disregard. "If you're so smart, I wonder why you don't have any friends? Hm?"

He put his knife down and looked at her.

"You know everything, Mister Informed, so can you tell me why you never go to any dances? Tell me why you don't have a girlfriend? Because you're so much smarter than everybody else, you must know."

He stood from the table. She saw the shadow fall around her plate, but wouldn't look up. Sharon was nearly trembling from what he might say.

His voice shivered with disgust. "You can't even see how diseased you are." He walked away.

How could someone say that to his mother? What cure was there for a boy given every blessing, except perhaps a good father, who still insisted on seeing darkness in everything? She thought he was actually begging for Christ's light, and part of what upset him was his inability to see it. So she prayed that night that Christ's light would find him.

Two days later he was gone, a brief note explaining that he would not be coming back.

Over the playground, a thundercloud broke, and the children screamed and ran to the pavilion's cover. The rain grew heavy quickly, and she saw the three boys, Eaton, Lester and DeRay, standing out in it. They were watching her.

Coach Phelps began yelling at the boys, and he scattered them under the awning.

Sharon would not go searching the avenues for graffiti today.

That night she ate some leftovers and went to bed early. As she was drifting to sleep, the words of the Our Father in her head, she kept seeing the three boys as she'd seen them the afternoon they'd been chasing the small dog.

The dog was thin, with clumpy fur, and its right front leg was held just above the ground, unable to bear any weight. They were chasing the creature down the empty lot across from the school, around old chairs and a refrigerator left in the grass. The dog swerved like a rabbit trying to lose them. White teeth spread out on the boys' dark faces, and they broke stride only to hurl a stone at the fleeing animal.

She'd screamed at them. Told them to stop immediately.

From across the street they'd looked at her, not talking, not moving. They'd seemed to be judging their own distance from the schoolhouse, gauging the weight of her power. Almost as one, they turned around and continued after the dog, who'd slowed a little, stunned by a rock Lester had thrown. She'd watched the dog and the boys disappear into a web of buildings. The next day she'd taken a stack of comic books from them.

Now, in her sleep, what she saw most clearly was the face of the dog, worn, fatigued by the chase and unable to understand why it was being pursued. In her dream she could see its tongue flopping as it ran, a pink flag, the small head, the black eyes.

Three days passed. She was in the part of town where Timpanica Gardens could be seen. She left her hand inside her purse, lightly touching the metal object, remembering it was there for her. She walked close to walls, moved discreetly around corners, and she allowed her back to hunch. She'd thought she saw Eaton Slavin a few blocks back, but kept to herself. She tried hard to disappear.

A few people sat on stoops, smoking, a mother yelling to her two small children who were in the street. Behind them was the Timpanica compound, absorbing an entire square block. When Sharon passed the tenement, she turned into an alley that cut left at its end, and she stopped in front of an overturned plastic garbage bin. She stared at a red brick wall.

The most distressing thing during Adam's disappearance was her powerlessness. There was no action for her to take, nothing she could enact that would bring him back or even allow her to know where he'd gone. Until this morning. Her idea this morning had to do with communion, a sharing, a sympathetic fellowship. Perhaps in a bad moment he might see one of her symbols and come home. That was the part that kept returning to her mind. She imagined him destitute, sick, perhaps robbed, and in his moment of greatest doubt he might chance to look up and see her message, like a divine sign, and know that she was still here, still loved him, and he would return. The bottom line was that she had to do something.

She looked over both shoulders and slid the stencil from her purse. She stepped close to the bricks and laid the stencil flat, holding its edge. She turned her back to the street, to block any view of what she was doing. Then she pulled the metal can out of her purse, fixed her finger on the nozzle. She'd chosen red.

She'd hardly had to move her hand, and it was done. She lifted the stencil and now the tank and the words were hers, her mystery glowing red on an alley wall. Sharon stared, wanted to add the note, 'Mom,' but she reminded herself of where she was, of the need to hurry. She wiped the stencil with a tissue, turned around to the street and saw him at the mouth of the alley. Small, black as shadow, Eaton Slavin stood directly in front of her, blocking the street, his yellow shirt risen above the tiny gut.

"Oh," she said. "Eaton?"

The boy walked toward her, slowly, dragging his hand along the side of the wall.

She fought an urge to retreat. He kicked at the ground with his oversize sneakers. Sharon moved her purse to the crook of her arm and clutched it tightly. Behind Eaton a tall strip of daylight showed the world beyond the alley.

"Eaton?"

He didn't answer, and didn't seem to really be looking at her. His eyes lolled down to the corners behind her feet.

When he was a few yards away, he stopped, twisting a heel, and looked up at the wall. He reached out and touched the red paint, came away with a wet finger. Finally he looked up at Sharon, who didn't know what to expect in this confrontation.

Eaton said, "You was one of them?"

His voice was so childlike, she exhaled relief. "One of who, Eaton?"

"Them in camouflage."

"I don't know—are you saying the people that paint these wear camouflage?"

He nodded his head vigorously.

Sharon winced as she bent toward him, her back full of needles. "Eaton? Do you know where these people are?"

He shook his head and stared at the ground.

"What are they called?"

He shrugged. "I can show where all they do this." He motioned to the paint on the wall. "Ain't you one of them?"

"No, dear," she said. "I'm looking for one of them."

She turned him gently toward the street, and kept her hand on his back as they walked out the alley. Their forms were insignificant against the buildings, as if they walked the floor of a concrete canyon.

She stayed close to him as he led her up the cracked sidewalk. Sharon could feel the people on stoops staring at her, but she kept her eyes forward with stiff resolve. Her ankles were swelling, she could tell, and worried what her feet would look like when she got home.

They walked less than two blocks. Eaton led her through a maze of interconnecting alleys. She could see the boy playing here, searching and mapping each strange new road the alley created, entire summers spent alone, navigating these inner channels. She knew that he might only have seen one person in camouflage spray-painting something, once. Adam had a camouflage shirt, but she couldn't remember if it was among the clothes he'd taken.

They came out near a Thai grocer's, and Eaton pointed up to the wall beside him. At least twenty copies of the stencil had been painted in close succession along this wall. Blue.

Sharon let her eyes drift over the graffiti. The first tank was a bit runny, blue tears stretching down from its treads, flowing into the words *Police State*. The next two were lighter, fading at their edges, created with quick bursts of the nozzle. Eaton stood beside her, kicking the wall with his toes. The entire front half of his shoe now appeared to be empty. The last two tanks were the clearest and best defined. All of them had been set on a fairly straight line. He always could draw a straight line.

She turned around. The street was narrower over here, a few tiny houses set beside quiet stone buildings, fewer people around. She looked left and right, the lean sidewalk empty, a dusky white sky set low over the roofs. She took the can and stencil up and moved close to the wall, laid the stencil under the blue graffiti.

Eaton said, "What you doing?"

She'd almost forgotten about him. "I'm looking for someone. You wouldn't understand Eaton. But it's very important. Go play."

"Who you looking for?"

"Eaton, please! Be quiet. I'm trying to find someone, and I need you to be quiet. This is very, very important. Go play. Run home."

She turned back to the wall and touched the nozzle lightly twice, two poofs of paint dusting the wall through the stencil, a little freckling her hand. Her sign sat just below the blue ones.

She moved back to Eaton, who was standing near her, still watching.

She was bending forward again, her shoulders tight now, to insist that the boy promise to keep her secret. She was going to offer him all the comic books she'd taken from him and his two friends. But as her face lowered, over Eaton's shoulder she saw a policeman exit the alley. In five steps he was next to them.

The policeman was short and stocky, his dark blue uniform tight across his chest, red hair visible below his cap. He nodded to her and stood close behind Eaton, who'd been staring at Sharon. Then Eaton turned around and saw the cop.

"So what's this? You're tagging again, Eat?" The policeman pointed to the can and stencil in Sharon's hands. He shook his head with disappointment. "I don't think your mom's gonna like this. I don't think your case officer's gonna like that."

For the first time she could remember, Eaton showed a dramatic emotion, his eyes wide like lanterns, head shaking furiously. "I didn't! I didn't do anything!"

The policeman looked at the fresh paint on the wall and back to the can in Sharon's hand. "Then what's all that?"

"She did it! She was doing it!"

The policeman looked back at Sharon, her lumpy form. She wore flared eyeglasses, and the brown dye she used on her hair made it dry, so she kept it in a short, feathered style. She herself thought that, with age, her face resembled a softball. Her cardigan was clean and her big purse was a yellow quilted bag she'd made over three decades before.

"Who are you?" the policeman asked. The uniform, its authority, caused a panic in her she'd never felt, because she'd never broken the law before.

She could feel her eyes welling up, her voice choked. "I'm his schoolteacher."

The cop looked back and forth at Eaton and the cans in her hand. He adjusted his hat, and seemed to understand something.

He took Eaton by the arm.

"She did it!"

"Uh-huh. Let's go talk to your mom, Eaton." The cop nodded to her. "Don't worry. I'll get him home." He reached out and took the paint can from her hand. He took the stencil, and she let it pass out of her fingers without resistance, her open mouth offering no voice.

The policeman showed the objects to Eaton. "Think your mom might want to see this."

Eaton was almost howling now. "Tell him! Tell him! It wasn't me!"

A few people had opened their doors and were looking out on the scene. Their faces stayed shadowed in the doorways, the barest glint of eyes. Out on the street a gray light prevailed. Eaton pleaded as the policeman guided him down the sidewalk. She felt terrified, needing so badly to take action that she was stuck with only the need. Her feet had not moved from the spot, and her mouth only gaped a little. The policeman turned a corner with Eaton, and the two of them disappeared. She looked down at her spotted, knotty hands, flecks of orange along the fingertips, and she heard him once more. *"She did it! She did it!"*

She realized, again, that the stencil was gone.

School became strange after that. Eaton was absent for two days, and when he returned, he was quiet and didn't speak in class. She'd seen him talking to Lester and DeRay, but that was the only evidence that he was not mute.

She returned the stack of comic books she'd taken from them, placing them on his desk. Eaton didn't touch them, and he didn't look her in the eyes. He just stared around her, toward the chalkboard in the front of the room. His two friends raided the comics and Eaton did not complain.

Her hair had been thinning lately, and her feet became numb and tingly during the day.

The boys stared at her during recess, from across the soccer field, and she felt that now when they saw her, they knew her, knew her in a way she didn't yet understand. Above all, she could not abide the idea of an unearned fate.

She'd closed the door to Adam's room and left it that way, feeling the space had become accusatory, and she felt guilty when she passed it, as if she'd lost something that had been entrusted to her.

Fall arrived. The leaves on the scant trees became a luxuriant, glossy collage of intense color. The streets became wet. Flyers were pulled down, walls were repainted. Eaton did not come back to class after Christmas break.

The final trial happened in early February.

She'd been sitting in front of the television, next to an electric heater, eating a can of soup. She now kept her hair in a shower cap whenever she could. Her feet were soaking in Epsom salts and baking soda.

The lead story on the news was about a bomb that had gone off in the city that day. The screen showed shaky footage of a department store, one she'd used to shop at, and its whole facade had been obliterated, with small fires dancing in the wreckage of glass and brick. The video was fuzzy, people screaming, crying. She listened closely, already feeling a nearly imperceptible twinge at the base of her neck. She set her spoon in the bowl, and set the bowl down. She lowered her glasses.

The reporter was a deeply tanned woman of that vague ethnicity Sharon was starting to see more and more. The reporter spoke about a message given to authorities, a message wherein a group of terrorists claimed responsibility for the explosion. The group called themselves "True Freedom." They claimed that this chain of department stores was owned by Saudi Arabian interests who contributed heavily to the president's reelection campaign. Four people died in the explosion. Eleven more were injured. Sharon's face hovered in the green glow of the television.

The reporter's face gave way to three portraits, black-and-white drawings of three men whom the police were trying to identify. The sketches were crude in some ways, but she still gasped in recognition. The third sketch depicted a young man with light-colored hair, his eyes glaring, his features familiar, gaunt, projecting.

No, she told herself. That was her imagination.

A phone number was posted at the bottom of the screen, telling viewers to call if they recognized any of the men. It was ridiculous, she thought, lifting her glasses off as she looked back at the screen. No, definitely not, she could see now. But still. Her heart was hurting its chamber, pounding away at its walls of tender bone. She turned off the television.

She took her bowl to the kitchen, rinsed it out, and set it aside.

Through the window above the sink, the night was black, faintly whistling. She imagined the people in the explosion, the pockets of flame, the force of the blast.

Outside the window, she began to hear a dog barking. She still saw the limping creature being chased by the boys. She heard the barking again, different, higher, as if in distress.

If there was an unearned fate, she nevertheless knew that somehow this had been deserved. A vague guilt had replaced her will, but not, so far, her faith. Her faith she kept intact. She could not say why over the years things should flee her, why she should be allowed so little, but she practiced accepting this as part of a just and far-reaching plan. And her guilt was not the kind she could atone for, because she had no idea what it was she'd done.

The dog outside continued to bark, and the wind tightened its soft whistle. In her thoughts, she could clearly see the dog resting beneath a tree, wounded, nestled beside a stone, a dry place. She could feel the animal curled somewhere with its injuries, waiting out the night, unable to recall how it had arrived at this shelter.

CHITLINS

Robert St. John

I once wrote a semi-controversial column about eating possum. I was unexpectedly bombarded with phone calls and e-mails from proud and angry possum eaters. I had never eaten possum. I still haven't eaten possum. I began to worry that there were other controversial Southern delicacies that I had been missing out on.

I had never eaten chitlins, either. Chitlins are a very divisive food. You are either a chitlin lover or a chitlin hater. Actually, you are "on the fence" until you eat your first bite, and then you quickly hop on one side or the other. I wondered about all of the fuss. Being the acutely intuitive investigative food journalist that I am, I decided to delve further.

I hesitated to write about chitlins after the possum incident; for fear that some readers might think my column had moved in a different direction, and that my eating habits had headed down into the deep, dark, endless depths of the culinary root cellar. Some might say I was already in the cellar, and an in-depth treatise on the glory and wonder of the almighty chitlin was an improvement.

The official name for chitlins is "chitterlings," but I don't use that spelling since no one pronounces it that way. It's silly. It's sort of like insisting on the correct "opossum" for what everybody calls a "possum." Nobody does it, and I won't start here.

Chitlins are pig intestines. And we all know what runs through intestines. Needless to say, chitlins must be thoroughly cleaned. My friend Banks Norman eats chitlins. He has tried to talk me into eating them. Last week, he told me how they were cleaned: he slings them against a tree stump, runs a hose through them, picks off the fat, and boils them for four hours, draining and changing the water three times during the boiling process, while skimming and picking more fat. (Banks says the slinging is the best part. He's a pro. He's been slinging the same stuff verbally for years, long before he cleaned his first chitlin.)

Four hours? Slinging intestines against a stump? Having to drain a boiled ingredient three times before frying it? Chitlins must be extremely tasty to go to all of that trouble.

Banks is a kidder. He keeps a few spare kernels of corn in his shirt pocket while eating chitlins. When no one is looking, he will slip the kernels into his mouth and wait for the perfect moment during the meal to spit them out into his hand. "Hey! Who cleaned these chitlins?"

Never having eaten pig intestines, I imagined they would have the consistency of crispy-fried calamari with the flavor of smoked bacon—a slight-rubbery texture with a nice hint of piquant pork surrounded by a crispy-fried breading of seasoned French bread crumbs. Sounds good to me. I have eaten bacon-wrapped Diver scallops, Oysters en Brochette, shrimp wrapped in bacon, and broiled oysters stuffed with a bacon dressing. The seafood-pork pairing is well-known. Maybe chitlins—and this imagined calamari/pork combination—would taste like those familiar dishes.

Andouille sausage is made from chitlins and tripe. I love Andouille sausage.

One of my favorite catfish houses is Rayner's Seafood House. The Rayners have been frying fish in the same location on US 49 north of Hattiesburg since 1961. Rayner's is home to some of the best fried catfish in Mississippi. They serve fried green tomatoes, fried dill pickles, excellent coleslaw, and some of the best hushpuppies you will find.

While eating catfish at Rayner's, I noticed a sign that read:

Chitlins Tuesday Only
Fried or boiled – All you can eat $12.95
Half & Half – All you can eat $14.95
Dasani Water $1.00

At first I wondered if anyone ever took full advantage of the all-you-can-eat promise. I can't imagine anyone consuming more than one plate of chitlins. I also wondered what bottled water had to do with eating chitlins. Those two foodstuffs seem diametrically opposed. As an uneducated chitlin eater, I wondered if bottled water was required to eat chitlins. I began to worry. Does bottled water make them cleaner? Does bottled water make them taste better? Does it have something to do with the cleaning process that I don't know about? Is there something in chlorinated tap water that interacts with pig intestines and makes you grow hairy ears, a snout, and tusks? Note to self: When eating chitlins, order bottled water.

And why is the combo platter (fried and boiled) two dollars more? I have a theory, but we will get to boiled chitlins later.

I decided to return to Rayner's on the following Tuesday and boldly go where no St. John had gone before— into the culinary root cellar that is the underbelly of the pig...chitlins!

Chitlins night at Rayner's is busy.

I ordered an all-you-can-eat plate of fried chitlins and a glass of sweet tea. Sensing that I was a virgin chitlin eater, Kim Rayner asked if I wanted them "fried crispy." Sensing Kim was a veteran chitlin server, I replied, "Most definitely yes." I also ordered a small sampling of boiled chitlins (just to see what they looked like) and an order of fried shrimp (every good businessman has a contingency plan).

In short order, Kim Rayner delivered my plate of chitlins. "How do you eat them?" I asked. "Oh, I don't eat them. But you'll be fine, just use a lot of hot sauce." I should have known right then that something smelled fishy. Well, not actually fishy.

Sitting there on the plate, chitlins looked like any number of fried foods. But there was a smell. I can't quite identify the smell, but I can report that I have never smelled anything quite like it. It is a distinct smell, make that a distinct funk.

The funk drifted up from the plate, surrounded my face and dug into my nostrils, where it kidnapped each individual pore of both sinus passages for the next twelve hours. I went home and changed clothes, still smelled it. I washed my face, still there. I jumped in the shower—lathered, rinsed, and repeated—still there. I had to snort two bottles of Neo-Synephrine to deliver me from that chitlinized trip to nasal hell.

Gathering up all of the epicurean courage I could muster, I took a bite. Actually, I only ate a small piece off of one individual chitlin (singular: chitli)

Friends and neighbors, chitlins don't taste anything like calamari. I used hot sauce and ketchup on my chitli and it still didn't taste good. To me, chitlins taste like they smell. Hot sauce doesn't help.

I glanced over to the bowl of boiled chitlins. I don't know what I was expecting boiled chitlins to look like, maybe Faith Hill's legs or the seat of Jennifer Lopez's jeans. No such luck. Boiled chitlins look like...well, like...boiled intestines! I resorted to the backup plan and ate my fried shrimp.

I am sure Mickey Rayner cooks world-class chitlins. The restaurant was crowded, so, as chitlins go, I am sure his are outstanding. I found out from his wife, Kim, that Mickey is not a chitlin eater, either (every good businessman gives the people what they want).

There were a couple of sweet little ladies seated at a table near me. Each of them had finished off a large plate of chitlins. One lady told me to take the chitlins home and "reheat them for two minutes in the microwave." Thanks, I'll pass.

Then the night began to turn ugly. Other customers began chiming in. One lady said she cooked them in "celery, onions, lemons, salt, pepper, and carrots." "Doesn't that smell bad?" I asked. "I boil them outside, baby." Yes, but doesn't that smell bad outside?

"When it's hot, you don't cook them. Fresh pork makes your blood pressure go up." Frozen pork makes your blood pressure go up too, lady.

Another nearby customer said, "There are as many ways to cook chitlins as there are cooks that cook chitlins." Yes, sir. There are also as many ways to torture small animals as there are small animals, but you don't see me doing it.

Banks boils chitlins in crab boil. When I complained to him about how my chitli tasted, he said, "Mine taste like crab boil." "Why not just eat crabs or shrimp?" I asked. He looked puzzled for a minute and then said, "I don't know."

I am not a food snob. But, if it means I will be labeled a food snob if I never eat chitlins again, then I will proudly wear that moniker like a gastronomic badge of honor.

Before this chitlin research project I was asking myself how I could have lived in the Piney Woods of South Mississippi for forty-one years and not eaten chitlins. Now I know. Maybe I will let forty-one more years pass and try them again. The year will be 2044 and I will visit the next generation of Rayner's, and eat more than one chitli. Then again, maybe I'll just have my usual, catfish and shrimp. An eighty-two-year-old heart can't take that much stress.

THE TURKEY HUNT

Philip Shirley

JACK

Henry Jackson Gaines Jr., who chose to go by Jack, like his father before him, stepped down from the chrome running board of his Ford F-350 onto dew-soaked grass and looked up. "Damn, I miss seeing the stars," he said. "Stay in the city too long and you forget how many stars there really are." His fraternal twin brother, Charles Johnston Gaines, dubbed CJ by the family before he could even walk, had downed three cups of black coffee during the fifty-minute drive from the city and now stood on the passenger side of the truck peeing. CJ didn't look up. "Seen one night sky, you've seen 'em all," he said.

Jack stared over the truck bed at CJ, unsure what to say to his younger brother. A middle-of-the-night birth had given the twins different birthdays, and Jack had gotten lots of miles out of being the older brother. But that was when they were growing up, and now Jack saw that six years as a Ranger and two tours in Afghanistan had transformed his pudgy, timid brother into a lean, hard man, a quiet confidence reflected in his eyes. In the few weeks since CJ arrived back home, Jack had found that his brother's demeanor was nothing like the shaky twenty-two-year-old who'd boarded a bus to join the army that bright June morning years before. The easy smile he'd left home with had been lost somewhere in the cold Afghan mountains above Khyber Pass on the Pakistan border, doing what he'd described, when asked by their father, only as "Special Ops."

Jack said nothing more about the stars.

CJ zipped up his army camo pants and turned to open the half door to the truck cab. "You hear any birds yet?"

"Nah, but I think we're on time. Let's get on down this hollow before light starts breaking." Jack tilted his coffee cup back for a last swallow, shook a few drops on the ground, and tossed the cup onto the truck seat.

Jack began pulling hunting equipment from the backseat, checking off items from his mental list: owl call, mouth call, box call, extra chalk, shells, water bottle, Snickers bar, face mask, gloves, knife, flashlight. He reached into the truck and grabbed a camo thermos, and dropped it into a camo backpack.

Jack glanced sideways as CJ slid an age-worn, but immaculately kept, Parker A-1 side-by-side shotgun from its case and ran his fingers slowly down the smooth twin barrels, then leaned the expensive weapon against the mud-caked rear truck tire. Jack wondered what his father would say. The borrowed weapon was their father's favorite shotgun, with a field scene hand engraved into the metal receiver and a fleur-de-lis carving in the wood stock. Their father had never let Jack hunt with one of his prized guns. As he watched his brother, something in the way CJ touched the shotgun seemed unnatural, too much like a caress.

Jack arranged the items in his pack, enjoying the preparation and anticipation of the hunt almost as much as the hunt itself. His routine had been largely unchanged in the fifteen years since he and CJ had first turkey hunted together when they were barely teens. He thought back to the days they'd taken to the woods on clear summer mornings with BB guns in hand, their Boy Scout packs stuffed with bottles of water, a knife or two, kitchen matches, extra BBs. Jack smiled into the morning darkness, remembering how CJ had once sneaked two foil-wrapped potatoes from their mom, later roasting them in the coals of a twig fire, deep in the woods behind the golf course.

Jack picked up a can of Deep Woods Off and sprayed heavily around his ankles and at his waistline to fend off the chiggers that were so bad every spring. He could taste the foul chemicals in the air. "You ready?" he asked after clearing his throat, his tone easy, almost a whisper, as he handed the spray to CJ.

"If you're waitin' on me you're backing up," CJ said.

Jack pulled back the breech on his Browning 3-inch Magnum 12-gauge autoloader and slid a load of number sixes into the magazine.

CJ

CJ used his callused thumb to shove a reloaded 2-inch shell into his 12-gauge. The night before, he'd used his father's equipment to reload the shell with number-two shot, along with enough powder to create a high-velocity, lethal load. The larger shot meant fewer pellets, but he preferred the extra knockdown power over a few extra pellets that poorer shooters needed.

After dropping shells into both barrels, CJ slammed shut the breech. He smiled, hearing the solid click of the tightly engineered metal on metal. He nodded to himself as he weighed the heft and balance of the gun in his left hand. His Special Operations training as a sniper for the 75th Ranger Regiment had taught him to make a weapon so familiar it became an extension of his own arm. If needed, he could take apart the shotgun in the dark amid a driving rain and put the weapon back together in seconds.

A breeze on his neck made CJ shiver as he started briskly down a path in front of the truck, not bothering to use a flashlight. After nine months in Bosnia and two years in Afghanistan, he'd learned to walk sure-footed without a flashlight, to avoid the enemy snipers who would creep through the rocks around U.S. encampments looking for a careless soldier.

Walking in darkness under the full moon took him back to his last week in Afghanistan and the shock of coming face to face with someone walking toward him. At a distance of only inches, the moonlight revealed the scraggly beard and look of astonishment in the dark eyes of the young warrior with a sniper rifle over his shoulder. CJ reacted without thinking and thrust his long knife upward under the man's rib cage, ripping the blade forward to sever the heart like he'd practiced so many times with a straw man during his training. It was him or me, CJ told himself again, but the face hovered there in the faint mist of memory, refusing to fade in the month since the incident. The kill was his ninth confirmed, but all the others were at distances of at least two hundred yards. With the others there'd been no gurgling sounds of lungs struggling for air, no rush of hot body fluids over his wrist, nor the coppery smell of fresh human blood.

"With this full moon the gobblers will be up early," CJ said, picking up his pace a little. The bright moon just above the tree line took him back to the hours he'd spent talking to the man in the moon, leaning motionless against a large boulder at the edge of his most recent mountain camp in Afghanistan, practicing what to say when he saw Donna again. Until his return he'd not spoken to her since her wedding to Jack, the day before he boarded the bus to report for basic training.

Walking through the knee-high grass and weeds, CJ thought for a moment about the old pair of snake chaps lying in the back of the truck, but remembered how weighty and cumbersome they felt. He heard Jack's pant legs swishing through the grass a few steps behind. Five minutes later CJ stopped. The heavy breathing behind him as he reached the top of a hill told him Jack was out of shape. CJ smiled to himself, but said nothing. He thought back to their days in high school when Jack, two inches taller and three steps faster, had been the star quarterback in football with the perfect physique. While CJ mostly sat on the bench as a defensive guard, Jack was starring on the field and winning a scholarship to Auburn. CJ remembered how proud their father'd been when they all gathered around the dining room table as Jack sat with Coach Pat Dye to sign a scholarship commitment. Now CJ was the one with the six-pack abs, arms bulging beneath his shirt and legs as strong as fence posts, while Jack had added a few pounds to his middle and a slight double chin while sitting behind his bank desk all day in suburban Irondale on the edge of the city.

CJ looked down on two big draws drained by sparkling, shallow creeks that merged below the point of the hill. He squatted and breathed slowly through his nose. He scanned the opposite hillside with sniper-trained eyes that would catch the movement of a single leaf. In the still, quiet morning he heard the sigh of water trickling over dead branches in the creek.

Jack walked up beside him, leaned over with his hands on his knees and gulped for air. The sky lightened as pink and orange streaks rose in soft-edged layers behind a black silhouette of trees scrawled above the horizon.

CJ reached into the front pocket of his Mossy Oak camo vest and slid out an owl call. He put the string around his neck and placed the wooden call to his lips. He blew hard into the call four times, followed by five more calls, repeating in his mind the mantra, "Who cooks for you, who cooks for you all" that helped him imitate the barn owl so hated by turkeys on the roost.

CJ sat in silence for ten minutes as Jack's breathing returned to normal. He listened to the world waking up around them. The familiar bird songs of morning were a stark contrast to the silent arrival of dawn in the desert after all night on his belly, anxious for the sun to rise behind him as he hid near an enemy encampment to watch for his target, usually the leader of a rebel group or a small al Qaeida cell. He blew the call again.

Several hundred yards east, an owl answered, "Who cooks for you?" Almost immediately two others responded, followed by a faint but distinct gobble. Before the first gobble was finished, a second bird thundered down an answer to let everyone in the woods know that he was the Boss Gobbler.

Curling his eyebrows into a question mark, CJ looked at Jack. Jack pointed toward the gobbler's roost. CJ had hunted with Jack enough that a nod, a tilt of the head or a shrug was adequate. The silence between them might last for an hour as they plodded through the woods. But the hush today seemed different, deeper, and CJ wondered if his brother had his own demons to argue with as the turkey hunt drew them farther down an unfamiliar road.

CJ nodded agreement at the bird's location, rose to his feet, and started off at a trot. The two men half-walked, half-ran down the hill, jumping the three-foot-wide creek at the bottom and following separate paths up the other side of the gully. Limbs of young sweet gums still wet from the humid night air slapped their cheeks. They stopped some two hundred yards from their original spot and listened.

Nothing. Two minutes passed. Still nothing.

The sweet fragrance of early spring wildflowers hung thick in the air, and CJ thought of Donna's perfume, the way it had surrounded him like fog as she hugged him when he got off the plane. He'd tried to prepare himself, but he found few words when he saw her standing there between his father and Jack, holding Jack's hand. When CJ hugged her, the feel of the firm muscles along her spine and the tuck of her waist were painfully familiar. CJ still couldn't understand how Donna had so casually dropped him for his fucking brother. A flock of blackbirds swirled into the trees above CJ, lighted for a moment, then flew as one into the sunlight, sounding like rustling paper and disappearing as suddenly as they had come.

CJ watched Jack hold up his owl call and look at him with a shrug. CJ nodded. Jack started the familiar "who cooks for you" owl-calling routine, and before he finished, the big turkey answered with a triple gobble.

CJ picked up his father's shotgun and eased quietly up the ridge to peek over the hill. The sky was filling with yellow light and the woods around him were now fully awake. His pants from the knees down were soaked through from the moisture on the weeds, and tiny black seeds from wild grasses stuck to his army boots. A squirrel darted in front of him and clutched the side of a tree twenty yards ahead to stare at the intruder, barking his alarm.

The air rumbled as the turkey gobbled again. Although the thick hardwood forest made distances hard to judge, CJ knew the bird was close now. It's almost time, he thought. CJ moved forward another forty yards. He stopped to listen and leaned the gun against a tree as he squatted to scan ahead with his binoculars.

"CJ, don't you think we're close enough?" Jack asked, walking up behind CJ, his chest heaving again. Jack had his mouth open, sucking in as much air as he could without making noise. CJ enjoyed the workout his brother was getting. "All right, let's set up here. Take that tree up there," CJ said quietly, pointing. "That red oak will hide your outline. I'll set up behind you and call."

Like his brother, CJ sat against a large tree to hide his silhouette, gun propped across his knees pointing in the direction of the turkey to minimize any movement needed to get off a shot. He would be facing the sun, which went against his training, but there was too much risk in trying to circle around the bird now.

CJ slid his box call out of his pocket, found a small piece of chalk, and rubbed it over the smooth surface of the wooden striker attached to the box at one corner with a long screw. He moved the thin piece of wood gently across the walls of the box to imitate the soft cluck-cluck-cluck sounds of a hen in a tree.

In response, three gobbles shook the ground, all from the same turkey. CJ waited two minutes and repeated his soft hen calls. Two more gobbles. He placed the call beside his leg. Now the hunt became a waiting game.

CJ sighted down the barrel of the shotgun resting on his knee, toward the side of his brother's head leaning against the big oak. "Bang," CJ said, his finger lightly on the trigger.

Five minutes later the gobbler let them know it was still interested in the hens, rattling the woods with its gobbles.

CJ watched as Jack turned his head to look back over his shoulder. He knew Jack might be able to see him smiling through the thin camo face net, but Jack would never guess why.

JACK

Being this close to a hot turkey, Jack's heart did a double-time march in rhythm with his breathing. When the time came, he thought, he'd be the one quickest with a shot, just like the old days. Sweat ran into his ears, but he dared not move. Any minute he would hear the turkey drumming the ground to signal the hen he was hers, and soon the big bird would walk over the hill for its last time. Jack had a vision of a twelve-inch beard; he had a vision of maybe even a double beard, and spurs two inches long. Jack had a vision that he would be the one showing his prize plump gobbler and trophy beard to his father and Donna.

After another half hour, he fought the urge to stretch. He felt his leg and back muscles tighten from sitting absolutely still and wondered if CJ, with his military conditioning, felt the same way. He'd noticed how much easier the walk had been for CJ that morning, and Jack resolved he'd soon get back in shape. He'd been meaning to get back on the weight machine anyway. Jack closed his eyes, wondering how his life could change so much in just the few days since his brother had been home. His dad seemed obsessed with CJ's opinion about this military strategy in Fallujah or that offensive on the northern front. And did CJ think Bush would strike Iran or Syria next to root out terror around the world? Donna talked about CJ's handsome good looks, about how he'd come back very different. When his wife mentioned his brother's cute butt, Jack had shouted at her for the first time. At some point in the screaming match that followed Donna blurted out that she and CJ had been more than friends while Jack was away at college. Jack stopped yelling and just stood there quietly as the words sunk in.

A breeze swept the leaves around Jack's feet as he opened his eyes to scan the woods for movement. Jack knew that a silent gobbler was often moving closer. The tom could be strutting just over the hill, its feathers puffed up and wings dusting the ground, or watching from behind a bush down the draw in search of the lonesome hens he and CJ were imitating with their calls. He decided not to risk the hand movement required to operate the box call. Slowly, shifting his hand to his mouth, he put a diaphragm call between his teeth and sat there soaking the plastic. He tried a series of four soft yelps. His patience was rewarded when the gobbler answered. The bird was no closer, but hadn't moved away either.

After another fifteen minutes, Jack knew the gobbler wasn't coming in. Sometimes a gobbler simply wouldn't cross a creek, or go down a hill, to reach a hen. The bird would sit there for hours gobbling, but come no closer. He placed his calls in his shirt pocket and crawled slowly back to CJ.

"He's hung up," Jack whispered.

"If you're that impatient, Junior, we can ease up here and see what's over this hill."

Jack took a deep breath, but said nothing.

Jack crouched beside CJ and made his way up the hill, pushing branches aside and stepping over dried sticks to avoid giving away their location. As Jack surveyed the woods ahead, the gobbler offered a single gobble. The bird sounded just beyond the next hill.

Jack crept down an embankment, waded a stream, and started up the other side. CJ was five feet to his left. On hands and knees the two made their way through underbrush and briars, aiming for an opening just below the crest of the hill. A stand of tall, straight poplar and thick-limbed shagbark hickory trees created a canopy that had killed most of the undergrowth.

Before they reached the opening in the woods, Jack's shirt had soaked through in the humidity. He said nothing and moved as quietly as possible, knowing they were close and fearing the turkey would spot them if they made a sound. He was determined not to be the one to screw up. He pictured the family seated around the large formal dining table Donna would have prepared, him at the end near the window, Donna to his right where she always sat. Who saw the turkey first? Who called best? CJ's voice brought him back to the moment.

"Why don't you set up in front?" CJ said. "I'll be back here to the side." Jack stared for a moment without replying, then went and stood with his back to a wide white oak tree.

CJ

CJ held his hand beside his mouth to muffle the sound and made four short hen clucks on the mouth call. From just over the hill CJ heard a desperate series of gobbles. He felt his pulse speed up as he held his shotgun to his shoulder, cheek pushed hard into the stock at ready. This is it, he thought, as he watched the woods beyond his brother's outline.

CJ thought his calling sounded just right, even though he'd been away from hunting—at least hunting game—for years. Despite all the ways a turkey could make a hunter doubt his skills, this time CJ knew he'd succeed. He heard a sound and caught movement in the leaves just to his left side. He felt his breath catch in his throat as he saw the thick snake only two feet away, slithering side-to-side toward his outstretched legs, its probing tongue flicking at his boots.

For a moment he'd hoped the creature was a gray rat snake, but when his movement caused the snake to raise its head and open its mouth he saw the vertical slits of the eyes. The cream and black lines on the wide pointed head and the diamond designs along its broad back confirmed his fear. He didn't need to see or hear the rattles that had begun clicking their warning. The eastern diamondback rattler showed him its inch-long fangs. CJ carefully moved his shotgun barrel toward the snake. The snake lunged and struck the cold steel. CJ pressed down with the barrel and pinned the snake's head on the ground. He reached over and gripped just behind its head. The snake wriggled furiously in his hand. Its glistening mouth was open and its dripping fangs were extended, but CJ only gripped tighter as he slid his Ranger knife from his boot with his left hand and severed the head in one stroke, kicking the still gasping mouth away from where he sat. The snake continued to twist in his hand. He tossed the squirming body behind him and wiped the dark blood off the back of his hand onto his pants leg. He looked up; Jack had witnessed nothing.

CJ raised the shotgun and clucked a single time on his mouth call, and again the turkey cut loose with a string of gobbles. As the minutes passed, CJ had to raise his knees to hold the heavy gun, but he dared not lower the barrel and risk missing the shot. He slowly swung his aim left until he could see Jack's head behind the tiny bead sight. Bang, he mouthed again.

Twenty minutes later, CJ lowered his shotgun, puzzled, after he saw Jack do the same. Had they misjudged the distance? What had made this gobbler hang up so badly? Ten minutes more, he told himself. You've waited six years. Be patient.

JACK

Jack had been listening for the turkey, but he couldn't get last night out of his mind. Donna had rolled over and pressed her breasts into his back, and slid her hand between his legs. He'd first willed himself to respond, but after a moment pushed her hand away. "I'm too tired," he said weakly, realizing as he was saying the words that he even lacked the resolve to fake being tired. He kept thinking of her with CJ. She'd gotten mad after he pushed her hand away. He had lain there not sleeping, staring up at the faint image of the slowly turning ceiling fan. The images he stirred up kept circling through his mind.

Finally Jack's patience evaporated like the sweat on his arms. He looked at his watch. Ten forty-five. They'd been chasing this turkey for four hours. Enough is enough. He lowered himself onto his stomach and began slowly, painstakingly crawling forward. Minutes passed.

He inched forward. The turkey kept gobbling.

Jack kept crabbing ahead. He neared the high point of the hill, taking ten minutes to cover just twenty-five yards. As he raised his head to peer over the hill, he heard the gobble that was now all too familiar as his eyes found the beautiful bird in full strut, chest puffed up, and dusting the ground with outstretched wings.

The bird was every bit the majestic tom that would be the center of the family's attention around the dinner table that night.

But this was one turkey Jack wouldn't be shooting. He closed his eyes for a few seconds in disbelief, then rolled onto his back. This is the perfect ending to a perfectly ridiculous day. At first he chuckled, his hand over his mouth, but soon enough an eruption of rousing laughter echoed through the woods.

CJ

CJ was baffled by Jack's laughter, and pissed. He propped his shotgun on his knee, looking over the barrel in the direction of Jack who was out of sight on his belly. Just stand up, Junior. Accidents happen all the time.

He removed his camo mask. As he stood, he reached back for the snake and gripped the thick middle, feeling it squirm as if still alive. Walking toward Jack, he spotted the huge gobbler strutting thirty-five yards ahead, a trophy beard dragging the ground, with Jack directly between them. The gobbler's head showed a brilliant red in the morning sunlight.

CJ jerked up the Parker with one hand, watching Jack's eyes grow wide and his entire body become rigid as he looked into the dark open ends of the barrels pointed his direction. CJ saw Jack's eyes lock onto his, held there by some invisible chain. He saw the look of fright pass over Jack as if the sun had shifted its orbit, creating a shadow that moved across Jack's face like a veil.

Neither man moved or blinked, as time seemed to stop for that instant. Jack's eyes narrowed and the wrinkles in his forehead relaxed. CJ saw Jack nod and his tightly pressed lips soften into a smile. CJ squeezed off quick shots using both barrels. Jack slumped face down into the leaves and dirt, and was still.

Within seconds the woods grew calm as the echo of shots faded. The breeze ceased. Small birds hopped nervously from limb to limb. Shafts of sunlight pierced the dense trees, illuminating specks of dust drifting to the forest floor. At the base of the hill, a bloody turkey quivered and kicked its death dance inside a chicken-wire pen behind a light blue mobile home in a well-kept yard carved into the edge of the lush, green forest bordered by a red clay road.

CJ tossed the snake inches in front of his brother's head, turned his back on the scene and started to the truck.

Hearing leaves rustle, CJ looked back as Jack raised himself on both arms, his cheeks glowing crimson and jaw clenched tight. The veins in his neck bulged. Mildewed leaves stuck to his quivering chin.

"Let's go, brother," CJ said over his shoulder "I guess I've got my limit." He walked quickly to keep ahead of Jack, allowing the breeze to dry the moisture gathering in his eyes.

Down There on a Visit

Charles Simic

For years now I've been looking at a photograph Walker Evans took
in the summer of 1936 in the South. I thought of it again while getting ready to travel to the South a few weeks ago. At the intersection
of two dusty, unpaved roads stands a dilapidated building with a small
porch and a single gas pump. There's no human being in sight. The
intense heat and the bright sunlight must have made the locals, a few
of whom can be seen standing on the very same porch on another oc-
casion, seek shade. The shutters of the two upstairs windows are
closed except for small openings where the slats are broken or have
been removed. The postmaster and his wife, who run the pump and
the store, are most likely napping, their heads covered with newspapers to protect them against the flies.

Downstairs, in the small side room with a scale and rows of bins
for the mail, there are a few letters whose recipients live too far or receive mail too rarely to bother making the trip. With so little to see
and so much to imagine, a photograph like this is an invitation to
endless conjecture. There's nothing more ordinary, nothing more
American than what it depicts: a small town one passes with barely a
glance on the way to someplace else.

This June, driving around Mississippi, Alabama, and Georgia, I
decided to pay a visit to Sprott and Hale County, where Walker Evans
and James Agee collaborated on *Let Us Now Praise Famous Men*, their
photographic and verbal record of the lives of three dirt-poor tenant
farmer families in the region.

I wanted to, as it were, poke around the photograph on my wall.
I drove from Mobile past a series of tiny little towns with names like
Sunflower, Wagarville, Sunny South, Catherine, and Marion. It was
early Sunday morning, so my daughter and I were a bit dressed up,
hoping to find a church along the way and attend a service. We saw
plenty of houses of worship, but oddly, not much activity around them

yet. Driving through one of the bigger towns, we were surprised to find a huge Wal-Mart open at 9:20 with dozens of cars parked outside.

The other puzzle was a number of abandoned churches both in towns and in the countryside. I recall a small, unobtrusive, white wooden church sunk in the earth, the grass and weeds grown tall around it. It had a thick, squat steeple, a single door, two windows on each side covered up with boards. The sky over it was cloudless, the quiet so deep we could hear the crows flap their wings as they flew over our heads in alarm. The people who came to pray there must have died or moved away years ago, but the spirit they sought after lingered on. I wondered if there was anything left inside the church, a hard bench, a hymnal, a suspended oil lamp, a skeleton of a dead bird.

The landscape of central Alabama alternates between patches of woods and rolling fields of cultivated land that open onto long vistas before closing up again. We found the crossroads Evans photographed and a small shut-down country store where the old one most probably stood. It did not appear that much had changed in sixty-eight years. There was a large sign announcing a rodeo in nearby Marion, two half-collapsed barns across the road, and a cat that came out of the bushes hungry and lonely, but ran away every time my daughter tried to make friends with it. The population of Sprott today is reputed to be 10 people and that sounds about right. Hale County has 17,185 inhabitants, and the county seat, Greensboro, only 2,731. I have no idea how many people lived there in the 1930s, when the cotton plantations were in full operation, but there must have been more. The impression one gets is that there's not much work to be had on the farms that remain. Most of these are large and require a small number of people to work the machinery. Whoever can pick up and leave the county does so, or if they decide to stay, they commute great distances to their jobs. On weekdays, the traffic to Tuscaloosa, Birmingham, and Montgomery tends to be heavy. Most of these commuters are heading to low-paying retail and service jobs in numerous shopping malls at the outskirts of these cities.

We headed south to Selma. What we found there surprised us. Its spacious downtown, where some 30,000 people once gathered with Martin Luther King to make a march to Montgomery, is badly run-down. It's a shell of the town it once was. Many of its beautiful turn-of-the-century buildings and storefronts appear in part vacated while others are completely closed. This I found almost everywhere to be the case. The heart of Montgomery has broad avenues, a restored Greek Revival state capitol atop a hill where Jefferson Davis took the oath of office on February 18, 1861, as the president of the Confederate States, and the famous civil rights landmarks, like the Baptist church where the bus boycott was organized in 1956, but there are few people there even on a Monday morning.

The capital of Mississippi, Jackson, is deserted on Friday afternoon. No one walks its streets. There are no restaurants or bars and no hint of where people who work in its many offices get fed. Old photographs of all these places show streets teeming with pedestrians, stores big and small, signs and marquees advertising cafés, drugstores, tobacco shops, and five-and-dime emporiums. The centers of many of the most interesting Southern cities, the neighborhoods that make them most distinct and attractive, have been forsaken for fast-food places, gas stations, and shopping centers at the outskirts, which resemble any other place in the United States.

The middle classes and the rich reside in well-maintained old and new suburbs and vote Republican, while their impoverished neighbors, who tend to be mostly African-American and who outnumber them in many counties, live in rural slums. While there's no official segregation between the races, there is a caste system with clear class distinctions and accompanying inequality that is apparent wherever one goes. There are towns like Jonestown, Mississippi, that in their shocking poverty make one gasp. Weathered, sagging, and unpainted houses, boarded-up windows, others covered with plastic, yards full of dismantled rusty cars, their parts scattered about amid all kinds of other junk and trash, are everywhere. Idle people of all ages lounge on collapsing porches or stand on street corners waiting for something to do. In the countryside with its fertile dark soil, soybeans have become the chief crop, poultry farms are a major business, and there are nine gambling casinos in the next county. All that has increased per capita income in the region, but there was no evidence of it among the blacks I saw.

In Clarksdale, the former capital of the cotton kingdom, which President Clinton visited during his 1999 tour focusing on the nation's poorest communities, I saw in a parking lot of a closed supermarket two ancient cars parked side by side with their four doors wide open. Over their hoods, roofs, and doors, spread out and draped, someone's once-pretty dresses and worn children's clothes were covering every available space. Two black women sat on low stools, one on each side, waiting for a customer. This is the town, they say, where the blues began. One of its legends, Robert Johnson, was reputed to have sold his soul to the devil at a crossroads nearby. There's a blues museum in town and an excellent restaurant and juke joint called Ground Zero owned in part by the actor Morgan Freeman, a part-time local resident. The downtown buildings of what was once clearly a flourishing city reminded me of towns in the Midwest and New England after their industries went broke in the late 1960s and their factories were shut down. Clarksdale has the despoiled look of a conquered and sacked city. Ranking conditions of poverty is a risky business, but what I encountered in Mississippi surpasses anything I've seen in a long time in this country. That the people here vote Democratic and have a liberal black Democratic congressman has not been of visible help to them.

When one enters the small store that also serves as a post office in nearby Belen, one first comes upon shelves cluttered with ancient TV parts. On one side, in the half-dark, an old black man sits poking his screwdriver into the back of a black-and-white set that must be at least forty years old. Beyond the TV repair section, there's a grocery store selling a few absolute necessities like canned beans and white bread, and finally in the back, the post office itself with its single oval and barred window where one can purchase a stamp. The old white storekeeper who shows me and my friend around could have walked out of one of Eudora Welty's Depression-era photographs. He is so pale; he probably rarely leaves the premises. In the meantime, he is happy to chat. It's not a cliché that people are courteous in the South. Many of them tell memorable stories, love words, and can make something unexpected out of the simplest verbal ingredients. No wonder so many great writers have come from Mississippi.

My first acquaintance with the South was in 1961, when I spent four months at Fort Gordon, Georgia, being trained by the U.S. Army to be a military policeman. On my weekly passes, I went into Augusta, where there was little to do beyond getting drunk in dives frequented by soldiers. With the news of men and women who protested segregation being beaten and occasionally murdered all over the South, it was not the most comfortable place for a Northerner to be. Without even trying, one inevitably got into arguments with the locals. The place seethed with hatred, I thought then. All that changed, of course, over the years, and so did my own understanding of the complexities. There were plenty of racists, to be sure, but there were also people of conscience who did their best to alleviate the wrongs in their midst.

Fifty miles from Jonestown, Mississippi, is William Faulkner's Oxford. It has a pretty courthouse square, a bookstore that could match any in New York City or Boston, fine cafés and restaurants, most of which have second-story porches with tables and chairs overlooking the square. People laze there for hours sipping a drink and gabbing. One could live here—one thinks—in a kind of timeless present. Bank, church, a few elegant stores, a barbershop, and a hotel—what more does one need? In the afternoons, when the shadows lengthen and the heat subsides a bit, one has the overwhelming sense of well-being as if everything were just dandy everywhere and one really had no cause to make oneself a nuisance to strangers with whom one happened to strike a casual conversation.

Unfortunately, the local newspapers brought me out of my reverie. The *Clarksdale Press Register*, which I'd bought earlier that day, had the following letter:

Dear Editor:

I am a Jesus freak.

Jesus said that you can't serve two fathers. Either you serve God the Heavenly Father or you are damned and serve Satan. All true conservatives will be against homosexuality. It's not acceptable in God's house. I believe they can be saved and change this lifestyle. Anyone that says it is OK to kill babies is damned. God made human life in His own likeness. We as Christians expect Americans to be against us. They were against Jesus. God has blessed us, but for how long? For America's weakness is turning its back on God. We better not think that God won't put his wrath on America soon. America better thank God for Christians who are praying for this country. The rest of the people are not getting what they can get in riches. May God heal the churches and people. It's time Christians take a stand in voices and elections. Get these liberals out of government, and get conservative Christian leadership in government.[1]

During my trip, I was asked several times point-blank whether I was a Christian. The first time it happened, I was so surprised I didn't know what to reply. Finally, I mumbled that I was brought up in the Eastern Orthodox Church and to further buttress my credentials, I mentioned that I had priests in my family going back a couple of centuries. As far as I could tell, that didn't seem to make much impression. What people were eager to find out was whether I had accepted Jesus as my Savior. For the writer of this letter, and for others I met, Christians are to be distinguished from the rest of Americans, who are something else—liberals, secular humanists, Catholics, atheists, abortionists, etc. They all share one thing in common, however: they are all going to hell.

The absolute certainty of that outcome, I found, is a source of deep satisfaction to the believers. They enjoy hearing about the torments that await the damned. That must be the explanation for the great success of *Glorious Appearing* by Tim LaHaye and Jerry B. Jenkins, the twelfth and final book in a series that recounts the story of those left behind when the Apocalypse arrives and the Rapture gathers the elect into heaven. The first eleven novels have sold forty million copies and the new one is also a best-seller.[2] The blood and gore of the final battle of the ages between Jesus and the legions of the Antichrist are described at great length and in loving detail:

"Tens of thousands of foot soldiers dropped their weapons, grabbed their heads or their chests, fell to their knees, and writhed as they were invisibly sliced asunder. Their innards and entrails gushed to the desert floor, and as those around them turned to run, they too were slain, their blood pooling and rising in the unforgiving bright-ness of the glory of Christ.

"For My sword shall be bathed in heaven; indeed it shall come down on Edom, and on the people of My curse, for judgment.

"The sword of the Lord is filled with blood. It is made overflowing with fatness. For the Lord has a sacrifice in Bozrah, and a great slaughter in the land of Edom.

"Their land shall be soaked with blood, and their dust saturated with fatness."[3]

It was reported that President Bush tried to enlist the Vatican for help in his reelection when he paid a visit to the pope last month. He has no need to make a similar appeal to the churches in the South. During the many hours of listening to Christian radio, I was assured again and again that the Bible is the best source of information on contemporary events and the only guide anybody needs on how to vote. When I watched religious talk shows on TV at night, I heard that the many wars that the president has promised us have happily been foretold in the Bible. "Let us restore to God the thunder," the poet John Crowe Ransom wrote in 1930,[4] and the people who called in would have readily agreed. Peace on earth went unmentioned. What excited the people I heard was the force of deadly weapons. I got the impression that it was a greater offense to believe in evolution than to bomb a city into rubble. As a letter to the Mobile Register signed "Addison DeBoi" put it:

"What the left has not come to realize is that most of today's suffering is the result of the left's continued efforts to remove horror and pain from war....The point is, war is hell, and it should be. The more respectable we make war, the more we make it less horrific, the more we seek to not harm civilians, then the greater the risk and frequency of war."[5]

Skepticism, empirical evidence, and book learning are in low esteem among the Protestant evangelicals. To ask about the laws of cause and effect would be a sin. They reject modern science and dream of a theocratic state where such blasphemous subject matter would be left out from the school curriculum. Their ideal, as a shrewd young fellow told me in Tuscaloosa, is unquestioning obedience and complete conformity in matters of religion and politics. The complaint about so-called secular humanism is that it permits teachers and students too much freedom of thought and opinion. If evangelicals haven't gone around smashing TV sets and computers, it is because they recognize their power to spread their message. Aside from that, they would like to secede intellectually from the rest of the world.

As if to alert me of the danger of such sweeping statements, I stumbled on a magnificent exhibition of Baroque art at the Mississippi Arts Pavilion in Jackson. It came from the State Arts Collections in Dresden and included porcelain, costumes, sculpture, armor, and paintings by Rembrandt, Rubens, Titian, Mantegna, Velázquez, Van Dyck, Lucas Cranach, Vermeer, and a few other Old Masters. It was fairly well attended. There were even families with kids. I've no idea what they thought of the sensual teenage Madonna holding a mischievous-looking two-year-old. The museum guides and attendants appeared to be volunteers. They stood at various points of the huge exhibition and kept asking each visitor if he or she was enjoying the show and were exceedingly pleased to hear that we did. It sounded as if there had been complaints and that they needed confirmation that they were, indeed, taking part in something worthy.

At the Mississippi Museum of Art there was another imported show—"Paris Moderne," art deco works from the 1920s and 1930s. Almost next door, Confederate flags were flying over the state buildings, often in close proximity to landmarks commemorating the civil rights struggle. A few well-known participants in the most gruesome events of its bloody history are still alive in nearby towns and remain unconvicted, as columns in newspapers on the anniversary of their crimes reminded their readers.

On another cloudless day, I drove south toward Hattiesburg and Mobile. The roadside fruit stands were overflowing with baskets of ripe peaches, tomatoes, and watermelons. There was also something called "boiled peanuts," which I was wary to try. On the radio, the burning issue was the new policy just passed by the Mississippi legislature that will drop from Medicaid eligibility 65,000 of its neediest elderly citizens and chronically ill patients with severe disabilities, leaving them to rely solely on the federally funded Medicare for their drugs. The governor, Haley Barbour, the brains behind the rollback, is the former chairman of the national Republican Party. In his view, taxpayers ought not to have to pay for free health care for people who can work and take care of themselves and just choose not to.

Most callers to the show sounded scared. The host of the program maintained that their fears were exaggerated, that Medicare would help out; but they were not buying it. They griped about the difficulties they already had signing up for the federal government's new prescription drug discount cards. The host of the show blamed the fiscal crises in the state on a teachers' pay raise and so did some of the other callers. He was willing to admit that there might be some inconvenience to the elderly, but he wanted them to realize that in the end nothing could be done. What came through were the inability and the reluctance of more than a few people to grasp the kind of hardship that faced their fellow citizens. The familiar Republican Party line—less government, no new taxes—eventually silenced the most stubborn of the complaining voices.

The lack of compassion for the less fortunate is also to be found in New Hampshire, where I live. Our politicians are as heartless as the ones in Mississippi and see themselves, despite their assurances otherwise, as being elected primarily to serve the well-to-do. Let the fittest survive is their attitude. However, they don't invoke God as they go about ensuring that the poor stay poor. As for the losers, both in the South and in the North, their outrage is not directed against the politicians. This is one of the great puzzles of recent American politics: voters who enthusiastically cast their vote against their self-interest, who care more about "family values," school prayer, guns, abortion, gay marriage, or the teaching of evolution than about having decent health care insurance and being paid a living wage. They squabble, as they did in Alabama recently, over whether the Ten Commandments ought to be posted in a courthouse while the education of their children continues to be underfunded and their overcrowded public schools are violent and dangerous places.

The result of these dogmatic inconsistencies of belief—which I found wherever I went—is fragmentation: "the growing social, physical, economic, and cultural separation of Americans from each other," as Sheldon Hackney points out in a fine collection of essays by thirteen different authors, *Where We Stand, Voices of the Southern Dissent*.[6] Even Pentecostals don't see eye to eye when it comes to theology. A town with no more than five hundred inhabitants has a dozen churches lining the highway. They stand barely fifty yards apart, all belonging to different schisms and factions. One of them is just a large trailer with a hand-painted name of the church tacked to its side. The door is open. Three old-model cars are parked in front.

A dozen miles down the highway is Mobile with its modern skyscrapers, and not too far beyond, the pretty little town of Fairhope on the eastern shore of the bay with its elegant boutiques, art galleries, and good restaurants. Fairhope was founded in 1884 as a model community inspired by a belief in land as common inheritance and as a cooperative commonwealth free from all forms of private monopoly and opportunities to prey upon one another. In his bittersweet reminiscence of growing up in Fairhope, included in *Where We Stand,* Paul M. Gaston, whose grandfather was one of the founders and guiding forces of the community, laments its transformation into what it is today, an upscale resort town where one of the shops for the well-heeled women is called Utopia without any irony. He writes of the morally benumbed citizenry unconcerned about disparities of wealth and the social apartheid such towns as Fairhope seem to serve.

It's easy to put all that out of one's mind as one cruises past the sandy beaches of Mobile Bay. The end of a long pier with a gazebo at Point Clear seems a good place for an afternoon siesta on a bench with the blue sky and sea birds for company. It's hot, but there's a breeze from the water. After a while, I hear the sound of chamber music. It's live, coming from the spacious lawn of the resort hotel next door where a wedding, it appears, is about to take place. There are some fifty chairs lined up in rows with a pulpit in front but no guests yet, only a string quartet playing Mozart. Eventually, as the guests begin to emerge from the hotel, I draw closer. They are a distinguished bunch, the men in tuxedos and the women in stylish, well-cut summer dresses. They come alone or in pairs strolling across the rich lawn to take their seats. With the quartet playing a lovely minuet, the four bridesmaids, all wearing dark red dresses, come out one by one, trailed by the groom and his parents. The bride, on the arm of her father, is the last to appear. She's a very pretty blond.

I'm too far away to hear the minister, but I can see them exchange rings. On a platform by the edge of the water, I see people setting up tables, decorating them with flowers for what I assume will be the wedding feast. It's all very proper, very charming, and very inviting. The servers are mostly black, and I realize that they are the first people of color I've seen since I drove into the Fairhope region. By now the wedding is over, the sun is setting over Mobile Bay, and the photographer is in a hurry to have the newlyweds pose against it. He wants them smooching and they oblige again and again, each kiss more lusty than the last one, to the joy of the younger members of the wedding party and the disapproving glances of the old. After that's over, they all file by me on the way to dinner, smiling and nodding in a most friendly way.

Yes, people told me on my trip, the American dream has been going wrong somewhere. I saw TV evangelists bring thousands of ecstatic believers to their feet. These programs were a mixture of old camp meetings, revivalist tents, rock concerts, and sales pitches on how to make millions in real estate "without spending a dime of your own money." The huge crowds were made up of well-dressed, middle-class people of all ages and races. Their piety was touching. Their eyes grew moist when Jesus was mentioned. God frets about them individually and they count on his guidance in practical matters. So many of the sermons I heard were about turning one's life around, overcoming financial worries, achieving worldly success. The men doing the preaching had made millions saving souls and had no qualms offering themselves as a model to emulate. Their lack of humility was astonishing. I'm flying high, the faces said, because God has time for me.

"There is going to be trouble in this country," a lawyer warned me. He wouldn't tell me from what direction. Like others I had met in the South, he kept a gun in his car; he had, he said, several more at home and worried that the government might take away his arsenal. What are they for? In one of his books, the Mississippi novelist and short story writer Barry Hannah suggests an answer:

"The gun lobby, oh my peaceful friends, you may hate, but first you had better understand that it is a religion, only secondarily connected to the Bill of Rights. The thick-headed, sometimes even close to tearful, gaze you get when chatting with one of its partisans emanates from the view that they're holding a piece of God. There is no persuading them otherwise, even by a genius, because a life without guns implies the end of the known world to them. Any connection they make to our 'pioneer past' is also a fraud, a wistful apology. Folks love a gun for what it can do. A murderer always thinks it was an accident, he says, as if a religious episode had passed over him."[7]

There are fireworks for sale in almost every town in Alabama. Small rockets wrapped in red, white, and blue paper. People are all set, I was told, to celebrate George W. Bush's reelection in November. He is liked a lot in the South, especially when he speaks about American moral supremacy and our right to kick someone else's ass in the world. I did not encounter many people able to entertain the thought that we could ever be at fault as a nation or that our president could be a fool leading us into a mess. When I asked what Kerry's chances were, even friends looked at me as if I had three heads. Near Flatwood, Alabama, I almost ran off the road after seeing a small "Elect Kerry" sign. It's the only one I came across. In fact, I didn't see any Bush signs either—there's no need for them since he's following God's plan, as everybody there knows. We have always had professional true believers, but in the past their apocalyptic views were marginal and never had such strong support in Congress and the White House, where they are now regularly invited and consulted on matters of national interest. Nor did they ever before have fans even among Catholic and Jewish intellectuals on the right, who find them to be model citizens even with their fanaticism and their love of violence.

"The grungier the town, the better the music and the ribs are liable to be." So I heard. Unfortunately, as I discovered, this is not really true. Most poor people eat mostly poorly prepared food and the better musicians tend to gravitate to cities where customers have cash to spend. The best ribs I had on my trip were not in any of the smaller towns, but in Atlanta. Fat Matt's Rib Joint is a small, unassuming place that promises little from the outside. It serves slabs of pork ribs on paper plates with slices of white bread. There are also bags of potato chips, bowls of rum-soaked beans, and plenty of paper napkins to wipe one's fingers and lips. The crowd is socially and racially mixed. Sitting side by side at long communal tables, eating and drinking pitchers of beer, are well-dressed men and women who could be doctors, lawyers, truck drivers, gas station attendants, and undertakers. The ribs are delicious and cheap, and there's live music. A terrific band is playing a little blues, a little country.

The four white musicians look as if they have day jobs. Three of them are grizzled men in their early sixties who could have come out of an R. Crumb drawing and all of whom one would guess have had plenty of ups and downs in their lives. The songs they play are bawdy, funny, and have a tough realism about them that any serious writer would envy. "A woman gets tired of one man all the time," an old blues song says. Cheating wives and husbands, bad luck, and trouble are the themes. The musicians are enjoying themselves and so is everybody else. That's what our protectors of virtue find so scandalous about the cities. The way diverse classes of people and races get together, drink beer, dance, and make whoopee. But as one of my tablemates, a woman from south Georgia, told me, "Atlanta is not the South."

FOOTNOTES

1   *Clarksdale Press Register,* June 3, 2004.

2   See Joan Didion's essay on the Left Behind series in these pages, "Mr. Bush & the Divine," November 6, 2003.

3   *Glorious Appearing: The End of Days* (Tyndale House, 2004), p. 226.

4   *Religion in the American South* (University of Carolina Press, 2004), p. 167.

5   *Mobile Register,* Sunday, June 6, 2004.

6   NewSouth Books, 2004, p. 189. The title recalls that of *I'll Take My Stand,* the collection issued in 1930 by the Southern Agrarian writers, including John Crowe Ransom, Allen Tate, Robert Penn Warren, and Randall Jarrell.

7   *Bats out of Hell* (Houghton Mifflin, 1993), p. 83.

SHADOW AND SOLOMON

Mac Walcott

There was a goat funeral at our place today. It was Shadow, the old
ebony Nubian. I drove the new black front-end loader slowly, mostly
trying to keep her from jostling out of the bucket, hoping she
wouldn't bust open. That was all I could do for her now, deliver her
to a final resting place without further incident—no better treatment
than a pauper received in our world. In her world, though, her real
family, the other eight goats, kept their distance, munching more of
the bonanza of withered leaves from the downed popcorn trees,
averting their eyes when I tried to talk to them. I know her new smell
meant something to them. They had probably already made their
peace with her when they let her take over the Bird House, the little
winged structure in the trees. It was a shelter made on a lark, in an afternoon, a bird-shaped contraption with thin plywood wings and a
horse-skull head. We thought our clever bird house was about art and
about rain. Shadow used it for travel, to fly where she next needed to
be. The kids found her there, dead center, day before yesterday.

I like to think Ivan did Shadow in. I saw her in the middle of the
east field a week after the storm: alone, belly down on all fours, head
still up like a sphinx. Her recent son, her common-law husbands, and
all her sisterhood stayed away for the two days that she was there,
conducting her own vigil in the center of her three-acre world. I then
saw her again Tuesday morning, a hot, humid October one, hobbling
heavily to the bird house, her weight dropped off, pain in her joints.
I thought of taking her to Dr. Heilmeyer, but knew he'd probably say
the same thing he did last year about Emogene: "Man, this is an old
goat," as he gave her lots of shots. "Looka here. She ain't got any
teeth." Emogene was gone within a week. Shadow had a better idea.
She knew where she was going, and how to get there.

Over the years, the goats have been laid out in random places
around the pasture; sometimes it's where they sighed their last; some-

times it's dragged to a place where it's easy to dig. I chose a special place for Shadow, in a mulch hill mounded up ten years ago around the time that she was "loaned" to us. Father Pat Brockman, all five foot two of him, taught me that loaning is the honest way to share the lives of the animals we think we have tamed. A navy man, Pat can tell you most of what you need to know in about ten minutes. The day he delivered Shadow and five of her friends, he sat down on the fender of his rusty horse trailer and quickly dissected the idea of "owning" anything in our world; he next lamented that goats really get a bad rap from that single passage in Matthew that seemed to link them to the dark side of things. He then asked if we had ever heard of the "Goat Man," a bearded wanderer who traveled the whole country in a small covered wagon pulled and surrounded by hundreds of goats. Pat said the last time he saw the Goat Man was in Bay Minette in 1978. Cars pulled over and children gathered as the Goat Man and his train tinkled and bleated down the highway. What Pat remembered most was the huge crude sign on the wagon: "Jesus Wept." Pat then said, "The stewards of the world usually make peace; it's the masters who make war." Finally, as his amen, he pronounced, "I love goats, and sinners." All that in eleven minutes. I need to call Pat and check on him.

I dug her grave partly with the new loader, but mostly by hand. While I worked, I sipped on a tall Genuine Fine Life Beer every now and then, the next one in my front pants pocket, like Daddy used to do. I think about him fairly often now; a glimpse of his ashes on my desk at the office is usually enough to make me talk to him, mostly just a fond "how ya doin'?" but sometimes a more specific question, or a more specific curse. At Shadow's grave I thought about all the pet graves we dug at home, growing up, about how well Daddy instructed us in the digging, but never held the shovel in his lotion-soft hands. I wished again he hadn't been blind the last few years before he passed, so that he could have seen once more what he had wrought here. Son Charlie and I dug the last grave together this summer for Coco, a child goat resting now under the corral. Charlie's grown up into this special country chore now, and buried Bob and Harley and

Purdy alone. He made Bob a nice two-by-four cross.

My thoughts wander widely through the whole world of good and evil when digging these graves, thinking unbreathable thoughts sometimes, just like I do in church. Mostly, I start with some attempt at human reverence for the deceased, although I always feel the other goats may be snickering at me as they peek out the corners of their averted rectangle eyes. My mind always cycles back around again to, "Is it deep enough yet? It's just an old goat."

And always I wonder: why not lay the carcass in a cool, shady corner of the pasture, downwind of the house, and let things continue as they started? The world knows what to do, the bugs are already waiting. Then, in the spring, when we find the bones scattered around the field, we will pick them up, guess what they are, and think of her. Most bones we will lay back down; big bones we'll take back to the shed to add to the collection. There are lots of bones in the woods outside the fence from the coyotes, from the seasons past when they patiently picked off the herd.

With Shadow, I found myself dreaming of a simple service in a simple sanctuary, the kind where people rise to speak about what moves them. I dream of the miracle of her long life, of all lives, of all survivals. I see a small shiny farmer stand up alone at the back of the bare room.

"Shadow was a spooky one. I never even touched her in the ten years she was with us. She was smart and polite. Her son will need our help. Shadow was a good goat. We will miss her." The brothers and sisters murmur their blessings. The shiny man sits back down. The service continues.

An old pine root brings me back to the hole. I chop with the shovel, flip mud up on my glasses, cuss, and go sit on the tractor while I clean them and calm down. From the padded seat I imagine the cheap obituary that might be in *Goat World* next month.

The deceased was a female domestic, dehorned, about sixty pounds; age approximately eleven years, mother of several kids, one recently weaned, her udder not dry. It appears to have been a natural, expected death, accelerated by parasites and exposure.

It was easy digging alone into the mulch hill, a cool, late afternoon. I was into the yellow damp sand, full spades each try. My thoughts drifted again, across the east fence under the canopy of the giant sugar pine. All the goats from up our road are there, laid down in a circle on the thick pine straw carpet. It's another gathering for Shadow. Mingled among the goats are children, some using the goats for pillows, some footrests. At the trunk, a wooly, dirty man rises to his knees. It's the Goat Man himself, Ches McCartney.

"Thank you, Sister Josephine. Most of you didn't know Shadow. I barely did, and she was one of our own. She always kept to the edge, shy and aloof; but I knew she was wise, because she survived all these years, coyotes included. All we really need to remember about Shadow is that she knew love. I saw it with my own eyes that morning last spring when she let me watch her and Solomon together. She was laughing like Sarah. It was beautiful." Ches pauses for a moment, and stokes one of the kids.

"Friends, Dostoevsky said most of us spend our lives looking for love in the empty firmament of our minds, but Shadow showed me again that love is all around us. Amen." The goats are silent. The kids stare up into the limbs above. Ches lies down on his back.

My foot slipped off the shovel, and I was back in the damned hole again, breathing hard now. Reaching for a little bit more, just to make sure, I always fear it is never deep enough. And I always dream those nights of festering carcasses rising from the mud or of Poomba the pig rooting his way down to rescue his old friends. When I finally hit ground water, I knew I was there.

Shadow waited patiently in the loader the whole time, feet up. Gentlewoman that she is, she slid perfectly out of the bucket into the hole, legs folded under her torso, head tucked down like she's forever butting the east wall of the hole. I dropped three loads of mulch ungently on her, and it was done, it was finished.

I formed the top of the grave into a rectangle with sloped sides, just like the professionals, imposing one last bit of dominion over the timeless stew that had already started below. The last rite is the sprinkling of the whole pound can of black pepper on top to keep her friends away. The spice only works for a week or so, but maybe that's all the preservation she will need. The pepper made me think of Father Pat again. We've discussed such funeral cakes before, and he always makes me think I'm overdoing it. "Pigs need to eat too," he would say with his preacher's grin, or "People are the only ones that make a big deal out of funerals; don't fret about an old goat like Shadow; it's the sheep that we need to worry about." I'd like to show him Oreo, the beautiful boy blend of black Shadow and white Solomon, to let him know that his line continues. I'd tell him how much they loved each other. I'd like to remind him that we still have his old lariat from ten years ago when he presented Shadow to us. I thought, again, to call him when I get back to the house.

The smell didn't wash away easily. I rubbed a cut lemon all over my hands to kill it. From the kitchen sink, I looked north to see Shadow's fresh black mound, as intended. So, each day now, I can think of Shadow and of Solomon; and then I'll think of Pat and his blind wife, Judy, sixty years together, lives lost and lives found, children buried, buildings named in their honor, 170 years of life between them; and I think of all they may need, nine miles away, alone in their farmhouse full of birds, trees down everywhere on their forty acres, storm skeeters whining through the busted screens, hot fall sun on a roof that's only known shade. I'll call them right now and take them some honey this weekend. Then I think of Shadow again and I'm reminded that they will be all right. They know love. They know life.

A Full Boat

Daniel Wallace

I'll never forget the day that tree fell on my father, crushing him like a fly beneath its massive trunk. We were sitting on a park bench together, on a beautiful—albeit windy—afternoon. My father: dried and withered. Hopeless in a pleasant way. But bitter: very, very bitter.

"I have nothing," he said, "nothing but unbridled contempt for the two-legged bastards who promenade about as if walking were something everybody could do."

He spit the thin, dry spit of an old man. A pigeon examined it, balked, and flew away.

"Yes, the wooden leg suits me," he went on, nodding, agreeing with this assessment of himself. "In some ways it's proven to be a great asset. If nothing else, it can certainly start a conversation!" And he gave me the raised-eyebrow look, his facial exclamation mark. "But I just can't walk around all la-de-da like these goddamn fuckers." He nodded toward the innocent people who had chosen this bright, clear, cool day for an outing to the park. "I suppose it would accurate to say that I perambulate, and in that way they are no different from me. But I don't so much walk as *limp*," he said. "Limp and drag, limp and drag."

"That's true," I said. And I might have added that the sound was quite horrific to me, waking up in the middle of a dark night and hearing it, in the hallway, coming closer and closer to my very own room. *Limp, draaaaaag. Limp, draaaaaag.* Over and over I had to keep repeating to myself, *It's my father out there. It's only my father.*

He leaned in toward me a bit. "I appreciate it, of course," he said, "how you accommodate me in that way. Limping the way you do. I really appreciate it."

"It's not a problem."

"*Can* you walk? I mean, in a way that's regarded as normal?"

"Yes, I can."

He nodded. "Good, good. You're versatile. You can limp, you can not limp—it's up to you. Me, I have no choice, but it would seem my handicap is either completely ignored or I am made a figure of fun."

"People—they don't know what it's like."

This seemed to make him feel good for a moment. But the moment passed. "Too true," he said. "The fuckers don't know a goddamn thing. Were they to open their eyes for but a second, and look this way, they would see A MAN WITH A WOODEN LEG!"

That last part he spoke quite loudly. People opened their eyes and looked. I felt sorry for the small, elderly African-American lady who had the misfortune of being the closest fucker to us at that time.

"What are *you* looking at?" he said. She turned away. "No, please! Gawk! Your eyes do not deceive you, madam. I am a man with a wooden leg. I hope the sight of me enlivens your otherwise predictable, boring life."

She moved on. He watched her derisively until she disappeared around a bend in the pebbled path.

"What a sad person," he said. "She has no idea how lucky she is! She must have had those legs her entire life, and yet, no doubt, given the opportunity she would regale us with stories of hardship and discrimination. But I'll tell you something, and it's the truth: I would rather be black than have just one leg. I'm dead serious. I would give up my natural skin color if it would mean I had my leg back. Doesn't that tell you something?"

"It does," I said.

"What? What does that tell you?"

"That you're a racist?"

"No!"

"Well, then I would say what it tells me is that you would do almost anything to get your leg back."

"Oh no!" he cried. "You're not going to get me with that one!"

"*Which* one, Dad?"

"The one where you give me a wish and I get my leg back but it's fifty years old and rotted through and smells bad? I've been around the block, son, don't try that with me. But. If I could get a brand-new, healthy, strong, nicely proportioned leg, well-fitted on my body—the whole nine yards—then, yes, I would happily become an African-American."

I tried to imagine my father as a black man. I looked at him and he looked at me.

"I've always liked you," he said. "I hope you know that."

"I'm your son, Dad."

"Even so," he said.

We sat there for a while longer, watching the people, the pigeons, thinking our own private thoughts. Inevitably, this was where we found ourselves, exploring the dark and confidential corners of our lives, in silence. He was a man of few words when I was growing up; we ate our meals in a solemn quietude, and an entire evening might pass before he said anything at all—usually *Good night.* Sometimes there was music—he liked to hum. But no conversation. "What are words," he told me once, after I curiously questioned his affinity for absolute silence, "but a random combination of letters, resulting in a recognizable sound? And what are letters but a meaningless scrawl of circles and lines?" When I was six I had no idea what this meant. But now I think this meant he thought language was an invention, a product like any other, and just because it was a common and accepted thing to speak to other people, it didn't mean he had to do it himself. He was a kind man, a good man. He just didn't have much to say. This changed of course when he became old. All the words he had denied in his young life began pouring out of him like water from a broken pipe. Once he was old there was really nothing he wouldn't say, to anybody, and I looked back fondly on the silent years.

"You know how I lost it, don't you?" he said.

"Lost what?"

"The leg," he said. "The leg, goddamn it!"

I thought about it. "I remember something about a whale," I said.

He shook his head. "That was just a story. The truth is, I lost it in a card game."

"A card game?"

"A very-high-stakes card game," he said. "I feel like an utter fool now, of course, as I have every day since. But at the time, I thought there was no way I could lose."

"You bet your leg in a card game?"

"You wouldn't understand," he said. "It was a different time, a time when men were men and cards were cards and men played card games. For *keeps*. Most of my friends had lost some body part or other. An eye, an ear. A couple of fingers more often than not. One of the people we played with, he was a doctor. Performed the surgery then and there."

He rubbed the joint, the place where his flesh and blood leg ended, and his wooden one began. It was a bit like a pool cue: he could unscrew it when he wanted. He usually unscrewed it right before bed. But if there was some household chore that needed doing, and he didn't want to do it, he'd unscrew it then as well.

"It was a painful procedure. But you knew that going in. 'Don't bet your leg if you're not prepared to lose it.' That's something I've tried to teach you." He looked at my legs. "And in that respect at least it looks like I've been successful."

"I don't think it ever would have occurred to me, under any circumstances, to bet a part of my body in a card game."

He looked at me, misty-eyed. "That's something a father longs to hear," he said. "Thank you, son."

"You're welcome."

"My father—hell, he didn't care whether I had my legs or not. Sad as that is. He never thought to tell me one way or another what I should or shouldn't bet. When the moment came, I wasn't prepared. And I bet the leg."

He reached into his back pocket and removed his wallet. He opened it up, and showed me an old, dog-eared black-and-white picture of himself dressed as a sailor, smiling, his arm around a girl whose laughter it seemed I could almost hear. Women were happier back then.

"I didn't know you were in the navy," I said.

"I wasn't," he said. "But it was a good look for me and the women, they loved it. That's not why I'm showing you this, however. I'm showing this to you because it's the last picture taken with me in it. All of me, I mean. Look at that smile: so hopeful. Full of life. That young man didn't know that in less than two days he'd lose his right leg to a guy with three jacks and two tens."

"A full boat."

He settled into the bench, as his mind seemed to be taking a stroll back in time; his eyes had that VACANCY sign. Even when he talked it wasn't like him talking; it was the voice of the ghost of the man he used to be, reporting the past to the present.

"It was Saturday night, of course. Two A.M. Everyone was smoking cigars, and the room was so smoky it was like playing cards in the clouds. We'd been at it for the last four hours or so, and let me tell you, son, I was on a roll! I couldn't lose! It didn't matter what I played—I won a hundred-dollar pot with a pair of threes! People couldn't read me. I bluffed like hell. By midnight I was up seven hundred and fifty dollars. I thought about leaving and taking my winnings and buying something special for myself—a new wallet, a nice bottle of Scotch, a warm pair of socks. But with things going so well I thought they could only get better. I decided to quit when I hit a thousand.

"I won the next hand—Montana Low-Hole, roll your own. That brought me up to eight seventy-five. I lost the next, but won the next two. Grand total: nine hundred and sixty-two American dollars. One more hand, and that was it: I was out of there.

"The dealer, winking, choose my favorite game: seven-card stud. This is the game I was born to play, son, it was like magic with me and everybody knew it. I figured I didn't even have to look at my cards to win this one. But I looked. I was confident. I thought it was my lucky day. And everybody folded—except for one man. DeSoto Moriarty, we called him."

"Why'd you call him that?"

277

"Because that was his name. DeSoto knew how to play a hand of cards. We kept at it, raising each other until we'd gone through all our money. I tried to call, but he would have none of it. *Chicken*, he said. *If you really had something there, you'd be willing to bet more than money. Me, for instance, I know I got you beat. That's why I'm betting my thumbs. Both of them.*

"I didn't blink. I could tell he was just trying to scare me. *Name the leg*, I said. *Right or left.* He smiled. *Right.* And we showed our cards. And that's all she wrote, I lost my leg." He paused. "A full boat beats two pair any day of the week."

I looked at him. "You bet your leg on two pair?"

"I was young," he said. "Reckless."

"But I still don't understand," I said. "What did he want with your leg? What did he do with it once he had it?"

My father shook his head. "That was his business. After the doctor cauterized the wound, I said good-bye to the leg and I never spoke to it again. It was DeSoto's now. He took it with him every-where. That's why I eventually stopped playing cards with those guys. I couldn't stand the smug smile on his face, and the way he rested his hand on my kneecap."

His eyes began to glow with an old man's sadness. He sighed. "A salamander can regenerate his legs," he said. "A newt. Sometimes—"

"Sometimes you wish you were a newt."

"That's right," he said. "Sometimes I do."

We sat there a moment. I was thirty-three years old on that day; my father was eighty-seven. I had known him all of my life and I had never heard this story, or imagined that he had ever lived through such a macabre experience. It just goes to show you, I guess. Some-thing.

"What a story," I said. "On the one hand, you were stupid to even be there, but on the other hand you were kind of brave. I would never play in a game like that. The stakes are too high."

He looked at me. "It works both ways, though, doesn't it? You can either lose big, or you can win big. Losing is the worst, but winning—

there's nothing like it."

And he stared at me then, for as long a time as I ever remember him staring at me in all our lives, taking in the details, the parts that made me real, as though he had never seen me before.

"Winning?" I said. "Winning what?"

He smiled, his eyes shining in wonder. "How do you think—you and me—you don't know?"

"Know what?"

"Ever wonder why you never met your mother?"

"Of course I've wondered. Why didn't I ever meet her?"

"Because neither did I. Son," he said. "Four Aces, King high...the best hand I ever had...are you telling me I never told you that story—*your* story?"

And that's when the tree fell. A big, towering, ancient oak, rotting from the inside, hanging on by its tenacious roots, teetering there for who knows how long—a cross-wind hit it just so, and before either of us could move, limp, or drag, the man I called my father—tiny already, shrunken by age—disappeared beneath it in a bloodless moment of finality. Crushed. But, save for a jagged branch scrape across the cheek, I was left unharmed, completely.

I guess it was my lucky day.

THE FREDDIES

M. O. Walsh

Frederick the Third slept in a house of mannequins, half dead himself until the phone rang. His mother had to whisper. "Look Freddy," she said, "don't come. I just wanted you to know." Then she hung up. The news, of course, was that his grandfather Frederick the First was dead, a massive coronary on the ninth hole of the Colonial Golf and Tennis Club.

Freddy dropped the receiver and rolled off the couch. Then he stumbled to the bathroom and pissed blood. He had kidney stones again, and this particular batch moved like broken china through a bendy straw. Freddy thought about cleaning the rust colored spots that dotted the rim of the toilet, as well as wiping the pink runners that dribbled the side of the bowl, but then remembered that Clara, his reason for cleaning, had left him. Just that morning, in fact. In the pouring rain, maybe.

Freddy sat on the side of his bathtub and attempted to cry, not only over the loss of Frederick the First, but also over his newly re-membered split with Clara the Fourth. If there was any natural time for tears, Freddy figured, this was it. But before any water could come, it's likely that Freddy found shelter in the abundance of his grief, an idea that no one person could possibly mourn two such simultaneous and tsunamic losses in any proper way. So, Freddy wondered, why try? What did he have to give, anyway? Drops of salt from his eyes? What does that change? What did they do in places like Asia for grief? Fall on their swords? Eat their own bowels with chopsticks? Something like that was needed here, because Frederick the First was the rock. Frederick the First was the glue.

And so the last time Freddy had cried seemed ridiculous to him now, maybe a fishhook through the web of his palm. He wondered how this act could possibly serve as the exit for both the orbital pains in his heart and the barbs in his hand. It seemed unjust. This thought

M. O. WALSH

quieted Freddy, and soon the obligation of it all turned heavy and distant. He sat there stone-faced. And here I imagine him grabbing the
shower curtain for balance and the whole thing crashing down on his
head.

So Freddy threw the curtain off his shoulders. "You don't come?"
he said. "They tell *me* don't come? Don't come for Frederick the
First?"

Freddy then stood up from the bathtub, full of a new and lam-
poonish energy. He ran down the hall like a kid to a swimming pool.
He hit the bedroom door with his shoulder and tripped onto his own
unmade bed, his face buried deep in the comforter. "Clara!" he yelled
into the feathers. And then let's say the room became silent, except
for the sound of thrown pillows, sliding off the nightstand.

At what couldn't have been more than thirty-five years old,
Freddy was four times married and soon to be four times divorced. He
eased off the edge of the bed and pulled the sheets down with him,
wrapping them around his head. He stared at the full-length mirror
Clara dressed in front of every day, and, perhaps through a film of pain
pills and mirror dust, Freddy saw in his reflection a shepherd.

"Listen everyone," Freddy said. "The good man is dead. Tell the
flock. Lower the flag."

With the expanse of his forehead and gobble neck hidden, Freddy
would look young and clean. So he pulled the fabric tight around his
face and crawled towards the mirror. "ClaraBell," he said. "Frederick
the First is gone! The good man is deader than denim. And they say
for me not to come."

Freddy felt these words intensely, especially since his wife was a
seamstress. And, since it was her phrase about denim that leaked from
his mouth when he spoke of his grandfather, this multiplied his anguish in invisible ways. Because he had meant what he said about the
good man, no matter whose words he used. As soon as they passed
from his lips, however, Freddy's face resumed its sleepy-still posture.
This was a fierce bother to him, that his features could lie blank in the
wake of legitimate sadness, so he squinted his eyes to say it again.

"He's dead, Clara-britches. My namesake! Gone." He held a frown for a second and then relaxed, his face back to nothing. He tried this several times.

"Hell," he said.

Freddy breathed heavy towards the mirror. He made crying noises like a baby. *Waa*, he said. *Waa.* Then he fell asleep on the floor.

Even after three and a half divorces, one miscarried child, and two bouts with AA, this was the first thing Freddy had felt deep in his guts since he kissed his first wife Shelly Fremont through a chain-link fence in the eighth grade. So it is likely that he dreamt about her on the floor that day.

Of course he would go.

Freddy had nothing to wear to a funeral. He found all sorts of khaki pants Clara had brought home to hem. He put on the pair that fit the closest and grabbed two neckties of his own. He threw blue socks into a suitcase with some dress shoes and put a button-down shirt over his shoulder. Then he went to the kitchen and gathered his pills. Freddy ate two more white ones for pain and did what any good grandson would do. He thought of his grandmother, and searched for reasons she should live from here out.

What had it been, sixty-three years of marriage? What was that party he hadn't been invited to? What had his grandfather said on the phone?

"I had no idea you weren't coming, Freddy. Your sister did all the invitations. It was a surprise party. Sixty (one? two? three?) years, can you believe it? I spoke to her about all this mess," he said. "I'm trying. But you know how she can be."

How many years ago was that? And where was Freddy when he called? What house? What wife? Regardless, Freddy remembered the call, and he remembered the sound of his grandfather's voice. The man had the voice of a giant, the voice of a bull.

"You know we love you, Freddy," he said. "You know I don't care for broken relations."

This was a man who should never be buried. A man who completely forgave. A man who lit up old black-and-white photos. Perhaps more than that even, a full cargo of traits too difficult to catalogue. And so, to Freddy, his grandfather became a man who looked not dissimilar to the mannequin in his kitchen, dressed in a seersucker suit that Clara had yet to alter. The hard jaw was there, the stiff chest. Everything was close except the hands that, on the mannequin, looked unable.

Freddy grabbed this mannequin by the waist and hauled him out to his car. He placed him in the passenger seat. And after three trips back inside the house to collect his keys, suitcase, and five beers, Freddy drove to Jackson, Tennessee, the place it seemed everyone but him now lived.

On the drive, Freddy and the mannequin did not speak. Instead, Freddy reasoned that his grandmother would appreciate this gesture, this gift. He recalled that it was never the conversation of his past wives that he missed when they were gone. Instead it was the hump of a body under the sheets, the quiet closing of a door not to wake them. It was having two burgers on the grill instead of one. And, although he knew the mannequin itself could never reason, Freddy thought it looked comfortable in its seat, still standing in the place of something.

They arrived in Jackson at dusk. Freddy pulled up to the town house his grandparents lived in. Cars were parked along the side of the road. It was pouring rain, so Freddy turned off his wipers and finished the last of his beer. He saw the car of his sister's husband, a tall blue SUV with a faded Republican bumper sticker. This was not good.

All told, it was this man's sister who was Freddy's second wife, the woman who had miscarried the child and stopped drinking. The one who forced Freddy's first bout with AA. The one who involved the police. The one who became best friends with Freddy's sister, and the one Freddy left on the day she found Jesus.

Had it all gotten so complicated? I imagine when Freddy thought of it, he didn't think so. To him, this ex-wife was a woman he could barely remember, an anecdote he found no reason to tell. But Freddy's sister Shirley was of a different persuasion. She was made of scissors, and had since cut the ties of her brother's belonging.

The garage door of the town house opened and a young man stepped out. Freddy watched him from his car. The kid stood in the garage and lit a cigarette, no more than fifteen, sixteen, seventeen years of age. He blew smoke out into the rain.

Who was this kid? Freddy wondered. What did he know about mourning Frederick the First? Freddy thought about his cousins, but couldn't place any so young. He thought maybe his grandparents had adopted this boy, to show him the golf courses of America. This is the type of people they were.

The kid spotted Freddy in his car and waved, then shouted something back at the house. Shirley appeared in the doorway, threw Freddy a look that was terminal and then went back inside.

"Here we go," Freddy said and unbuckled the mannequin. He got out in the rain and slid its body through the driver's side door. The town house was on a hill, and as Freddy ran up the slick driveway he fell. The mannequin tumbled down the concrete and into the street, its head in the rush of drain water.

Freddy picked it up and started back toward the house as Ronald Hutchins, Shirley's husband, bolted out of the door. He told the kid to go inside and unbuttoned both of his shirt cuffs. This is how bad it had gotten. He charged toward Freddy in the rain.

"You shit-eating bastard," he said, and went to punch Freddy in the face. This was an awkward thing though, as Ronald's foot slipped from underneath him. He opened his fist in a panic and, instead of landing one on Freddy's jaw, only grabbed hold of his T-shirt. All three of them fell and Ronald got the worst of it. Freddy landed on top of him, dug his knee into the man's crotch, and rode him back down to the sewer. The mannequin smacked the ground hard and slid to a stop. The kid blew smoke from his nose because, at that age, he thought everything was beneath him.

Freddy got up and saw that his khakis were ripped at the knee. Ronald lay in the water, holding on tight to his privates. "Jesus,

Ronald," Freddy said. "This isn't about us here at all. I told you a thousand times I was sorry! Tell your sister to call me or something. Look what you did to my pants!"

The kid threw his cigarette into the yard. "Uncle Freddy?" he said.

Freddy dragged the mannequin into the garage and wiped the water from his own eyebrows. The kid pulled a small camera from his jeans pocket and snapped a picture of him doing this. His pose was the kind seen in tabloids, the guarded face of a celebrity on trial, the Yeti peeking out from the woods. And with that, Freddy's existence, or at least this moment of it, became indisputable and permanent for the boy.

"Shit," the kid said. "*It lives!* I mean, I always kind of thought they were making you up."

That this young man was Nat Hutchins was probably no easy blow to Freddy. He had seen this kid born. This was his nephew, his godson. But Freddy remembered him only as a circumcised penis, a hungover eight A.M. baptism. Had it been that long? Could Freddy only be in his thirties? At what point did he become a ghost to his family, I wonder? Surely he was too young for it then.

Freddy didn't answer the boy but leaned the mannequin against his grandfather's new Buick, parked in the same spot he remembered the old one. He straightened the mannequin's sport coat and tried wringing the water from its sleeves.

Ronald rolled around in the street. He yelled that Freddy was some "piece of work."

"Want your uncle's advice?" Freddy asked. "Your father is the Olympics of asshole."

"Tell me about it," the kid said. "You should smell his farts. It's like he's rotten inside."

Freddy slapped at the pants of the mannequin and straightened him up. He held onto his chest like a brother.

"You have any beer?" the kid asked.

"In the car," Freddy said and then headed into the house.

The kitchen was swarming with people, all quiet, none of whom Freddy first recognized. He stood on the floor mat and wiped his feet. He heard someone say, "Christ."

Shirley came at him from the crowd, snapping her claws like a sea creature. "Where's Ronald?" she said. "What did you do?"

Freddy spotted his mother by the sink, washing out an empty coffeepot.

"Honey," she said. "I thought I told you not to come."

"You called him?" Shirley yelled. "I can't believe you called him!"

"Shirley," his mother said.

"Where's grandma?" Freddy asked.

People made a path through the kitchen and Freddy saw his grandmother at the table. She had her head in her hands and two stacks of paper in front of her. As he walked toward her, Shirley grabbed the arm of the mannequin.

"Don't you dare!" she yelled and jerked hard on the mannequin's wrist. But the replacement grandpa was strong and Freddy just yanked it away.

"Have some respect!" Freddy said. "What did *you* bring? I don't see you with anything."

Shirley pulled at her hair, and ran outside to get Ronald.

When Freddy reached the kitchen counter, the pain of his stones roared back to him. He bent over and toppled some snack trays. Someone asked if he was all right, if maybe they should call 911. Then Freddy held up a finger, and made his way to the table.

Despite all the time in his car, Freddy had never thought of what to say when he got there, how awkward the exchange might be. To Freddy, the thing was all but finished when he devised it, but now seemed littered with complications. He sat the mannequin down on the chair and knelt beside his grandmother. He shut his eyes. But instead of crafting tender words, I imagine Freddy could only conceive of the pain, now scraping a path through his tubing. And by the time that Freddy could focus, his mother was standing there too, rubbing the shoulders of a widow. He heard her say his name. He heard someone else diagnose him with appendicitis. He tried to block out each of these noises, every other voice but his conscience, and said the first thing that came to his mind.

"I brought this for you," Freddy said. "I know it's kind of wet."

Freddy's grandmother wiped his head with her handkerchief. She combed his hair with her nails. "I remember when you used to take the train here," she said. "After your father left, and your mother moved down to Memphis."

Freddy remembered this too. He would walk through the train and to the snack car. He would order a ham-and-cheese sandwich and they would give him silver packets of mayonnaise, with pictures of old-time cabooses.

"And Frederick would tell you that joke about molasses," she said. "Right when you got off the train. Remember? I'd get so upset with him for telling you those dirty jokes. Doesn't that seem silly now? But you always got so tickled. I know that you loved him so much, Freddy. I know this is hard for you too."

"Mole asses," Freddy whispered.

"That's the one," his grandmother said and Freddy put his head in her lap. He heard his mother begin to sob.

Just then, Ronald Hutchins came in through the doorway.

"I'm calling the cops," he said. "You could have done permanent damage!"

Shirley was right behind him. "Get out of here, Freddy!" she said. "Nobody wants you here."

"Shirley," his mother said.

"It's true isn't it? Even you told him not to come!"

"Shirley!"

"It's just like Ronald says. You are some piece of work, Freddy. You know that? Some pathetic piece of work!" She walked up behind Freddy and poked him in the back. "And take this goddamned thing too," she said, and pushed fake Frederick out of his chair.

"Honey," his mother told Freddy, "Maybe you *should* go. Just until things settle down. We can see you tomorrow at the funeral. Just until things settle down."

"He's *not* coming," Shirley said. "It's a disgrace."

A bunch of people in the kitchen said, "Shirley!" but Freddy couldn't stand to hear that name once more. And it still has a hissing-sharp edge to it, I think, *Shirley!*, because this was a woman who never gave in. Her unforgiving came from a place no one knew and rendered her ugly for years, eventually gashing spaces between her husband, herself, and her son, setting the table for many other stories than this one.

So Freddy got to his feet and dug his knuckles into the small of his back.

"Go!" Shirley said.

Freddy picked up the mannequin by its armpits. "Just let me know if you want this," he told his grandmother. "I thought maybe it would be something to sleep with. I don't know, someone to cook for. I thought the jaw looked just like him."

His grandmother studied the mannequin's jaw and pressed at her cheek with the handkerchief. "We both thought the world of you, Freddy," she said. "We tried to call. You know we did. Let us see you tomorrow, okay? Let us get you cleaned up."

Shirley pinched Freddy's side. "Don't even bother," she said.

Ronald yelled into the phone. "We have a trespasser in the house! A goddamned intruder!"

Freddy edged his way through the crowded kitchen and took his fake grandfather with him. The last voice he heard upon leaving was a stranger's, a woman who said, "Now, who was that man again?"

When Freddy got outside, his nephew was still in the garage. "You've got the right idea," he said, and asked the kid for a smoke.

"There wasn't any beer in your car," the kid said, and shook a cigarette out of his pack. "I got soaked."

"Sorry." Freddy adjusted the mannequin on his hip. "You're just going to have to give me a break on this one. I mean it's Clara, it's your mother. Maybe it's just women in general. You know anything about that?"

"Well, I know it's kind of creepy," the kid said. "Lugging a wooden person around. Maybe you should bring it to the funeral. I love to see my mom get pissed."

"So I guess you heard all that in there?"

"I can imagine," the boy said.

Freddy let the kid light his cigarette and stared out into the rain. He probably already knew that there was no way he could show up tomorrow, despite what his grandmother had said, and despite what she felt when she said it. Because what would he even wear now, anyway? Now that those pants that never fit had been ripped? And what would it be like later, the moment the funeral ended? Would he caravan back to the house? Would he follow these people back home? Or would he let cars get between them in traffic, and slip off on an exit to Georgia? Freddy would do the latter. And so his mourning, he figured, would have to come soon, and take place while those he loved slept. So Freddy decided to go to the body himself, and asked the kid where it was.

"Just look for the place with headstones," Nat said. "It's next to the Long John Silver's."

Freddy took another long drag off his cigarette and looked his nephew all over. He had large veins that ran the side of his neck, and a silver ring that pierced the top of his ear. He looked strong but wet, and water dripped the elbow of his sleeve.

"I'm sorry you didn't get to know your great-grandfather," Freddy told him. "He really was a hell of a man. The type of man we should all be."

"I knew him," the kid said. "We live right down the road."

Upon hearing this, Freddy had to fight back a playground form of jealousy. After all, this kid probably did know his grandfather better. He might have even seen him that morning, cleaning his sand wedge and backing his cart out of the shed. But to say that Freddy became impossibly jealous would be wrong. Maybe with his first three wives whom he fled from, and maybe with this last one who fled him. But Freddy wasn't impossible in this moment, no matter what people say,

THE FREDDIES

because unlike his sister, Freddy found no strength in his hating. Instead, he soon saw in his nephew an ally, a believer.

"See, *you* know what I'm talking about!" Freddy said. "You want
to get out of here? You want to come with me? Go see the old man
one last time?"

The kid lifted up his pant leg. He showed Freddy an electronic
bracelet on his ankle. It weighed exactly two and three-quarters
pounds. "House arrest," the kid said. "I ran a buddy's car into a lake."

"Ouch," Freddy said, and again rubbed the small of his back. "I
guess we're both a bit friendly with trouble."

"You're not all that scary," the kid said. Although now he wishes
he'd said more.

It's easy to imagine Freddy's drive to the funeral home as mis-
guided at best. Freddy stopped to buy beer. Freddy stopped to hold his
testicles. Freddy stopped to dig pills out of his glove compartment,
and Freddy stopped to ask directions.

When he finally got to the home it was closed, and the rain had
not let up a bit. He told the mannequin to stay in the car, that he
would be fine, and then lurched to the only door he saw.

A heavyset man answered. He had bags, like pools of ink, under
his eyes. A Chihuahua barked in the background and the man hushed
it with only a look. Freddy doubled over with pain.

"No vacancies," the man said.

Freddy couldn't even look up.

"It's an old mortuary joke. Sorry."

"You have a man named Frederick Little in there," Freddy said.
"He was a great man."

"There are no great men in here," the undertaker said. "Just dead
ones."

"I don't think you understand," Freddy said. "My grandfather!
Not like you and me. He really was!"

Freddy meant to explain, but a wave of anesthesia overtook him.
Not the good kind either, he realized, not the kind he had lived on
for years. This one carried a dark consistency of purpose, and crept

terribly from his fingertips in.

"Listen," the undertaker said. "You'd be surprised how many people come here just like you, in the rain. But, trust me, there is nobody special in here. In fact, this is the only place where everyone's the same."

"You don't understand," Freddy said.

"I don't? Well, what did this man of yours do?" he asked. "Was he kind? Was he brave? Did he tell you jokes? Did he give you butterscotch candies? Did he drag three children through a jungle after accidentally killing their mother? Is your grandfather greater than that? That's what someone else's grandfather did. You want me to dig him up so you can see him? There is nothing great about him now."

Freddy got on his knees and crawled towards the doorjamb, as if trying to slip past the guard. The undertaker put his foot on his shoulder to stop him. "You'll be here soon enough," he said.

"You're a monster," Freddy said, and drooled a bit on the welcome mat, a scene of St. Peter at the gates.

"I think maybe you have a lot of monsters," the man said. "I think maybe what you should do is go back to your car. You've got someone inside of it waiting for you. I can see them. That's who you should go to. That's who you should touch. I don't know why people insist on touching the dead, anyway. They fix their hair, rub their cold hands. And this is after they've paid me to do it. I think maybe they imagine themselves dead when they touch them. Maybe that's the real kick."

Freddy placed his palms on the pavement. He felt the ground as a thing becoming dear to him, another thing to dream in, another thing to inhabit.

"Listen," the man said. "I'm not trying to be smart, but there's no reason to coat this with sugar. It's late. You feel like it's over. Maybe it is. Because if there's one thing I've learned it's that tomorrow there will be more of them, men twice the height of your grandfather. Children too. Because people are dying right now, you see, right now as we speak. There goes another one. See? And another. Maybe that was a doctor. Maybe there goes the cure for everything. So go to your wife or whoever. You'll get enough of me in the morning."

The man then closed the door on Freddy, but not out of any brand of viciousness. I imagine he *had* seen men like Freddy before, women too, and he recognized that look in their eyes, the look of idiots wanting meaning from death. In fact, he probably memorized that look those people held then, so he could change it when they came to his table.

Freddy tried to bang on the door again, but found himself nowhere near it. So Freddy cried onto the pavement. He vomited in the lawn by the sidewalk. Then Freddy slept for good in the rain.

Meanwhile, his fake grandfather sat lumped in the passenger seat, the engine still running. And I have to wonder what it was thinking, even though I know dead wood cannot think. Was it amazed by the turn of this day, that started so still in their kitchen? Did it feel anything at all for this man? Were there senses of loss, pity, rot? Or was it able to see through the rain, the way a body relaxes when it dies? The way stones just spill out from the bladder, and nestle in the cup of white cotton? And would it carry the mark of that evening, when finally returned back to Clara, or stood up in a department store window? Would Clara ask it for answers, and beg it to know if she was to blame? If so, how could it resist the temptation to say *Yes, Clara!* if only you could have stayed one more day, one more week, one more year? Could it not say *Yes, Clara! Yes, Shirley! Yes, Mother and Ronald and Nat!* How could this fake man not answer at all, I wonder? If only to say, *Yes,* I remember, in the car, when I felt so ashamed of my hands.

But they tell me this is the wrong type of thinking. They say this is the thinking of blame, and why I have all the troubles I do. Because I am on my third wife now, you see, and I haven't spoken to my parents in years. And we are in with this hot-shot marriage counselor, and I have crept up to the age of my uncle. They need to know what kind of person I am, my wife says, so they can tell me why I turned out like I did.

This week they had me bring in photos from my childhood, and said it would get to the roots. So I am looking at that snapshot from the garage now, the one with my soaking wet uncle. And I think they're right, because it's a funny thing about pictures, the way you notice new things in the background. With this one, I notice a reflection in the glass of the Buick. It is me with my stupid flash camera. It is me just standing there watching. It is me not doing a thing.

But you are getting ahead of yourself!, my wife tells me. Just describe *who it is* in the picture. Just look at them. Imagine them. Speak of them.

Don't pretend that they are speaking for you.

A MAP OF THE FOREST

Marly Youmans

This story hangs as a mirror on a wall opposite to another—
to Jack Stanfield's account, "Our Uncle Willem Stanfield,"
by Howard Bahr. Thus, inside each glass is a wilderness of
chambers, infinitely multiplied, utterly unmappable.
                                        —Nancy Stanfield, May 3, 2004

When I was twenty, my black hair changed to a silvery gray and hung
in a stiff metallic helmet, the kind that drops below the shoulders in
the back and rises toward the face in front. My brother would know a
name for that, and he would know all the different peoples who had
used such a helmet as a defense. In my case, that contrast with my
youth proved weirdly alluring to men. That, however, is another
though not less interesting story.

When I was thirty, my silver changed to snow.

I'm not a girl anymore, of course; by the turn of the millennium,
my face finally had made peace with my hair. My mother once told
me that her mother and grandmother and great-grandmother had
been like me, at least in their hair, though neither she nor my aunt,
Maeve, had inherited that gene.

Walk about with a girl's body and face joined to an old woman's
stiff and resistant locks, which will only hang like a sheath made from
thousands of strands of spun metal, and it will make one think. Not
that I needed a reminder of mortality. I remember lying at full length
in my brother Jack's tree house, back in the '40s, idly throwing pieces
of pecan hulls toward the graveyard where my father should have
been cached but was not. Our mother had buried souvenirs of him
there—the telegram, the Purple Heart, the flag—in some primitive
act of forgetting that became only another memory.

My brother always says that we think we are immortal, and
nothing we can do can convince us otherwise. Of course, he assumes

I feel the same—he's sure that I always did.

But that wasn't the way it was for me. I could close my eyes tight and be with my father, feeling the terrible rocket of pain as black insect-like specks swarmed in the air, and a tug somewhere near the solar plexus pulled me toward oblivion. A fright washed over me. I never spoke of this sense of annihilation, feeling it to be utterly private.

Later on I would smile slightly when Jack spoke of our utter inability to grasp mortality. Long before the Mona Lisa, women smiled that smile—the one that humors a man in his obsessions, whether it is for a Leonardo with his paintbrush or a Jack with his military history and philosophical reflections. For a while, I was married to a psychiatrist, and the one thing I learned from his practice is that there are many more aberrant men than women. In general, we women appear to lack the large numbers of cannibals, teenage shooters, mental defectives, and outright mad geniuses found at the high or low ends of the intelligence scale. While often depressive in middle age, his female patients tended to be healthy and smart and the ones who supported and took care of the men and boys at the top and bottom. Maybe that's why we're depressed...

I must have heard the story about how our father died and how our Uncle Willem came to be as he was a hundred times. I always pictured the event in a prospect of fields bordered by the thin, irregular spires of Lombardy poplars. This was wholly untrue and entirely dictated by some black-and-white photographs of Europe that I had seen in an exhibition at the local armory. Actually the men had been in the Hurtgen forest, about which I knew nothing, and the narrow lanes bordered by poplars were hundreds of miles away. I still have to make a conscious effort to change the landscape when I imagine what happened.

Because it is in me as a place in that other mode, and the atmosphere is always a little grainy and gray.

The way Jack tells it, my father and uncle and another boy from home were lost when a *Panzergrenadier* of fifteen or sixteen came up behind the jeep. He tossed a grenade at my father and shot our Uncle

Willem in the head with a Luger. The brothers had been muzzy from lack of sleep; they hadn't noticed anything amiss, and my father never would. It had started to snow, making the scene look even more like a photograph, stippling the air with dots. The other fellow with them was scouting ahead but not so far that he didn't manage to shoot the German, who was now hobbling away at the edge of the road. The boy sprawled in the ditch by the trees and bled to death quickly, while the sky awarded numerous cold stars for his bravery.

That's the way my mother became a widow and we were made into half-orphans. It's how my uncle arrived home the way he was, neither entirely with us nor absent.

When I think about this story, I remember that Jack said that they could not find the place on a map. The roads were simply not there. It is as though our father and uncle had wandered into a web that led inexorably to that sleepless blank where death was waiting for them. Even as a child, I imagined a labyrinth in the green absence on the map that meant forest. It seemed to me that three were intended to die: my father, Willem, and the flaxen-haired boy who, when the tommy gun burst into fire, did not even turn in the air but crumpled easily to the moss. My uncle was the teller: the surviving Ishmael of the family. He was meant to come back and say to my aunt Maeve and my mother what had happened. The bullet from the Luger spun in Willem's helmet and lodged in his brain and did not kill him.

In my childhood, Uncle Willem was the element that was unpredictable and did not make sense.

I was always trying to figure him out, trying to be a woman though I was only a girl. We were all propping him up, me and Mother and Maeve. We never thought about Jack helping. My brother's job was to discourse about "men things" with Willem: cars or the heifers in the pasture or the job at the lumber mill. They'd go squirrel hunting anytime, and sometimes workers from the mill would drive out in a flatbed truck, and Jack and Willem would set off coon hunting with these men and our unmarried priest, Father Girardeaux, and a passel of somebody's dogs. He didn't hold anything against guns, even after what had happened.

At first, everything at home must have seemed just as it had been when he went off to war, as much like itself as if reflected in a faraway mirror—identical, though chiral and behind glass. The twin houses separated by the graveyard with the rickety iron fence were exactly as they had been, white with long galleries, built by my great-grandfather and his brother. The view was tidy and symmetrical. There were the two matching houses. There were the two sisters, one of whom lived inside each of the houses, one married to father and one to Willem. The days of those marriages came before the South was ruined by its rebellion against zoning, before the squat brick ranches began popping up in the fields on either hand. So the home place appeared just as before, unless you wanted to dig in the corner of the cemetery where our mother had buried those remnants of our father's military glory.

Of course, it was all an illusion. My father was no longer in one of the twin houses, and in the glass, Willem saw that his own face was subtly wrong. He let his hair grow to hide the scar, but it was still strange to him, that image. One day I heard him talking about it.

"A dead man's face," he whispered, catching sight of himself in the triptych of mirrors over my great-grandmother's vanity.

I came up beside him and put my hand on his arm and looked into the mirror. It was true; he had a haunted look that was only emphasized by the presence of my young face, so close to his. I was barely thirteen, with dark eyes and hair. It seemed that I was going to resemble my mother, who was a handsome woman.

"What do you mean, Uncle Willem?" I glanced at him—at him, not at the reflection, which was not really him and might be in its reversals obscurely altered—but his eyes were fixed on the glass.

"I'm already—."

He broke off, his gaze jerking away and coming to rest on my fingers. He looked puzzled for a moment, then stroked them lightly.

"Little sister," he said.

"Are you all right, Uncle Willem?"

He looked me in the face then, gave me a long stare that was more intense and prolonged than any man had ever given me. It seemed like he didn't know any more how long or how hard a look should be, or when it made a person feel uncomfortable and uncertain.

"Youth is beautiful. Never forget that," he told me.

Since I was still a child, I didn't know what to say in reply, although by this time in my life I was accustomed to comforting adults.

"I love you, Uncle Willem," I said, leaning my head on his arm.

For a girl, it might be called a mistake to know and be fond of men who have been harmed; the practice gives one too high a toleration for defects in one's potential husbands. That, at least, is what experience has shown me. But I had loved Willem before he went away, and I was willing to care about what remnant of him had come home.

"That's not me." He bent and whispered close to my ear. "That man's not *me*." He was glancing sidelong at the mirror. In a minute he tapped himself on the chest. "This isn't me either."

I surveyed him. "Where are you then?"

Now what I believe is that the torturous inside of his brain, pierced by the bullet, resembled a map of Hurtgen forest with its mazy paths culminating in the house of death, which was a blank. That was where the bullet forced into nothingness all the neat windings of thought which had been gathered there. But at thirteen all I knew was that he had gone somewhere inside himself that I couldn't always reach. Maybe he was there in the woods with my father and with death in the shape of a boy. Maybe the two of them were calling to Willem from the other side of the road, where foe and foe are no longer opposite but the same.

He lifted one hand and traced the swirl of scar with a fingertip as if its thread were a way of getting somewhere.

"I don't know," he said finally. "Now and then I do, and now and then I don't."

"I think you're right here beside me, Uncle Willem," I said; "Let's go out to the field and visit the cows, and after that I can help you wash the coupe."

That's what we did, and the rest of that afternoon things were fine. I remember just as plain as plain can be how we ripped up fistfuls of clover to feed the calves by the fence. Their mothers came over, pushing their blunt heads at the wire. A sluice of green slobber splashed my shoes, and Uncle Willem dried them off carefully with his handkerchief. Afterward we fetched the bucket and the sea sponge and soap and wax and chamois, and we washed and dried and waxed the Chevrolet, every inch of it, even the staghorn steering wheel. It took us hours, but we did it, even though it wasn't a Saturday and the car had been as unsmirched as a just-polished mirror from the start.

It sticks in my mind, that afternoon flowing into evening. It's lodged in some long-lasting curl of my brain, probably only because of what happened the next day. I can see my aunt coming out the side door, and Uncle Willem hesitating only for a moment before he picked her up and set her on the hood for an ornament. They were laughing, and all the watchfulness seemed to vanish from Aunt Maeve.

But it was the very next day that Willem dismantled the car and put it piece by piece down the septic tank. I hardly need to tell about that evening, because Jack tells it so very often—my brother has told this story to my children as many times as he ever told me the tale of Hurtgen forest when I was young. They have never grown tired of the image of my uncle in his welder's mask with the acetylene blowing in a blue stream from his hand. I've never been allowed to forget the strangeness of Willem working through the night with the floodlights on him so that he seemed enormous and black against the flickering image of the second house, with the moths and long-legged flies and bugs whirling like a bright dust devil around him and the goatsuckers crying out and snatching at their prey. His Chevy coupe was the last of the many things he destroyed and buried, unless you count Willem himself.

Because that was the very last stroke he wielded against himself, and afterward he took to his bed with a vengeance and, in time, died.

In time.

Outside, the glittering pieces of the car were muted in the ground, like stars muffled by a cloudy night. The staghorn and metal wheel lay like an immense medallion for a chieftain. My vision of a jet-black Uncle Willem, arms upraised and winged with light, like the magnified silhouette of a nightjar, dwindled to a paltry thing—a shape found in the grass, its claws crimped and head bowed into the silence. It was all like something else, as curious and alien as if we had garroted one of our own and flung him to the goddess of a district bog. Everything of his that could be in the earth, everything that was cared for but not alive had already been offered. There was nothing more left. All his idols were broken and gone: the car, the collection of vinyl records and turntable, the woodworking tools, the favorite Browning. They had gone into a barrow grave, where he had belonged ever since that long-ago burst of noise in the heart of Hurtgen forest. A sense of the ancient world and of the brokenness of all things had crept into our lives. It seemed that the strewn constellation of a car had been burning in the darkness of the yard for more than a thousand years. Willem dwindled in his bed at the VA as the soil with its shining gifts and its once-companionable bones waited with its usual patience. What was earthly felt unearthly. Toward the end, he wandered in his mind on foreign paths until he became lost, and there his fair-haired death found him out.

The burial service was the mirror of one that had been performed in memory of my father, except that Maeve asked for a reading of Psalm 139, which has these lines: *If I say, "Let only darkness cover me, and the light about me be night," even the darkness is not dark to thee, the night is bright as the day; for darkness is as light with thee.* What they meant for Willem, who called the dark down on his head, I didn't know. Was he seen and yearned over as he passed into what we knew as blankness and blackness? *With God, all things are possible,* Father Girardeaux said; when he came near me, I could tell that he had been crying. I remember that he gave a single white rose to Maeve.

By that time in our lives, my brother had escaped to war. I had a snapshot of Jack leaning on a North Korean tank; a star on the turret hovered above his head. My mother was still angry that he had abandoned home, so I kept his pictures in a drawer under my slips and only occasionally took them out. Eventually I mounted that photograph on black paper, along with one of my father and one of Uncle Willem, and I tucked them in a dime-store frame. These were the three men of my girlhood—privately I called them *the father, the son, and the ghost*. One was murdered, one was hurt to madness, and one ran away. I had never felt any of the rage and despair that emanated from my mother, only a sorrow that poured out as freely as childish tears.

All this was 1954, exactly fifty years ago.

I was almost eighteen. With the first real money I had ever earned, I rode to the city and had my hair cut so that it curved just above my shoulders, a rich dark helmet without any of the waves the others girls wanted. Afterward, I bought myself a red coat that swung when I walked, some snug red leather gloves, and a pair of black pumps.

It was winter, and my new heels clicked on the sidewalk. For the first time in years, I felt a sense of adventure and well-being. I was pleased; not once had I accidentally strayed from my meticulously planned route. Far from being lost—for not once had I needed to ask for help—I had a sense of being *found*. A puff of breeze shifted strands of my hair, and it seemed like the touch of an invisible hand.

Armored in my new cut, defended by my coat, I felt as trim as a soldier in his first uniform: an unaccustomed glamour. Every inch of me was taut and expectant, waiting for some newness to spring forth and alter the world. Then I knew what Jackie had meant—that we don't quite believe in our mortality—because for one thrilling instant I felt my immortal youth stream from me like a flag. And there was still an hour until my bus would leave.

I took out a map of the city.

Perhaps this was where I belonged, I thought. I could work here, save my earnings, and go to college later on. Algebra, botany, chemistry: the alphabet of learning would be waiting for me in its orderly stacks. I perched on the steps of the public library to unfold the map, glad to see its grid of streets, so different from the loose tangle of dirt roads at home. The cartographical city on my knee showed nothing but an interlace of blocks and triangles, with parks that were snips of a wilderness green so civilized by benches and urns that no one could ever become lost there.

About the Authors

HOWARD BAHR was born in Meridian, Mississippi, and from 1976 to 1993 was on the staff at Rowan Oak, the home of William Faulkner, serving as curator from 1982 to 1993. He currently resides in Fayetteville, Tennessee, and is an associate professor of English at Motlow State Community College in Lynchburg, Tennessee. Bahr has published in *Southern Living*, *Civil War Times Illustrated*, the *Southern Partisan*, and the *Saturday Evening Post*. He is the author of *The Black Flower: A Novel of the Civil War*, *The Year of Jubilo*, and a children's book, *Home for Christmas*.

JOHN BOYER is a cardiothoracic surgeon, but would prefer to be a writer. In his spare time, he constructs morbid fantasies. His analyst maintains it's healthy for him to release his inner wickedness in such a fashion, but his wife still worries.

RICK BRAGG is the author of the best-selling memoirs *All Over but the Shoutin'* and *Ava's Man*, as well as a collection of his newspaper stories, *Somebody Told Me*. While a reporter for the *New York Times*, Bragg won the Pulitzer Prize for feature writing.

Books by ANDREA HOLLANDER BUDY include *The Other Life* and *House Without a Dreamer*, winner of the Nicholas Roerich Poetry Prize. Other honors are a Pushcart Prize and fellowships from the NEA and the Arkansas Arts Council. Before becoming the writer-in-residence at Lyon College, she was an innkeeper for fifteen years.

DAVID CAMPBELL writes from Franklin County in southwest Mississippi. After a career in rural electrification, he is now an instructor and associate director of alumni affairs for Copiah-Lincoln Community College. He also writes a newspaper column, "South by Southwest," for two weekly newspapers.

MARSHALL CHAPMAN (www.tallgirl.com) was born and raised in South Carolina. She is a singer, songwriter, and author. Her first book, *Goodbye, Little Rock and Roller*, was a 2004 SEBA Book Award finalist and 2004 Southern Book Critics Circle Award finalist. She lives in Nashville with her husband, who thinks she hung the moon.

A Louisville, Kentucky, native, RYAN CLARK is a Western Kentucky University graduate and winner of the 2002 Jim Wayne Miller Fiction Award. He currently writes stories about northern Kentuckians for the *Cincinnati Enquirer*. Ryan lives in Florence, Kentucky, with his wife, Manda, and their cat, Nelly—who only wants to be petted when Ryan is typing on the computer.

JIM DEES is a weekly newspaper columnist and the host of *Thacker Mountain Radio*, a literature and music program on Mississippi Public Radio. He is the editor of *They Write Among Us*, an anthology of Oxford writers. Dees lives in Taylor, Mississippi.

The recipient of the 2000 American Academy Award in Literature, ELLEN DOUGLAS of Jackson, Mississippi, is the author of many novels, including *A Family's Affairs*, *Where the Dreams Cross*, *The Rock Cried Out*, and *A Lifetime Burning*.

ANN FISHER-WIRTH is the author of *Blue Window* (Archer Books, 2003) and a prize-winning chapbook, *The Trinket Poems*. Another chapbook, *Mississippi*, appears online in *The Drunken Boat*. A new book, *Five Terraces*, is forthcoming in 2005. Her poems have been published widely. She teaches at the University of Mississippi.

KRISTIN GRANT (www.kristinannegrant.com) won the Grand Conference Award at the Ozark Creative Writer's Conference. She lives with her husband in Baton Rouge, Louisiana. She recently completed her first novel and hopes to find a publisher. When not attending fais-do-dos on the bayou, she serves as managing editor for a small subsidiary of the *Washington Post*.

JASON HEADLEY is the author of *Small Town Odds*, a BookSense Recommendation and one of Barnes & Noble's Best of 2004. He was raised in West Virginia and now lives with his wife in San Francisco, where he's working on his next novel—a tale of a husband and wife moonshining team.

INGRID HILL has published stories in a range of magazines and is the author of the novel *Ursula, Under* and the collection *Dixie Church Interstate Blues*. She has twice received grants from the National Endowment for the Arts. She grew up in New Orleans. She is the mother of twelve children, including two sets of twins.

SUZANNE HUDSON's first novel, *In a Temple of Trees*, was published in 2003. Her second novel, *In the Dark of the Moon*, was published in 2005. A collection of short stories, *Opposable Thumbs*, which was a finalist for the John Gardner Fiction Award, was published in 2001. She lives in Fairhope, Alabama, where she is a middle school guidance counselor and writing teacher.

CECILIA JOHNSON is an MFA student in creative writing at Ohio State University and the associate fiction editor of the literary magazine *The Journal*. When she's not writing, she enjoys painting portraits of bunnies. She is working on a collection of stories about extraordinary parallel worlds. Visit hers at downtherabbithole.com.

BRET ANTHONY JOHNSTON is the author of *Corpus Christi: Stories*. He can be reached on the web at www.bretanthonyjohnston.com.

SUZANNE KINGSBURY is the author of the novels *The Summer Fletcher Greel Loved Me* and *The Gospel According to Gracey* and co-editor of *The Alumni Grill*. She was born in Baltimore, Maryland. In 1999 she became a literary nomad, living and writing in Mississippi, Georgia,

Arizona, Panama, and Mexico. She currently lives in Brattleboro, Vermont, where she is at work on her third novel.

CHIP LIVINGSTON's writing has appeared this year in *Ploughshares*, *Apalachee Review*, the *New York Quarterly*, *Barrow Street*, *New American Writing*, *The Gay & Lesbian Review Worldwide*, *Cave Hill Literary Annual*, and *Hampden-Sydney Poetry Review*. He grew up in a red state; now he lives in a blue state.

HUMPHREYS MCGEE was raised in Leland, Mississippi, in the heart of the Mississippi Delta. Before resorting to the practice of law, he worked as a high school teacher, newspaper reporter, and cotton farmer. This is his first published work. He currently lives in Oxford, Mississippi, with his dog, Pike.

JEFF MCNEIL was raised in Mobile, Alabama. He now lives in Charlotte, North Carolina, with his wife and four children. "Jimmy the Playwright" is his first published story. He has just completed a novel.

DIANE MCWHORTER is the author of the Pulitzer Prize–winning *Carry Me Home: Birmingham, Alabama—The Climactic Battle of the Civil Rights Revolution*, and a young-adult history of the civil right movement, *A Dream of Freedom*.

CAROL MEGATHLIN was born in Americus, Georgia, and reared in Albany. She majored in geography at the University of Georgia, but the influence of her newspaper editor father was strong. She has had columns published in the *Savannah Morning News*, the *Atlanta Constitution*, the *Macon Telegraph*, and the *Albany Herald*.

JANET NODAR writes, teaches, and raises her family in Mobile, Alabama. She has been writing since childhood and sees no reason to stop. She recently completed a novel and is now working on a new one.

Anna Olswanger grew up in Memphis, the backdrop to many of her stories, including "Chicken Bone Man," which won Maryland's F. Scott Fitzgerald Short Story Contest. She now lives in New Jersey and is a literary agent with Liza Dawson Associates in Manhattan. Her website is www.olswanger.com.

Nic Pizzolatto was born in New Orleans and raised on Louisiana's Gulf Coast. His stories have appeared in the *Atlantic Monthly*, the *Missouri Review*, *Shenandoah*, and other journals. A collection of his short fiction will be published in 2006, to be followed by a novel he is currently writing.

Restaurateur-chef-food writer Robert St. John is the owner of the Purple Parrot Café and Crescent City Grill in Hattiesburg, Mississippi. He writes a weekly food/humor column and is the author of *A Southern Palate*, *Deep South Staples, or How to Survive in a Southern Kitchen Without a Can of Cream of Mushroom Soup*, *Nobody's Poet*, and the upcoming *Southern Seasons*.

Philip Shirley has received more than a dozen awards for poetry, fiction, speech, and feature writing, with work in *POEM*, *Wind*, *Aura*, *Southern Humanities Review*, *Epos*, *Art Gulf Coast*, *Thunder Mountain Review*, and others, as well as on public radio. He has two chapbooks of poetry, *Four Odd* (Baltic Avenue Press) and *Endings* (Thunder City Press). He's president of GodwinGroup, the South's oldest ad agency, in Jackson, Mississippi. This was his first fiction accepted for publication. Two stories have recently appeared in *Southern Gothic* and *Thicket*.

Born in Yugoslavia in 1938, Charles Simic came to the United States in 1954. Upon graduation from Oak Park High School in Chicago (the alma mater of Ernest Hemingway), he went to work for the *Chicago Sun Times*, where he started writing poetry. He has since published more than sixty books, won the Pulitzer Prize for Poetry, been a National Book Award finalist, and received numerous other grants and awards. Simic and his wife and their son and daughter live in Strafford, New Hampshire.

MAC WALCOTT is an architect in Fairhope, Alabama. Born and raised in Greenville, Mississippi (where there is something in the water), he would like to be a literate farmer like Wendell Berry or Noel Perrin in his spare time. The "literate" and "farmer" parts continue to elude him. He lives with his wife and three children at Big House Farm on Fish River.

DANIEL WALLACE is the author of three novels: *Big Fish* (1998), which has been translated into eighteen languages and was adapted for film by Tim Burton, *Ray in Reverse* (2000), and *The Watermelon King* (2003). His essays, stories, and illustrations have been published in many magazines and anthologies, and his illustrated work has appeared on T-shirts, refrigerator magnets, and greeting cards across the country. Raised in Birmingham, Alabama, he now lives in Chapel Hill, North Carolina, with his wife and son.

M. O. WALSH was born and raised in Baton Rouge, Louisiana. His work has appeared in *Greensboro Review*, *New Orleans Review*, and *Pindeldyboz*, among others, and has been anthologized in *French Quarter Fiction*. When not writing, he would rather be fishing or watching the LSU Tigers win at anything. He now lives with Sarah, his wife, in Oxford, Mississippi, and is an MFA student at Ole Miss. He is currently working on a collection of linked stories that he hopes someone will be drunk enough to publish.

MARLY YOUMANS is a native and longtime resident of the Carolinas who now lives in a snow heap near the Baseball Hall of Fame in Cooperstown, New York. She is the mother of three works-in-progress and the author of six books. Her most recent novel is *The Wolf Pit*

(Farrar, Straus & Giroux), winner of the 2001 Michael Shaara Award. In 2003 she published a collection of poems called *Claire* (Louisiana State) and *The Curse of the Raven Mocker* (FSG), a fantasy for young readers—to be followed up by *Ingledove* (FSG, 2005).